LOVE AND PEACE WITH MELODY PARADISE

First published in 1998 by
I.M.P. FICTION

I.M.P. Fiction is an imprint of Independent Music Press Ltd
P. O. BOX 14691, London, SE1 3ZJ

A catalogue record for this book is available
from The British Library

ISBN 0-9533275-0-7

Printed and bound in Great Britain by Guernsey Press Ltd.

Front Cover Photo: Martyn Goodacre
Back Cover Photo: Mandi Peers

Love And Peace
With Melody Paradise

Martin Millar

I.M.P. Fiction
London

Love And Peace
With Melody Paradise

To anyone who knows me, it would seem strange that I once helped to organise a festival. Strange because I am not the sort of person who enjoys festivals. I don't like tents, or benders, or tepees. I don't like travelling, or being in the countryside. I hate muddy fields. Even dry fields are a trial, though I'm not convinced that there ever really are dry fields at festivals. I don't like much except sitting in front of the television in my comfortable armchair, and reading books about the ancient world, and playing video games. I dislike the modern world, apart from video games.

It was the fault of Melody Paradise that I became involved. I liked Melody Paradise, though I would not have said I liked her to the extent of helping her organise a festival. I got on well enough with her friends even though these friends were, like Melody, members of a group of travellers who called themselves The Tribe Of The Last Free Moonbeam.

So I suppose that the hardships I suffered during this enterprise were really all my own fault. Any man of true wisdom and sagacity would not have got involved with a bunch of people who called themselves The Tribe Of The Last Free Moonbeam. It was bound to lead to trouble.

"I am not fond of the modern world," I said to Melody one day, sitting with her on the pavement outside the old red van that was her home.

"Why not?" she said.

I explained that everything about it was terrible.

"So terrible that I have decided to revolt against it entirely. From now on I'm going to pretend that I'm living in classical Athens. If you see me walking down the street in a toga, don't be surprised." Melody Paradise considered this.

"Didn't you tell me you spent all your time in your comfortable armchair watching television?"

"Yes, but I really hate all the programmes."

"It seems strange that you stay in the city though. You can't get away from the modern world in London. Why don't you come travelling with us? I mean, it's not like we have horse-drawn

7

carriages like Iris The Peaceful, but travelling around the country-side even in a bus must be closer to ancient Athens than watching television all the time."

"Travel? Me? Are you serious? In these things?"

I waved my arm disparagingly at Melody's ramshackle old van. Next to it was her friend Megan's bus, a vehicle in even greater disrepair. Megan's bus looked like it had carried troops into battle in the First World War and come off badly at the Somme. Megan was at this moment deep inside the engine, waving tools and cursing angrily.

Megan had no more idea than Melody how to fix an engine but thought that she should probably try, for appearance's sake, before calling in help.

"I wouldn't be safe. You break down everywhere and farmers chase you off their land with shotguns. And I don't like being cold and wet. Your van's got a hole in the roof. And that mattress you sleep on looks lumpy. I need a nice comfortable mattress or my back gets sore."

Melody laughed.

"My van isn't cold and wet, it's very warm and comfy."

I found this hard to believe, but let it pass.

"I think you'd have had a hard time in classical Athens," said Melody, "you're too used to modern conveniences. No televisions there."

"I'd do without."

"No telephones."

"A blessing. Everyone who phones me up talks rubbish."

"The ancient Greeks kept slaves. You wouldn't like to keep slaves would you?"

I frowned. Despite the fact that Melody Paradise was an out and out hippy who often showed little sign of being in touch with the real world she had an annoying habit of displaying her intelligence at inappropriate moments. In between joints she could be extremely acute.

I brushed aside her objection.

"I'd institute a few constitutional reforms. I imagine I'd have been a fine legislator in the Assembly. I can see me now, debating with Pericles, standing up in a toga and making a terrific speech about the issues of the day then going off to fight the Persians."

Melody had a prolonged laugh at the thought of me going off to fight the Persians.

"Socrates fought the Persians," I countered, "whenever he wasn't lecturing on philosophy. I'm sure I could have done it as well. Probably at the Battle of Marathon I'd have distinguished myself and they'd have put up a statue to me."

"So are you coming to our land rights protest next week?"

"No."

"Scared you'll be arrested?" said Melody, grinning.

"Yes. But being arrested on a land rights protest with The Militant Children Of Lemuria is not the same as fighting the Persians at the Battle of Marathon."

Megan's baby was sleeping contentedly in Melody's lap. Megan withdrew herself from the engine of her bus and swore loudly.

"I can't fix it."

Megan's bus, like Melody's van, was continually breaking down. So were the other eight vehicles belonging to The Tribe Of The Last Free Moonbeam. None of The Tribe seemed to be competent mechanics. When they were in London resting from their travels they were always going round looking for someone to help them with repairs. I would have thought that such extreme mechanical incompetence would be a severe handicap to travellers but they always seemed to get by somehow.

Melody and Megan rolled up a spliff which became oily from Megan's hands.

"If The Galactic Navigators arrive, Catherine will fix your bus," said Melody.

Catherine was Melody's sister, and by reputation a very fine mechanic, as was her boyfriend Nemo. The Galactic Navigators were another group of travellers.

"So you're reading at the Chelwyn Literary Festival?" said Melody.

I nodded. I'd been booked to do a reading next month. I wasn't looking forward to it but I'd get paid. I'd never heard of Chelwyn before but apparently it was somewhere near Canterbury.

"Well, that's a happy coincidence," said Melody.

"Why?"

"We're organising a festival of our own near there at the same time. In a little valley we sometimes go to. Do you want to help us organise it?"

"No," I replied. "I don't like festivals. Also, I'm a terrible organiser."

"Well, you wouldn't really have to do much organising, just help out. And I could do with your help, for our proposal. And you could read to us as well."

I had known Melody Paradise and the rest of The Tribe Of The Last Free Moonbeam for a few years. As far as I could remember they had never shown any interest whatsoever in my writing before. Why they would want me to come and read at their festival was a mystery, particularly as I had received the impression from Melody that it was to be a small affair: just her, her friends and her family.

Melody's friends and family included many groups, in particular the twelve separate tribes with whom her sisters and brothers travelled. This amounted to several hundred people but as festivals went it would still be small.

"I thought the festival was just for you to plant a new Wishing Tree? Do you want me to read something to the Wishing Tree? I think The Tree Planters would be better for that, they're more used to talking to trees than I am."

"No, I don't want you to read to the new Wishing Tree. Not unless you want to, of course. Now you mention it, it would be a nice idea. Would you like to write something specially for it?"

"No, Melody. My career as an author depends on keeping up some semblance of sanity. If word got out I was reading to trees critics would mock."

Melody and Megan both said it would be a very nice gesture for me to read to the tree. I declined in the strongest terms.

"Well, we'll let that one go for now," said Melody. "I expect when you actually see us and Iris The Peaceful planting the new tree you'll be moved to compose something. And the tree would enjoy it."

Melody Paradise was a fine person, but occasionally when talking to her I got the urge to bury my head in my hands. I dragged the conversation back on course.

"You were saying you wanted me to read?"

"That's right. You see there's more to this festival than planting a new Wishing Tree. I want to clean up the valley, for one thing. The valley and the Peaceful Grove were my favourite places and now they're a shambles. The Wishing Tree dead, other trees damaged, rubbish and junk everywhere. There's even a couple of buses rotting down by the river. I can't leave the place in such a state."

I nodded. I already understood that the valley had held special significance for Melody Paradise and her travelling friends, and I knew the sad story of their last visit. The valley was some way from the nearest civilisation but even so the local council had objected to their being there and the police had evicted them in a dawn raid. Melody Paradise was scrupulous about not leaving mess behind her in the country but this had been a very sudden and violent eviction and there had been no time to clear up.

"That was almost a year ago," said Melody, "I still get upset thinking about it."

"Well, it's a nice idea to clear up Melody, but how are you going to do it? If you go there again you'll just get evicted. And the council won't give you a licence to hold a festival. Are you planning to hold an illegal festival, the way things are now?"

This seemed to me like an insane idea. Travellers had been having a very hard time at the hands of the authorities for some years. Councils and police forces now had new laws at their disposal to make things even harder. It was extremely difficult for them to even stop for the night in many parts of the country. Organising a festival would surely be impossible. I knew that travellers in the past had successfully organised such affairs but any attempt to do so these days seemed bound to be crushed from the outset.

Melody Paradise grinned, and shook her head.

"It'll be all right. The festival will happen. We'll have a good time, and clean up the valley, and make peace."

"Make peace?"

"Between my family. Everyone's arguing. That's another reason for the festival. I want to make sure everyone is friends before I leave the country. Like I said, I could do with your help for the proposal."

"Proposal? What's that?"

The pavement darkened with spots of rain and Melody hurried to check the section of tarpaulin she had fixed over the hole in the roof of her van.

"Unfortunate," muttered Megan.

"What?"

"Unfortunate. This is Saint Swithun's day. If it rains on Saint Swithun's day it'll rain continually for forty days and forty nights."

"To hell with Saint Swithun," said Melody, rather inappropriately.

16th July (Day 2)

Melody Paradise came to visit me the next day, enquiring about my participation in the festival.

"Well, Martin, what about it?"

Melody, who I guessed was around twenty five, though I am poor at guessing people's ages, had very dark eyes, a very slender frame, and very fine, pale skin which her travels had not darkened. She was pale but healthy, unlike some of her fellows, who were pallid and slightly the worse for wear. On her forehead the faintest of wrinkles had just begun to form, two tiny lines which showed only when she frowned, which wasn't often.

She could have been a year or two younger, or older. I never ask anyone's age, for fear that they might ask mine. She wore old clothes that covered her from shoulder to ankle in bright and ragged layers, yellow and orange and green, and black boots with red laces. Her hair was done in dreadlocks, a style which had become popular, dominant even, among young whites in Brixton, and many other places as well. There were ten members of The

Tribe Of The Last Free Moonbeam and every one of them wore their hair in this way. Every one of them had layers of old ragged clothes, some bright like Melody Paradise and some dark like Megan. They travelled around Britain, and sometimes abroad, calling back to south London occasionally to meet old friends. I had little real idea of what their life on the road was like though their time in the city seemed to be spent almost entirely in having fun which was something I could only approve of.

There had at this time been some protest against new legislation aimed at making life more difficult for people like The Tribe Of The Last Free Moonbeam, and demonstrations in London would now comprise a sea of bright, ragged, dreadlocked figures dancing down Park Lane in the wake of open trucks playing techno music. Rather more enjoyable than demonstrations used to be, and just as ineffective I suppose. Still, I had several times shuffled along in the demonstrations myself, although I no longer had the energy to dance all the way from Hyde Park to Trafalgar Square.

Among those dreadlocks there would be some of outstanding length, colour and decoration. Among those outstanding examples there was Melody Paradise, surely the brightest-haired person ever to be photographed by tourists as she danced her way into Trafalgar Square with the rest of her tribe.

No description can do justice to the psychedelic jungle that was Melody Paradise's hair. When her locks were eight inches long she dyed them red. When they were eighteen inches long the intervening space had been dyed blue and yellow and the next foot or so was orange and violet. The next twelve inches were all the hues of the rainbow and above that was a range of sea greens and blues and above that was a foot or so of pinks and purples crowned with another layer of yellow, so it sometimes seemed to me that ninety per cent of the effort and time spent by The Tribe Of The Last Free Moonbeam must be in maintaining and extending Melody's hair. Woven amongst this incredible display of length, luxury and colour were countless coloured beads and small silver rings that flashed in the sunlight. Her hair reached down to her thighs. If she knelt on the ground nothing but hair was visible.

Anyone appearing at that moment might have thought that rather than a person they were witnessing a tepee made of dreadlocks.

This would not have been such a ridiculous thought. In the alternative arts centre in Brixton many stranger things were on view than a tepee made of dreadlocks.

I made Melody some tea; unlike some of her friends, she didn't demand some strange herbal concoction. She admired my copper bracelet, which pleased me. It was a pleasant bracelet, even though I'd bought it in a chemist's shop rather than a jewellery stall. I was wearing it because my right hand and arm were sore, strained from writing and playing music and playing video games. A copper bracelet is meant to be good for rheumatic pain.

Once dismissed as a fallacy, this idea has gained some scientific credibility, albeit on the wilder shores of the scientific community. The idea is that some of the copper rubs off the bracelet and into your system, thereby benefiting your joints which need a little copper every now and then. Traditional scientists still ridicule this theory however, and so do I. It seems to me far more likely that wearing a copper bracelet attracts the Copper Fairy, and naturally having a nice little Copper Fairy dancing on your forearm works wonders for aching joints and tendons, as fairies are by nature beneficial to your health.

How pleasant fairies are. I wrote a book about them once, and will do so again, as soon as public disapproval for the first one dies down.

While drinking her tea Melody Paradise asked if she could look at my arm. Immediately I was a little uneasy. Melody was a natural healer and I suspected that she might be about to try some natural healing on me. I didn't really trust natural healers.

"Is this sore?" she asked, prodding my wrist.

I nodded.

She prodded it further up.

"How about that?"

I nodded again. She prodded and poked it some more then examined my fingers.

"Is that sore?"

I started to lose patience at all this painful prodding.

"Melody, just assume that everything is sore. And rapidly getting worse."

Melody Paradise, now in healing mode, was oblivious to my ill temper. After a little more manipulation of my arm she announced that I was suffering from long term stress of my muscles and tendons due to too much writing and playing computer games.

"I knew that already."

"But you don't know how to get it better. I can heal it."

"Right now?"

Melody said that it would take about a month. I didn't really believe it but as nothing else had any effect I accepted her offer, though possibly with less grace than I should. We arranged that my first treatment would be tomorrow.

Melody spoke again of her festival.

"One important reason we're going there is to clean up the valley. It used to be beautiful and now it's a mess. Evictions are never much fun and this one was terrible. Lots of our things got damaged. Even some trees got damaged when the police towed away our vehicles. Loads of other stuff got left behind. I always try to leave land in the same state I find it in but this was a mess. There's all sorts of rubbish there now."

Melody looked pained at the memory.

"I love the valley and the Peaceful Grove so clearing it up is one major objective. Another of course, is having fun. What about the reading, do you want to come and do it?"

"Why are you having readings?"

"I'm having lots of things. I figure it will be nice if one evening we have poetry and storytelling. Another evening we're all going to help with The Clan Of The Night Time Elves' Unicorn Survey. Then there's The Tree Planters, they always make sure the trees are happy so I thought we could all spend an evening being nice to the trees."

I wanted to protest but was rendered temporarily speechless.

"Not that I want to do too much organising of course, people wouldn't like being too organised. Anyone that just wants to hang out doing nothing can hang out and do nothing. And Mary and The Golden World Eternal Party Tribe will be there with their rave tent so we can all dance all night anyway, which is what I like best. But a few other things will help give everyone a good time. Remember, I'm keen for everyone to have a good time so that they'll stop arguing. The Universal Leyline Protectors will be coming with their space pyramid so we might spend another evening astral travelling."

At this further outrage I managed to regain my voice.

"Astral travelling? Being nice to trees? Hunting for unicorns? Melody, even by your standards this is ridiculous."

"Why?," said Melody brightly. "They all sound like nice things to do to me. And we'll plant the new Wishing Tree in a big ceremony. So what about it, you want to come?"

There was no way that I was going to participate in Melody's dumb festival. I decided to strongly discourage the idea right from the start. Any weakening and I might find myself sharing a damp field with lots of horrible dogs, all roaming free while their owners floundered about in a mushroom-induced haze.

"It sounds like an incredibly stupid scheme from start to finish. Nothing would induce me to travel to some rain-splattered field with The Tribe Of The Last Free Moonbeam. I don't like rain-splattered fields."

"We're holding it in a beautiful little valley," said Melody Paradise.

"No difference. It'll still be terrible. Being nice to the trees and hunting for unicorns indeed. And festivals are always full of dogs aren't they? I don't like dogs. I'm scared of them. Especially travellers' dogs. What if they've travelled somewhere foreign and come back with rabies? Surely you can't expect me to risk catching rabies when they haven't discovered a cure for it yet? And the toilets would be disgusting. I'm too old to cope with disgusting toilets any more. Is it going to be legal? I don't want to be arrested and truncheoned over the head by a squad of armed police. And I'd have to stay in a tent. I don't like tents. I can't put them up and they leak and blow away and I always worry that it might catch fire and I'll get roasted in a sleeping-bag fireball. Me and tents just don't get on. Why don't they make them easier to put up?"

Melody Paradise laughed. She often laughed. Normally I would find this irritating but with her it was quite disarming, which was one reason to like her. Everyone I knew liked Melody Paradise.

"Don't bother with a tent," she said. "Tents are awful. We'll help you build a bender."

"A bender? Are you serious? You expect me to live in an old bit of canvas held up by a few twigs? No chance."

"Okay, bring a tent if you insist. We'll help you put it up."

"That's what you say now. Come the time it would be different. You'd all be too busy doing something else and I'd have to put it up myself. I know, it's happened to me before. Back when I was younger and more adventurous I went to a festival with a friend who swore he'd help me put my tent up and when the time came he just lay on the ground with a flagon of cider glued to his mouth and said it was high time I learned how to do it myself. It was terrible. I'm hopeless with a mallet. Why don't they make tent pegs so they don't bend in half when you try and knock them in the ground?"

"Pick a soft piece of ground," said Melody. "I promise we'll help you."

I shook my head.

"I'm not coming. Think of the dogs. It's just too dangerous."

"It won't be dangerous. It'll be lovely."

"Lovely? That's not the word I'd use. I just don't understand why you like festivals at all Melody."

"Lots of reasons. I meet all my friends. I have a good time. I get to relax. I get to forget the outside world for a while."

This took me by surprise. I wasn't aware that Melody Paradise paid any attention to the outside world.

"You think I can avoid it when I'm travelling around?"

Melody pointed out to me that as a traveller she came face to face with unpleasant reality all the time, generally when she was being forcibly ejected from some piece of uninhabited and unwanted land. She also pointed out that although I had gone with The Tribe Of The Last Free Moonbeam to protest against the government legislation banning raves, gatherings and suchlike, it was comparatively easy for me to avoid the effects of this legislation.

"But we face it all the time. Any time the police decide they don't like the look of us they harass us under the Criminal Justice Bill. And things have already been more difficult since councils stopped providing sites for travellers, and banning our free festivals, and stopping anyone earning a living. Too difficult really, that's why I'm leaving the country."

Melody stopped, smiled, and apologised for lecturing me. I didn't mind, she lectured very pleasantly. I was interested in what she said about forgetting the outside world for a while. Quite a reasonable aspiration, I had to admit. Everyone needed a break. Conservative politicians, for instance, during their long, well-paid vacations, could holiday abroad in exotic locations. People like Melody Paradise could go onto common land and enjoy themselves. Until the Conservative politicians made this illegal of course.

"Well, Melody, I'd like to help you out but it's just not the sort of thing I'd enjoy."

"We'll pay you," she said, which startled me.

"You'll pay me? I don't believe it. How much?"

"One hundred pounds now. And another hundred when it's done."

I looked at her suspiciously and could not help commenting that the prospect of Melody Paradise and The Tribe Of The Last Free Moonbeam ever having two hundred pounds to spare seemed very remote unless they all happened to get their benefit cheques at the same time and a miraculous act of God prevented them from spending it immediately on hash and cider.

Melody retorted that this was a terrible view to have of travellers and how dare I suggest that they never spent their money on anything else except hash and cider?

"I didn't say all travellers did. No doubt there are many abstemious travellers roaming the country in a blameless fashion. But that doesn't include The Tribe Of The Last Free Moonbeam. You are not abstemious. Last night in the pub I spotted two of your Tribe asleep under the next table and three more unconscious in

18

the garden. And it's not just the people. What about the time your dog drank your mushroom tea and ran into the police station biting policemen right and left and they had to call out the emergency team from the RSPCA? You had to drive away to Wales till all the fuss died down. The poor animal ended up under armed guard in Battersea Dogs Home. Face it Melody, you're not the most sober group of people ever to block up the nation's roadways in a broken down bus."

She smiled at me, ending the argument. Melody could often end unpleasantness with a smile, an attribute I had never encountered before. Not only that, she never seemed upset if I mocked and abused her and her friends. A fine character trait which others would do well to copy.

"Maybe, maybe. But I'll get the money."

I couldn't understand Melody's persistence. It wasn't as if The Tribe Of The Last Free Moonbeam and The Universal Leyline Protectors and everyone else were clamouring to hear me read. They'd all managed fine up till now without paying any attention to my literary efforts. In the face of her persistence I was forced to find more excuses, and explained to her that I was a busy man.

"Are you writing something just now?"

"Not exactly. But I am planning my next book and that takes immense concentration. It's going to be a romantic comedy. Next to fairies I like romantic comedies best. I don't like books with problems in them. I hate reading about other people's problems. What have all these writers got to complain about anyway? Stick them in the middle of a tribal war in Rwanda, then they'd have problems, that's what I say."

Melody sipped her tea, each movement of her head causing her locks and beads to clink on the table. Her face, when visible behind her hair, was slightly angular and very beautiful, although I was never sure whether the two gold rings through her lower lip added to the effect. But her nose stud and eyebrow piercings were universally admired. Her eyes were very dark, black almost, and large. She painted her eyelids with kohl and wore a jewel on her forehead.

"It doesn't really sound like you're that busy. You could plan your book at the festival."

"Other matters detain me in London. I'm waiting to hear the outcome of my 'Young Socrates' proposal for children's television."

"Young Socrates?"

"Yes. A stirring and challenging cartoon."

"Why 'young'?"

"Everything on children's television has something 'young' in it these days. When they bring back an old cartoon like Scooby Doo or The Flintstones there are always some new young characters like a puppy or a baby or something. And there's a funny one about a penguin who's also young. Just the other day I saw a cartoon called Dino Babies about these dinosaur babies who were really cute. I wish I'd thought of it. If I could come up with a really good idea like Dino Babies I wouldn't have to keep thinking of ideas for books."

"Write about us." suggested Melody.

"I might."

"Isn't Socrates a bit old fashioned?"

"I don't think so. He's more modern than dinosaurs. Anyway, I don't like the modern world. Leading children back to the time of Socrates can only be good for them."

Melody Paradise looked dubious.

"I still think you should try something more modern."

"What? Like Plato?"

I scanned briefly through this idea. 'Young Plato'? Not bad, quite a nice ring to it. I could turn it into a series. 'Young Aristotle'. 'Young Diogenes'.

Melody looked me in the eye, something which I always find disconcerting.

"Apart from your fear of perishing in a sleeping-bag fireball, there's really no reason for you not to help us, is there?"

I was forced to admit that this was true.

"But you could get someone else."

"I don't know anybody else who's been published. How did you get published anyway?"

"I slept with the owner of the company."

"Was it fun?"

"Terrible. And afterwards I had to accept very low royalties."

Melody Paradise applied some slight moral pressure.

"Remember," she said, "I was the only person who sat through your whole rendition of the Emperor Claudius' *History of Rome*."

This was also true, although the memory gave me little pleasure. In ancient Rome some historians, appreciative of their Emperor, had staged an annual reading of Claudius' history, a fine idea which I had tried to revive by staging a reading in a Brixton pub. An admirable effort, but not one which the general public had warmed to. Melody did sit through it all, until the landlord came and threw us out. Quite a tragic occurrence really, though not as bad as my attempt to read Euripides in the middle of a rave at the alternative arts centre.

"Well, Melody, the offer of money does put a different light on things. I suppose I could consider it. But why do you need a published author? I thought you were just planting a tree, saying goodbye and heading off to the continent?"

"And ending the arguments," said Melody.

"Is me reading going to end your family's arguments?"

"I doubt it. But it's all part of the scam I'm working," she explained.

This surprised me. Melody Paradise had never struck me as the scheming type.

"Do you know anything about Chelwyn?"

I admitted that I didn't, apart from that I was going to do a reading there.

"It's a village outside Canterbury, not far from the valley. Very pretty. There aren't many actual villagers living there now, it's mainly weekend homes for rich people from the city. Every year they stage a summer fair, and there's lots of money for this summer fair because the bankers and stockbrokers all make big contributions to try and make the locals like them. It's not the sort of place I'd normally go, in fact the village pub has a 'No Travellers' sign in the window, but Rupert's aunt lives there and through her

21

I got involved in helping restore the stained glass in their church, which is how I met them. Anyway, this year their summer fair comprises a big traditional circus and the literary festival you're reading at. They're also going to have a small alternative circus, provided by us, though they don't know about it yet."

"Why?"

"Two reasons. One, we'll get a load of money for just one performance, and two, we'll get a licence from the council to stay in the valley for a week. Not to hold a festival of course, we'll have to pretend we're just there getting things ready for the circus but it won't make any difference, the valley's quite a way from the village so everyone'll leave us alone. Which means I can have my festival in peace. I'd rather not have had to go to such trouble but you know what things are like these days: if we just go onto some piece of common land and try holding it there without a licence the police will move us on immediately."

"Won't they move you on anyway when they suddenly find a big festival on their doorstep?"

"It won't be big. Just my family, about a hundred people or so. We could easily be the advance workers for the circus. So I've solved two problems at once. I'm going to make sure my festival is allowed to go on undisturbed and also get money to make it fun for everyone. I'll get loads of stockbrokers' cash to spend on drugs, beer, and whatever else seems necessary. And we'll all get to stay in the valley."

Melody held her arms aloft, inviting heaven and earth to acknowledge that this was indeed a brilliant scheme.

"But what about the circus? You'll have to do it and you're not a circus."

"Well, yes," acknowledged Melody, "but that's no real trouble because I know lots of people with circus skills. The Motorbikes Of Merlin, for instance, and The Flying Dementos."

"I don't really understand why the Chelwyn Village Summer Fair Committee is going to pay you to put on an alternative circus, Melody."

Melody smiled.

"I had the idea talking to Rupert, after he'd been to see his aunt. Even in prosperous villages there is adolescent unrest. According to Rupert, various young sons and daughters of stockbrokers have been complaining that a traditional circus is too dull for them. So I got Rupert to make some enquiries to the Summer Fair Committee about providing something with roaring motorbikes and fire-juggling and stuff like that and they're actually quite keen. All we have to do is send in a good proposal, which is the first piece of help I want from you. Could you do it on your computer?"

"I suppose so."

"Good," said Melody. "It doesn't have to be much, just a few pages about what a terrific affair the Melody Paradise Circus is, and maybe some forged reviews from newspapers around the world."

"Forged reviews?"

"Sure, why not? It'll have to sound good or they won't hire us. And if we pretend some Australian newspaper said we were fabulous they're hardly going to check are they?"

I already felt like I was heading for a lengthy period of imprisonment but Melody brushed aside my objections. Against my better judgement, I agreed that I would make up the proposal for Melody, although I insisted she would have to forge the reviews herself.

"Good," said Melody. "That's one problem out the way. I can already feel my festival starting to happen."

"You're not going to have much time for your festival are you, if you have to organise a circus at the same time?"

Melody told me that she wasn't going to spend any time at all organising the circus because Rupert was going to do it all.

"Why him?"

"He's done this sort of thing before, he's a good organiser. With him taking care of it I won't have to spend any time on it, which is fine, because I'm going to be busy clearing up the valley, helping everyone have a good time, and dancing."

I frowned. I didn't like Rupert.

"Rupert is awful."

"He's not so bad," said Melody. "Anyway, he's keen to do it, and he's got experience."

"He'll do a lousy job."

Melody Paradise shrugged.

"It doesn't matter. The alternative circus can be a complete disaster. I don't care. I'll have had the money by then and we won't be staging it till the end of the week so it really doesn't matter what it's like, just so long as it happens. There's no pressure to put on anything good. Anyway, it had to be Rupert. He's a respected member of the community, or at least his aunt is. How else could I persuade the Chelwyn Summer Fair Committee to let us do it? Mrs Fitzroy, the chairwoman of the Committee, likes me after the good job we did on the stained glass, but she's not going to go throwing their money around if she doesn't think it's going to be properly spent. Rupert's a businessman, he's rich, he's got aristocratic relatives."

"He spends every summer pretending to be a travelling hippy," I interrupted.

"No matter," said Melody. "You have to accept everyone for what they are. What's more he won't mind that all the money is going to me."

I didn't need to ask why Rupert was doing all this for the angelic Melody Paradise. It certainly wasn't out of any love of the circus.

"And this brings me to the second reason why I want you to come," continued Melody. "Instead of just doing a reading at the literary festival, could you do a creative writing class?"

I felt myself going weak and clutched at the arm of my chair for support.

"A creative writing class? Me? Certainly not."

"You'd be doing us a big favour."

"How?"

"Because on the last day you could bring the people from the class out to the valley and then they'd see what nice people we were and stop evicting us. Why are you laughing?"

"That's the most naive thing I've ever heard. You think if I ferry a load of stockbrokers' wives out to do a creative writing class at your festival they're suddenly going to say, 'Wow, these travellers are nice people after all, let's get the council to stop evicting them'?"

"Exactly," replied Melody. "I couldn't have put it better myself."

Despite feeling that Melody Paradise was again losing touch with the Planet Earth, I skated over this for the meantime and pointed out the more obvious objection.

"I haven't been booked for a creative writing class, just a reading."

"Rupert says Mrs Fitzroy would change it round if he asked. You write about Brixton and stuff, that's probably quite interesting for young stockbrokers, or maybe their wives and children."

"I doubt it."

"Nonetheless," Melody Paradise said, "Rupert can arrange it. So what about it?"

I was appalled. I couldn't believe that Melody Paradise had been plotting behind my back to get me to do a creative writing class.

"Haven't you done it before?" she asked, innocently.

"Of course I haven't done it before. I've never been near a creative writing class. I hardly even know what it means. You expect me to go to some rich stockbroker's place and spout some rubbish about creative writing and somehow make them like you?"

"No. You can just spout rubbish and I'll make them like me. You know how good I am at spreading love and peace."

I shook my head. Melody was surprised at the strength of my feelings on the matter. She apologised for my distress but pointed out that not much could go wrong really.

"I mean, it'll be your workshop so you can just do anything you want. Just bring them to the valley and be creative. Make them all write about fairies, you'll like that. It might do your career the world of good. Anyway, it won't take you long and it doesn't really matter what it's like. You've only got to do it on the last day and all the rest of the time you can spend having fun with us in the valley. It's a beautiful valley. It contains the Peaceful Grove, with the Wishing Tree. Or did, till the tree was destroyed. But Iris The Peaceful is bringing a new sapling. Planting it will be a wonderful event. So how about it?"

I frowned.

"You are not really planning to use the money for what it's

intended are you? It all sounds like fraud to me. And I'll be involved if I do the proposal."

"Do you mind a little fraud?"

"Will I get arrested?"

"Of course not. It's not so serious. All it means is that Chelwyn Village will get a rather cheaper alternative circus than they anticipate. But so what, they've got a great big circus performing for a week anyway. And we'll all be ready to leave by then so who cares?"

Melody smiled, and told me that the success of her festival was vital to her. I pondered her proposal but could not work up any enthusiasm.

"And as well as participating in this fraudulent proposal you want me to do a creative writing class, something I know nothing about, with stockbrokers, at your festival, surrounded by your demented family?"

"That's right."

"I won't do it."

"Please."

"Absolutely not."

"It's important to me."

"Something will go wrong. The police will arrest us as soon as we turn up in the valley."

"No they won't, we'll have permission to be there."

"In that case we'll all be arrested for fraud."

"We won't. No one will know we spent all the money ourselves. It's just some small local thing, no-one'll care."

I shook my head, and put on a resolute voice.

"I'm sorry, it all sounds too horrible."

"Remember," said Melody Paradise. "You'll be getting paid."

And thus it was that I became involved in the free festival as organised by Melody Paradise, and the huge travelling family of Melody Paradise, and the tortuous romance of Melody Paradise, and the doomed literary event, and the even more doomed circus. The desire for money is a terrible curse.

"I wouldn't exactly say that Melody Paradise is burdened down with worry," said Megan, "but she's not as carefree as she used to be."

I nodded. I had noticed that Melody Paradise was not quite the bright spirit she'd been last year. She was subdued to some extent. A subdued Melody Paradise was still more vibrant than almost anyone else however, and she was imbued with the happy attribute of brightening up any place she happened to be.

"She tells me that her brothers and sisters and friends arguing all the time gets her down."

Megan nodded.

"It's been like that since the Wishing Tree died. It used to be everybody's favourite place, the valley, and the Peaceful Grove. Every time you went there you felt good. It was a kind of home to the whole family."

"Did the Wishing Tree actually grant wishes?"

Megan shrugged. She seemed not to think so.

"But some people believed in it. Either way it was a nice tree. Or bush rather. It was kind of small. Everyone loved it. After it died, everyone fell out with everyone else. Ever since then things have gone badly. It's like we're all cursed or something."

Megan's baby started to cry. I was about to depart as I'm no good with crying babies. I only upset them more. Fortunately Megan managed to soothe him quickly, taking him from his pushchair into her lap where he seemed happier, and fell asleep again.

Megan asked me about the creative writing class.

"What are you preparing?"

I admitted that I wasn't preparing anything.

"Shouldn't you be?"

"I don't know. I'm trying not to think about it. I don't really know what happens at creative writing classes."

Megan suggested that I should give it some thought. I shrugged, cushioned by Melody's assurance that it didn't matter what it was like. There didn't seem much point in me going to a lot of trouble

27

over my part of the affair. After all, the main thrust of Melody's scheme was the alternative circus and as Rupert was organising that it was bound to be terrible.

"No sense me turning up with something good if everything else is a shambles. I'm just planning to take the money and depart. Melody Paradise is a fine employer. Her complete disinterest in whether it's any good or not is quite refreshing. But I'm extremely dubious about her idea that I have to take the class out to the festival."

"Why?"

I explained that in my opinion Melody's idea that this might lead to some sort of new understanding between local inhabitants and travellers was naive, foolish even.

"Not at all," retorted Megan. "Wait till you see Melody in action. She'll charm them completely. Probably after they've seen Melody Paradise at home in the valley they'll beg her to stay."

"Not if Melody is collapsed unconscious from drug abuse they won't."

Megan dismissed this, saying that while it was not unknown for Melody Paradise to collapse unconscious from drug abuse, she only did it on special occasions.

"Usually when she's happy. Not when she's busy spreading love and peace to stockbrokers."

"I wish Rupert wasn't involved in the festival. I hate Rupert. He spends the winter on the continent selling private jets. Any artistic enterprise staged by him will be a disaster."

"I thought disaster was fine?"

"Apparently it is. Which is just as well. Rupert will make a mess of it."

"He might ask Magwyn The Grim to help him," said Megan.

"Magwyn The Grim? And Rupert? What a dreadful combination of people."

Megan agreed that it was but pointed out that there was no one better qualified to help put on a circus for no money. Whatever staging and props needed to be made, Magwyn would do it. He was an experienced artist and craftsman in many fields. He'd often produced miraculous sets on no budget for events at Glastonbury and other festivals.

"And then outraged everybody by going around being drunk and violent from what I hear. Has he started speaking yet?"

Megan shook her head. Magwyn The Grim was legendary for his brooding and hostile silence. I was not wholly looking forward to meeting him again. He was a hard person to get along with, largely because he almost never spoke. He had a well-deserved reputation as a bitter and hostile soul, more given to drunken violence than friendly co-operation. I couldn't think of anyone who was less generally liked. With his virtual silence and hostility to the world Magwyn's name and reputation were well known, but he was now seldom seen. I had met him only once. He spent long periods travelling alone abroad, nursing his dislike of the world.

Magwyn The Grim also had a reputation as an excellent fine artist, but I had never seen any evidence of this. Nor had Megan. If Magwyn had ever produced a good painting or sculpture he'd kept it well hidden from the world.

"I can see he'll be a useful helper if he can keep his behaviour in check, but why did Rupert ask him? Everyone hates him. There must have been someone else."

"Not as talented as Magwyn," replied Megan.

I got the impression that Megan was leaving something unsaid here but did not pursue it.

We were sitting in Sweep's kitchen. Whenever The Tribe Of The Last Free Moonbeam arrived in south London it was common for them to descend on Sweep's kitchen. As Megan left, Sweep arrived home from signing on so I stayed a while more.

Sweep, keen on Melody Paradise, was also keen on the idea of the festival.

"Brilliant idea of Melody's," he said, "getting money from the Village Summer Fair Committee. You should see that village. I drove through it with The Moonbeams last year. You can't move for Volvos and Audis. And antique shops. I doubt there's a native inhabitant left in the whole place, they've all been chased out by executives. Defrauding executives is a fine thing to do. And

Melody's festival is bound to be great, especially as Melody is now extra-dedicated to spreading love and peace. I love it when Melody Paradise spreads love and peace."

I admitted to Sweep that I wasn't really looking forward to it.

"Why not? I love festivals. And this'll be a nice small cosy festival. We'll all have a great time."

"I hate the country. Especially camping in it. It's too dangerous." Sweep scoffed at this.

"It'll be fine. Not dangerous at all. And remember, Melody's going to get all this money so she can make it comfortable."

"How can I be comfortable without electricity?"

Sweep said that there would be electricity because lots of Melody's travelling friends had generators, which was news to me.

"I expect they'll break down all the time."

"Then Melody will hire new ones. I expect Melody Paradise will provide you with every home comfort. Unless she's just planning some wide-scale drug abuse. I don't know, I haven't seen the actual breakdown of the budget yet."

I mused aloud for a while, wondering if Rupert could mount a credible circus, at short notice and with no money. Almost certainly not. It would be a disaster, a debacle from start to finish. As would be my writing workshop.

"It doesn't matter, does it?" said Sweep.

"Apparently not. All Melody really wants is an uninterrupted week in the valley, safe from police and bailiffs. I suppose it's quite refreshing in a way. I'm continually under pressure to come up with high quality work in all my other fields of endeavour, for instance my 'Young Socrates' idea for children's television, but at least this is free from stress. Nobody cares if it's rubbish. Just accept that it will be a catastrophe and take the money. I find that quite a relief."

"When is it exactly?"

"Festival starts 17th August, performances on the 23rd."

"With a whole week of enjoyment in between," said Sweep, blissfully.

In 304 BC, Iris The Peaceful, sister of Melody Paradise, rode her unicorn round the seven wonders of the world. This tale she related to me twenty three centuries later, in Camden Market. She was selling painted sea shells and Nepalese hats at a market stall.

"In a previous incarnation?" I enquired politely.

"I suppose so. Though I tend to think of all my past lives as running into one long one. I remember it so well it could have been last week. But as the seven wonders are mostly long since gone, it can't have been."

Iris The Peaceful's favourite among the seven wonders of the ancient world had been the statue of Artemis at Ephesus, though they were all impressive. Philida's statue of Zeus at Olympus was magnificent for its divinity, and the Pyramids were stupendous for their size and antiquity.

"The Hanging Gardens of Babylon were very beautiful. They were my unicorn's favourite."

Apparently she had got into some trouble with the authorities when her unicorn nibbled too many plants. I could believe this. If you rode a unicorn all the way over the desert to Babylon it would be bound to be hungry.

"Everyone loved my unicorn. They hadn't seen one before, although unicorns used to be around in the East. They weren't just made up in Arthurian legends. My fabulous unicorn kept me safe, even when I visited the Mausoleum in Halicarnassus during a terrible food riot. Fierce citizens would rush up to me waving spears and shouting abuse but as soon as they saw my unicorn they calmed down and started to pet it, and give it scraps of food."

According to Iris The Peaceful, the Colossus of Rhodes did not straddle the harbour, as commonly imagined, but stood beside it. Iris made a complete circuit of it and scraped a little dust from the cement that joined the bronze statue to the marble base. She put the dust in her pocket, along with the cuttings she took from the Hanging Gardens, and the small mirror that had reflected the light from the huge lighthouse at Pharos.

All these items she still had, she claimed, and kept them in her bag as she rode her horse-drawn carriage round the world. After making some money selling exotic sea shells and floppy hats she had headed off on her travels again, this time with the purpose of finding a new Wishing Tree. She was last heard of in Portugal.

Melody Paradise was depending on Iris to bring back a new tree. With a new Wishing Tree growing, it seemed likely to Melody, and to her friends, that things would start to go better for them. Another reason for wishing Iris The Peaceful to be there was that she, with or without a unicorn, was even more adept than Melody Paradise at quelling arguments, and pacifying the troubled.

Which reminds me. Willis Elf of The Clan Of The Night Time Elves was one of Melody's brothers. Whilst telling me about his Unicorn Survey of Britain and Ireland, he had wondered out loud if Iris's present horse might actually be a unicorn in modern disguise.

"It could only be pretending to be a horse," he reasoned. "It doesn't have a horn on its forehead but it is white. If anyone would have a unicorn these days it would be Iris The Peaceful. Unicorns would just naturally gravitate to her."

I agreed with him, which was simpler and easier than telling him he was a lunatic who should be locked up for his own good.

"What does Iris say about it?"

"She denies it's a unicorn. But Iris The Peaceful might say that anyway, not wishing to draw too much attention to herself."

Afterwards I was entertained by the thought of anyone who claimed to have ridden a unicorn round the seven wonders of the world more than two thousand years ago not wishing to draw attention to themselves. Iris The Peaceful, The Clan Of The Night Time Elves, Melody Paradise, they were all as mad as each other. But I liked to think about Iris's journey, and wondered if she would show me the dust from Rhodes, and the cuttings from Babylon, and the light from the lighthouse at Pharos.

Iris The Peaceful was at this moment in southern Portugal. She and her friends were heading unhurriedly back towards Britain to go to the festival.

Their four wagons were parked by a river. Iris and her friend Fernhadzi walked barefoot along the bank, admiring the flowers.

"What a beautiful daisy," said Iris.

"It is," replied Fernhadzi.

"You ridiculous hippies," said a harsh, rasping voice, as they rounded a large tree. There sat Magwyn The Grim, staring into the depths of the river.

"Why, Magwyn," said Iris, "how nice to see you again. What brings you to this pleasant riverbank in Portugal?"

"Trying to avoid people like you," retorted Magwyn.

Fernhadzi looked worried at this unexpected meeting but Iris was unperturbed.

"Will we see you at the festival?" she asked.

"No," said Magwyn sharply, and stood up, turning his back on them. He started to walk away. Iris swiftly caught up with him.

"You should go to the festival," she said. "It'll be a very good place to be."

Magwyn The Grim snarled.

"I'm taking a new Wishing Tree for the Peaceful Grove," said Iris.

At this Magwyn snarled even louder and clenched his fists. Iris carried on serenely.

"And I'm taking presents for everyone. Here, I'll give you yours now."

With that she produced something from her bag.

"Only a postcard, I'm afraid. But it's a beautiful picture."

Magwyn took it unwillingly and looked at it without expression. He did not thank Iris for the present.

"The roof of the Cistine Chapel as painted by Michaelangelo. Newly renovated. Isn't it beautiful? I thought you'd like it as you're a painter."

Magwyn scowled deeply, crumpled up the postcard and dropped it on the ground. Iris produced another one from her bag.

"I bought lots of them in Rome," she said cheerfully. "Have another."

She forced it into his hand, wished him a pleasant goodbye, and rejoined Fernhadzi.

"Why did you do that?" asked Fernhadzi.

"Why not?"

"He's so horrible."

"Even Magwyn deserves a present," Iris said, "and it's such a nice picture. Full of angels and saints and madonnas."

They hitched up their horses and returned to their quest, the hunt for a new Wishing Tree, leaving Magwyn The Grim behind them, silently scowling at Iris's present.

19th July (Day 5)

Sweep was what at one time would have been called a 'suitor' to Melody Paradise: he was attracted to her, he spent as much time as he could with her, he tried to help her with whatever she was doing whether she wanted help or not.

Sweep lived in a council flat in Brixton although he was rarely there. He earned his living by performing and this took him all over the country. Sweep was a master of juggling and tumbling and stilt-walking and suchlike, and did his act at festivals or students' fairs or alternative cabarets and got by without ever threatening to be very successful. He was a spectacularly talented juggler. Some years ago this would have been sufficient to make up an entertaining performance but the last few years had seen a quite drastic decline in the popularity of jugglers, due to an enormous increase in their numbers. Practically everyone could juggle. Even I can juggle with the basic three balls. Sweep had consequently extended his act to include other circus skills such as fire-eating and unicycle riding. This gave his act variety, although again there was no shortage of other performers doing much the same.

His best professional attribute was his cheerfulness and extrovert nature on-stage which was fairly endearing. While watching him, the audience could be assured that he was not suddenly going to do anything mean or distressing like demand a volunteer to step up and be humiliated. When some stunt went hideously wrong and Sweep collapsed in a tangle of juggling clubs, fire hoops and unicycle parts, his cheerfulness contrived to make it as entertaining as a successful performance.

Unsurprisingly, as is often the way, for a man who had no qualms about walking a tightrope juggling four flaming fire-clubs in front of a large crowd, Sweep was rather shy in daily life. Off-stage he was quiet and awkward. This made his courtship of Melody Paradise difficult. Melody Paradise was herself not such an extrovert as to demand that anyone in her company be continually entertaining her with humorous anecdotes but neither was she sufficiently introverted as to be entirely comfortable with a companion who seemed most of the time to be too tongue-tied to say anything at all.

I knew Sweep quite well, and I knew he wasn't happy. I also knew that he attributed his unhappiness to his lack of a female companion. This had for some time been a general misery but since the appearance of Melody Paradise it had become very specific. Sweep had set his heart on her, and fallen in love with her. Every time I saw him these days he would tell me of his hopes, dreams and unhappiness.

Watching him in pursuit of Melody Paradise was a generally sad experience. He was eager to please but his shyness made it impossible for him to tell her why. Sweep could not come out and say to Melody Paradise that he loved her. In some ways this was just as well, as any such sudden declaration would probably have put her off. But I could not help feeling that rather than running around buying drinks for Melody, bringing her small presents from his tours, paying her over-frequent visits and too constant attentions, it might be helpful to actually tell her he liked her. Unfortunately Sweep was far too diffident to do anything of the sort.

Melody's company was much sought after and would have been even more so had not her beauty put some men off. Generally only those young men with a very good opinion of themselves made any serious attempts to win her affections. When some man who did have a very good opinion of himself came along, Sweep would retreat into the shadows, and watch in mortification. On various occasions I had been obliged to comfort him after a distressing evening in the pub or at a party where some more confident admirer of Melody's had paid her attention and dominated her company for the whole night, and amused her.

Melody Paradise did like to laugh. In some ways this was in Sweep's favour. Unable to express his true feelings to her he would frequently resort to acting out his stage persona in her presence, which was entertaining. However I didn't really feel that this was of much use. It seemed unlikely to me that he would ever be able to clown Melody Paradise into bed. It also seemed to me that his continual attentions might start to bore her. Fortunately this had not yet happened and she still seemed to like his company. More fortunately she had not started going out with anyone else. When Sweep asked anxiously for advice I would be as helpful as I could but if I encouraged him to be a more active admirer he could only shake his head before descending into a gloomy silence.

"It's no use hanging around her in a crowd," I'd tell him. "Ask her out somewhere. She likes dancing. Go raving with her."

This made Sweep even gloomier. Melody Paradise was famous for her dancing. While in London, if she could afford it, she'd go out to clubs or warehouses and dance the night away, and the next day and night as well. Sweep told me that he was first attracted to her at an outdoor event put on by The Golden World Eternal Party Tribe when he saw her gyrating on the back of a truck where her sister Mary was DJ-ing at the time.

"She is a fabulous dancer," sighed Sweep, "and I'm not. If I end up on a dance floor with Melody Paradise I feel completely useless. The sight of me dancing is more likely to put her off than attract her."

Sweep's passion, and also his good nature, meant that The Tribe Of The Last Free Moonbeam were welcome in his council flat any time. When they were around it was quite normal to find the entire Tribe crowded into his small kitchen, drinking herbal tea.

"Well, next time she's around ask her out somewhere that won't involve any dancing. Go to the pictures."

Sweep shook his head, dismissing going to the cinema with a date as a strange and old fashioned thing to do.

"Perhaps. You could at least try taking her to a different pub where you don't know anyone and then just say you like her or you dream of her or something. I know you're shy but you have to make some sort of effort. In my experience you can't win a woman's heart with public juggling routines."

I was wasting my time. The chance of Sweep ever asking Melody Paradise to the pictures was negligible, even though at any moment she might take up with some other man and break his heart completely. If she didn't take up with some other man she would certainly leave the country. The festival she was planning was by way of a goodbye. After it was over The Tribe Of The Last Free Moonbeam was heading across the Channel to France, Spain or wherever things might seem better.

"And then you'll be sorry," I told Sweep, and he agreed that he would, and shook his head sadly. His blond hair flopped over his forehead. That at least was in his favour. Sweep was quite nice looking. In my long observation of such matters, being quite nice looking and having floppy blonde hair can take a young man a long way, and make up for a great many character defects.

20th July (Day 6) Saint Arild's Day

Megan's bus was parked outside Sweep's flat. Melody Paradise had moved her van round the corner onto a piece of waste ground beside a railway bridge. Melody's road tax was out of date so it was illegal for her van to be on the public highway. The Tribe Of The Last Free Moonbeam often had problems with not being able to afford road tax. What happened when they were on the road with expired tax discs on their windscreens I didn't know.

There was a great deal about their lives I didn't really know. Where they went and how they lived when they were travelling was something of a mystery to me. I didn't even know where they came from or why they took to travelling. Some people are born on the road but I don't think this applied to Melody Paradise. I understood from her, vaguely, that there were different types of travellers. Romany Gypsies who'd travelled for generations for instance, and workers following the remnants of the fruit picking season, and families who'd lost their homes and now lived in caravans in lay-bys and trailer parks, and travelling showmen, and young people who just felt like wandering, and no doubt others. I wasn't at all clear about it, but it would be fair to say that The Tribe Of The Last Free Moonbeam were at the 'stoned hippy' edge of the range, and quite content to be there.

As I arrived at Sweep's, it again started to rain. Before I could knock on the door Megan suddenly burst out looking flustered.

"I've lost my keys" she announced, and began scrabbling around in the cabin of her bus. Her many layers of black clothes were disarranged, presumably where she had hunted repeatedly through her hundreds of pockets

I looked on, gaining some pleasure from Megan's agitation. I'm always losing things. It's always a relief to know you're not the only one.

Beer cans, torn maps and bits of clothing flew around the cabin of the bus as Megan hunted.

"Here it is," she said triumphantly, emerging not with a set of keys but a book. I was puzzled, and glanced at the cover.

"A book of saints?"

Megan nodded, and opened it to scan through the index. The book was well-used, crumpled and dirty.

"I've lost my keys."

I couldn't see the connection.

Megan, no longer flustered now she had the book in her hands, explained to me that there was a saint for any emergency and she was looking up the correct one to appeal to when looking for a lost item.

"Here it is," cried Megan, happily, pointing at something in the index.

"For locating lost objects, appeal to Saint Anthony of Padua."

"Are you serious?"

"Of course I'm serious."

She consulted the index again.

"And this is Saint Arild's day, also famous for her miracles. Good."

I took a step back, giving Megan some room. I had no idea what this appeal to a Saint might consist of and wouldn't have been surprised if Megan had suddenly produced some candles and an altar from her bus and started singing hymns. The rain dripped down onto me, Megan and the book. I braced myself for the impending ceremony.

"Hey, Saint Anthony and Saint Arild," said Megan, loudly, "I've lost my keys. Would you help me to find them please?"

She turned round, tossed the book in the bus and headed back inside leaving me wondering about the briefness of it all. I had imagined something much more impressive.

I followed her inside. Obviously Megan had suddenly turned into a mad woman but she didn't seem dangerous.

I reached the stairs and was just preparing to tell Megan that that was one of the most ridiculous things I'd ever seen when Rag appeared at the top of the stairs waving Megan's keys which had just been discovered inside someone's discarded boot.

"Good", said Megan, showing no surprise, and put them in her pocket.

"Thank you Saint Anthony and Saint Arild."

Upstairs Melody Paradise was grinning.

"Always works for her," she said.

21st July (Day 7)

What had become of The Magic Hat was an impenetrable mystery. The Mushroom Clan were strongly suspected of knowing of its whereabouts but this they denied utterly. They claimed it was irretrievably lost on the night of the notorious sinking of the boat belonging to The Riverboat Tribe. However Magwenwy of The Riverboat Tribe claimed that before flinging herself to safety as her narrow boat went under, she noticed the hat was no longer in her cabin. She believed that someone had stolen it.

"But Magwenwy was in a panic," Melody Paradise would say,

whenever the subject was raised. "Quite understandably, after The Mushrooms crashed a double-decker bus into her boat. She can't be sure what she saw."

So no one knew for sure what had happened to The Magic Hat. Rumours had placed it variously with The Galactic Navigators, The Nomadic Daughters Of Lilith, The Clan Of The Night Time Elves and numerous other individuals, some of whom were no longer in the country.

Bernadette of The Mushroom Clan believed it had been taken by an ex-Mushroom called Matthew who was now travelling in India. The Nomadic Daughters Of Lilith claimed that it had been fished out of the river by The Galactic Navigators who now carried it secretly in one of their trucks. The Galactic Navigators denied this but a few of them muttered that if anyone had it would be bound to be The Clan Of The Night Time Elves, who were notoriously untrustworthy, and keen on all things mystical. Still others said that it must be at the bottom of the river, and blamed The Mushrooms for their carelessness in putting it there.

Even before it had been lost, The Magic Hat had been a cause of controversy. Woven into it was a sprig from the Wishing Tree, the last remnant of that now dead icon.

"I made it so we'd have something to remember the tree by," explained Melody Paradise, "but needless to say, everyone started arguing about who should have it. The Galactic Navigators said it should be theirs because they'd been going to the Peaceful Grove the longest. The Tree Planters said it should be theirs because they loved the tree best. The Universal Leyline Protectors said they should have it because they could regenerate it with their pyramid. I said we should all share it. Some chance."

"What happened?"

"Everybody kept trying to steal it. Nobody trusted anyone else by then. They all thought if some tribe got it they'd keep it. I tell you, that last night with The Riverboat Tribe was a nightmare. You wouldn't believe the cunning and depravity displayed by The Nomadic Daughters Of Lilith in trying to get their hands on it. Florimel swam underwater for a hundred yards grasping it in her teeth. She'd have got clean away with it except Magwenwy spotted her white dreadlocks in the moonlight. We had to mount a guard to keep her away, and then The Night Time Elves tried sneaking it off concealed in a plastic model unicorn. The Militant Children Of Lemuria tried bribing The Riverboat Tribe with grass and mushrooms. Despicable, just despicable. Appalling behaviour all round. What would have happened if the boat-sinking-disaster hadn't diverted everyone's attention I can't imagine."

"So it's lost for good?"

"I think so."

Despite her opinion that it was now lost, speculation was still rife, and the fate of The Magic Hat was a continual topic of conversation among the friends of Melody Paradise.

22nd July (Day 8)

Finan had just come back from a land reclamation protest. Generally a dour character, Finan was in an unusually good mood. Despite being utterly bedraggled he claimed to have had a wonderful time. As this protest involved going illegally with The Militant Children Of Lemuria onto private land somewhere outside London and staying there for four days in a bender, risking assault, arrest, and death from hypothermia, I was surprised to hear such enthusiasm. Presumably the protest had some success, at least in terms of attention from the media.

"No," said Finan. "The newspapers didn't show up. Neither did the TV people."

"Then why was it such a success? Has the government agreed to change the law on access to private land?"

"Don't be stupid. Of course they haven't. Anyway, I didn't say it was a big success, I said I had a good time."

Finan had short purple locks with a few longer ones dangling down the back. He generally dressed in very dirty and ripped combat clothes. His topmost T-shirt which appeared to be torn was, on closer examination, simply rotting away with age. The socks he wore were ruined beyond description. He was generally unshaven, which suited his character.

Finan was involved in some sort of dance music project with Mary from The Golden World Eternal Partyers. He was often busy programming drum machines, sequencers, samplers and his trusty Roland 303.

Despite his fondness for making dance music, Finan seldom appeared to be having a good time.

"You had a good time with The Militant Children Of Lemuria? Are they fun to be in a field with?"

Finan shook his head and said that The Militant Children Of Lemuria were not a lot of fun to be anywhere with unless you found it amusing to padlock yourself to a tree and defy the might of the oncoming bulldozers. The Militant Children Of Lemuria were always doing this sort of thing, organising or appearing at doomed and near-suicidal protests against new roads or country-devouring housing projects. Breed, Melody Paradise's sister, was one of their members, and she was a fierce and uncompromising campaigner. A warrior in fact.

Finan supported these causes himself but would not have claimed to be anywhere near as active as The Militant Children Of Lemuria. He was too busy programming his music, or getting stoned, or doing nothing.

"No, there was not a lot of fun to be had in the field. What made it good was the girl I met when we stopped off on the way home to picket a 'Big And Beefy' burger restaurant."

There were some congratulations to Finan from around the table at meeting a nice young woman. Everyone approves of romance and Finan, like Sweep, had rarely been known to have a girlfriend.

"Who was she? Was she at the land protest?"

"No, only at the restaurant."

"Just came along for the picket?"

Finan looked uncomfortable.

"Not exactly. She worked in the restaurant."

"What?" exclaimed Megan, wonderingly. "You've fallen for a woman who works in a burger restaurant?"

"She's a waitress."

42

Melody Paradise, Megan and myself burst out laughing at the thought of Finan, a famously strict vegetarian, falling in love with a waitress in a beefburger restaurant. Finan was offended and informed us sharply that she was a very nice young woman.

"The only person I've ever met who actually has a job," he added, which I could certainly believe.

"Not much of a job I admit, but I think it says something for her character. Imagine. She gets out of bed every day and goes to work. How would anyone do that?"

"Finan," said Megan, "you're a dedicated vegetarian. You feed your dog vegetarian food. How are you going to have a relationship with a beefburger waitress?"

"I'll win her over."

"What's that funny smell?" asked Megan, looking pointedly at Finan.

"What smell?"

Megan reached swiftly over and drew a crumpled parcel of paper from his pocket.

"What's this?"

"A cheeseburger," admitted Finan. "I had to accept it when she offered. I didn't want to seem rude. But I never ate any of it. Don't worry. I'll win her round. I've asked her to the festival."

He threw the cheeseburger into the bin, which was an old paint tin, always overflowing. It spilled out onto the floor and one of the numerous cats that frequented the house came to investigate. Despite having some success with dogs, neither Finan nor Megan nor Melody Paradise could ever convince any of the cats to become vegetarians.

17th August (Day 34) First Day Of The Festival

At the festival Melody Paradise is besieged by lovers and suitors. Sweep sets up his bender on one side of her van and Eko pitches his tepee on the other. Rupert drives his truck up as close as he can and keeps a watchful and jealous eye out for the movements of the others. At the far end of the valley, as far away as he can be without actually leaving the festival, Magwyn The Grim broods alone.

What Melody Paradise makes of all this attention I'm not sure. She professes herself to be uninterested. Love, romance or sex are not on her mind.

Neither are they on mine. I am fully occupied with mere survival. Obliged to live for an entire week in a tent in a muddy and rain-soaked valley, I give myself only a fifty/fifty chance of coming out of it alive. The grim prospect of this struggle to survive in a field full of crazed travellers, crazed travellers' dogs, malicious insects and vindictive plant life is more than enough to command my full attention. If I can just make it alive through seven days in the country away from all the comforts of home, I don't care how great a disaster the reading is. Fortunately for me, no one else cares either.

And yet, I can't help reflecting that there is an extraordinary amount of romance going on around me, most of it painful to the participants in some way or other. All of Melody Paradise's suitors hate and fear each other. This is interfering with Melody's declared intention of spreading love and peace.

To be honest, her family are proving extraordinarily resistant to the idea. I've never seen such bad-tempered hippies. The festival in the valley, supposedly an occasion of harmony, friendship and general enjoyment, is already a place of suspicion and bad feeling. To Melody Paradise this is a disaster.

"I can't leave the country while my family are all arguing with each other," Melody tells me rather sadly, outside my tent, as the rain pours down.

"The whole point of this festival was to make them all friends again."

"Flee while you can," I advise her. "You have too much family and they're all determined to hate each other. It's all that travelling round the world in old vans and buses. It's driven them mad. Just accept it and escape to France."

"I can't. I have to make them like each other. What's the matter with them all? The century's coming to an end. It's a new era."

"Is it the age of Aquarius yet?"

"Possibly," says Melody, "though I'm not really sure. Astrology isn't my strong point. Anyway, it should be an excellent time for love and peace. Oh well, I'll just have to keep trying I suppose. I can't leave before Iris The Peaceful gets here with the new Wishing Tree."

"What if she doesn't make it? I thought she was going to be here at the start?"

"She'll make it. I can sense she's close. I'm sure she'll arrive tomorrow."

I nod. If Melody Paradise says it, it's probably true. She has a talent for prediction.

"Can you do something to keep the dogs away from my tent? They're persecuting me because they know I'm scared of them."

"Just be friendly to them," says Melody, which is as ridiculous a piece of advice as I've ever heard.

18th August (Day 35) Second Day Of The Festival

The valley is a mess. Near the top, where a dirt track leads down from the road, some of the smaller trees have been uprooted, destroyed when the police towed away the travellers' vehicles. Other damaged trees seem not to have regenerated themselves and lurch sickly into the sky. Beside the small river which runs through the valley are two trailers and a caravan, left behind to rust and decay. Bits of furniture lie rotting on the ground. The whole of the wall of the valley is strewn with rubbish ranging from ragged clothing to old tyres. As the rain pours down it all looks very depressing.

The Peaceful Grove, further up the valley, is undamaged but the Wishing Tree is now only a blackened stump. This depresses Melody more than anything else. On our second day in the valley there is no sign of Iris The Peaceful and the new Wishing Tree.

"I thought she'd be here by now," says Melody, "although it doesn't really matter as no one else is either. Where is everyone?"

Apart from The Tribe Of The Last Free Moonbeam, Melody Paradise's family stretches over eleven other groups. She was expecting them all to arrive yesterday or this morning but so far only The Tree Planters are here.

"Looks like there won't be anyone to help The Tree Planters in tonight's 'be nice to the trees event,'" she sighs.

She confesses to me that she feels slightly depressed. I've never known Melody Paradise to be depressed before.

"No wonder you don't feel so good, Melody. We're living outdoors and it's raining. More than enough for anyone. My tent is already a disgrace to the civilised world."

Melody brushes this aside.

"I'm depressed because the place is such a mess."

Melody is carrying a plastic bin liner into which she has been putting rubbish. The effort of her and her friends in clearing up is already making some impression but until more people arrive, particularly The Galactic Navigators with their lifting equipment, nothing can be done about the larger blights on the landscape.

"I'm worried no one will come."

It's unusual for Melody's optimism to slip to such an extent. Perhaps all this activity is getting her down. Melody Paradise is not generally noted for her activity. She is far keener on hanging out with her friends, travelling peacefully, and dancing when the mood takes her. Organising a festival is quite out of character. Organising people is not really something Melody likes doing, preferring generally to spread love and peace in an anarchic fashion, just 'letting it flow' as she says. She would not have contemplated such an arduous endeavour were it not for unusual circumstances surrounding her family. Melody is adamant that she cannot leave the country without making some attempt at bringing peace to them all.

"I think you've done well so far Melody. All your organisation has worked out. I mean, here we are, in the valley, festival starting up. Rupert's arriving soon to take care of the circus which leaves you free to hunt for unicorns, astral travel and spread peace and love amongst all your feuding friends."

"What if no one comes? It'll all be a disaster."

"It won't be a disaster," I say.

Melody tells me that I am an unconvincing liar.

"Not true. Most times I'm a convincing liar. It's just that you are unusually perceptive. Okay, so I am expecting disaster, but only a personal one when the stockbrokers of Chelwyn chase me out of the literary festival. Apart from that I'm fine. Well, I'm a bit worried about the rain, to tell you the truth. Have you noticed the river's rising? When the valley floods I expect you to rescue me. Personal disasters aside, I can't see why things will go wrong for you. Once all your family's tribes arrive they're bound to start talking to each other again."

Not for the first time, Melody Paradise says that I don't know her family.

The tales Melody has told me of the feuds and disagreements between the tribes are baffling in their number and complexity. For instance, The Militant Children Of Lemuria are annoyed with The Universal Leyline Protectors for refusing to help them resist bailiffs in the final stages of a road dispute. While The Militant Children were occupying houses due to be demolished to make way for a motorway, and chaining themselves to the railings, The Universal Leyline Protectors had, despite being in the area, refused to join in. Instead they sat in a nearby undisputed field. They claimed that this field was an important point in the leyline running between England and the Crab Nebula. It was news to The Militant Children Of Lemuria, and to me, that leylines actually extended to the distant galaxies. It had caused some bad feeling. I could understand this. While there would have been no chance whatsoever of me occupying a house against the police or chaining myself to a railing and defying a bulldozer, I could well see that to anyone prepared to do such things the sight of a bunch of fellow travellers sitting in a nearby field gazing up at the sky must have been very frustrating.

The Militant Children's ire extends to other members of the family. Both The Golden World Eternal Party Tribe and The Clan Of The Last Free Moonbeam have aroused their displeasure for allegedly refusing to help them in their struggles.

"Very unfair," Melody pointed out. "It's not everyone who is capable of standing up to the police and bailiffs. The Militant Children Of Lemuria should understand that. Besides, speaking personally, The Tribe Of The Last Free Moonbeam did not refuse to turn up at the protest as they allege. We were just late getting there. Six days late I admit, but we did our best."

The Golden World Eternal Party Tribe are themselves involved in more than one dispute. One of these is a fierce disagreement with The Clan Of The Night Time Elves over damage done to their main generator. The Clan Of The Night Time Elves are themselves fighting a rearguard action against The Tree Planters who have made the very serious allegation against them that they have been cutting down trees. This is not the only tree dispute engaged in by The Tree Planters. They blame The Mushrooms for the notorious Oak-burning-incident. This painful affair also involved The Militant Children Of Lemuria who, in another defence of a wood, had been forced to jump for their lives after finding their tree houses blazing beneath them and The Mushrooms wandering around below shouting apologies for letting their camp-fire get out of hand. As The Mushrooms are also held responsible for the notorious boat-sinking-incident it is not hard to see why they are so generally disliked. Even Melody Paradise with her mission to spread peace cannot keep some small touch of bitterness out of her voice as she relates the desperate circumstances of her sister Magwenwy being forced to swim for her life.

"They are so irresponsible. Wherever The Mushrooms go, chaos follows. What do they expect? You can't eat a whole carrier bag full of magic mushrooms at the same time as trying to park a double-decker bus next to a slippery riverbank and imagine nothing bad will happen. It took The Galactic Navigators six days to get that bus out of the river. Magwenwy's still trying to repair her boat."

These are only a small portion of the arguments that Melody tells me about. All of them have been exacerbated by the suspicions roused by the affair of The Magic Hat, with everyone suspecting everyone else of having it. Some of the disputes are so serious that she is worried about where to put everyone when they arrive.

"I know that The Nomadic Daughters Of Lilith will absolutely refuse to park next to The Galactic Navigators. They don't like us much either. The Elemental Sunshine Family won't want to be close to The Universal Leyline Protectors. I tell you it's all getting too much for me. I wasn't made to be a parking attendant."

She sighs.

"I wonder if it was all a bad idea? Maybe I should have just left them all to get on with it."

"Why not let someone else do it?"

"No one else will. Everyone else seems content to go on arguing. But it's got to stop. When The Tribe Of The Last Free Moonbeam heads across the Channel we're not going to leave chaos behind us. My family is going to get on if I have to kill some of them."

She sits in silence for a while, just toying with her breakfast joint. It's a little past midday. There was some idea that every day around now there would be a friendly meeting of everyone around a camp-fire. Whether the friendly camp-fire meeting will ever take place I'm not sure. Apart from anything else, it's still raining heavily.

Melody continues her rather moody reflections. While it worries her that everyone who arrives will immediately start arguing, it also worries her that some of them might not appear at all.

"The Nomadic Daughters Of Lilith are terrible for holding grudges. They might just refuse to show up. And The Mushrooms will probably get lost somewhere along the way. I've known them take three weeks to travel four miles and even then it was in the wrong direction."

She sighs.

"I'm dreading the arrival of some of them."

"You don't think they might have made up their differences on the way here?"

"Not a chance. More likely they've been studying road maps to find out how to avoid each other. For free and easy living travellers, my family are a stubborn lot."

Melody Paradise has a brother or sister in each of the twelve groups she has invited to the festival but I have the impression that when she refers to her family she actually means everyone connected with these groups. This means that Melody now regards herself as a member of an extended family of more than a hundred people.

What her precise family background is, in more conventional terms, I'm not certain. Not all of her eleven brothers and sisters are blood relations. Some were adopted by Melody's parents whilst they were children and some others seem to have been picked up along the way, granted status as honourary members.

Melody Paradise rarely speaks about her childhood. I have heard her say only two things about her life when she was young. One was that she and her brothers and sisters were renowned for talking to each other all the time, even when they were very small, and the other is that her father had a fearsome temper.

"I can hardly bear to think about what will happen when The Riverboat Tribe and The Mushrooms meet again..."

Melody winces. Obviously this is a particularly painful memory.

"The only thing worse would be the arrival of Magwyn The Grim," continues Melody, shuddering.

"Magwyn The Grim?"

Melody nods.

"It would be bad if he arrived?"

"A total disaster. He must be the only person everyone hates more than The Mushrooms. And as for him and me..."

She makes a face.

I consider this information.

"I don't suppose there could be two people called Magwyn The Grim could there?"

"I wouldn't think so."

"No, it would be an unlikely co-incidence, even in a universe so full of marvellous co-incidences. Yes, I suppose it must be the same Magwyn The Grim that Rupert was going to ask for help."

Melody Paradise groans, and starts to give her joint more serious attention. Outside the rain beats down. Already it is seeping into my inexpertly erected tent, giving me some bitter thoughts about Megan, and Saint Swithun.

Peggy and Eko from The Tree Planters arrive.

"I just checked with my runes," Eko tells Melody. "A very favourable reading. It'll be sunny tomorrow and everyone will show up and start having a good time."

"Did your runes really say that?" asks Melody.

"Absolutely. I picked out the characters for a Viking raid and a huge battle."

"That doesn't sound very good."

"You have to interpret them in light of the modern world," explains Eko. "It means that The Riverboat Tribe will arrive and everyone will start partying."

Immediately I'm depressed. If Eko predicts good times ahead it can only mean the world is about to end. Eko is the worst fortune teller ever to walk the earth. I don't believe he has any skills whatsoever, he just keeps making up these good predictions to impress Melody Paradise. Like a great many others, Eko is always keen to impress Melody Paradise.

There is a small pool of water at the entrance to my tent. Melody Paradise, for no apparent reason, drops her joint into this pool.

"Damn," she says, staring mournfully at the ruined spliff. "I'm so clumsy these days."

She departs with Eko, muttering darkly about Magwyn The Grim though without offering any explanation as to why his appearance would be such a bad thing. Presumably he had one time driven his van over a neighbouring tribe, or started a forest fire at a 'Green Planet' ecological gathering. I wonder how any of them are still alive. Melody Paradise claims to have travelled all round the world but personally I would not trust her or any of her friends to drive me to the nearest Post Office.

The Tree Planters have been doing some tree surgery, cutting off dead branches and suchlike, but apparently the physical damage is not the trees' only problem.

"They're unhappy," she says. "All the trees in the valley are sad because the Wishing Tree was killed. The ones that got damaged

51

just aren't recovering properly."

The Tree Planters have been trying to cheer them up, with limited success. There is one tree in particular, a fig, about which they are very worried.

"Its neighbour got knocked down and it's been lonely ever since. We've been trying to raise its spirits but it doesn't seem to be working."

I enquire how precisely they've been trying to cheer up the fig tree.

"Telling it stories mainly. Roxanna's up there now telling it some Arthurian legends so maybe that'll help."

As Peggy departs, Sweep's head, wet, appears in my tent. Sweep generally appears shortly after Melody. He will then work the conversation round to her without delay. I inform him that Melody has gone back to her van to have another attempt at fixing the hole in the roof. Sweep nods his head in the vague way he does when unsure what to do. His vast green jersey hangs damply around his slight frame.

"Why don't you go and offer to help?"

"Do you think I should? I might get in the way."

It is fortunate that I am good friends with Sweep or his diffidence would long ago have driven me mad.

"Why not? Melody is hopeless with practical things. She's been trying to fix that hole for months. If you waltz in and repair it she'd be bound to appreciate it."

Sweep looks cheerful at the thought, but only for a few seconds.

"I wouldn't know how to fix it," he admits. "I'd just get in the way. Anyway, Eko was with her. I expect he can fix it," he adds gloomily.

Eko is a rival to Sweep for Melody's affections. Despite the fact that he has been known to call himself 'Eko the Great, Master of the Cosmic Winds', he is a rather more practical person than Sweep. He only uses the Master of the Cosmic Winds title while trying to earn a little money at festivals and suchlike making predictions by means of the runes, tarot, I Ching or whatever system he's using at the time.

"You know he's been predicting that him and Melody Paradise are destined to end up together?" says Sweep indignantly.

Despite dismissing Eko as a fraud, Sweep can't help being worried. Whether or not Sweep should be concerned about Eko's fortune telling, there is no denying that Eko is a much more practical person than the juggler. Eko has years of experience of travelling and is used to dealing with attendant problems like vehicle repairs. The only time I can remember Sweep trying to help out with a vehicle repair was some months ago when he managed to drop a small spanner inside Megan's fuel tank and the whole tribe took four days to sort out the problem. After this he had to promise never to go near any of their vehicles again.

"He's always hanging around Melody offering to repair things for her. Do you thing she likes him?" asks Sweep.

"Probably not. I expect he's driving her mad. I mean, think how annoying it would be if every time something went wrong someone just came and fixed it for you."

"Why would that be annoying?" demands Sweep.

"Well, I suppose it wouldn't be annoying at all, now you mention it. Rather pleasing in fact."

Now very worried that Eko is at this moment pleasing Melody Paradise, Sweep hurries off to see if he can get in the way. On his way out he brushes past Megan.

"Your tent's leaking," she says, to which I make quite a sharp reply.

"Why not come and sit with us in my bus?"

"Because the air is an impenetrable fog of marihuana smoke and I don't smoke marihuana. God knows how your baby survives. I'd be surprised if he's ever spent a day when he wasn't stoned. Also the bus is full of dogs with grudges against me. Also I might get involved in some of the problems Melody is trying to sort out and I have sworn to myself that I won't get involved in any problems this week."

"Still the grim struggle for mere survival?"

"That's right."

Megan is a pleasant young woman, about the same age as Melody Paradise with dreadlocks of almost equal length, though uniformly black. Megan is Melody's closest friend. As such, she occasionally discusses with me the vast army of prospective lovers who hover perpetually around the multi-coloured queen of the festival.

"Sweep still hanging on to her every move?"

"Yes. He's just gone to get in the way while Melody tackles the hole in her roof. He's worried that Eko might fix it first. I wish Sweep was more confident. If he keeps hanging around Melody being too scared to speak his mind I'm sure she'll end up annoyed at him."

Megan agrees. The charm of a shy suitor is strictly limited.

"Of course, Megan, if Melody Paradise likes him enough she could just take the initiative. Scoop him up in her arms next time he offers to carry water for her or fetch her firewood."

"I think Melody has too much on her mind to scoop anyone up."

"What does she have to worry about? Compared to me she's having things easy. I'm the one suffering here. Melody's used to this sort of thing. I'm not. Staying in this wet tent is already having a detrimental effect on my health. Do you know what the first symptoms of pneumonia are? I think I can feel it coming on. And I'm worried that the children's TV controller might be trying to get in touch with me about my 'Young Socrates' idea. It's making me anxious. I wish I could afford a mobile phone. It was madness for me to come here. Of course it wouldn't be so bad if you hadn't made it rain."

"What do you mean?" demands Megan.

"All that Saint Swithun stuff. Probably if you hadn't mentioned it was Saint Swithun's day no one would have noticed anything and the sun would have come out. But no, you had to go ranting on about how it was going to rain for the next forty days, which will, I calculate, take us right up to the end of the festival, by which time I will be either drowned or dead of pneumonia. I'm convinced it's your fault."

Megan laughs.

"It doesn't depend on anyone mentioning it. It just happens naturally. Or it's meant to. Anyway, I didn't say that I seriously believed it."

I'm not convinced and maintain a suspicion that the rain is Megan's fault.

"It was a risky thing to do anyway, you probably invoked the rain without knowing it."

"I didn't invoke anything."

"Yes you did, you invoked Saint Anthony when you lost your keys."

Megan, slightly defensively, says that this was altogether different.

"Altogether stupid," I reply, feeling a quite reasonable desire to be criticising someone.

"Well, it worked didn't it?"

"No."

"Yes it did. I found my keys right afterwards."

"You'd have found them anyway."

Megan refuses to argue the subject any further which I find even more aggravating. Megan has not dispensed with the Catholicism of her childhood but is generally unwilling to discuss it. I'm forced to return to general criticisms of the world.

"How is a man supposed to survive in this? You're all mad being here. I'd never have come near the place if I'd known I was going to be marooned in the middle of a biblical flood. None of us will come out alive. The only ones with any chance are The Riverboat Tribe, providing The Mushrooms haven't sunk all their boats. Are they really going to sail here?"

This seems unlikely to me, although Melody says that the river in the valley is connected to some canal that will enable them to do so. Megan assures me that they are indeed going to arrive by boat.

"Good. That's one bunch of ridiculous hippies I'll be pleased to see. If this deluge continues I'll hijack a barge and sail right out of here."

From somewhere outside comes the plaintive and irritating sound of a tin whistle. This will be Rooster, who plays the whistle very badly.

"How's the literary workshop coming on?"

I wave a plastic carrier bag at her.

"This is it."

"That's it?"

"Yes. I just bundled some books and a pencil into this bag. I haven't decided quite what to do yet. I'll make up my mind closer to the time."

"Maybe you should have got someone else to help you," suggests Megan. "Some other authors."

"Well, I didn't want to go to a lot of trouble organising things," I tell her. "Anyway I don't know any other authors. I could hardly write to some complete stranger asking them to come and stay in a wet valley for a week and help me out at a creative writing class, it's not that attractive a prospect."

I did actually once write to Martin Amis asking him to read with me at an event to raise money to help the Campaign Against The Criminal Justice Bill. Some time later, when the event was over, he wrote me back a friendly letter to say he was sorry he was too busy to do it. At least he wrote. All I got from Jeannette Winterson was a brief postcard from her PA saying that she was in America.

I can see Megan is a little doubtful about my workshop but I point out to her that the real disaster is waiting in the form of Rupert's circus. About this she expresses some genuine concern.

"It's all very well for Melody to say it doesn't matter what sort of shambles it is but what if hundreds of tourists turn up on the day expecting something really good? The Village Summer Fair Committee has paid out quite a lot of money. I'm sure they're not going to be very happy if all they get is one or two motorbikes and Sweep doing a bit of juggling."

Megan again seems to have some moral doubts about taking money for something and then doing it badly.

"It'll be dreadful," I state, quite confidently. "Rupert sells jet aircraft to businessmen. Hardly the right qualification to go around putting on circuses."

Megan agrees. She expresses more worry about the non-appearance of Iris The Peaceful.

"Iris promised she'd be here for the start of the festival. I hope nothing's gone wrong."

Melody is looking after Megan's baby but as it is feeding time and Megan likes to take care of this personally she crawls out of my tent and heads back to her bus.

I eat a piece of flapjack and muse about the circus. I don't like circuses, traditional or alternative, so I don't much care what it's like, but I agree with Megan that there may be some problems with Melody's plan. This sort of modern circus, with chain-saws and motorbikes and explosions has been quite well done for a number of years. It seems likely that Chelwyn village will be expecting something considerably more spectacular than Melody and Rupert are planning to provide, with their budget of nothing. Melody has diverted all of the money to her festival so presumably there is nothing left for staging the event. Magwyn The Grim might be able to build whatever is needed but no one is sure if he's coming.

"I used to go out with Magwyn The Grim. It was terrible," says Melody Paradise, astonishing me.

Her voice rises.

"Why did Rupert ask him of all people?"

Water drips down through the trees which shelter the higher part of the valley. These trees have prevented my tent from being washed away but even here the constant rain has made the earth slippery and treacherous. I have fallen over several times. So has Melody. She's right, she is becoming clumsy.

As if to remind us that there are potential broken hearts in every direction, Rooster and Rag both approach Melody and ask her eagerly when The Nomadic Daughters Of Lilith are due to arrive.

"Soon," replies Melody, with little enthusiasm. Rag and Rooster stare at each other suspiciously before going their separate ways.

"It's unfortunate they've both fallen for Florimel," I say.

"Damn Florimel," snaps Melody, her hair billowing behind her in the gathering wind and rain.

Despite some slight dismay at her anger I am intrigued to learn that the angelic Melody Paradise once had a relationship with the dreaded Magwyn The Grim. I'm keen to find out more. Surely any such relationship must have been a disaster from start to finish. It's always enjoyable hearing about other people's disastrous relationships. Melody looks like she has a lot more to say on the subject but we are interrupted by a shout from Livia who is sitting on top of Megan's bus, oblivious to the rain.

"Someone's coming."

The Tribe Of The Last Free Moonbeam had travelled down with The Tree Planters, there being no dispute between them, but no one else had arrived on that first day. Now, well into the evening of the second, the failure of anyone else to arrive has caused some concern. Melody has again wondered aloud if feelings were now so bad as to prevent some of them coming at all.

The Tribe Of The Last Free Moonbeam are such harmless people that it is surprising to learn that even they have enemies, but they have. They have a long standing dispute with The Elemental Sunshine Family arising out of some domestic violence between two of their members who went out together. There is also the persistent bad feeling caused by the accusation from The Militant Children Of Lemuria that they had failed to support them.

Furthermore, although I had been under the impression that everyone liked Melody Paradise, it turns out that she is personally responsible for another dispute. After promising to sign on illegally for Florimel, while Florimel was travelling abroad for a few weeks, Melody had forgotten to do so. As a result of this, Florimel's claim for welfare benefits was closed down causing her endless trouble when she returned home. As the best excuse Melody Paradise could offer for this failure was the honest admission that she had been too drunk the night before to remember to turn up at the benefit office, or even to get out of bed, Florimel had not been pleased. Florimel apparently is a woman who holds a grudge.

Florimel and Mirabel travel together in a Land Rover, still in its original camouflage colours. Everything I have heard about them makes me wish that I was not going to meet them. They are by repute aggressive and unfriendly, and much given to bad language. This makes it strange that Rooster and Rag are both besotted by her. It also makes it awkward for Melody Paradise. Rooster and

Rags' attentions to Florimel give her plenty of opportunities for putting Melody down.

Fortunately it is not The Nomadic Daughters Of Lilith who are at this moment negotiating the narrow track down into the valley in four old vans, three buses, an estate car and a caravan, but The Clan Of The Night Time Elves. They are immediately recognisable by the green pennants that flutter from their vehicles.

As far as I know only two of the tribes of Melody's relations wear any sort of recognisable uniform. The Militant Children Of Lemuria wear floppy blue hats with long tassels, and The Clan Of The Night Time Elves wear green leggings, or green socks, or green spray painted boots.

Melody is pleased to see The Night Time Elves. She forgets her anger over Magwyn The Grim and runs to meet them, seeking out the bus belonging to her brother Willis.

Behind me there is some muttering. Standing around their benders – igloo shaped constructions of hazelwood covered with canvas – The Tree Planters don't look pleased. They're reviving memories of the time they caught The Night Time Elves cutting down trees. This still rankles. It will, I imagine, be the first dispute that Melody Paradise will have to deal with. Never being much of a diplomat myself, I shall be interested to observe her technique. Whatever method she adopts I've no doubt that Melody Paradise will be able to settle the disagreement, being such an agreeable person herself.

"Damned Night Time Elves," mutters Peggy. "The trees are depressed enough already without them arriving."

"Still no luck with the fig?" I enquire.

Peggy shakes her head. Roxanna's rendition of the Arthurian legend has failed to cheer it up at all.

"It's a very depressed tree," says Roxanna, but vows to keep on trying.

I'm not qualified to judge whether or not the fig tree is actually depressed but it certainly doesn't look healthy. I really should keep my mouth shut but I'm unable to prevent myself from saying that if I was a depressed tree, Roxanna telling me Arthurian legends would not cheer me up at all. This does not go down very well.

"It's always worked in the past," she says, defensively.

"Maybe it's missing its home," suggests John. "The fig tree is native to Italy after all."

"Well, there's your problem," I say confidently. "No point trying to cheer it up with Arthurian legends is there? Obviously if it's missing Italy it needs something a little more familiar. Why not try entertaining it with a few of the Latin classics?"

Sensing my sarcasm The Tree Planters frown at me. I frown back, and depart.

Behind The Clan Of The Night Time Elves comes Rupert in his pristine and costly Mercedes Mobile Home. I frown again. In fact, I groan. As this gathering is primarily for Melody's family it has not been advertised anywhere and does not appear in any of the lists of festivals that circulate each spring. I might therefore have reasonably expected to avoid Rupert had he not been recruited to direct the circus. A tragic mistake I feel, and one of which no good will come.

I won't admit to prejudice against anyone simply because they are rich but when a man spends the winter months going round Germany, France and Switzerland as a representative for a company selling private jets, thereby raking in vast amounts of money for himself and the family business, and then reverts for the summer months to the persona of travelling hippy, it does make me wonder. Rupert, who appears from his Mercedes wearing a mixture of Indian prints and faded denim, very clean faded denim, is absolutely rolling in money and has been since the day he was born.

Well, as I say, I don't like to hold anyone's birth against them. I am aware that several of the people with whom Melody Paradise travels were not born poor by any means, and may in fact merely be going through a brief youthful rebellion before departing back to the safety of their family wealth and job prospects. Finan for instance, for all his rotting clothes, comes from a very nice part of Richmond and his family bought him most of his musical equipment. However, as Rupert is actually the son of an extremely wealthy business magnate and related by marriage to several members of the House of Lords it strikes me as somewhat disingenuous of him to adopt the persona of travelling hippy.

To make things worse, Rupert seems to be very well in with whatever network of people organise festivals. Melody has told me tales of Rupert rolling up to various sites, having been given the job of organising or producing something or other, then shifting other people's tents and benders and ordering people around before going back to the comforts of his extremely well-equipped mobile home. For this sort of officious behaviour he is not well-liked.

As soon as Melody Paradise disentangles herself from the embrace of her brother Willis, or Willis Elf as he is commonly known, she finds herself embraced by Rupert. He informs her loudly that he's come down to sort everyone out and he's looking forward to putting on the circus, even though it's on a rather smaller scale than he's used to.

According to Megan, Rupert's real motive for helping out is that he too is in pursuit of Melody Paradise. She suspects that he has already asked Melody to leave The Tribe Of The Last Free Moonbeam and travel round Europe in comfort with him.

The rain intensifies. I have been wet for two days. I long for my comfy armchair. Rupert takes Melody's arm and ushers her into his luxurious home. I trudge back to my tent, keeping a watchful eye on the pack of dogs which are gathered under a tree on the far side of the valley. This pack includes several lurchers, which are hunting dogs, and fast runners. I hate them.

As I pass Megan's bus she leans out of a window and invites me in for some food. I decline, having previously determined not to touch anything cooked here. Who knows what might be in it? Strange organic ingredients and harmful vegetables no doubt.

The Clan Of The Night Time Elves set up camp down in the valley, close to the river, far away from their enemies The Tree Planters. Obviously they have no thoughts of letting bygones be bygones.

Not long afterwards, Melody emerges from Rupert's mobile home and approaches The Elves with a purposeful gait and a determined air. She interrupts Willis Elf who is helping to put up one of their large green banners and points up the valley to The Tree Planters. They talk for a few minutes. Willis seems dubious but Melody is not to be put off. She takes him by the arm and starts leading him towards The Tree Planters.

This seems like a good start. I'm impressed. Melody Paradise is obviously going to waste no time in putting things right.

Three more of The Clan Of The Night Time Elves join Melody Paradise and Willis as they walk up to the encampment of The Tree Planters. I'm interested in the outcome so I tag along. Willis has been complaining to Melody about being forced to make peace but under Melody's benign influence he is now coming round to the idea.

"We must start getting on with each other," says Melody. "Think how shocking it'll be if no one is speaking to each other when Iris arrives with the new Wishing Tree? We'll be disgraced. The new tree won't like us at all. I can't stand the thought of the new Wishing Tree not liking me, I'll feel terrible."

As no one wants Melody to feel terrible, there is a general consensus among the four Elves that they might as well make peace.

Willis Elf is wearing a pair of Doc Martens which have been painted green and decorated with a constellation of silver stars. These stars are already disappearing behind a nebula of mud. Such is the detrimental effect of being in this place that I am now capable of holding a conversation with a man who calls himself Willis Elf and paints stars on his boots, and not minding too much. A very poor state for me to be in.

In the long summer twilight The Tree Planters are gathered round their camp-fire. Mark is playing an Irish jig on a mandolin. The Tree Planters are quite a genial group, if given to bouts of idiocy like relating Arthurian legends to fig trees. Their collective spirit has been slightly dented however by a bitter dispute between John and Alistair.

John and Alistair, formerly as pleasant a couple as ever exchanged eyebrow piercing studs, have argued vehemently about under which tree it is most spiritually beneficial to park their van. John has thrown Alistair out of the van, claiming to be shocked beyond measure by his boyfriend's assertion that in August you should park your van under a birch tree instead of an elm. Alistair, forced to seek refuge where he can, is now reduced to sleeping in the open, wrapped up in a piece of polythene. Despite this, he refuses to back down. He states in the strongest possible terms that he would rather sleep in a piece of polythene under a birch tree than in a van under an elm, particularly in August, when birch trees are at their most spiritually beneficial. He is predicting a bad end for John and says that he would not be at all surprised if the elm tree came crashing down on his van, which would serve him right. This argument is now threatening to spread to the rest of The Tree Planters.

John and Ali are both seated at the camp-fire, but as far apart as they can be. Ali has his roll of polythene beside him. I notice he's taken out the eyebrow stud John gave him as a winter solstice present.

The Tree Planter's encampment smells of freshly baked bread. They knead their own dough and bake it in an oven in one of their vans. Quite impressive, I think. Their bread is warm and appetising although I have not tried eating any of it. I don't trust anything here and am still expecting to be stricken down by disease. Before leaving home I did stock up with medicines at my local chemist. Rather disappointingly, he told me there was no general antidote to poison freely available over the counter.

Melody's sister Peggy, sometime called Pretty Peggy after a song, shouts a greeting to Melody.

"Come and join us," she says, "but kindly don't bring these Elf-pigs near our camp-fire."

Melody Paradise looks pained.

"Peggy, that's not the spirit. I've organised this festival so we can all get along together and this is a good place to start. So why don't you and The Clan Of The Night Time Elves make up your differences right now? It'll be a good example for everyone else.

"Who is she calling an Elf pig?" demands Willis.

"You," says Peggy.

Melody holds up her hands. She smiles, which quietens everyone's temper.

Now Melody has previously explained to me that the reason The Tree Planters dislike The Clan Of The Night Time Elves is because they once caught them in the act of cutting down a silver birch. The Clan Of The Night Time Elves had justified their action by saying that it was an old and sick tree which was soon going to fall over anyway and they were going to use the wood for fuel and there was nothing wrong with that. The Tree Planters however had been of the opinion that there was nothing the matter with the tree that a little love and attention would not have soon put right and, besides, there had been plenty of dead wood lying around for making fires. I couldn't really see what all the fuss was about and agreed with Melody that it should be easy enough to sort out.

"I'll just suggest that The Clan Of The Night Time Elves promise to plant a few trees somewhere or other and The Tree Planters stop calling them Elf-pigs and it's bound to be all right."

In this Melody is sadly mistaken. Despite her pacifying presence, the moment the subject is broached they all start arguing again.

"That was a perfectly healthy tree," states Peggy forcefully.

"It was sick as hell," retorts Willis. "Practically dead."

"Well, it was when you finished with it," says John. "But we would have saved it."

"Saved it? You? I've seen healthy trees keel over and die the moment you approach."

"No doubt shortly after you'd taken an axe to their trunks. The way you Elves go on I'm surprised there's a tree still standing in the country. The Militant Children Of Lemuria should forget about road contractors and just follow you around, trying to salvage what's left."

"And who made you such big experts on trees?" demands Willis's friend Parrot. "The Clan Of The Night Time Elves commune with nature. We know a sick tree when we see one."

Peggy is furious at anyone casting aspersions on her vast knowledge of trees.

"Tree murderers," she shouts.

"Elf-pigs," shouts John.

At this Willis Elf looks quite violent and strides forward purposely before being halted by Melody Paradise.

"Stop this at once," she demands.

"Whose side are you one?" says Willis Elf. "I tell you I'm fed up with these people going round like they think they were the only ones in the world who like trees. The Night Time Elves love trees. We talk to them every night. I know more about trees than all these people put together. Look at that idiot who's parked his van under an elm in August. Doesn't he know that's an unlucky thing to do?"

"Aha!" says Ali The Tree Planter, rising to his feet in triumph. "Just what I've been saying. A terrible mistake which can only bring misfortune."

John is outraged by his ex-boyfriend's treachery and has to be restrained from attacking him.

"You see?" says Willis Elf, as John and Ali struggle to come to blows. "They can't even behave sensibly among themselves. What chance would a sick larch have in their hands?

By now, the whole mass of The Tree Planters, some twelve or so people, is on its feet, either struggling to restrain John and Alistair or shouting abuse at the four indignant Night Time Elves. Abuse flies in all directions. People slip and slide in the mud which adds to the confusion.

"Please!" screams Melody, "Stop this!"

Such is the force of Melody's positive aura that even in this melée a sort of peace does break out, although one that is laced with anger and recriminations.

"So now we've sorted out our main differences," continues Melody Paradise, "Let's say we just bring this to a satisfactory finish. Willis Elf, I suggest that you and your friends just promise to plant a few trees to make up for the one The Tree Planters are upset about, and Peggy, why don't you just admit the birch was sick and allow for the fact that The Night Time Elves do know quite a lot about trees?"

I take a step backwards. Even I, who make no claim to be any sort of diplomat, can see that this is a poor time to make such a suggestion. Willis explodes. Peggy explodes. John explodes. Ali stands on the sidelines adding fuel to the fire by siding with The Night Time Elves. Several of his friends who were hurt in the struggle with John now seem to be on his side and scream at their fellow Tree Planters to stop making such a fuss about nothing.

After a further brief exchange of views, Willis and his companions turn on their green heels and storm back down the valley. When Melody pleads with them to reconsider, they are quite abusive. They tell her that they are by no means pleased with her for siding with The Tree Planters and demanding that they plant some trees to make up for the one they cut down. When Melody turns to The Tree Planters her sister Peggy tells her stiffly that if she had known that Melody was going to spend the whole time lecturing them on how much more The Night Time Elves knew about trees than they did, they'd never have come to the festival.

Meanwhile Alistair and several others are packing up their belongings to move to another part of the valley. They say that they no longer wish to be associated with such a stupid collection of people as Peggy, John, and anyone else foolish enough to park their van under an elm in August.

"We're moving down to The Clan Of The Night-time Elves. When it comes to trees they certainly know what they're talking about."

Melody spends a few hopeless moments staring at the departing factions before walking sadly back to her van. I stand alone in the mud for a while, shaking my head. The preceding scene was nothing like what I had imagined. Rather than making anything better, Melody Paradise's attempts at reconciliation made things worse. They all still hate each other and The Tree Planters have now split in half.

Everyone seemed so eager to fight that I wonder if there might be something in Melody's theory that they were all cursed after the Wishing Tree died. I reject this though. The problem isn't a curse. The problem is that they're all demented.

Melody Paradise did not actually seem to be very good at

reconciliation, which opens up whole new terrors for me. While prepared for the endless suffering entailed in coming to the festival, I had at least expected to be surrounded by a genial crowd of people. If Melody can't do better with the other feuding factions I'll be in the middle of a tribal war. The factions will end up killing each other. Any innocent author caught up in the middle will fare very badly indeed. Once again I curse myself for ever getting involved.

Peggy taps me on the shoulder.

"About this fig tree," she says. "We've been considering your idea. And you know, you might be right. Maybe Arthurian legends aren't the thing to cheer up a Mediterranean tree. So how about it?"

"How about what?"

"How about telling it some tales from the Latin Classics? Like you suggested."

I burst out laughing.

"I didn't suggest any such thing."

"Yes you did."

"Well, I wasn't serious."

The Tree Planters all look at me seriously. Surely they can't actually think I'm going to start telling stories to sick trees? Completely outrageous. I bid them a swift goodbye and hurry off into the damp evening gloom.

As the second day of the festival draws to a close I find a rather sad Melody Paradise being comforted by Megan in the Peaceful Grove. The Peaceful Grove is a small and secluded area at the highest part of the valley. The tops of the trees hang over the clearing, giving some shelter. In the middle of the grove are the pathetic remains of the Wishing Tree.

"A bit small for a Wishing Tree, wasn't it?" I comment.

"I suppose so," agrees Melody Paradise. "More of a Wishing Bush really. But Wishing Tree sounded better. And that's what Iris called it. It was she that discovered it was a Wishing Tree in the first place."

Before or after visiting the Hanging Gardens of Babylon,

I wonder, but don't say it.

Next to the stump is a large standing stone around six feet tall. It's grey, heavy and slightly sombre in the twilight. Each time I see it I try to picture the lives of the stone age tribe who fashioned it and placed it here but I can never form a clear image. It's too long ago. I can't imagine what they were like. Whoever they were, their obelisk has stood here for the past three thousand years, upright, majestic and unmovable.

Melody and Megan are smoking one of the largest joints I've ever seen, including even the vast bazooka-like constructions once favoured by reggae stars.

"What a disaster."

"Abandon the enterprise," I advise her. "Your family are all mad. Flee while you can."

Melody Paradise refuses to flee, although when I inform her that Magwyn The Grim has just arrived in his army truck it seems like she might be wavering.

It is time for my treatment. Melody rubs the usual herbal concoction on my arm and wrist. When she places her hands on me, the familiar heat flows through. It was at first very strange to me how heat flowed from Melody's hands but I'm used to it now. So used to it in fact it seems to me that today it is not as strong as usual. Melody's hands have cooled a little.

I try and cheer up Melody by entertaining her with the story of The Tree Planters asking me to help treat the sick fig tree with the Latin classics.

"Imagine," I say, slapping my thigh and chortling. "Imagine me standing next to a tree and quoting from Livy. Isn't that the stupidest thing you've ever heard? These Tree Planters have got to be the most ridiculous people on the planet."

I guffaw with laughter, only stopping when I notice Melody Paradise staring at me rather intently. I realise that my attempt to entertain her has backfired somewhat when I find myself being led up the valley to read to the tree.

"I absolutely refuse to do it Melody. I don't care what you say, I'm not reading Horace's *Odes* to a fig tree."

"But it's such a good idea," says Melody. "Absolutely brilliant. It was so clever of you to realise that Arthurian legends were the wrong thing for a Mediterranean tree. You have to help now."

"Let someone else do it."

"No one else here knows any ancient Roman stories. It has to be you. Think how pleased The Tree Planters will be. Remember, tonight was my 'be nice to the trees night', which isn't going to happen now as there's hardly anyone here and The Elves have argued with The Planters already. It'll entirely make up for the mess I made of things earlier."

"I won't do it. Not under any circumstances."

"Peggy," says Melody Paradise, as we reach her encampment, "Martin has agreed to help you."

The Tree Planters clap and cheer. I scowl round at everybody. I seem to be trapped.

"Well, don't blame me if the damned tree dies," I say, resigning myself to my fate.

So I spend the second evening at the festival talking to a tree. I give it a version of Terence's first play, *The Girl From Andros*, a pleasant, light comedy.

"I think I should probably avoid the heavier Latin works. Light comedy seems more in order for an invalid. Tacitus would be too much for it to follow if it's not feeling well. Juvenal might finish it off entirely."

Melody Paradise and The Tree Planters gather round as I relate *The Girl From Andros*, an ancient Roman romance between Pamphilus and Glycerium, a romance which is complicated by the interference of Simo, Pamphilus's father and Chremes, a neighbour. It all works out well in the end. Feeling fairly self-conscious about the whole thing, I would not say my performance is all that good but The Tree Planters seem pleased.

"I'm sure the fig tree enjoyed it," say Peggy and Roxanna. "It's definitely perked up a bit."

The tree looks the same to me. After all the trouble it's caused me I won't be sorry if it keels over in the night.

23rd July (Day 9)

A week or so after Melody first asked me to help at the festival, I realised that I should be getting on with things. If I was to hold a creative writing class I should surely get something creative ready. I couldn't think of anything. What happens at a creative writing class anyway? I decided to think about it later.

I was, at the time, deeply engrossed in the building of a vast city on a new video game I'd just bought. So what with grappling with pollution problems and trying to attract more citizens into the city, I was spending around ten hours a day at my games machine and did not want to have to start doing any writing or researching. I was meanwhile sinking further into debt but was still confident that my 'Young Socrates' idea would be taken up by children's television. When 'Young Socrates' was being networked round the world I would have plenty of money.

Finan was much happier than he had been. The beefburger woman had decidedly improved his moods. I suppose I should stop calling her the beefburger woman. Her name was Irene. That very day they were off to join a road protest in north London where The Militant Children Of Lemuria were defending a row of houses and a small meadow against a proposed bypass.

I saw them set off. They made a slightly incongruous couple: Finan with his purple locks, shabby clothes and pierced nose and Irene in the quite normal attire of someone going to work in a restaurant. She wore a cream blouse and a blue skirt. Her hair was plain brown, uncluttered by dreadlocks or beads. There were no rings through her ears, nose, lips, or eyebrows. Her sole concession to Finan's world was a pair of strong boots, themselves a little incongruous beneath her knee length skirt.

Before they left she confessed to being a little nervous about attending the protest. She'd seen pictures on television of people being arrested and dragged away into police vans. Finan reassured her. He told her they'd keep out of the way of any trouble. Irene had never in her life attended any sort of protest; despite her nerves she was looking forward to it as a new experience.

Irene had proved popular with The Tribe Of The Last Free Moonbeam and was well-liked though they still teased Finan about her working in a beefburger restaurant and being completely straight. He defended her, saying she'd handed in her notice, as well as secretly distributing anti-beefburger propaganda around the tables. They went off quite happily together.

Melody Paradise was looking as spectacular as ever. She'd just had the newly grown two inches of hair round her head dyed a lovely deep green, with every seventh lock or so a contrasting light blue. I complimented her on the additions and she thanked me brightly, and smiled.

"How's the arm?"

I told her there was some slight improvement after her treatment, which was true. I arranged to come round for more treatment later. Melody had at this time just cured a young woman of eczema, which had been famously resistant to all conventional medicines, so I was prepared to place some confidence in her abilities. Melody informed me that the money from the Chelwyn Village Summer Fair Committee had arrived. I was impressed. I'm used to people planning things and then nothing happening. For a scheme to actually work was unusual, almost unique.

"I hope you haven't been playing video games. Very bad for your wrist."

I assured her I hadn't been. It was a mistake ever to have mentioned it. Like all doctors or healers, Melody Paradise would insist on patients stopping doing the things they most enjoyed.

24th July (Day 10)

The Famous Romance of Melody Paradise and Magwyn The Grim, as related by Mary from The Golden World Eternal Party Tribe:

"Magwyn first saw Melody Paradise at a rave put on by The Golden World Eternal Party Tribe at a small circle of standing stones in Somerset. He wasn't called Magwyn The Grim then, just Magwyn. He wasn't ever what you would call cheerful or talkative

71

but he didn't used to be quite so bad. No one liked him much though. No one was particularly pleased to see him because he was not really a fun person to have around. He drank a lot, and caused arguments, and got into fights, and if he wasn't doing that then he was criticising someone, or giving them a hard time. It's no fun for anyone being criticised by Magwyn because he has quite a sharp tongue and a sarcastic manner. Well, he used to have, when he spoke. All in all, he was never well-liked.

"One time, for instance, a few of us were together on a hill in Spain watching the sunset and telling stories. When Iris The Peaceful told everyone about the time she rode on a centaur to Sparta, Magwyn burst out laughing and said it was the most stupid thing he'd ever heard. Which wasn't very polite. No one could ever remember anyone being rude to Iris The Peaceful before. If she says she rode on a centaur to Sparta then I'm sure she did.

"We all wished we hadn't run into Magwyn. He was over in Spain selling some stained glass. He's very good at stained glass, when he's sober enough to do it properly. When he's not he gets it all wrong then breaks it. Everyone was pleased when he got in his truck and drove away.

"Every time I heard of Magwyn he'd been upsetting someone or other. The Galactic Navigators don't like him because he ran one of their vans off the road when leaving a festival instead of just waiting till he could pass, and The Universal Leyline Protectors despise him because he threw a cider bottle at their pyramid and made a hole in it.

"The Golden World Eternal Party Tribe wasn't organising such big events back then," said Mary. "We're much more successful now, but the event at the stone circle wasn't very large, about three or four hundred people. It was good, even with Magwyn there. He'd arrived on his own. Magwyn was always on his own, he never had any friends. He drives that old army truck with the small metal sculptures stuck on the back. One time Peggy admired them and he said he wasn't aware she had any talent as an art critic. He paints as well, but I've never seen any of his pictures. He's usually covered in paint, and dirt.

"While everyone else was dancing or sitting around, Magwyn just wandered around on his own swigging on a bottle and shoving past people and scowling at them if they protested.

"Eventually he crashed into Melody Paradise. He was pretty drunk by this time. I know, because I was standing right next to Melody. Naturally, he didn't apologise or anything like that. In fact he insulted her hair, which was another bad thing to do. The entire Tribe Of The Last Free Moonbeam rose to her defence, outraged, because you just can't go around insulting Melody Paradise's hair. They've all put too much effort into it. They love it. I love it. I love her. Melody is the most beautiful of my sisters, without a doubt. No one insults her. Apart from Magwyn of course.

"Soon they were all threatening to beat each other up and then Hawk and Mulberry from The Navigators got involved because they can never stay out of trouble either. In one instant Magwyn had spoiled everything. The Tribe Of The Last Free Moonbeam are a pretty peaceful bunch but Magwyn was so abusive they couldn't help being furious and it really seemed like there might be a fight until Melody stepped between them all and told them to stop arguing, which they did. Back then Melody could stop arguments just like that. I've noticed she isn't quite so good at it now. Her friends all calmed down. Magwyn just glowered at everyone then stumbled off."

Mary paused. She was one of the smaller members of the family, with very pale skin and thick red hair. Her clothes were among the most colourful, which is saying something, a patched and layered jumble of purples and greens and yellows and reds. So bright and striking was her appearance that I knew it well and recognised her figure long before I was ever introduced to her. I remembered her from the time I saw her. She was on top of a statue in Trafalgar Square. A demonstration against the Criminal Justice Bill had just marched into the square led by the music truck of The Golden World Eternal Partyers. Mary and Melody Paradise were dancing on top of the statue, and laughing at their friends as they played in the fountain below, splashing water up at them. It was a bright and sunny day and it was the most fun I've ever had in Trafalgar Square.

Usually all you do in Trafalgar Square is wait for a bus. Every time I saw Mary after that I remembered her on top of the statue, laughing and dancing with Melody Paradise.

"So that was how they first met. Not the best of starts, but Magwyn never made a good start with anyone in his life. He's a pig."

"But they ended up going out together?"

Mary frowned. She wasn't happy with the memory.

"They did. Which goes to show that Melody Paradise is just as stupid as everyone else when it comes to picking boyfriends, and maybe stupider."

25th July (Day 11)

Melody Paradise was the ninth daughter of a ninth daughter. This, she claimed, made her magical, and gave her healing powers. As well as eight sisters she had three brothers. Some were blood relations, others had just happened along. None of the eleven brothers and sisters claimed special powers, but like Melody they were all travellers.

Melody Paradise rode around in an old red van and was the leader of The Tribe Of The Last Free Moonbeam. Melody Paradise spread love and peace.

Her sister Pretty Peggy travelled with The Tree Planters, who looked after trees wherever they went. They were also musicians.

Her sister Catherine travelled with The Galactic Navigators, who plotted their route by the stars. They were a large tribe, and very practical, and many of them were vendors of various goods. They were talented at making and repairing things.

Her sister Mary travelled with The Golden World Eternal Party Tribe, who made music and held raves wherever they went.

Her sister Iris The Peaceful travelled with The Contemplators, who journeyed quietly in horse-drawn vehicles. Everyone liked Iris The Peaceful.

Her sister Magwenwy travelled in a narrow boat with The Riverboat Tribe, who sailed up and down the country's canals and rivers.

Her sister Breed travelled with The Militant Children Of
Lemuria, who fought with contractors and police when new roads
were despoiling the countryside, and fought with huntsmen when
they were chasing foxes, and fought with factory owners when
they were polluting the land.

Her sister Bernadette, who was the oldest, travelled with The
Mushroom Clan, who spent their days in a hallucinogenic stupor.
Everyone disliked The Mushroom Clan.

Her sister Florimel travelled with The Nomadic Daughters
Of Lilith.

Her brother Patrick, who was the oldest brother but younger
than Bernadette, travelled with The Universal Leyline Protectors.
They were concerned with preserving all leylines, both on this
world and throughout the universe.

Her brother Willis travelled with The Clan Of The Night
Time Elves.

Her brother Michael travelled with The Elemental Sunshine
Family.

That was the family of Melody Paradise, all of whom she was
going to meet at the festival.

26th July (Day 12)

I asked Mary to tell me how it came about that the blessed Melody
Paradise ever came to have a relationship with the cursed Magwyn
The Grim. Mary did not relate this with much enthusiasm. She
said that she had always disapproved of it and would rather have
seen her sister going out with a stockbroker or a Conservative
politician than Magwyn.

"It was all because he injured himself after stumbling off drunk.
Everyone had forgotten all about him. We thought he'd probably
just driven off although Magwyn wouldn't leave a place just
because everyone there hated him. He's too thick-skinned for that.

"Sometime around six in the morning I'd just finished my stint
at the turntables. I was sharing a joint with Melody and Megan

when someone came up and said they'd just found Magwyn lying beside his truck with his head cut open like he'd fallen down and hit the fender. This met with general approval. A bash on the head seemed to be just what he deserved.

"Melody didn't agree. She said we'd better take a look and see if he was all right. Very public-spirited of Melody. I suppose being a healer makes her feel obliged not to let someone lie around injured. Personally I wouldn't have cared if Magwyn had died. Would have served him right. But she thought we'd best check on him if only to stop him freezing to death overnight and then the newspapers giving us a hard time about someone dying at an illegal rave.

"He seemed quite bad. I couldn't really tell if he was seriously injured or just drunk and unconscious but Melody felt his pulse and looked at his aura."

"Looked at his aura?" I said, rather dubiously.

"That's right, looked at his aura," said Mary. "A good healer like Melody Paradise can see your aura. She said his was very weak, in fact she said we'd better help him right away. So we did. We carried him into his truck and Melody got busy with her herbs, her healing touch and whatever else she does. I don't really know what Melody does to heal people but I know she's good at it. She cured my asthma. After a while she had the wound cleaned and his head bandaged up and forced some sort of medicine down his throat and said he was out of danger. He was still unconscious but he had a bit more colour in his cheeks so I figured he was probably going to be all right. And do you know what happened then?"

I shook my head.

"He woke up and abused us for being in his truck," continued Mary indignantly, "accused us of stealing his stuff and shouted at everyone to get out. He even accused Melody Paradise of trying to poison him. Imagine!"

"So what did you do?"

"We left. Everyone had had enough of him. I think if he'd had a sudden relapse even Melody would've let him suffer. It was the most ungrateful thing I've even seen. We all got back to partying because it was about eight in the morning and things were heating up again. When the rave was finally over and I woke up in my bus, next day, or possibly the day after, I'd forgotten all about Magwyn. So had everyone else. Melody Paradise and Iris The Peaceful were cooking some breakfast over a fire and we were sitting round eating toast and drinking tea when to everyone's disgust Magwyn appeared again."

Mary paused.

"He was holding a bunch of wild flowers he'd picked from a verge. And that is the strangest thing I ever saw, Magwyn The Grim facing a hostile group of people with a bunch of flowers in his hand. We were amazed. We were more amazed when he walked up to Melody Paradise, gave her the flowers and apologised for his behaviour last night. He thanked her for healing him, thanked everyone else for helping, and said he was sorry for being rude and ungrateful."

I commented that it did not sound like Magwyn to be so charming. Mary said that he was not exactly charming because the words were coming out rather gratingly so it was obvious that this unnatural behaviour on his part was causing him a lot of effort.

"Still, the fact that he was making an effort impressed some people. Not me though. I disliked him then and I dislike him now. But afterwards when he got in his truck and drove away, Megan and Iris said that it had been a nice thing for him to do. Melody Paradise agreed although she was still insulted by his previous behaviour. No healer likes having a patient accuse her of trying to poison him."

After that, Mary said, Magwyn's behaviour became even stranger. The Golden World Eternal Party Tribe was putting on a series of events in Somerset. Magwyn started turning up regularly, and he never misbehaved. Everyone noticed that he had washed himself, washed his clothes and generally improved one hundred per cent.

"You know what his hair is like now? Horrible, greasy, filthy? That's what it was like before, but in this period when he was look-ing after himself it was like a huge black lion's mane and billowed out like some Celtic warrior's. He refrained from being drunk and

77

kept on making efforts to be friendly, again something which was unnatural to him. And difficult, because Magwyn's reputation was such that no one really wanted to be friendly back. Some people even made extra efforts to be unpleasant to him because he had been horrible to them in the past and now they saw a chance to get their revenge. Hawk and Mulberry, who aren't all that pleasant a pair, used to abuse him to his face. But Magwyn didn't react.

"It didn't take long for people to realise the reason for all this. He'd fallen for Melody Paradise in a big way. Being healed by her had obviously had a profound effect on him. I presume it was that. Melody is hugely attractive but so are other women and I never saw Magwyn show any interest in any of them. He'd always seek her out. One time he gave her a piece of stained glass he'd made and once he drove down to Brighton and gathered sea shells from the beach and brought them for her to put in her hair. He'd drilled little holes through them so she could use them as beads.

"Everyone thought this behaviour was funny at first, ridiculous even, but after a while it didn't seem so strange. In fact, with Magwyn now looking strong, clean, handsome and still smouldering somewhat with the effort to keep his behaviour in check, there were a fair amount of other young woman who started wishing that it was them he was bringing flowers for, and sea shells for their hair. Some people who'd only just started being around and hadn't met Magwyn when he was horrible wondered out loud why Melody Paradise didn't return his advances. There certainly wasn't anyone else around who could match him as a romantic hero, all dark, good looks and Celtic warrior hair and big dark eyes, very suitable for striding over Yorkshire moors or riding horses up to hostile castles.

"Melody was wary however. She was suspicious that at any moment he might revert back to his old character and start turning up drunk and abusive. I thought so too. Megan didn't. She said that this must be his real character and the old bad ways were just caused by loneliness. Megan likes to think the best of everyone.

"This went on for about six months or so. Melody started to waver. Melody Paradise likes having a lover as much as anyone else and she hadn't had one for a while. She was charmed by the sea shells from Brighton beach but what really won her over was when Magwyn arrived at a rave at five in the morning with an injured fox cub in his arms. He'd rescued it from a pack of hounds three hundred miles away and drove all night to bring it to Melody Paradise to see if she could save its life.

"What a scene that was. Melody Paradise, The Tribe Of The Last Free Moonbeam, The Golden World Eternal Party Tribe, The Universal Leyline Protectors with their pyramid, Iris The Peaceful sitting on the pyramid and hundreds of others all dancing in the moonlight and Magwyn The Grim suddenly striding through the crowds with a tiny little sick fox cub cradled in his arms. This was the man who one time picked up a rottweiler that barked at him and threw it in a river.

"Melody Paradise got to work on the fox cub. It was badly mauled, and very sick, which in itself was quite a drama. The whole night was spent with everyone dancing and having a good time and also worrying about the fox. We had to broadcast hourly health bulletins over the sound system. After an uphill struggle Melody Paradise saved its life. And after a similar uphill struggle Magwyn won the heart of Melody Paradise. Immediately afterwards they started going out together. Most people were pleased. By then it seemed like a good idea. They did make a good couple. I never liked him though."

27th July (Day 13)

The Riverboat Tribe were unable to set off for Melody's festival in time. Refloating and refitting Magwenwy's narrow boat after it was sunk by The Mushrooms was arduous, time-consuming and expensive. Many were the bitter comments directed at The Mushrooms as a result of this.

Magwenwy, at first grateful just to find herself alive after the bus had rolled down the bank plunging her boat to the bottom of the river, had now recovered enough of her spirits to be very angry indeed. Whilst drying out her belongings, engaging in repairs to the superstructure and supervising the refitting of her living quarters, Magwenwy brooded on the matter in a way quite alien to her character.

Floating gently along the nation's waterways at four miles an hour was normally sufficient to keep her happy. Mean and vindictive thoughts rarely entered her mind but the assault on her boat had hardened her. She could not prevent herself from thinking that really she was due some restitution for her trauma. Unfortunately there was no way that the hopeless band of Mushrooms could ever make her restitution. They never had any money. They never had anything, particularly sense. Had it not been for the money sent by Melody Paradise and the practical aid from The Tree Planters and Galactic Navigators, Magwenwy might never have been able to refloat and refit her home.

Magwenwy found her thoughts turning increasingly to revenge. While repainting her cabin she found herself thinking dire thoughts about bundling all The Mushrooms up inside one of their dilapidated buses and rolling it into a river. These thoughts she kept mainly to herself, not wishing to introduce any unpleasantness into her tribe.

Halfway through painting a silver moon on her wall she broke off and went to stand at the bow where she stared off into space.

"What are you thinking about?" asked Amesh, a fellow sailor with a bright boat of his own who was helping with the refit, repairing the rope matting which hung on the bows.

"Nothing," replied Magwenwy, not wishing at that moment to share her thoughts of dragging some of The Mushroom Clan along a canal behind her for a mile or two to show them what she thought of them.

During this time The Tree Planters visited The Riverboat Tribe and helped with repairs. Magwenwy was grateful for their assistance and the presence of another tribe cheered everyone and made the work go faster. The Tree Planters were excited at the prospect of the new Wishing Tree and could not let a fellow tribe miss the arrival of Iris The Peaceful.

"Where is the new Wishing Tree coming from?" asked Magwenwy.

"No one knows," replied Peggy. "There aren't many of them about. Iris just planned to roam the world till she found a suitable sapling."

"She's been gone a long time now. Has anyone heard from her?"

"Melody got a letter from the Lebanon. Iris thought that might be a good place to find a magical tree but apparently she was out of luck."

Peggy and Roxanna helped paint Magwenwy's cabin and John and Ali used what carpentry skills they had to help repair the superstructure. Magwenwy's narrow boat was seventy feet long and just under seven feet wide and most of this area was covered by the long wooden cabin. This provided her with a comfortable living space but it had been completely destroyed in the accident and needed to be rebuilt from scratch. The hull, being solid metal, had largely escaped damage but there was one large dent near the bows which had to be hammered out and this was difficult without the full facilities of a boat yard. All of the boat's fittings, its batteries, lights, cooker, chimney, ropes, windows and suchlike, had been destroyed.

Later, Eko found Magwenwy staring glumly at her grounded craft.

"Don't worry, Magwenwy, it'll be fixed in time for you to get to the festival."

Magwenwy was doubtful about this but Eko assured her that it was true.

"Did the tarot tell you that?"

"No, I asked the runes. Never fails. If the runes say you'll be at the festival then you will be."

"She'll get there quicker if you lend a hand instead of playing with runes all the time," called Peggy, good-naturedly, at which Eko wrapped a red cloth round his black locks and set to work.

Magwenwy was cheered by the prediction.

"Why did Eko start using runes instead of the tarot?" she asked Peggy.

"They gave him better answers," replied Peggy. "According to his runes Melody Paradise is guaranteed to fall for him at the festival."

"Really?"

"That's what Eko says. But I doubt he's being impartial."

"I didn't know Eko was after Melody Paradise."

"Why not? Almost everyone else is. Our sister always did have a kind of lethal attraction about her. Who else could have got Magwyn The Grim acting like a normal human being?"

At the memory of Magwyn they both shuddered.

"I think I favour Sweep," said Magwenwy. "Sweep is nice."

Peggy nodded.

"Better than Rupert anyway."

28th July (Day 14)

Iris The Peaceful was four years older than Melody Paradise. She travelled in a horse-drawn carriage. Her tribe had no real name but were always referred to by Melody as The Contemplators, this apparently being an appropriate description of their character. Iris was fairer than Melody with blonde hair and deep blue eyes and she was a devotee of all things natural. Her hair hung long and straight to her waist and she wore a plain green dress that covered her from neck to ankle. Over this she wore a large, functional army jacket and on her feet a pair of strong boots.

Like all of Melody's family she was attractive to look at and, unlike many of them, she had no detractors. No harsh words were spoken against Iris The Peaceful, no secret resentments were harboured against her. Nor was she in the habit of uttering harsh words against others. In her thirty or so years on the planet, Iris The Peaceful had entirely failed to learn how to be unpleasant to her neighbours.

Untroubled by the cares, woes and miseries that plagued most of the nation, Iris The Peaceful and her friends rode their four horse-drawn wagons from Scotland to England to Wales to Ireland, overseas to Europe, and by repute all the way to India.

Personally, I was a little dubious that anyone could actually ride a horse-drawn carriage all the way to India but that's what people said. Exactly how they got their horses overseas I don't know. Perhaps they left them here and hired new ones in France.

Before the festival I had never met Iris but Melody had told me some interesting things about her. She was a musician and played the flute. She wove material and made her own dresses. She had the talent of pacifying disturbed people, and also animals. As, in the run up to Melody's festival, I was plagued with visions of demented drug-crazed travellers brawling with demented drug-crazed dogs, I took this to be a good sign. Perhaps she could protect me from the otherwise inevitable mauling by roving packs of rottweilers, German Shepherds, lurchers and psychopathically inbred mongrels.

Furthermore, Iris The Peaceful had ridden a horse to the Stonehenge Festival in 1988. Rather incongruously, she had made a film about it on camcorder. Iris had borrowed the camcorder intending to record a druidic ceremony with which friends of hers were planning to celebrate the solstice but as the event was broken up by the police, the film had turned into something rather different.

I've seen Iris's film. It's very depressing. It is made up of endless scenes of violence as the police, faced by a field of peaceful hippies, don riot gear, arm themselves with long batons, and proceed to uphold the law. They uphold the law for quite a long time. Later, whilst the hippies are nursing their broken bodies and wrecked vehicles, one can only congratulate the police on taking decisive action against such a dangerous threat. As previously mentioned, I have decided to devote myself to romantic comedy. So I was interested in Melody's other piece of information about Iris The Peaceful, namely that her last boyfriend Simon had departed to ride round the world on a motorbike. Nothing had been heard of him for a year or so. No one was sure why he left. Melody Paradise suspected that life in a horse-drawn carriage had just been too slow for him.

"Iris doesn't talk about Simon much," Melody told me, "but I think she still misses him. I think she might secretly hope to run into him somewhere on her travels."

29th July (Day 15)

On an occasion when Melody's van and Megan's bus were both laid up for repairs, they found themselves near to a large supermarket in Camberwell. Unfortunately they had no money. They rarely had any money. The Tribe Of The Last Free Moonbeam did not used to be so poor. A few years ago they would spend their summers earning a living by selling goods at the series of free festivals held around the country. Doing this earned them enough to see them through the winter but as the Government had put a stop to the free festivals they were now obliged to spend the whole year signed-on for benefits, which was unsatisfactory, and full of problems.

When they did have money, The Tribe Of The Last Free Moonbeam bought food communally to share between them. While there were occasional disagreements over who had or had not paid their share, or whose turn it was to cook, this system worked reasonably well for them. The Tribe Of The Last Free Moonbeam was fortunate in that it contained no one who was overtly anti-social, unlike some of their friends. There were several groups who spent almost their whole time on the road arguing. The Galactic Navigators were especially notorious for this. There was never a moment when one Galactic Navigator was not arguing with another Galactic Navigator over something or other. If a Galactic Navigator turned up with cuts and bruises it was safe to assume that he or she had not suffered at the hands of unfriendly local residents, or over-zealous policemen, but had simply been involved in a dispute over whose turn it was to collect wood, or go to the shops.

Having no money, Melody and Megan were forced to resort to the time-honoured method of visiting the skip outside the supermarket to see what they could find. Supermarkets threw out a great deal of usable produce and The Tribe Of The Last Free Moonbeam had often fed themselves in this way.

Unfortunately the skip was now locked. A shiny new padlock had been put on it to prevent anyone from taking the unwanted food. A strong smell of bleach suggested that the supermarket had also contaminated the food before throwing it away, to further prevent it being used.

"It's a funny old world," said Megan.

Later they met Finan and Irene. Irene still wore her white blouse but had now put on an old pair of army trousers in place of her smart skirt. Earlier that week Finan had taken her to have her ears pierced as a present and Irene now sported two small gold studs.

Irene had enjoyed being at the road protest and had, according to Finan, enthusiastically hurled abuse at the bailiffs as they moved to evict The Militant Children Of Lemuria and their allies from the houses in which they had boarded themselves up. As some of them had chained themselves to railings, the eviction had taken a long time and was not yet finished. Further up the road more protesters were still holding out. Some of them had actually cemented themselves into cellars.

Irene was keen to return. Finan agreed, though normally he did not like to spend too much of his time protesting as he was often busy programming techno music or lying stoned on his bed.

"We should go back," said Irene, and Finan nodded. He seemed quite proud to have a militant girlfriend of his own to show off to Melody. Later Irene studied Melody's hair, asking her how she got it to go into locks and what dyes she used and suchlike, and wondered how she would look if she were to dread her own hair.

"Very good I'm sure," said Melody Paradise, and offered the help of her vast expertise if it was required, and also some spare beeswax she had in her van.

19th August (Day 36) Third Day Of The Festival

In the dreary early morning of the third day of the festival, The Golden World Eternal Party Tribe pull wearily into the valley. They had been travelling through the night having been the previous day playing music at a gig in Exeter. I am alone in witnessing their arrival. Everyone else is asleep but I have been wakened earlier by some unidentified country noise.

A torrent of water from the upper reaches of my tent cascades onto my head. I swear violently. Someone must be to blame for this. It has to be the wettest summer on record. Probably at this very moment the Government is recommending to the population that they all build rafts.

Even in the dim morning light, The Golden World Eternal Party Tribe are easily identifiable. They have 'GOLDEN WORLD ETERNAL PARTY TRIBE' painted on the sides of their vehicles. Mary's bus also has the word 'MARY' emblazoned on the side inside a giant daisy. There are eight vehicles in all, some trucks, some buses and an old Citroen pulling a caravan.

I'm glad they've arrived. The Golden World Eternal Party Tribe will no doubt liven up the place with their music which can only be to the good. So far there has been precious little enjoyment to be had here, even by people who like this sort of thing.

As the tribe drive slowly towards the near end of the valley where The Night Time Elves are camped, they suddenly change direction. Of course, they have an ongoing dispute with The Elves. More problems for Melody Paradise.

Just discernible, far away through the gloom, is the army truck of Magwyn The Grim. No one has yet parked near him, not even Rupert. Rupert's luxury mobile home is lodged close to us at the top of the valley. He has been in constant attendance to Melody Paradise, much to the distress of Sweep and Eko.

Eko is much more confident than Sweep. His runic prediction about his future partnership with Melody Paradise is well-known. Most people are amused by it. Sweep, whilst publicly denouncing Eko as a fraud and charlatan, has confessed to me privately that he is worried.

"What if the runes really have told him that Melody Paradise is going to fall in love with him?"

"Sabotage the runes," I suggest, an idea which Sweep seems to like.

Despite being a house dweller like myself, Sweep has entered into the spirit of things by building a bender. In retaliation for the attentions which Eko and Rupert are paying to the object of his devotion he is edging his bender closer to Melody's van, inch by inch. Quite a hard thing to do, edging a bender along a valley, and surely proof of his love. When Sweep can't think of an excuse to be near her, he sits at his door and stares forlornly at her van.

I decide that I really must take some positive steps to help Sweep if only to stop him complaining to me all the time. There must be something I can do to bring him into the arms of Melody Paradise. Beg and plead with her perhaps.

Sweep has already suggested to Melody Paradise that he should do a little juggling at the ceremonial planting of the new Wishing Tree. Melody was non-committal about this, probably feeling that juggling was inappropriate but not wishing to be impolite. Sweep will be performing at the circus and he is looking forward to this, as he always does.

I'm not sure what sort of ceremony Melody Paradise has planned for the planting of the tree. Nothing spectacular I imagine. Melody Paradise doesn't actually worship trees or anything like that. She's not concerned with their welfare above all other creatures like The Tree Planters. In fact, Melody is not extreme about trees in any way. She talks to them in a quite a matter of fact manner.

Glancing again around the valley I see that Magwyn The Grim is now standing outside his truck, staring. He's looking at Melody's van. I can't make out the expression on his face but I guess that it's not friendly. The well-known hostility Magwyn feels towards Melody Paradise has led some people to suggest that his real motive in coming to the festival is not to help Rupert but to spoil the whole enterprise.

I still don't know what happened after they started going out together. I'll have to ask Mary.

The rain pours down. I wriggle my way back into my tent, placing a damp foot inside my carrier bag and thereby putting a mucky footprint on the literary workshop. Cruelly, criminally even, while I'm trying to get back to sleep, a dog starts to bark. All the others join in. When not actively harrying me around the valley the dogs like nothing better than to practise their barking. Any quiet moment is sure to be enlivened by their efforts.

It was at one time so common for people like Melody's family to use leads made of string for their dogs that they were even defined in this way. 'Dogs-on-string-people'. There seem to be more proper leads now. Unfortunately the dogs aren't on them, and run around freely.

You can't have a dog as a pet in a city in China, it's against the law. I've always thought that the Chinese were a wise nation.

Later in the day The Universal Leyline Protectors arrive and start building a pyramid. I ignore it all and succeed in going back to sleep.

It is a mistake to pitch my tent so close to The Tribe Of The Last Free Moonbeam. A natural mistake, as Melody Paradise and Megan are the people I know best here, but a serious one. Not so much because it puts me close to a bunch of crazed and noisy hippies – that would be the case anywhere in the valley – but because it puts me too close to the centre of responsibility. By this I mean that if anything goes seriously wrong the problem will swiftly arrive on Melody's doorstep. As things are almost bound to go seriously wrong I would have been better advised to place myself as far away from that doorstep as possible.

This is brought home to me forcibly when I waken for the second time in the day and emerge from my tent to find myself kneeling at the feet of three policemen, never a pleasant experience. Instinctively raising my hands in case truncheons are being wielded, I scramble to my feet and make ready to flee.

Once on my feet I see that immediate flight may not be necessary. Melody appears to be talking to them affably enough.

"Yes, we're building the stages here before taking them over to Chelwyn at the end of the week," she says. "The performers aren't here yet, we're just the advance crew."

At this she notices me and waves in my direction.

"And here is one of the main figures in the literary festival. Just off to fax some last minute instructions to his organisational team, I imagine."

I curse under my breath. How dare Melody Paradise introduce me to senior policemen first thing in the morning. She knows I'm not strong. I'm forced to go along with it and greet them politely, endeavouring to look like a main figure in a literary festival.

"A very famous author," adds Melody, which is certainly the first time she's ever said any such thing. Megan sniggers behind her hand.

Melody Paradise leads them off to see some other part of the valley. I sink down on the ground followed quickly by Megan who seems no more sanguine than myself about the experience.

"What was all that about Megan?"

"They came out to see what was going on."

"But isn't everything all right? We're allowed to be here aren't we?"

"We are. But the police got reports of lots of strange people in the valley and came to take a look. Somehow they got hold of the idea that there might be an illegal festival going on here."

"There is."

Megan nods.

"But Melody sorted it out. As advance workers for the circus we have a perfect right to be here. Melody's a very good talker. Charmed them in thirty seconds. Charmed them even more when she slipped and fell into the Chief Constable's arms."

"Deliberately?"

"I'm not sure. Have you noticed how clumsy Melody is these days?"

I nod, and I tell Megan that Melody is no longer transmitting such heat during her healing sessions.

"That's worrying," says Megan. "Perhaps it's all the stress of organising the festival. It didn't show when she was talking to the police though. She even managed to convince them that the Universal Leyline Protector's pyramid over there is part of the scenery for the circus.

I gaze over at the pyramid, which The Universal Leyline Protectors have erected in a single morning. It's about nine feet tall, made from cane and withy, wired together and covered with tissue paper hardened with PVA. It is stone grey coloured like a real Egyptian pyramid. The Universal Leyline Protectors, as I may have already mentioned, are very keen on pyramids. They carry the pieces of this one around with them in their trucks, erecting it wherever they are. They claim that the pyramid serves a vital function in connecting them to some galactic leyline, though whether this is the one running between here and the Crab Nebula or some other stellar body I'm not sure. According to them, keeping the interstellar leylines in good order is important for the well-being of the planet. It's the first time I've seen their pyramid and I'm quite impressed. It looks rather grand in the field, quite majestic in the drizzle.

"That'll be more trouble," sighs Megan.

"Why?"

"The Eternal Sunshine Family. They build pyramids too and they're not going to be pleased to find that The Universal Leyline Protectors have beaten them to it."

"So on top of everything else we're going to have a fight about pyramids?"

"Afraid so," says Megan. "Probably quite a bitter one. The Universal Leyline Protectors and The Elemental Sunshine Family haven't got on for years. They make a point of avoiding each other. They never go to the same festivals. I'm surprised they've both agreed to come here."

"Melody's benign influence," I suggest, and Megan agrees.

The police depart and Melody Paradise returns, bright and cheerful after dealing easily with the problem.

"They thought we might just be a bunch of travelling hippies who'd attached themselves for no good reason to the circus," she says, laughing. "I put them right. Now they're rather looking forward to the event. The Chief Constable is quite a fan of modern literature, Martin. He's coming to your creative writing class."

I frown deeply at Melody. In fact, I scowl. In fact to be honest I start to panic. This makes her laugh even more. She admits she's only joking. The Chief Constable is not really a fan of modern literature and is not going to turn up at my class. Which just goes to show how dangerous even Melody Paradise can be, making cruel jokes and endangering my health.

It is a relief that Melody dealt with it all so well but it does occur to me that she may have to cope with more of this sort of thing than she intended, now she's taken the money. It's fine in theory to leave everything connected with the circus to Rupert but surely any serious problems will soon arrive in Melody's lap.

Later in the day I help with the clearing up operations, carrying rubbish up the valley in bags for transportation to a dump. It's still raining and the whole enterprise is not much fun.

"Cheer up," says Melody Paradise. "Tonight we're all going on a unicorn hunt."

I fail to cheer up. Sweep however is agog with excitement. The thought of roaming through the woods hunting unicorns with Melody Paradise is close to his idea of heaven. As I'm trudging through the mud, fun unexpectedly breaks out all around me. The sun makes an appearance, The Golden World Eternal Party Tribe starts testing out their sound system and people take a break from clearing up the valley to stretch themselves, talk to their neighbours, run round with the dogs and children and even dance a little.

The music livens everyone up, as does the appearance of the pyramid. Inspired by the construction, The Clan Of The Night Time Elves have encircled their encampment with their largest green banners which flutter in the breeze like pennants at a mediaeval joust. The Tree Planters drape colourful ribbons from their neighbouring trees, after asking the trees if this is all right with them. For the first time it feels like there is something entertaining happening around me and for the first time I sense that perhaps this will not all be a complete waste of time. Perhaps Melody Paradise will be able to bring peace to her family. As people gambol around happily in the sunshine it seems like it might be possible.

I'm close to Rupert's Mercedes. Already bored with clearing up, I'm planning to hide in the bushes for a while. Sweep suddenly appears from the depths of the undergrowth, looking guilty.

"What are you doing here?" he demands.

"What are *you* doing here?" I counter.

"Nothing at all," says Sweep, "Can't a person go for a walk without you dogging his footsteps every inch of the way?"

I lay a reassuring hand on his shoulder. Sweep, uncharacteristically ill-tempered, brushes it off. After several more unsuccessful attempts, I give up on the friendly gestures and ask him what the problem is. I do, of course, already know what the problem is. Sweep is up here spying on Rupert because he suspects the hippy magnate of having designs on Melody Paradise. I put this to him and his anger fades away into gloom.

"She's in there now with him," he tells me. "He's plying her with wine."

"Expensive wine?"

"How the hell would I know if it was expensive?" demands Sweep.

"You could have looked at the label on the bottle."

"I was standing on tiptoe on a tree root," says Sweep, crossly. "I didn't have time to take an inventory of his belongings. And who cares if it's expensive or not, the point is he's plying her with it."

He looks sullen for a while before again turning to me.

"What are you doing here?"

"Nothing." I reply, not wishing to admit that I was about to hide from the public gaze. Not that I'm obliged to help clear up rubbish of course, it just makes me feel guilty if Melody and Megan see me lazing about while they struggle up the hill with sacks of rubbish in their arms.

Sweep looks thoughtful.

"You've been spending a lot of time around Melody Paradise," he says, polishing his glasses with a suspicious gleam in his eye. I immediately catch his meaning and vigorously defend myself against this slur.

"Sweep, how could you think such a thing? You imagine that I would try and muscle my way into Melody's affections?"

"Worm your way more like," says Sweep.

"Sweep, I'm shocked. Shocked and saddened. My interest in Melody Paradise is strictly platonic. You know I'd rather not be here at all, I only came to do the readings and earn a little money. The very idea of me and Melody Paradise is quite absurd!"

"Why, what's wrong with her?" demands Sweep.

"Nothing is wrong with her. Melody Paradise is terrific. An angel in human form. Speaking platonically that is. And you'd be a wonderful couple. My heartfelt wish is for you and her to get together and travel the world in a bus. Nothing would bring me greater pleasure."

Sweep is somewhat mollified. I risk taking a quick peek inside the mobile home, standing precariously in the bushes on an old tree root. I have only a few seconds before I tumble off, causing myself some injury and distress at the hands of thorns, brambles and suchlike, but in these few seconds I see that Rupert's home is luxurious inside, plushly outfitted in mahogany and velvet. It's rather staid but certainly expensive. Limping slightly from bramble injuries, I make my way back to my tent.

"Sweep," I say, as we sit down in the sun, "the time has come to take strong action. It's no good carrying on like this, loving Melody Paradise from afar."

"She's right next door to me," protests Sweep.

"Well, I mean 'from afar' in a spiritual sense. Silently worshipping her. Gazing at her van in the moonlight. That sort of thing. You have to do something else."

"I'm not asking her to the cinema," says Sweep, resolutely. "She'd laugh at me."

I wave this aside.

"What I have in mind is much more impressive than asking her to the cinema. It seems to me that Melody Paradise is too used to seeing you around to regard you as a prospective lover. I mean, she obviously likes you, she just doesn't think of you in that way. 'Here's Sweep,' she says to herself. 'Now we'll see some good fire-club juggling.' Or 'Look, Sweep is doing something funny with a trick bicycle.' Which is fine in a way, but just not impressive enough. It's moving away from the trick bicycles and into her arms that's the problem. What you want her thinking to herself is not 'Here's Sweep, now we'll have a good laugh, but 'Here's Sweep, now there's a man I'd like to fold me in his arms and kiss me like there's no tomorrow. You see what I mean?"

At this keen analysis of the problem, Sweep looks quite impressed.

"Well, what would you suggest? How can I make her think of me like that?"

"I'm glad you asked me that Sweep. Because I've been giving the matter some thought and it seems to me that you really should perform some dramatic, forceful action which will change you from the pleasant but diffident soul you are now into something more like a romantic hero."

Sweep, who is fairly realistic about himself, doubts that there is any chance of him suddenly being transformed into a romantic hero.

"Left to yourself, no. With me helping, it's a different matter. Remember, you're talking to someone who is *au fait* with all the romantic heroes of the past from Orpheus and Theseus through Galahad and Gawain to Romeo and Heathcliffe."

Sweep urges me to elaborate. What, he demands to know, should he do?

"Something dramatic, and full of human emotion. Remember, the single verifiable instance we have of Melody falling for someone in a big way was when she slept with Magwyn The Grim right after he rescued a sick fox cub."

At the mention of this Sweep looks pained. I remind him that far from being a rival for Melody's affections, Magwyn is now Public Enemy Number One.

"Forget about Magwyn. Just concentrate on the story of the fox cub. She'd resisted all his advances till he found the sick animal and drove three hundred miles through the night so she could heal it. An escapade of such high drama and romance that I'm not surprised Melody fell for him. How could she resist the sight of Magwyn striding purposefully through the dancing, hedonistic crowds, ignoring his own comforts to save the baby fox? Melody Paradise has a very soft heart. Expending such effort to save a fox was bound to impress her. Strong and manly but caring and gentle as well. It was a master stroke. It wouldn't surprise me at all if Magwyn injured the fox himself just so he could fake the rescue. Probably ran it over a few miles up the road and then lied about the rest. Nonetheless it worked."

"You're right," says Sweep, "but where can I find a sick fox?"

"Well, I think we'll have to take a slightly different approach. We can't keep bombarding Melody Paradise with sick fox cubs or she'll get suspicious. But if you were to pull off a dramatic rescue right in front of her, say for instance, pulling a drowning man out of the river and struggling ashore gasping 'Don't worry about me, Melody, attend to this person first,' I'm sure it would have a dramatic effect. Even better, rescue a drowning child."

"What if no children start drowning while we're here?" asks Sweep, quite reasonably.

"There's quite a lot of them about," I point out. "Lots of these travellers seem to have children in tow and they play at the riverbank. I'd say there was a fair chance of one of them being swept away."

"But what if none are?"

I muse on this for a while.

"Perhaps you could set it up. Get a friend to pretend to be drowning and then make a heroic rescue."

"You mean you'd really do that for me?" says Sweep. "I'm impressed."

I hurry to correct his mistake.

"No Sweep, I wouldn't do it for you. Nothing would get me into that river. I meant some other friend. Rag or Rooster."

"That's no good. They might tell Melody. Then I'd look like a fool."

Faced with this difficulty Sweep is frustrated, and again appeals to me to be the victim. I refuse, and Sweep lapses into a perplexed silence.

Suddenly he leaps to his feet.

"I've got it! Megan's baby!"

"What?"

"Pookie. I take him out every day. It gives Megan a break. I could rescue him from the river. No chance of him telling the truth afterwards, he hasn't learned to speak yet."

"Eh, Sweep," I say, trying to bring him back to reality, "I don't think you can reasonably throw Megan's baby in the river."

"Why not?"

"It's too dangerous."

"Not if I'm right there to make a rescue it's not. Imagine it. Little

95

Pookie about to be swept away on the current and me dragging him out just in time. Melody can't help being impressed by that. I mean, what's a measly fox cub compared to Megan's baby?"

"Well, that's all very well Sweep, but what's Megan going to say? She might be pleased you rescued her baby but isn't she going to get round to wondering how he fell in the river in the first place? If you take him out to play and he ends up six feet under water it's not going to look very good for you is it?"

"It'll look fine for me," says Sweep, a maniacal gleam in his eye, "because I'll say I left him with you. You drop him in, I'll do the rescue."

I tell Sweep that this suggestion is absolutely out of the question.

"Please."

"Not a chance."

At this moment Melody Paradise dances past us. She is a fabulous dancer. The sun glistens on the beads and sea shells that play in her hair and the anklets that jangle around her bare feet. Sweep is enraptured.

"Please do it," he says.

I can't stand to see Sweep so miserable. I'm forced to agree. Appropriately enough the sun disappears and it starts to rain.

I believe Megan's child was originally christened Luke. Why he has acquired the nickname of Pookie I don't know. Undoubtedly it will send him to a therapist in later life. Sweep procures the baby. The baby is happy about this. Pookie and Sweep get on fine.

"No time to waste," says Sweep "I just saw Melody heading for the river with a water container in her hand."

"What's Megan going to say when Pookie comes back completely drenched?"

"He won't get drenched. You don't think Megan would let him out in the rain without his waterproofs on do you? She's a very careful mother. I've double checked all the fastenings. This baby would stay dry in a monsoon."

"Perhaps we should reconsider." I say. "It might be dangerous."

"No it isn't. It's not as if we're going to toss the baby in the middle of the Atlantic ocean. It's only a little river. Just shoot young Pookie a few inches out into the water and then start screaming for help. I'll come pounding down the bank, leap in and drag him out. Nothing to it. Look, Melody's getting water upstream. When she sees me in action she's bound to be impressed. Like I said, what's a fox cub compared to Megan's baby?"

Sweep hands the child over to me and the instant he does this Pookie starts to protest.

"Quiet. Start screaming now and you'll ruin everything."
As I take the disgruntled infant into my arms I notice two dark green Land Rovers descending into the valley.

"Who's that?"

"The Nomadic Daughters Of Lilith," answers Sweep. "Florimel, Mirabel, Belladonna and Anorexia."

"Florimel, Mirabel, Belladonna and Anorexia?"

"That's right. Florimel, Mirabel, Belladonna and Anorexia."

Four young women in army clothes and boots get out of the Land Rovers and gaze around them with a truculent air.

"More arguments," mutters Sweep.

Melody Paradise is still filling her water container, a large clear plastic jerry can. Not wishing to lose the moment Sweep shoves me forward. I am again seized by doubts but reflect that the baby is probably not in any real danger. He's not going to have much more than a paddle really.

Without further ado I set matters in hand. I hold Pookie a few inches out in the stream and let go, meanwhile preparing to shout desperately for help. To my surprise, once he's released in the water, rather than struggling about in a panic Pookie calmly paddles his way back to the shore. I shove him out in the river again. Unperturbed, he paddles back. A few more attempts produce similar results. Pookie laughs and smiles. For the first time in our relationship he seems to be enjoying himself.

I pick him up, very displeased, and give him a talking to.

"Pookie, this is not what is meant to happen. How is Sweep going to dive in and save you if you keep swimming back to the shore unaided? Try and show a little consideration. At least pretend to be drowning."

Sweep slithers down the bank behind me.

"What's the delay?" he demands anxiously.

"The baby appears to be a champion swimmer," I tell him. "One of the strongest infants ever seen in the water."

"Hurry up," hisses Sweep. "Melody's going away."

I send him back up the bank and try again. The rain picks this moment to intensify. The baby gurgles with delight.

Feeling that stronger action is needed, I prepare to toss Pookie further into the river. With luck, once caught in the current he will be unable to show off his command of the breast stroke. Unfortunately at this moment Sweep, in a characteristic piece of idiocy, slips from the top of the bank. He crashes into me from behind, taking my legs away. We fall very heavily and end up in a tangle of bruised limbs and riverside mud.

This is too much for me. The man is just too incompetent to be helped and I let him know it.

"No wonder Melody Paradise doesn't want you. You're a menace to public safety. You can't even stand on a riverbank without causing an accident. God help anyone who comes close while you're juggling fire-clubs."

Sweep is rather abashed. He apologises, saying that he lost his footing on the wet grass. He tries to placate me but I am by this time feeling very hard done by. I'm just pointing out to Sweep exactly how painful my bruises are when he suddenly starts yelling and waving his arms about.

"Pookie!"

Pookie, his infant limbs having finally succumbed to the current, is now floating along the river, some way off. In all the confusion I would appear to have dropped him in without noticing.

"Help!" I scream. "The baby's drowning!"

Sweep dives into the river. However, before he has travelled more than three yards he is overtaken by a figure in brown who thunders down the bank and leaps into the water like an Olympic athlete. While Sweep slowly makes his way towards the drifting child this figure cuts through the water like a shark. Only seconds after the crisis began the newcomer has it under control and is hauling Pookie back to the shore. Rescuer and baby arrive safely back while Sweep is still floundering around in the river. The rescuer is Florimel from The Nomadic Daughters Of Lilith. I'm indignant. Who does she think she is, butting in and ruining everything?

Uproar has spread round the festival site and people are appearing from all directions. The Tribe Of The Last Free Moonbeam arrive at a gallop and Megan scoops her baby up in her arms and hugs it tightly to her breast.

Melody Paradise, the intended recipient of all this, arrives just in time to see a very bedraggled Sweep hauling himself out of the water in front of a crowd of onlookers who don't know whether to be shocked, outraged or amused. One thing they are not is impressed.

"What did you do to my baby!" screams Megan.

I shake my head despairingly.

"I can't understand it" I say. "Sweep insisted on taking him for a swim then he got into difficulties. I tried to prevent him but..."

I raise my eyes to heaven in wonderment at such folly. Megan glowers at Sweep and starts to berate him for his foolishness. I take the opportunity to leave, although not before I hear Megan breaking off from berating Sweep to thank Florimel for rescuing her baby.

Florimel accepts this thanks with little grace.

"The Tribe Of The Last Free Moonbeam," she sneers, "can't even look after a baby without half-drowning it."

As she departs Rag and Rooster look on adoringly and enthuse about Florimel's courage and athleticism. Melody Paradise thanks her as well but Florimel doesn't even acknowledge her presence.

Melody looks disappointed. Rupert takes the opportunity to put his arm round her. I depart. The rain is pouring down. I am wet through. It will be completely impossible to get dry. I feel that I will never be dry again. I wish I hadn't come to this stupid festival.

Mary is in her van, rummaging through a box of records. Around her are more, all neatly stored, and a DJ's double turntable. Mary also has a television and video, run off a large battery, bought with the proceeds of the increasingly popular raves run by The Golden World Eternal Party Tribe. They are starting to do well, and Mary is proud of their success.

I have heard one or two mutterings against The Golden World Eternal Party Tribe. For instance, some of the quieter members of The Tree Planters deplore the way that techno rigs turn up at rural gatherings and then play loud music twenty four hours a day. Various mandolin-playing Tree Planters do not enjoy a thundering electronic beat going on all day and all night. Mary refutes this charge, claiming that The Golden World Eternal Party Tribe do not play for twenty four hours a day except at techno events organised by themselves. She says they are quite prepared to fit in with the vibe of any gathering, and blames house-dwelling DJs for any problems. Although there are many rigs playing all over the country, The Golden World Eternal Party Tribe are unusual in that they are actually permanent travellers, carrying their whole equipment with them on the road, rather than living in town and only visiting the country at weekends.

When Mary and Finan find time to do their recording together they plan to put out dance records on their own label. Mary has quite an entrepreneurial spirit and I have no doubt she'll succeed in this as well.

I ask her to tell me the rest of the story of Magwyn The Grim and Melody Paradise which she does, sitting on the floor rolling cigarettes.

"Although everyone knew that Magwyn was in pursuit of Melody Paradise, it was still quite a shock when they actually got together. Even though Magwyn had moderated his behaviour he still wasn't exactly what you'd call pleasant. I know The Tribe Of The Last Free Moonbeam weren't at all happy about it at first. They thought Melody Paradise was making a big mistake, even though Melody told them that she knew when Magwyn saved the fox cub that he was a nice person at heart, just bad at getting on with people. They were dubious. They expected him to revert back to his abusive self.

"But Magwyn didn't revert to his former self. Going out with Melody Paradise he improved all the time. He stopped his drinking, reduced his drug intake, continued washing and started being more or less civilised. Even to the point where he wouldn't kick dogs. He used to make efforts to play with Megan's baby. So after a while everyone got used to it."

"But you never liked him?"

Mary shakes her head.

"I always thought he'd relapse. And I was right in the end. Well, sort of. But for about six months everything was fine. Magwyn and Melody Paradise became a well-known couple. Melody Paradise grew more beautiful than ever and Magwyn continued to look like a celtic prince. Melody used to wrap black ribbons in his hair and he made fine coloured glass beads to add to hers. He gave her another beautiful stained glass panel to hang in her van, and painted the walls inside. After Magwyn finished decorating, the inside of Melody's van looked like The Garden of Eden.

"He travelled with The Tribe Of The Last Free Moonbeam and ate with them so he didn't look half-starved any more, and he was healthy, and friendly. Being accepted by Melody Paradise meant that other people were willing to give him a chance so he wasn't lonely any more. Now, no one minded him turning up at events, particularly as Melody Paradise seemed happier than ever. When Melody Paradise is happy, any event is guaranteed to be fun. At our Ben Nevis get-together, she danced on the side of the mountain for fourteen hours without a break. Afterwards Magwyn had to carry her to her van because her feet were bruised.

"And this relationship, incidentally, is really why this festival is happening. Melody met the Chelwyn Summer Fair Committee after Magwyn took a commission to replace some stained glass in one of their churches. Rupert introduced him to some woman there, a Mrs Fitzroy. She's rich, but I think her son went off travelling which probably made her a bit more sympathetic. Anyway, Magwyn's stained glass is good and Chelwyn Village was extremely pleased with his work which is probably why they were willing to believe Melody and Rupert could organise the circus for them.

"But now things were becoming difficult for travellers. New laws, councils closing caravan sites, farmers and policeman chasing them here and there, Stonehenge and other places being fenced off. The Tribe Of The Last Free Moonbeam decided that it was time to leave the country. Some of their friends had already gone. Melody and Magwyn decided that they'd try their luck in France and Spain, and if they didn't like it there just travel on and see what they found. It was arranged that Magwyn would sell his army truck and move into Melody's van, which was sensible.

"I never saw a happier couple. Ever since Melody healed him, Magwyn had practically idolised her. I suspect no one was ever kind to him before. And Melody seemed to love him. She was certainly happy, and I never knew her spend so much time with a lover."

I find this tale of Mary's interesting but slightly dispiriting. Tales of famously happy couples generally depress me.

"So what went wrong? Did Magwyn get drunk and crash the van? Did he fall under the evil influence of The Mushrooms and start misbehaving again?"

Mary shakes her head.

"No, Magwyn didn't do anything. It was Melody Paradise. The day before they were due to leave Magwyn arrived home and found her in bed with Tuffy."

"With Tuffy? Tuffy the demented Mushroom?"

"Well, that would be one way of describing him. You could also call him the cute young Mushroom. He's not actually demented, just over-fond of mushroom tea."

I'm astonished.

"So the tragic break-up was all Melody's fault?"

"I suppose so. Though I'm sure they could have sorted it out. Magwyn just overreacted. It was simply a misunderstanding. Melody Paradise had a perfectly reasonable explanation. She was merely comforting Tuffy because he was upset after a terrible argument with his girlfriend Fluffy. You know Melody is devoted to spreading love and peace, she couldn't just let Tuffy suffer."

"Wasn't actually getting into bed with him going a bit far?"

"Well, it was a cold night. But they didn't have sex or anything. Naturally Magwyn didn't believe that."

"I'm not surprised. Few people would."

"Why not? You don't think Melody Paradise would lie about it do you? If she says she was only comforting Tuffy as a friend you can believe her. It was a complete overreaction for Magwyn to go and kill the Wishing Tree. How horrible can you get?"

"Magwyn killed the Wishing Tree?"

"Yes, didn't you know? To get back at Melody. He took a bucket of weed killer that The Tree Planters had liberated from a garden centre – The Tree Planters don't approve of weed killer and steal it if they can – and dumped it on the tree. It never had a chance.

"Melody went berserk. Nothing else could have got to her like killing the Wishing Tree. She threw his stuff out of her van, told Magwyn she hoped he'd die young, then drove off to India. Afterwards, Magwyn went completely to pieces. The night after she left he was found by the police in the middle of a road, howling at the moon."

According to Mary, Magwyn's drinking, drug taking and hatred for all humanity subsequently grew to undreamed of levels. She claimed to be surprised he was still alive, the way he abused himself.

"He completely stopped speaking. A few people tried helping him out but he chased them away. They came back talking about his terrible silence and hostility and general madness and soon everyone was scared of him. People started calling him Magwyn The Grim, and dreading his arrival."

"What did Melody Paradise have to say about all this?"

Mary shrugs.

"Not much. She wasn't around when the worst of it was going on, she'd gone to India. When she got back she didn't want to discuss it. She's never really said much about it to me. Megan might know more."

I can't help feeling sorry for Magwyn, even though I don't like him. Surely many people would have been shocked to find their girlfriend in bed with Tuffy. I mean, Tuffy's only eighteen and he devours about a field of psychoactive mushrooms every day.

"I guess a lot of other people might have felt sorry for him if he hadn't poured a bucket of weed killer on the Wishing Tree," says Mary.

Melody Paradise and Magwyn The Grim haven't met since then. It's strange that Rupert asked him to help at the festival. Mary agrees that this is odd.

"Megan thinks he might be trying to scare Melody into going off with him. Maybe. He might have just wanted someone who'd do the work cheap. I'm more surprised Magwyn came. I'm worried he might be going to try and wreck everything. He hates Melody. I think he might try and kill the new tree just to spite her."

I muse for a while on the thought of Magwyn The Grim bulldozing the Peaceful Grove with his army truck during the planting ceremony. It would certainly liven things up.

"I wonder what it's like being called 'The Grim'? A strange title for anyone to have. What would you be called if you had a title?"

Mary considers.

"'Mary The DJ' I suppose."

"'Mary, The Brightly Clothed DJ,' would be better."

I suppose I would be 'Martin The Writer', which would be quite tedious. Actually, now I think about it, I quite like the sound of 'Martin The Grim'. It has a certain ring to it.

It seems wise to avoid Sweep for the rest of the day. He might be upset at me for putting all the blame for the baby fiasco on him. Tomorrow it will be fine, Sweep is not really capable of holding a grudge.

Walking towards Melody's van, I have a fierce frown on my face. I'm pretending to be Martin The Grim, the most feared mercenary soldier in the ancient world. With my help, the Athenians will defeat the Spartans and win the Peloponesian war. I pause outside Melody's van, slightly depressed by the thought of the disastrous Athenian naval adventure to Sicily in 411 BC. Why didn't they let Alcibiades command the fleet?

Melody opens the door.

"Stop worrying about ancient Greece and come in," she says.

"Melody, do you think if I concentrate about it hard enough I'll be able to re-incarnate backwards and have my next life in ancient Athens?"

"Of course," says Melody Paradise reassuringly. "Why not?"

"You might not be able to go backwards."

"I don't see why not. Anyway, if time is a circle, which seems likely, all you'll have to do is go a long way forwards. Either way I'm sure you'll get there in the end."

"Thank you. I always feel better talking to you."

Melody is also slightly depressed.

"Things don't seem to be going all that well." she admits. "I haven't solved any arguments yet. I seem to have made the one between The Tree Planters and The Night Time Elves worse."

"The Tree Planters still split into two factions?"

Melody Paradise winces. I ask her who is actually in the right regarding parking under an elm in summer but Melody confesses she has no idea. Tree mysticism is not one of her specialist subjects.

"But I'm sure it can't be all that important. It's John and Ali's fault. If they'd get back together then The Tree Planters would all get on and we might make some progress with ending their argument with The Elves. Have you read to the tree yet?"

"Pardon?"

"The sick fig tree. The Tree Planters were very pleased about your rendition of Terence. Said the tree was much happier afterwards."

"Surely they don't want me to do it again?"

"Of course," says Melody. "Any healing requires persistence. You can't stop now, not after you've made such a good start."

I sigh, and agree to visit the tree, after making Melody promise never to tell anyone in London about it.

"While you're there," says Melody, "perhaps you could encourage The Tree Planters to stop making fun of The Elves' Unicorn Survey."

"Of course. Delighted to help. It's so unreasonable of them. How could anyone make fun of people who are diligently searching the country for unicorns?"

Melody tells me not to mock, and assures me that I'll enjoy it tonight when we all join in the search. I nod, though in reality I have no intention of joining in. Nothing is going to induce me to wander through a dark wood in the middle of nowhere looking for unicorns. Compared to that, reading the works of Terence to a fig tree seems quite sane.

"I wish Iris The Peaceful was here, she'd sort everything out. I'm starting to worry about her. I hope she's found a new Wishing Tree."

"How is she going to transport a tree across the Channel?"

"It's only going to be a sapling. And I wish The Riverboat Tribe were here. Having boats around puts people in a good mood. The kids love them."

Melody Paradise lists those of her family that are here: The Tribe Of The Last Free Moonbeam, The Tree Planters, The Clan Of The Night Time Elves, The Golden World Eternal Party Tribe, The Universal Leyline Protectors and The Nomadic Daughters Of Lilith.

"I take it Florimel is still mad at you?"

Melody nods. After the business of Melody forgetting to sign on for her Florimel had endless trouble with her benefit claim. Consequently Florimel does not like Melody Paradise. As sisters they have apparently never got on all that well.

"That's what you get for trying to do people favours," I tell her, but Melody Paradise is not the sort of person who will ever stop trying to do people favours.

"The Nomadic Daughters Of Lilith don't get on with The Golden World Eternal Party Tribe. I'd like to sort that out."

"Why don't they get on?"

"Mary insisted they paid admission to a Golden World rave instead of getting in free like they normally would. The Nomadic Daughters were outraged. But everyone else had paid, even us. It was a charity event for some travellers who got their vehicles confiscated.

Melody carries on with the treatment for my arm. Her hands are no longer hot. I don't know if she realises she is losing her healing powers. She wishes the rain would stop because so much bad weather is preventing people from getting together. Apart from today's brief interlude of sunshine, the continual downpour has meant that everyone is sticking to their own vehicles, or huddling around them in tepees and benders.

"I never bargained for this. I assumed that once everyone was together they'd all just naturally start getting along better. As it is they're all just hanging around in their own corners of the valley hating each other. We were meant to have a big friendly gathering every day at noon but how can you do that when it's so wet?"

"They'll have to get together soon. Rupert wants some help for organising the performance tomorrow."

Melody Paradise is pleased to hear this.

"One thing about Rupert, he does get things done. He's not such a bad guy, you know, once you get to know him."

Hearing Melody say this makes me wonder if his plying her with wine and expensive hash has had some effect. This is a worrying thought. I couldn't stand it if Melody Paradise started going out with Rupert. Sweep would make my life a total misery.

Mary arrives to invite Melody over for some food. She informs us that they'll be erecting their giant marquee tomorrow, which cheers Melody considerably. This at least will be a large dry area for people to congregate in. As we leave Melody's van, we run right into Magwyn. He's standing on his own in the gloom, staring at us. Melody Paradise walks straight past him like he wasn't there.

"He's got a nerve coming here after he killed the tree," says Mary.

"He came down this morning and told me he was sorry about it," says Melody.

"Really? What did you say?"

"I told him it was no use being sorry now."

They head off to eat. I head off towards The Tree Planters encampment. I have a little glass lantern with a candle inside it which is meant to light my way in the dark. It is completely useless and I will no doubt plunge into a mine shaft at the first opportunity. As it is, I'm almost mowed down by another collection of vans, buses and caravans winding their way down the narrow track into the valley.

"The swines have put up a pyramid already!" comes an irate voice through an open window.

It has to be The Elemental Sunshine Family, pyramid rivals of The Universal Leyline Protectors. As they pass, I hear many bitter comments and promises of swift action to counter this affront.

"So Syrus helps Clitipho to trick his father out of a thousand drachmas. Syrus is a sort of house slave and a cunning operator. Clitipho gives this money to Bacchis the courtesan, thus getting himself out of trouble and leaving himself free to marry Archonides's daughter. Meanwhile Antiphila is found to be Clitipho's sister so Clinia can marry her and they all end up happy. Another fine romantic comedy, though quite a confusing one. I hope you could follow it all. First performed at the Megalensian Games in 163 BC, held in honour of the Great Mother Goddess Cybele."

I'm standing in front of the sick tree. Round me sit The Tree Planters. They all look pleased. Any mention of the Great Mother Goddess always goes down well with them.

"What a nice play," says Roxanna.

"The tree liked it," says Mark.

"Definitely reminded it of Italy," says John.

"Same time tomorrow?" says Peggy.

I sigh, and nod my head. I wonder what bad thing is going to happen as a result of all this. You can't go around entertaining fig trees with early Latin drama without suffering for it in some way or other.

Around one in the morning my wandering brings me close to Magwyn's truck. Although other parts of the valley are still noisy, particularly the part occupied by The Golden World Eternal Partyers, there is no sign of life around Magwyn's isolated encampment.

The dense clouds overhead make the night very dark, far darker than I'm used to in the city. This is disconcerting. Stuck in the mud outside Magwyn's truck is a large outdoor candle on a stick but this provides very little light. The back door of the truck is open. I hold up my lantern to take a look. I have no excuse for this peering into someone else's space, apart from being nosy. Inside is a mess, a grim mixture of broken furniture, half-made props, paint tins, bits of glass, pieces of unidentifiable scrap and other assorted junk. Magwyn's living space and work space are jumbled together in one chaotic shambles. Everything is either ripped, broken or falling apart.

No other traveller's vehicle I've seen inside has been anything like this. It's all so horrible that it's quite a shock when the light from my lamp strays onto a panel of stained glass lying propped up to one side, and this panel of glass turns out to be a particularly fine work of art.

The panel is about four feet square, stained glass cased in lead, and painted before being fired. Even in the dim light of my lamp, the colours stand out brilliantly and the figure depicted is so perfectly painted that I might be standing in the Renaissance section of the National Gallery rather than in Magwyn's horrible old truck.

The subject matter is interesting too. It's a picture of Melody Paradise sitting in front of a tree, smiling.

I'm astonished. I had no idea that Magwyn The Grim was this good an artist. It's easy to see why his work impressed the people of Chelwyn. His depiction of Melody Paradise is of such high quality that it would not seem out of place in a Renaissance cathedral. Well, perhaps that's not quite true: few women depicted in Renaissance cathedrals are sitting naked with the makings of a joint lying at their feet, but apart from that it's a classical masterpiece. The painting of Melody's hair alone displays amazing workmanship. Magwyn's panel actually changes my whole opinion of stained glass. Before seeing it, I'd regarded it as something rather dull. I'd no idea anyone could produce such beautiful effects.

It strikes me for the first time that Magwyn The Grim is still in love with Melody Paradise. An interesting thought. I don't get the opportunity of discussing it with him. He arrives back and throws a cider bottle at me. I dodge the bottle and depart at speed, not stopping till I reach the pyramid at the foot of the valley. Melody

Paradise and Mary appear out of the darkness and I launch into a lengthy and bitter complaint.

"Melody, Magwyn The Grim just threw a cider bottle at me for no reason. What sort of way is this to treat someone's who's come to put on a literary workshop? I knew it would be dangerous but I didn't expect violent lunatics to leap out of the grass and assault me. I insist you do something about it. What a nightmare this is all turning out to be. First, I have to do a creative writing class for stockbrokers and then I have to recite Latin plays to fig trees and now Magwyn is throwing cider bottles at me."

I pause, noticing even in the darkness that Melody Paradise is staring stony faced into the distance and Mary is glowering at me in an unfriendly manner. Rather too late I realise that launching into long complaints about Magwyn The Grim in Melody Paradise's presence is not the most tactful thing to do.

"Don't mention that name to me," says Melody. "You know he tried to pick a fight with The Nomadic Daughters Of Lilith today? He's going to ruin everything."

"I don't know how he had the nerve to come here," adds Mary. "We should chase him off."

I drop the subject. Melody is on her way to visit The Clan Of The Night Time Elves.

"About The Tree Planters?"

"No, about The Golden World Eternal Partyers. Mary's coming with me to sort it out. It shouldn't be too hard, it's not very serious. Afterwards we're going searching for unicorns. Want to come along?"

"I wouldn't miss it for the world."

With so much discord everywhere it will be pleasurable to see some of it ended. I accompany them in the direction of the encampment of The Clan Of The Night Time Elves, recognisable by the large green banners which hang limply from flagpoles in a circle around it.

Our feet squelch in the wet grass. Although there is now less rubbish strewn around the valley it still doesn't look very pleasant. The ruined caravan and trailers still lie by the river and the continual rain has softened the grass to such an extent that parts of it are now turning to mud under our feet. To avoid the worst excesses of this, Melody is instructing as many people as possible to park up by the road where there is an area of gravel. Even so, some tyre marks are now carved like ugly scars into the sides of the valley.

"Will it ever stop raining?"

"Of course," says Melody Paradise. "I can smell some better weather on the way. I think it'll be fine tomorrow."

Our welcome from The Clan Of The Night Time Elves is muted, to say the least. Melody has been unpopular with them since her disastrous attempt at ending the disharmony between themselves and The Tree Planters, and they have a grudge against Mary as representative of The Golden World Eternal Party Tribe. The genesis of the argument between them and the Partyers is as follows: three months ago, at the time of the benefit which had so outraged The Nomadic Daughters Of Lilith, The Golden World Eternal Partyers had travelled with The Tribe Of The Last Free Moonbeam and The Night Time Elves to the site of the rave. The Elves and Moonbeams were helping out as their charitable contribution.

Mary had left them to look after some equipment, including their main generator, or gennie, as she called it, while she and her companions departed to DJ at a previously arranged gig in the next town. Before leaving she gave clear instructions that they were not to use the generator. It was an old machine, prone to malfunctioning, requiring constant care from people who knew it well. Additionally they were short of petrol to run it and money was scarce.

"We arrived back to set up next afternoon," says Mary, "to find everything in ruins. No petrol in the generator, none to be had nearby, and when we managed to siphon enough from my bus to get it going again it wasn't working anyway. Which was bound to happen if anyone else tried to use that generator, it's very temperamental."

By her own account Mary had completely lost her temper,

which was understandable in view of the difficulties they were now in. People were already starting to arrive and there was no power for lights or music. It took the whole engineering skills of The Golden World Eternal Party Tribe plus the help of Nemo, Catherine and Cinderella, ace mechanics of The Galactic Navigators, to get it running again. The event started late although it had then passed off very successfully.

"I shouldn't have lost my temper so severely I suppose," says Mary, "but putting on these things is pretty stressful. And we hate to do it badly. The Golden World Eternal Party Tribe don't put on shabby events, we take pride in doing them well. Our reputation depends on it. I can't stand it when things go wrong."

Unfortunately, by the time Mary calmed down and apologised the damage had been done. She'd cursed The Clan Of The Night Time Elves and violently accused them of using the generator to power a huge arc lamp to help them scan the woods for unicorns. The Elves vehemently denied this and it soon degenerated into a slanging match, as happens on any occasion The Night Time Elves feel themselves mocked about the Unicorn Survey.

Finally a young Night Time Elf called Boot did admit that he had used the light to finish off a drawing of a butterfly though he swore that the generator had already been switched on by someone else and he'd only used it for half an hour. Boot was known to be eccentric, particularly on the subject of butterflies. He had undoubtedly been using power from the generator to hunt them all through the night.

I know Boot. He is rather a nice young man, and not really eccentric. Just very quiet, with a passion for poking around in hedgerows looking for butterflies. Oddly, in a world where things do not usually work out so well, he has a pleasant young girlfriend called Caddy who shares his passion. Any time The Night Time Elves are around you can find him and Caddy stuck in a hedgerow somewhere, enthusing about the local butterflies.

He is popular with The Clan Of The Night Time Elves. Not surprisingly they had stood up for him against Mary, even if in truth they had thought it quite likely that he had damaged the generator.

"It was infuriating at the time," concludes Mary, "but as it all worked out well I shouldn't have been so annoyed and I'm going to apologise."

Mary does this, quite graciously. Unfortunately The Clan Of The Night Time Elves don't seem inclined to accept her apology quite as graciously. They are still stung by her insulting them and abusing Boot.

Boot himself is fine about it. Sitting beside Caddy he tells Mary not to worry, he wasn't really insulted.

"I shouldn't have used the gennie. But I needed a good light to finish off a drawing of a Red Admiral before I forgot the details. And I really thought it was only a half hour."

Tempers soften. In the dim light of the Elvish lamps, a reconciliation seems close. Melody Paradise smiles broadly at everyone.

"Well, it's time to forget all about it," she says. "No harm was intended. I expect you used the generator longer than you thought Boot, because I remember me and Megan interrupted your butterfly drawing to come and help with my hair."

"That's right," says Boot. "I'd forgotten that. Of course, that must be it. You were doing a major job on the new purple locks weren't you?"

"That's right."

Mary looks thoughtful for a moment.

"Melody," she says. "How long did this major job on the new purple locks take?"

"Quite a long time," replies Melody Paradise, brightly. "All night in fact. I had the tribe doing some complex new colourings for me and putting in some new sea shells and some nice terra cotta beads. I wanted my hair looking good for the charity event."

Mary taps her foot on the ground.

"And how exactly did you see what you were doing, working on your hair through the night? The lights in your van aren't strong enough."

"Ehh..." Melody Paradise pauses. "Ehh...we borrowed your big arc lamp."

"And used the generator for ten hours?"

"Closer to twelve I think. It was a big hair operation."

Mary explodes.

"It was you! You broke the generator! It was your fault we had all that trouble!"

Melody looks surprised.

"I suppose it could have been," she admits. "I never thought of it before."

"You and your damned hair!"

Willis Elf is now laughing heartily at all this which does not please Mary at all. She fires some abuse at him, lets Melody know in strong terms that she is not pleased about her behaviour, less pleased to be made to look a fool in front of The Night Time Elves, then storms off. Melody Paradise is perplexed at this turn of events.

"Oh dear," she says. "I seem to have caused another argument."

Boot and his girlfriend Caddy try to make things all right by again telling Melody Paradise not to worry, it will soon blow over.

"We'll try and patch things up with The Tree Planters to make up for it."

This is not what Willis, a more hardcore Elf, wants to hear.

"No, we won't," he says.

"Yes, we will," says Boot.

"No, we won't," says Willis.

"We should," says Caddy.

"Call yourselves Elves?" says Willis. "You're a disgrace."

A fierce argument breaks out around the camp-fire. Strange insults involving butterflies and unicorns rend the air.

Peggy and Roxanna arrive on the scene.

"Hi, everyone," they say, cheerfully. "We've come to make friends. So when does the unicorn hunt start?"

Willis Elf, completely enraged, is not in a mood to make friends.

Melody sinks her face in her hands as he furiously tells The Tree Planters that if they don't leave immediately he'll personally start chopping trees down just for fun. A brief yet furious altercation follows. The previously conciliatory Tree Planters storm off after informing everyone that they are going to place a tree curse on Willis and he'd better be careful next time he walks under an oak.

All of this leaves Melody Paradise rather stymied in her efforts to spread love and peace. She withdraws, sad and defeated. I presume that tonight's mystical unicorn hunt has now been cancelled.

"I just made things worse again," says Melody, gloomily.

I'm forced to agree.

Quite disturbingly, Magwyn The Grim appears silently out of the darkness and stands in front of Melody. They don't speak, just stare at each other in hostile silence. After a minute or so Magwyn turns his gaze on me.

"I'm sorry I threw a bottle at you," he says.

"You ought to try controlling your temper," says Melody, "and don't pick fights with The Nomadic Daughters."

"They pick fights with me," replies Magwyn.

Melody's temper, already strained, starts to give way.

"What are you doing here anyway?" she demands.

"Working for Rupert."

"Right," says Melody. "As if you enjoy working for Rupert. You just came here to see me fuck up, didn't you? Well, fuck you."

"You ignorant bitch," says Magwyn.

He departs without another word leaving Melody trembling with anger.

It strikes me once more that Magwyn The Grim is still in love with Melody Paradise.

Melody shakes her head, and mutters sadly that there is no doubt that she is cursed, what with old boyfriends trying to ruin everything and her family wilfully arguing all the time. She sighs, and puts her hand out to rest on the pyramid. Unfortunately the pyramid has been weakened by the rain. Her hand goes right through and Melody Paradise disappears up to the neck. She wails as I struggle to free her.

"Oh no," she shrieks, "I've ruined The Leylines' pyramid."

"Only one side," I point out, encouragingly.

"What'll they say? They practically worship this thing."

"Let's just depart quickly and pretend it wasn't us."

"I can't do that. They'll go mad when they find it's damaged. I'll have to sort it out now."

But Melody doesn't sort it out now. All of a sudden her energy seems to flag. She troops off home, muttering that she'll sort it out tomorrow. I stare briefly at the now three-sided pyramid then depart quickly, not wishing to be blamed for the damage. Close by my tent I find Sweep scrabbling in the wet earth.

"What are you doing?"

"Burying Eko's runes. That'll teach him to go around making phoney predictions about him and Melody Paradise."

I leave him to it. It is now the early hours of the morning. The drizzle is thickening into heavy rain. My tent is surrounded by a sea of mud which would sink a tank. The valley is now silent, a wet gloomy silence which holds little promise of anything better. Things don't seem to be going very well.

30th July (Day 16)

Iris The Peaceful and her companions rode their horse-drawn caravans through northern Portugal. There were four caravans in all. The Contemplators, as Melody Paradise called them, totalled only seven people. Iris rode without a companion; behind her were Gail, Green, Maddy, Miguel, Hugh and Fernhadzi.

They halted for provisions in a small village, drawing their horses up in the dusty street in front of a tiny store. After making a few purchases they retired to a small common at the end of the village where they unhitched their horses, fed them with oats and molasses, and rested a while.

Iris The Peaceful had so far been unsuccessful in her mission. She had not found a new Wishing Tree. Her companions were starting to worry.

"I didn't think it would be so difficult," said Miguel.

"There aren't that many Wishing Trees about these days."

"I know. But we've looked everywhere. We should have just brought that one from the Lebanon."

"It didn't want to come," Iris pointed out. "It was happy where it was."

"Maybe we could have persuaded it."

116

"I think we should have just taken it," said Maddy. "How did it know it wouldn't like England? Just obstinate, I reckon."

Iris The Peaceful dismissed this, pointing out that no tree was going to take kindly to being kidnapped.

"And if it's not happy it's not going to grant any wishes is it?"

The problem was that Wishing Trees were so rare. Furthermore, they were very difficult to recognise. Everyone was helping in the search but it was really only Iris who could be sure of recognising a suitable tree. The chances of finding one young enough to be moved, and willing to go, were starting to seem very small. Iris had scoured the south of England before moving abroad to continue the hunt, deeming this better than heading north. Her companions wondered if she might think there was more chance of meeting Simon on his motorbike if they crossed the Channel.

"What if we don't get to the festival on time," asked Fernhadzi, who for some days had been concerned that they might not.

"Melody's festival doesn't start for another eighteen days. That's plenty of time to reach Chelwyn."

"Not if we keep going on detours looking for trees."

Fernhadzi, known to her friends as Fuzi, was a young Pakistani woman who had travelled with them for the past six months or so and was keen not to miss the festival. What could be more enjoyable than a week-long party with the whole family and friends of Melody Paradise? Though Fernhadzi had never met her, reports of Melody's fame had reached her from many sources.

"Is she really such a fabulous dancer?"

"Definitely," replied Iris. "She never tires. Like you, Fuzi. You can dance together for the whole week."

"Is her hair really so spectacular?"

"Yes," said Gail. "Spectacular beyond description."

"And is she as good a healer as people say?"

"Better," said Hugh, and told the story of her healing his foot after he was forced to jump from a blazing tree at the notorious oak-burning-incident, an incident which had precipitated his leaving The Militant Children Of Lemuria for the quieter life of The Contemplators.

Fuzi heard all this with admiration.

"What does she look like?"

Iris rummaged around in her bag, pulling out the bundle of postcards she'd brought on her travels to decorate her wagon. She handed one to Fuzi, a detail of the Cistine Chapel in Rome.

"Like that angel," she said, "but with longer hair. And rings through her lips and eyebrows."

They sat and listened to the birds singing. Hugh made a few small repairs to the rather complicated harness which hitched his horse to his wagon. Like the other wagons, it was pleasingly fat and rounded, and decorated in bright colours. The Contemplators made their own wagons, a skill first learned by Iris in Ireland from Tinkers.

After a while Fuzi rose, saying that now their horses were fed and watered perhaps they should be moving on. Iris smiled. By The Contemplators' standards this was rash and hasty action.

"Relax," she said. "There's plenty of time."

Fuzi relaxed.

"Still, it might be a good idea to get there early," suggested Hugh, who was now gently rubbing oil into the harness.

"Melody Paradise could probably do with your help."

"What for?"

"To end all the arguments. You know you're best at that."

"Melody can cope. No one likes to upset her."

"What about Florimel?"

Iris gave a slight nod. This was true. Florimel, one of her louder sisters, didn't seem to mind upsetting Melody Paradise at all. Florimel was peculiarly resistant to love and peace.

The evening was hot, slightly too humid to be pleasant, though a faint breeze from the hills suggested that it would soon be cooler. Iris took a wooden flute from her caravan and blew through it softly for while. The others lay back and relaxed, listening to the long notes floating away into the evening. Some children from the village wandered up and sat down nearby to listen.

After a while, Iris put down the flute and turned her deep blue eyes northwards. She gazed into the distance, her body so still and her expression so intent that she might have been gazing all the way from Portugal to England. She couldn't see a Wishing Tree. Nor could she see Simon on his motorbike. Either of them might be anywhere in the world. Wherever Simon was he would be bound to be going too fast.

She did think she caught a glimpse of Melody Paradise.

"Perhaps you're right," she said, eventually. "Melody might need our help. We'll start searching for the tree earlier each day, and going a little further in the evenings."

With that she rose gracefully and began to harness her white horse onto her caravan. The local children watched with interest as The Contemplators hitched up their wagons and rolled quietly out of the village. Later they played in the ruts left by the caravan wheels, and wondered about the strange creatures who had ridden in and out of their village so peacefully, like mythical visitors from another age.

31st July (Day 17)

By this time, sixteen days after Melody Paradise first asked me for help, I had decided on a plan for my creative writing class.

"I'm not going to prepare anything," I told her. "I'm just going to say whatever comes into my head."

Melody thought this was a good idea.

"It sounds very creative."

It was time for my treatment. Melody pressed my arm and studied my aura, frowning all the while.

"That's strange. Two days ago it was getting better. Now it's bad again. What happened?."

I shrugged.

"It's difficult to rest your fingers when you're a working author. I had to do an emergency rewrite of my 'Young Socrates' proposal. It was hard going, almost too painful to bear, but I suppose we creative people just have to suffer for our art sometimes."

"Has your city reached five hundred thousand people yet?" asked Megan.

"No, there's still too much pollution..."

This, I immediately realised, was something of a blunder. Melody Paradise launched into a long lecture about playing video games for hours on end when I was meant to be resting my arm. There is something about healers that makes them just love lecturing their patients for any little misdemeanour. Even Melody Paradise, a model of good humour, would go on for hours if any of her patients stepped out of line. A least she hadn't told me to stop drinking or anything like that.

"Perhaps you should stop drinking for a while," she said. "Help your body to heal naturally."

My arm and hand grew hot under Melody's touch as she transmitted her healing energy to me.

Finan arrived with a woman I didn't recognise. She looked much the same as everyone else round here, with green dreadlocks, two rings through her nose and a ragged old jersey the size of a tent. One of the neighbours I supposed. Some time later, after listening to her enthusing about the animal rights demonstration she and Finan were going to the next day, I realised that this was in fact Irene the beefburger woman, only recently seen in cream blouse and navy blue skirt. I was amazed at the change. Surely one of the quickest waitress-to-new-age-hippy transformations on record.

When I asked Finan how his music was coming along, he told me he hadn't really done much as he'd been away protesting with Irene most of the time. I noticed he was looking at his feet in a rather dissatisfied manner.

"New shoes?"

Finan nodded.

"Good, aren't they?" said Irene. "Finan had to get a new pair because his old boots were made of leather. Imagine a vegetarian wearing leather boots!"

She laughed heartily, as did Finan, but I couldn't help thinking that he did not look particularly impressed with the natural fibre articles he now wore on his feet.

Rag and Rooster sat silently in the corner. Both of them had been depressed since reports reached The Tribe Of The Last Free

Moonbeam that Florimel had taken up with a new lover. Melody Paradise kindly pointed out to them that these reports were only unconfirmed gossip and could well be false, which cheered them a little.

"Don't despair," Melody encouraged them. "There's every chance Florimel will be single by the time of the festival, and just raring to meet you."

"And God help Rooster and Rag if she ever is raring to meet them," said Melody to me later. "I don't think either of them exactly recognise the force of my sister's personality."

"What do you mean?"

"I mean she's unpleasant, aggressive and mean."

"Sounds horrible."

"Not horrible," protested Melody, "none of my family are horrible. Just unpleasant, aggressive and mean. She has her good points as well. Don't tell Rag or Rooster I criticised her. I don't want to upset them."

"Well, one of them is going to be upset anyway if the other succeeds."

Melody Paradise agreed that this was true but thought there was little chance of either of them ever securing the affections of Florimel.

"Romances rarely seem to work out well these days," she said. "It makes spreading love and peace very difficult."

1st August (Day 18)

It was around this time that I first became aware of the Unicorn Survey. Melody's brother Willis called to visit his sister when The Clan Of The Night Time Elves were passing through London. I found him sitting on the floor of Melody's van with her and Megan, drinking some dubious-looking liquid.

The inside of Melody's van was much as I would have pictured the living space of Melody Paradise to be: messy, but colourful and pleasant. It was a comfortable place. The warmth from the stove reassured me that I would not necessarily freeze to death at the festival. A wooden bed was constructed high up at the end nearest the driver's compartment. The space underneath the bed was used for storage. A sink and cooker fitted neatly along one side. The hard metal floor of the van was carpeted and covered with bright cushions and rugs. The walls were painted with pictures of trees and rivers. Beside the trees, Melody had hung small pictures and ornaments garnered from her trips around the world, an exotic and eclectic collection of Eastern and Western art. Between her bed and the driver's compartment was a panel of stained glass, two feet long and two feet high. This, Magwyn's work, looked as if it may have been fine at one time, but it was now cracked and broken. Melody Paradise introduced me to Willis.

"This is Martin," she said. "He's coming to read at my festival. This is my brother Willis, from The Clan Of The Night Time Elves. He's going to Yorkshire to look for unicorns."

Now I can't say that hearing that a brother of Melody Paradise was going to Yorkshire to look for unicorns came as a terrific surprise. It was, however, a little surprising to hear Melody relate it in such a matter-of-fact tone. After all, Melody Paradise was not out of touch with the real world. She might not like it that much, and she might be keen to hide from it whenever possible, but she hadn't lost contact with it. While she was well-up on studying people's auras, and fairly keen on the Tarot, she was not a party to any of the wilder theories that some of her companions were wont to propound. She would not openly mock anyone who claimed that it was now scientifically proven that aliens were among us, making circular patterns in corn fields in Wiltshire, but she wouldn't really believe it.

"Tell me about the survey," I said to Willis, meanwhile putting my mental notebook into gear, because if someone tells me anything strange, I'll eventually steal it and put in into one of my books, even if it means mocking them in the process. That is a large part of how I make my living, stealing ideas and experiences from other people and putting them into books. Recording them for posterity, I call it.

On occasion, realising that they have shared some private

experience with me and that I am now going to share it with a great many more people, people have implored me not to do this. I have never listened to their entreaties.

"Please don't write that," they say, "I don't want everyone to know."

"It'll be fine," I tell them. "I'll handle it sensitively."

Afterwards they are upset. I've lost friends this way, and made enemies. But they can take comfort. I know that in some manner I will get my come-uppance in the end. God or karma will work out a revenge for them.

"Tell me about the unicorns, Willis."

"We're carrying out a systematic survey of Britain, to see how many unicorns are left."

"How long have you been doing this?"

Willis-Elf looked thoughtful. He was a large and powerful looking young man. His hair was shaved very short apart from two long dreads which trailed down his back. Now around twenty five, his cheeks were still mottled by teenage acne which gave him a slightly rough, outdoor look. He wore green socks, thick and long, which he folded down over his star-painted boots.

"About a year."

"How many unicorns have you found?"

"None," he admitted. "They're very elusive."

"Weren't unicorns mythical creatures?"

That was a bad thing to say. Willis gave me a long lecture on unicorn sightings through the ages. He did have a comprehensive knowledge of the subject. Apparently unicorns were mentioned by the Greek writer Ctesias in 400 BC and also featured in the ancient myths of India and China. They were depicted in early Mesopotamian art and even feature in the Bible, though Willis said that scholars were now of the opinion that the Biblical creatures were wild oxen rather than unicorns.

"But I think they were unicorns," said Willis. "It seems quite reasonable that they'd have appeared in the Bible. Did you know it was the only animal which could defeat an elephant?"

"I thought they were peaceful?" said Melody.

123

"They were. But their horn was very sharp. They could defeat an elephant in a crisis."

Willis moved on to later accounts, leaving me with the clear impression that at one time you couldn't move in Britain without treading on a unicorn.

Willis Elf certainly believed in unicorns. I was entertained, but not convinced. There again, who knows? In 98 BC, Sylla, a Roman general saw a satyr. It was found in a cave and brought to him as he marched with his army back from Thessaly. He examined it for a while before dismissing it, displeased at its unpleasant behaviour. Sylla Lucius Cornelius is a well-documented historical figure. There is no particular reason to doubt any other story about him; his battles and campaigns, his political career in Rome and suchlike are not in question. The story about the satyr is recorded by Plutarch, who is occasionally frivolous, and Pausanius, who is not. So perhaps it is reasonable to believe that Sylla and many of his Roman comrades actually saw a mythical creature.

After I wrote my book about fairies, various people told me about fairy experiences they'd had. Unfortunately these experiences all took the form of 'We'd just spent five days in Ireland whacked out our heads on magic mushrooms and then we came to a stone circle and it was full of fairies dancing about! But they were really there, it wasn't anything to do with the magic mushrooms.'

No one told me a convincing fairy story. I'm still hopeful. How pleasant fairies are. I'll write another book about them, once public disapproval for the first one dies down.

"We're sure there must be some unicorns left somewhere," continued Willis. "In a wood in Wales, Starshine, Sunshine and Moonshine saw a white horse-like creature disappearing through the trees which might have been a unicorn. Moonshine thought she saw a horn on its nose but wasn't sure. And we saw something that might have been a unicorn in Cornwall when we were coming back from a festival at Treworgy a few years back, but the nearest person was Boot and he had his head stuck in a hedgerow looking for butterflies so it got away. You can't really rely on Boot to look for unicorns, he's too interested in butterflies."

"Yes, Boot is a bit of a dreamer."

Megan showed me a letter that had just been forwarded to her from the Social Services in Leeds. The letter stated that she had to attend a hearing during which the father of her baby would apply to have custody of the child granted to him. Megan did not want to attend the hearing. It seemed to her quite likely that custody would be granted to the father. If, however, she did not attend, the social services would immediately apply for a care order and put her baby into a foster home pending a legal judgement.

"I wish I could ride away on a unicorn," said Megan.

2nd August (Day 19)

By the time The Tree Planters departed much of the work was done but the continuing rain and bad weather prevented Magwenwy from completing her repairs. Some days the downpour was such that it was impossible to do any work at all and The Riverboat Tribe could only huddle under the black sky in their narrow boats, waiting for the weather to improve. Magwenwy fretted with impatience. Grown used to a life on water, she could not feel at ease if her vessel was not in good shape. She cursed the weather, and The Mushrooms.

Amesh sat with her, sharing her herb tea and her frustrations.

"How long to the festival?"

Magwenwy studied her diary for a while, counting the days with difficulty on her fingers.

"Fifteen," she answered, finally.

"If this rain keeps up we're not going to make it."

"We have to make it. We can't possibly miss Melody Paradise's festival. Not when she's leaving the country straight afterwards."

Magwenwy cursed The Mushrooms again. Amesh sympathised, as he always did. He knew that Magwenwy was harbouring thoughts of revenge. He did not entirely approve of this but found it understandable.

"Who did it?"

Magwenwy shrugged. Which particular Mushroom had caused

the calamity had never been established. As the hand brake on the bus was known to be loose, there had been a large wooden wedge under the rear wheel to prevent it slipping. Someone had removed the wedge, thus allowing the bus to roll onto the boat. It was Bernadette's bus but Bernadette was unconscious on the other bank at the time. Fluffy, Tuffy, Bug and Simple all thought they had been somewhere else but couldn't really remember where. Really, any one of the demented Mushroom Clan could have suddenly removed the wedge without realising what they were doing.

"Do you think The Magic Hat is really lost forever?" said Amesh, once more voicing the question which was never satisfactorily answered.

Magwenwy shrugged. It certainly hadn't turned up after the sinking. "But I'm sure someone took it before the boat went down. I swear it wasn't in my cabin where it should have been. I suspect Florimel."

Magwenwy rose, frustrated at her enforced inactivity.

"This time last year I was sailing through Germany on my way to Poland. Since I started living on the water I haven't spent more than three days in the same place. Until now that is. We've been stuck here for weeks and I don't like it."

Magwenwy paced round the cabin.

"I'll get them back," she muttered.

3rd August (Day 20)

Before the festival, Sweep had complained to me about Willis monopolising Melody Paradise.

"You'd think he might let me get in a word or two seeing as they were all sitting in my kitchen drinking my tea. That Willis talks too much. How am I meant to charm Melody Paradise when she's obliged to spend the entire evening listening to him rambling on about unicorns and other such rubbish?"

I reminded him that Willis was Melody's brother so at least he didn't have to worry about it so much.

"Better for you that she spends the evenings talking to Willis about mythical creatures than some other young man about more personal things."

Sweep agreed, but reluctantly. Apparently he did not think it was impossible that Willis might be in pursuit of Melody.

"But he's her brother."

"How do we know for sure?" said Sweep. "He might just be using that as a cover story to get close to her."

"Wouldn't Melody notice if someone was only pretending to be her brother? Strike her as a little odd, surely?"

"I suppose so. Unless he was very cunning about it. I don't trust him anyway. There must be something wrong with a man who travels round the country looking for unicorns. Who's to say he's not suffering from incestuous lust?"

I saw that Sweep's jealously was starting to run out of control and hastily changed the subject by asking about Livia. Livia was a young Italian woman who left The Tribe Of The Last Free Moonbeam after forming a relationship with Cabot from The Elemental Sunshine Family. This relationship had turned out to be brief. Livia had arrived back with two black eyes and a cracked nose. For a New Age traveller, Cabot had proved to have some very old fashioned ideas about how to treat his girlfriends. Livia had her nose set in a casualty ward and afterwards Melody Paradise nursed her bruises and her spirit till she recovered.

The Elemental Sunshine Family banished Cabot in disgrace but The Tribe Of The Last Free Moonbeam were less than pleased with them for allowing it to happen. Cabot's reputation for violence was known to many people, though perhaps not often talked of. Why Livia ever went to live with him was a mystery to me, but many relationships were a mystery to me.

This bad feeling between The Elemental Sunshine Family and The Tribe Of The Last Free Moonbeam counted as one more thing for Melody Paradise to sort out. When I was not actually terrified by the thought of spending a week in a lonely valley with all these people, I could actually find the ever-mounting arguments of Melody's family quite entertaining.

Sweep reported that Livia was now recovered. He had been

doing his bit to aid the recovery by teaching her some new juggling tricks.

"Very good for the spirit, juggling tricks."

Sweep reported that Magwyn The Grim had departed the country, having refused Rupert's request that he help at the festival. Everyone was pleased, particularly Willis. Magwyn had apparently stolen Willis's parking space, quite a serious matter since Willis's bus was not taxed and it was necessary for him to park it somewhere off the road. Around Brixton and Clapham there were not that many patches of waste ground where a large bus could be safely parked. True to his reputation, Magwyn had just driven in while Willis was away somewhere then refused to move. There was nothing Willis could do. Neither he nor the combined forces of The Clan Of The Night Time Elves were a match for Magwyn's capacity for aggression and violence.

"Tell me something cheerful Sweep."

Sweep considered this.

"Iris The Peaceful once rode a Sacred Buffalo round the North American plains. In a previous incarnation of course. When she was a Lakota Indian. I always thought that was quite cheerful."

"Yes, Sweep, that's a fabulous story. Better than the three little pigs."

"Don't knock Iris The Peaceful," said Sweep. "Remember, she's bringing a new Wishing Tree. I'm depending on it."

"Why?"

"So as I can wish for Melody Paradise, of course."

Sweep, suddenly afflicted by an unbearable sadness about his hopeless love for Melody, found himself unable to talk, and unable even to juggle. He sat and stared at the carpet. Thinking it better to leave him alone with his thoughts for a while, I got back to my video game. I was building sports stadiums to attract new citizens but they were still reluctant to come to my city. The population was up to seven hundred thousand but refused to grow any more. Well, they had better be careful. If they kept complaining about pollution I was quite liable to lose patience entirely and destroy them all in a gigantic earthquake.

The rain poured down. It had now rained every day for the past three weeks. It was generally agreed to be a very poor summer. Everyone was bored with the rain, or depressed, except Melody Paradise. She maintained her optimism.

"It'll be sunny soon. I can feel it. It won't rain at my festival. The weather will be perfect and we'll sleep under the stars."

Two cats wandered over. One leapt on Melody's lap and paced around for a while before making itself comfortable and going to sleep. The other cat looked on jealously. After a while it settled on Sweep's lap, making it quite clear that this was a poor second choice.

"Are we going to be in the circus?" asked Megan.

Melody Paradise said she didn't know.

"Rupert is organising The Flying Dementos and The Motorbikes Of Merlin and some others but he might need a few people as extras. I'm not sure, I'm leaving it all up to him and he hasn't been in touch for a while."

"Too busy selling jets to Swiss bankers, I imagine. The circus is going to be a disaster."

"It doesn't matter if the circus is a disaster," chanted Melody and Megan in unison, and laughed, as this had now become a well-known phrase.

The door bell rang and Finan appeared in the kitchen, looking tired. He accepted Sweep's offer of a cup of tea.

"But I'll have to be quick. I have to meet Irene in Brixton in five minutes. We're going down to Dover to protest about live animal exports."

"Weren't you meant to be showing Mary how to programme your 303?"

"No time for that. I just called in to ask you to tell Mary I'll do it later."

"But Mary drove up specially."

Finan said he couldn't help it, he had to go to Dover. Irene was very keen to attend the demonstration. He yawned.

"You look like you could do with a good sleep rather than going off to Dover," said Megan.

"I could," agreed Finan, "but I haven't got time."

He sniffed his tea suspiciously.

"Is this real milk?"

Sweep nodded.

"Can't drink it," said Finan. "I've given up all animal products. I'm a vegan now."

"Since when?"

"Since Irene suggested it. It's a good idea. What's the point of being a vegetarian and claiming not to abuse animals if you go around stealing their milk?"

Finan looked rather wistfully at his cup of tea, put it down undrunk, and departed.

I had met Melody Paradise in Sweep's house for my treatment, which was now going well. Both Sweep and the cat in his lap now looked on jealously as Melody ran her hands over my arm. Sweep at this moment had no injury which could require her touch although he managed to sustain them with surprising frequency. In fact, the amount of times Sweep claimed to be in need of treatment from Melody Paradise you might have thought he was lucky to still be alive. Even now I could see him gazing at his own arms, wondering if perhaps they might be starting to develop a few strains that would require immediate attention.

Megan's baby cried. Megan herself was very stressed after receiving the letter from the Social Services about her court appearance. Courts were notoriously unfriendly to travellers. Megan would not be the first traveller to be deemed unfit to look after her child, and have it taken away. I wasn't sure if she was planning to attend. So far, all I'd heard her say about it was that she hoped Iris brought a good Wishing Tree so she could wish the problem away. To me a good lawyer would have seemed like a better option but Megan seemed to have some difficulty in facing up to the prospect of lawyers and courts.

Eko arrived, to Sweep's disgust, though he greeted him as politely as he could and made him a cup of tea.

"Past-life reading, anyone?" asked Eko, brandishing his pack of illustrated cards.

I declined. Eko did do a reading for me once but when he claimed that Sweep and I were brothers in ancient Egypt I found it just too difficult to believe. Particularly as Eko also claimed that he and Melody Paradise were father and daughter in a family of priests around about the same time, thereby implying that he and Melody had some sort of eternal tie between them. Of all Eko's various means of delving into the secrets of the universe, the past-life cards were by far the most stupid. I utterly refused to believe that Sweep, Eko, Melody Paradise and myself had once gambolled around under the same pyramid.

Another thing that strained my credulity was Iris The Peaceful's tale of riding a giant dingo round Australia at some time in the indeterminate past. As later repeated to me by Melody Paradise, Iris had apparently spent a whole lifetime travelling the Continent on the back of this huge animal before Europeans ever came to settle.

"So Iris The Peaceful was once an Aborigine?" I said, rather cynically.

"Yes. Or rather, according to her, an Andigari. Her tales of visiting all the tribes and going to Uluru are fascinating."

"I refuse to believe that Iris The Peaceful was ever an Aborigine," I said, "or an Andigari."

"Why not? You should hear her play the didgeridoo, she's a natural."

"That's hardly conclusive proof. Do you seriously believe all this stuff?"

Melody Paradise answered quite emphatically that she did.

"Wait till you meet her, then you'll understand. When she was injured in the Himalayas after visiting the Dali Lama in Eighth century Tibet, she bled gold."

"Bled gold?"

"That's right. Tibetan Lamas do that if they're very spiritual. And get a cut."

The conversation was getting worse.

"Did I tell you about her last life when she met Janis Joplin riding in a pink cadillac between Texas and San Francisco?"

I was now convinced that Melody Paradise was mocking me and refused to participate in the discussion any more. Janis Joplin in a pink cadillac indeed.

Melody Paradise had come to Sweep's to use the phone. She was ordering some portable toilets for the festival. This was good news to me although Melody Paradise had not been bothered one way or the other. She had assumed that they would just bury their excreta as they normally did on their travels but found that as the council were licensing the use of the land they were providing temporary toilets, and a standpipe for water. I was certainly pleased to hear this. I hadn't been looking forward to using a ditch.

Melody made the call and placed her order. She was surprising efficient at this sort of thing. Phoning up a company and briskly hiring a few portable toilets was no problem for her, even in the middle of a conversation about her sister Iris The Peaceful bleeding gold in Eighth century Tibet.

5th August (Day 22)

Every day Alexander sat in his wheelchair on the pavement in Norwood High Street dressed in a shabby old track suit too thin to keep out the cold. He held a polystyrene cup in his hand, begging for money. Round his neck there was a cardboard sign saying 'Please talk to me.'

Few people talked to him. Few people took the leaflets he handed out either but if they did they would read the following photocopied message:

'I ask you to help me. My life is terrible: no family, no relatives, no friends. I am disabled. Only a true happy family can solve my situation. I ask you to make copies of this letter and help me find a family. I will really care about my future wife and children. Also I need any friends.'

The note finished off with an appeal to write to him at the temporary bed and breakfast accommodation in which the Social Services had now housed him.

Poor Alexander. I couldn't describe the true extent of his misery. He was the son of Russian immigrants, and still had a strong Russian accent. He had been injured at birth and spent most of his life in a wheelchair. He was around forty five. Now his family was dead he had not one person in the world to talk to.

I used to talk to him but I found it difficult. He had one subject uppermost in his mind and that was to find a wife. Nothing else in the world interested him, although many things caused him pain. Every time I stopped to talk he would ask me, quite seriously, if I had found a wife for him yet. Not wishing to say that I would never in my whole life meet anyone who wanted to marry him, I would try and change the subject but Alexander wasn't interested in anything else. He actively disapproved of books, films, television, music, cars, shops, money, sport, religion, entertainment of any sort, everything. He had a lot of time to grow into his fixation. This made conversation almost impossible. Perhaps that was why few people talked to him, despite the pleading of his pathetic cardboard notice.

He looked anguished as he sat in his wheelchair. His wheelchair was very old fashioned, a more antiquated model than I ever saw anywhere else. Alexander was the unhappiest person I ever met. He used to say that his daily life was torture, and I believed him.

One time I found him in his usual place, but without his wheelchair. It was broken and no one had organised its repair so he had crawled from his home to his usual place in the street. As Alexander's legs didn't work at all it had taken him two hours to crawl there. He didn't want to miss his usual place in case a wife happened along that day.

When I passed by again later in the evening his strength had deserted him and he was unable to sit upright. He couldn't get home. My friend Angus and I carried him there. It was a very difficult and distressing task. Alexander was heavy and in pain and getting him back seemed to take for ever. All the way Alexander was half-concerned with thanking us and half-concerned about whether we had found a wife for him yet.

I bought him food and included him in my prayers. Neither

seemed to do him any good.

One day he wasn't in his usual place. I haven't seen him since. Poor Alexander. No family. No one in the world at all. No wealthy relation to pay for private nursing care. No convenient relative in Lambeth Council to push him up the special needs housing queue. No Melody Paradise to make things better for him.

20th August (Day 37) Fourth Day Of The Festival

Living in the valley destroys my metabolism. My body-clock goes haywire and I start waking up at ridiculous times in the morning. As the fourth day of the festival dawns I stick my head out of my tent to find a light drizzle falling and not a person in sight. Everyone else is still asleep. In the poor light, the scattered and ragged collection of benders, tepees, cars, caravans, trucks and buses surrounded by oozing mud, makes for a desolate sight.

There is a slight noise some way off. The door of the single caravan in which the four Nomadic Daughters Of Lilith sleep opens slowly. Florimel, Mirabel, Belladonna and Anorexia emerge, yawning. Despite the rain and the cold wind, each of them is lightly clad. They wear green vests, army trousers and their feet are bare.

They walk down the side of the valley till they reach a patch of level ground. Silently and with little ado they begin to perform Tai Chi Chuan in the mud and the rain. The movements and steps of Tai Chi Chuan are very slow and the four women go through the form in graceful defiance of the elements though they are soon wet through and their hair hangs limp and waterlogged around their shoulders.

I watch, almost hypnotised by the long series of movements performed in perfect unison. They glide from one posture to the next, their actions seeming sometimes like martial arts and sometimes like dance. Punches and kicks alternate with gentle waving of the hands and spiralling turns of the body. Each movement flows smoothly into the next in an unending stream. They are all performed at such a slow rate, with such apparent oblivion to the outside world, that the four women might all seem to be in a trance, or even dreaming.

This lasts for twenty minutes. I am so fascinated by their grace that I forget that I too am being soaked in the drizzle. They finish as they began, in perfect unison. Each stands with her arms crossed over her chest. A minute or so later they sit on the ground, apparently to meditate. Eyes closed, legs bent beneath them in the lotus position, they sit in peace as the wind blows the rain in the faces, and their bare feet and legs settle into the surrounding mud.

This performance leaves me with the strong feeling that I have misjudged The Nomadic Daughters Of Lilith. They can't be entirely bad to be capable of such an impressive feat of skill and grace. Parts of the Tai Chi Chuan form required such precise balance that I would have thought it impossible to do in these conditions. It's hard enough just to walk around in this quagmire yet even while spinning round slowly on one leg none of them had looked unbalanced for a second. Rather they looked like they might have been born just to do Tai Chi Chuan in the wind and the rain.

While they are still meditating, I creep back into my tent, try to dry myself, and go back to sleep.

I next awaken to chaos. Children scream, dogs bark, voices are raised and threats are uttered. The Universal Leyline Protectors have discovered the hole in their pyramid. The resulting uproar has roused all but the most determined sleepers from their benders. Festival go-ers, unclad and drowsy, emerge into the cold morning to see what all the noise is about.

All twenty of The Universal Leyline Protectors are marching down the valley to confront The Elemental Sunshine Family. The Sunshine Family, tumbling from their vehicles, set themselves stoutly in position to repel the attack. A large bearded Leyline Protector brandishes a stick and hurls abuse, condemning The Elemental Sunshine Family in the strongest possible terms for sneaking out during the night and sabotaging their pyramid.

The small hole caused by Melody Paradise has now grown into a huge gaping gash, torn open by the wind and rain. It does look as if someone has committed deliberate pyramid terrorism.

Melody Paradise is herself nowhere in sight. This is not so surprising since Melody does figure highly among the world's most determined sleepers. Toughened by a life of raves, festivals and travelling, she is a hard person to rouse in the morning. This capacity for resolutely sleeping through any disturbance is something she shares with most of her tribe. If a crisis happens before lunch time, it's no use expecting The Tribe Of The Last Free Moonbeam to sort it out.

"A whole night's energies from the Crab Nebula lost forever!" cry The Universal Leyline Protectors. The Elemental Sunshine Family retort that it was nothing to do with them but I can see that passions are already too high for them to be believed. When some of them add that The Universal Leyline Protectors are well-known for their shoddy workmanship so their pyramid probably just fell apart from natural causes, it doesn't help matters at all.

Mary sprints across the valley towards the still slumbering encampment of The Tribe Of The Last Free Moonbeam. She hammers furiously on Melody's door and screams for her to get up.

"Come quick before they all start fighting!"

After a great deal of banging, the door opens and a dazed looking Melody Paradise appears. Scuffles are now breaking out between The Leyline Protectors and The Sunshine Family. Mud and stones start to fly. Realising what is happening, Melody, wearing only a silk dressing gown with more holes in it than material, stumbles from her van and hurries with Mary towards the affray.

The Nomadic Daughters Of Lilith are on the sidelines, enjoying the spectacle. Muttering a curse at them and everybody else, I withdraw from the scene. For a long time, I lie thinking bitter thoughts about the miserable chain of circumstances which has brought me to this wet valley to be tormented by ever-increasing amounts of mad people. After a long time the tumult fades away. I presume they have all killed each other, which is fine with me.

Footsteps sound in the mud outside my tent.

"Can I come in ?" calls Melody Paradise.

"Have they all killed each other?" I ask, quite hopefully.

Melody Paradise shakes her head but says it was a close thing.

"The Universal Leyline Protectors are furious. They regard their pyramid as a religious icon. They thought The Elemental Sunshine Family had deliberately damaged it."

"So what happened?"

"I managed to get myself in the middle and stop the fight. But it was difficult. The Elemental Sunshine Family and The Universal Leyline Protectors are itching for a chance to get at each other. They hate each other because each claims to have started building pyramids first."

"Really? Aren't pyramids quite common at festivals?"

Melody agrees that they now are but informs me that both tribes claim to have been the originators of the idea.

"To hear my brother Patrick talk you'd think The Leyline Protectors got there some time before the Egyptians. Also they accuse The Elemental Sunshine Family of being frivolous because they build pyramids just for fun."

"As opposed to The Leyline Protectors, who build them for a serious purpose."

"Absolutely. Connecting and preserving the energies of the universe."

"They're mad."

"I know," says Melody Paradise, too upset by the proceedings to mount her usual defence of the family. She is very upset. When Rooster starts emitting painful shrieks on a tin whistle somewhere nearby, she actually sticks her head out the tent and yells for him to shut up.

After Melody had quietened everyone down she'd done the frank and honest thing you'd expect of her, which was to admit that she was the culprit.

"But they didn't believe me. Patrick said he appreciated me trying to make things better but it was no use me taking the blame for it, he knew that The Sunshine Family were behind it. I spent ages trying to convince everyone that I'd done it but even then I'm not sure they believed me."

"They all expect you to stop arguments, not start them."

Melody nods. "Though I can't think why, the way things have been going. Have you noticed how every time I get involved, things get worse?"

I nod. Melody sinks closer to the ground and looks depressed.

"Well, there's a reason. Things like this never used to happen to me. I never used to be so clumsy that I'd stick my hand through a pyramid, or fall over dancing. I never used to say the wrong thing and make everything worse like I did with The Tree Planters and The Elves. I'm cursed."

"Cursed? That's putting it a bit strongly, isn't it?"

"No, I mean it. It's all because of..." She pauses, looking round her in some despair. She checks outside the tent to make sure that no one is listening.

"I have to tell someone this," she says, unhappily.

I wait with interest, wondering what grim crime Melody Paradise can have to confess.

"Have you heard about The Magic Hat?"

"Incessantly."

"Well, I've got it."

"What?"

"I've got it. I stole if from Magwenwy's boat."

"Why?"

"Because everyone else was trying to steal it. It's the last remnant of the Wishing Tree. I made it so it could be shared by everyone but no one seemed to want to share things any more. No one's wanted to co-operate at all since the Tree died. I knew if I left it someone else would take it so I just took it myself. But I feel terrible about it. The Magic Hat was for everyone. I was going to put it back but then the boat sank and it was chaos everywhere and everyone was rushing about trying to rescue people and it was too late. Ever since then I've been cursed. The spirit of the Wishing Tree has it in for me. That's why everything's going wrong."

I try and reassure Melody, telling her that preserving the hat doesn't seem like such an unreasonable thing to have done, and hardly worthy of a curse, and anyway surely she doesn't really believe in curses, but her guilt makes her resistant to my reassurances.

"I pretended I wanted to keep it for everyone but really I wanted it for myself," she says, miserably. "No wonder I'm cursed."

"I'm sure you're not really. You just think you are."

"Oh yes? You've seen how badly everything's gone. I used to be able to spread peace and love just by smiling at people and now I'm about as much use at ending arguments as Attila the Hun. And it's getting worse. Doom is creeping up on me. Magwenwy knows the hat went missing before her boat sank so now everyone suspects someone else of stealing it. More bad feelings, and I've caused them. Last night Eko told me he'd started asking the runes where the hat was. He thought he was doing me a favour. He'll find out it was me and then everything'll completely fall apart."

I scoff at Eko's powers of discovery but Melody says it doesn't matter because someone is bound to find out eventually. She can feel it.

"I thought I might end the curse by ending the arguments but now I'm starting to think it's hopeless. Everything will only get worse."

Megan sticks her head into my tent.

"Chelwyn Summer Fair Committee's here," she says, "and some men in suits. They want to see you right away."

A slightly haunted expression settles on Melody's face.

"I wish Iris would get here with the new Wishing Tree," she mutters.

"If that bastard Magwyn hadn't killed the old one none of this would have happened," she adds, very bitterly, which is the only time I've heard Melody refer to the unhappy incident.

Melody persuades me to accompany her. She is displeased at having to talk to the Committee again. She had assumed that Rupert would be able to take care of everything to do with the circus. The Committee are sheltering under a cluster of black umbrellas. I am reminded of a funeral. Melody shakes off her depression and readies herself to present a cheerful and confident face to the visitors. I admire her for this. Personally, the prospect of talking to them makes my heart sink. Alongside the members of the Committee are some men in very smart suits indeed.

"Melody, I think that man in a suit is a Member of Parliament."

"Really?"

"Yes."

I attempt to retreat. Melody grabs me and drags me on.

"Let me go," I whisper frantically. "We have to escape. The Government's got involved. We're finished."

Melody Paradise grins at me.

"Come on, stop worrying. MP's aren't that important."

Her resilience can be annoying at times. Rather than agreeing to immediate flight she rises to the occasion. Banishing all trace of her recent gloom, she strides forward confidently through the mire and greets everyone cheerfully. The greeting she receives in turn from the Chelwyn Summer Fair Committee is slightly muted. From the Member of Parliament it is decidedly frosty.

Perhaps it is not surprising he doesn't look happy. After all, his recent sessions in Parliament have been spent passing laws designed to prevent gatherings of the sort of people by whom he is now surrounded.

I fear the worst and am convinced the police have found out that Melody Paradise spent almost all the Committee's money on drink, drugs and vehicle repairs. How will the local MP react to the news that the money earmarked for acts and props went instead northwards to Scotland to purchase a large quantity of high-grade hydroponically grown grass? Not well, I fear, especially with the economy doing so badly.

When I reflect that I did the original proposal for all this on my computer, quite reasonable visions of newspaper exposés, national scandal, a swift trial and lengthy imprisonment flash through my head. Looking grimly around them, the Member of Parliament and his companions seem to be thinking along much the same lines. They are certainly not impressed by what they see. Again, this is not surprising. Bright, colourful and friendly as Melody Paradise and her associates are, I can tell that in his eyes they make a shabby bunch. Although most people have been washing at the standpipe or the river – The Nomadic Daughters Of Lilith undress completely and stride right in, again defying the elements – it is impossible to keep clean in this sodden valley. Melody's smiling face is smeared with dirt as she greets him. Her bare feet are completely sheathed in cloying mud. She is still dressed only in her torn dressing gown. She does not really have the air of a serious cultural ambassador. I myself, less than enthusiastic about washing in cold water, am utterly filthy.

To make matters worse, Magwyn The Grim chooses this moment to make a rare foray across the valley. Magwyn is by now very, very dirty, filthier even than me. His dark, shabby clothes are ripped, mud-spattered, greasy and totally appalling. His hair is worse, having now matted itself into one huge, filthy dreadlock. He smells of cider. His hands are covered in paint. Only his eyes, large, dark and belligerent, bear much relation to what humans normally look like. I can't imagine why he has chosen this moment to appear, unless he just felt like glaring rudely at some new faces. The MP blanches, and looks away. Melody Paradise looks briefly troubled but swiftly banishes her frown.

"How nice of you to visit us," says Melody to the MP, who explains that he takes a keen interest in all local cultural events.

"My husband," says one of the Arts Committee, the chairwoman I think.

There is a brief pause as Melody Paradise and myself struggle to come to terms with the thought that the chairwoman of the Committee from whom we have more or less embezzled money is in fact married to the local MP. Undeniably it's a bit of a blow. Somewhat of a blunder on our part.

He is introduced to us as Mr Colin Pitt. I shake his hand and try to look honest. Colin Pitt is obviously not impressed by what he sees around him. Few people would be. There is no chance of anyone mistaking this shambling collection of benders, tepees and buses for a visit from the Russian State Circus. In answer to his queries Melody says, rather hopefully, that really he should talk to Rupert as he is the director and is also in charge of the production company. Mr Pitt replies that Rupert has directed him here, which means Melody's stuck with it.

Melody Paradise does her best to put things right. She takes the initiative and the MP's arm and conducts him round the valley. Such is the force of her personality that she is almost able to carry it off. Talking confidentially about the rise of the modern circus, the complexities involved in staging such things, budgetary considerations, previous productions she has been involved in and a great deal else besides, she comes close to convincing even me that the whole thing is genuine. When she launches into an amusing anecdote about the problems she and Rupert encountered while organising a performance from The Motorbikes Of Merlin in Venice last year, when the bikes hopped from one gondola to the other, Mr Pitt is amused enough to laugh along with everybody else.

So charming is Melody Paradise that in a short time he seems to forget that, rather than a serious circus organiser he is actually being shown round by a mud-splattered, bare-footed hippy traveller with incredibly long dreadlocks in a ragged old dressing gown which she has to keep clutched tightly around her to prevent from flying open. All in all, it is a fine performance from Melody. She can even spread love and peace to Conservative MPs. I am terrifically impressed and wonder if I might not have to go to prison after all.

Rupert arrives. It is quite obvious that his nerve failed him when confronted by the Member of Parliament but now Melody Paradise has done all the hard work he is keen to demonstrate his importance in the scheme of things. I am sad to relate that he is actually quite good at this. He convincingly backs up Melody, dropping the names of some of his titled relatives into the conversation and implying that they will very probably be attending the performance, which goes down well. He is also able to talk on a grand scale about the productions he has been involved in and implies that he is a big name director who has flown in from

Switzerland specially for the occasion.

Things take a difficult turn when some toadying sycophant takes it upon himself to ask Melody Paradise why there are so many people already in the valley apparently doing nothing for the circus.

"The advance crew," says Melody. "It takes a lot of people to get a circus on the road these days."

It is unfortunate that Rooster now wanders into view. Rooster has twelve earrings and a bone through his nose.

"One of our finest acrobats," says Melody.

Rooster trips over his own feet and sprawls in the mud.

"He's a comedy acrobat," says Melody, laughing heartily. This saves the day, but not for long. The Golden World Eternal Party Tribe are at the foot of the valley struggling to erect their huge marquee. Mary decides that as everyone is up early she might as well liven things up with a little music and starts playing a record. Her speakers are still perched inside her van to protect them from the rain. The back of the van is pointing our way. Thundering techno music obliterates all conversation. The Member of Parliament looks confused then angry. He raises his voice to ask in a hostile manner if the audience at the circus is going to be deafened by this frightful racket?

"Not at all," shouts Melody, struggling to retain her charm at maximum volume. "That's just a little music to get the stage hands working."

She sends Rooster scurrying away to tell Mary to turn the music down, but we have again lost credibility in the visitors' eyes. The MP's assistant notices that despite there being a lot of people here, there isn't actually anything that looks like a circus.

"The rest of the performers are arriving soon," says Rupert, sounding less than convincing.

"That doesn't leave you much time to get ready, does it? Your proposal spoke of a large array of props, scenery and special effects."

I wince. It's true, it did. When I was typing it I got a little carried away and promised that The Motorbikes Of Merlin would appear at the top of a giant gothic castle and plunge down the ramparts on the back of a fire-breathing dragon.

There is another pause. Naturally, Melody Paradise cannot admit that the only scenery and special effects are going to be whatever bits of junk we can knock up for free. The entire edifice as constructed by Melody and Rupert starts to look shaky. Magwyn The Grim elbows his way to the fore.

"I'm in charge of the staging," he announces, flatly. "I've built all the scenery in sections and it's ready to be taken over to Chelwyn when our trucks arrive."

He glares at the Chelwyn Committee as if defying them to disbelieve him. As they look at his filthy countenance I can see that they are quite ready to disbelieve him. I groan. Nothing could have been more harmful to our cause than the appearance of Magwyn The Grim at this moment, claiming to be an important member of the team. Melody stares at him with something like horror in her eyes.

"Hello, Magwyn," says one of the Committee, weirdly.

She looks at Magwyn and smiles. I'm confused. How she came to be on first name terms with him I cannot imagine.

"How nice to see you again," she says, striding forward to shake his hand. "I'm glad you're involved here."

She turns to the others.

"This is the young man who restored our stained glass windows."

Mr Pitt's suspicions abruptly vanish. Warmly, and with apparent sincerity he congratulates Magwyn on his fine work. Suddenly everyone is happy. Magwyn's stained glass was obviously a great success in Chelwyn and his presence has reassured them. Quite by accident, Magwyn The Grim has saved the day. The crisis has passed.

They ask me a few questions about my creative writing class. I find these difficult to answer as I know nothing at all about the subject. I finally retreat into a silence which is meant to imply that my powers of teaching creative writing are not to be shared with just anybody. The Committee are not impressed. I can tell that none of them will be signing up for a lesson from me. Fortunately, this is only a minor part of their summer fair so my incompetence doesn't really matter.

I am spared further humiliation by the arrival of The Galactic Navigators who at this moment start pouring into the valley. Their long convoy of vehicles lurches down the dirt track towards us, skidding in the mud. Leaning out the window of the foremost bus is the easily distinguishable figure of Pixie, a fat, bald, bearded, genial, fifty year old hippy in a giant-size blue caftan.

Before Pixie or any other of The Navigators can ruin everything, Rupert quite cleverly announces that his production company has arrived. As The Galactic Navigators have in their convoy several heavy vehicles this is vaguely convincing. He hurries over to guide them further up the valley before they can do any harm. The Minister and the Committee depart, reasonably satisfied. Everyone sighs with relief. Mary starts up the music again.

I'm glad none of them are coming to my creative writing class. It would be completely wasted on them.

The population of the valley rises rapidly with the arrival of The Galactic Navigators. They have been on the road for many years and there are around thirty of them. Various others have travelled down with them so that more than forty vehicles now make their way towards us. These include the circus acts. The first of these is The Flying Dementos, a band of young female acrobats who perform impossibly dangerous stunts on trapezes. They arrive with a truck on top of which is built a sort of tower which can be raised to accommodate their trapeze equipment. I've seen them perform at community festivals in London and they're very impressive; they are also quite mad and will surely all plummet to their deaths sometime in the near future.

Behind them are The Motorbikes Of Merlin, another group of travelling entertainers. They do things like setting fire to their motor bikes and riding them over burning bales of hay, or standing four people on one bike and doing acrobatics. Next in line are The Ancient Secret Knife Society who are juggling friends of Sweep's. To make their act more entraining they dress up in mediaeval costume and juggle with knives, swords and axes, sometimes on stilts and sometimes blindfolded.

These are three reasonably entertaining acts, though hardly enough for an entire circus performance. Perhaps more are on the way.

Behind them comes the converted ice cream van belonging to the Druid Burger Wholefood Company. I'm told the Druid Burger Wholefood Company are a common fixture at festivals and have followed The Galactic Navigators down to supply food and cigarette papers to the masses. Behind them is Jane The Jeweller's bus which is good as Jane is bound to have some nice things with her and may well have some fairy pieces I can buy.

The Galactic Navigators apologise to Melody for their late arrival. They had been evicted from their last park-up on a disused aerodrome and some of their vehicles had been impounded by the council. It took them three days to raise the money to reclaim them. Melody thanks them for coming and promises to try and find some money to defray this ruinous expense.

The appearance of The Galactic Navigators, The Flying Dementos, The Motorbikes Of Merlin and everyone else puts the festival go-ers in a good mood. It's still raining, although not so badly, and the temperature seems to be rising. The giant marquee is now up so there is a dry place in which people can gather. Spirits are further raised when The Militant Children Of Lemuria appear at the edge of the valley.

The Militant Children Of Lemuria, while not exactly swaggering in, do carry with them an air of warrior righteousness due to their continual battling with the authorities. As every issue on which they battle the authorities is supported by everyone here they are well-thought of by most people. Only among those tribes with whom they are currently arguing are there some sour expressions and muttered derogatory remarks.

The Militant Children Of Lemuria, all wearing their long blue hats, drive in leaning out of their windows, whooping and hollering to their friends, shouting enthusiastic greetings and news of their latest exploits. They have about them something of the manner of soldiers returning from the battlefield for home leave which they are determined to enjoy. The bad feeling between some of them and The Tribe Of The Last Free Moonbeam does not extend to Breed and Melody Paradise, who hug each other like long-lost sisters, which I suppose is what they are.

Breed also apologises for their late arrival. The Militant Children had been obliged to wait around for a few days in Norfolk to bail some of their members out of prison after a road protest. This protest, over a decision by The Department of Transport to build a motorway across an area previously designated as one of outstanding natural beauty, has apparently gone well. Thanks to the vociferous mass protest led by The Militant Children Of Lemuria the matter has now been referred back to The Department of Transport for an enquiry. Everyone knows that this is just a means for The Department of Transport to decide the issue in their own favour and do what they want anyway, but it will at least cause a long delay in the building of the new road and preserve for some time the wildlife sanctuary over which it is to be built.

Breed is relieved to hear that Iris The Peaceful isn't here yet. The Militant Children Of Lemuria had been worried they might miss the new Wishing Tree planting ceremony.

Riding with The Militant Children is Finan. Irene insisted they attend the road protest before coming to the festival, as he rather apologetically informs Melody Paradise later. He looks rather weary as he gets out of his old estate car, behind which trundles a large caravan. His purple locks are drooping and his shoulders sag. Irene herself is full of energy and leaps about between Finan, The Militant Children Of Lemuria, and Melody Paradise, eager to tell of her recent exploits. It turns out that Irene was one of those incarcerated in Norfolk. She was arrested after padlocking herself to a tree to prevent it from being felled. This goes down well with The Tree Planters.

"Perhaps things will just go well on their own now," says Melody, seeing everyone congregating in the marquee. She sounds much more optimistic.

"Tonight we're all going to go astral travelling with The Universal Leyline Protectors."

"I hope it goes better than the 'be nice to the trees' evening and the unicorn hunt."

"I'm sure it will. But I'll have to have a word with people about the circus. We might have to take it a bit more seriously now."

Melody Paradise disappears, swept up by the gargantuan figure of Pixie.

Pixie, the fifty year old hippy, is a famous character. Now fat, bald and genial, he was, in 1967, thin, long-haired and spiritual; an original hippy who never gave it up even when times and fashion were seriously against him. For this, and for his laughing nature, most people like him and are prepared to ignore his bad points. These bad points include his unfortunate habit of greeting young women by placing his hands enthusiastically on some part of their bodies they would probably rather he didn't. Along with much else in the intervening years, the sexual revolution seems to have passed Pixie by.

Melody skilfully removes his hands from her hips, slaps his bald head in a friendly manner, and goes off with him to mingle with the other Galactic Navigators. Among them is her sister Catherine and her boyfriend Nemo, a burly, buccaneering figure, a long-time traveller who has barely stepped inside a house for fifteen years. I like Nemo. He's the sort of person you can imagine banging a brawny fist on a table in a tavern and laughing uproariously then quaffing down a flagon of ale. Catherine is a bit like that as well.

Most of the others I don't know, apart from Hawk and Mulberry, who I met recently at Sweep's. Melody was giving them some money to buy things for her, beer, I think. Hawk and Mulberry are both tall and lean, and not genial. Hawk wears a black silk bandanna over his long brown hair and Mulberry's hair is cropped very short. Both are heavily pierced on their ears and eyebrows and wear shirts ripped off at the shoulders which show their arm muscles and Book of Kells tattoos to their best advantage. They have about them a slightly aggressive air. Amongst Melody's travelling friends I would say that Hawk and Mulberry, and perhaps The Galactic Navigators in general, lean towards the macho end of the spectrum. I know they are not well-liked by The Nomadic

Daughters Of Lilith, and the feeling is mutual.

Sweep joins me. He is annoyed.

"Did you see the way Pixie was groping Melody Paradise?"

I nod, though if Sweep starts becoming jealous of Pixie then he will certainly be beyond all hope. He might be better advised to start worrying about a new stranger who I notice greeting Melody at this moment, very elegantly. I wouldn't pretend to be the absolute best judge of this sort of thing, but at a rough guess I would say the stranger is the most handsome man in the world.

This can only be bad news for Sweep. He is really going to hate it if the most handsome man in the world suddenly appears and starts being nice to Melody Paradise.

For a long time Melody Paradise is completely surrounded. Everyone wants to kiss her and embrace her. The Galactic Navigators' children pull at her dressing gown and hug her ankles. Melody laughs and smiles at it all. They all want to talk to her and tell her what they've been doing since they last met. It's almost as if their experiences aren't complete till they've related them to Melody Paradise. In addition to this, anyone who has anything wrong with them comes to her for healing and Melody makes a long list of appointments to see everyone and do what she can. So many people pass joints in her direction that it's a miracle she's still organised enough to do this, although I've noticed that Melody Paradise and the whole of The Tribe Of The Last Free Moonbeam do seem to have an infinite capacity for marihuana.

I'm pleased to see Melody being so well-loved. Perhaps now she'll forget about the supposed curse. I find myself next to Finan and ask him how his music is coming along.

"I haven't had time to do any. I had to spend all last week with Irene at the protest. Mary wasn't very pleased. But hey, there're more important things than music."

Eko wanders up and to Finan's surprise starts interrogating him about The Magic Hat. He asks him if he saw any clues to its whereabouts while he was away with The Militant Children Of

Lemuria. Finan shakes his head.

"What was that all about?" he asks me, after Eko leaves.

"He's on a mission to find The Magic Hat. He doesn't believe it was lost so he's been asking his runes about it. I think The Militant Children are his prime suspects."

Finan is not too bothered about it one way or the other, but Irene naturally thinks it is a great outrage that the Wishing Tree was destroyed and a greater outrage that anyone stole The Magic Hat. She promises to keep her eyes and ears open and pass on anything she might learn to Eko. The crowd around Melody has now thinned, allowing me to speak to her. I warn her of Eko's continuing interest in the great hat mystery. Melody Paradise is very displeased and wishes he'd drop the matter altogether.

"He's doing it to please you," I point out.

"He'll end up making me hated and despised by everyone."

"No one will hate you. You're not the sort of person that people hate."

"I will be if this gets out. Florimel will spread it everywhere. I'll be held up to ridicule. Melody Paradise – healer, spreader of love and peace, and thief of sacred items. Why did I ever take it?"

"Don't worry, Melody, Eko won't find out anything. For one thing, he's about to find out he's mislaid his runes. Anyway, I don't think anyone else really believes The Magic Hat still exists, they all think it was washed out to sea and eaten by a fish."

"Fish don't eat hats."

"Yes, they do. I read in the paper one time that a big fish jumped out the river and ate an angler's hat."

"That's the most ridiculous thing I've ever heard," says Melody.

"It's true. It was a pike. Pike can be very vicious."

"Are you sure you're not confusing it with a shark?"

"No it was definitely a pike."

"Preposterous."

"Well, that's rich coming from a woman who claims she can see the auras of dogs, cats, flowers and buildings. I haven't forgotten the time you told me Megan's bus was looking poorly."

"It broke down right afterwards didn't it?"

"Proves nothing. Megan's bus is always breaking down."

"The fact that Megan's bus is always breaking down doesn't mean a huge pike leapt out of a river and ate an angler's hat," says Melody, who is a hard woman to shake off in an argument. I concede the point.

"But even so, no one'll find out you've got the hat."

Melody points out that the discovery of her guilt is not the only issue.

"Discovery will merely be the final tragedy. I'm already cursed just for taking it in the first place."

She has a few hard things to say about Eko, and about Irene for offering to help him.

"Irene is turning out to be a menace. She's one of these obsessive characters. Four weeks ago she was a waitress at a burger restaurant, serving up hundreds of dead cows every day. Now she goes around criticising anyone who drinks milk or wears leather shoes. And she's well in with The Militant Children Of Lemuria. A day spent without chaining herself to an endangered tree is a day wasted for Irene. You know some of The Militant Children don't like me. They'd love it if they found out about the hat."

"Well, you only have yourself to blame," I say, seizing my chance. "It's bad karma."

"What bad karma?"

"Bad karma caused by persuading a mild-mannered author to type out a proposal for you thereby involving him in a serious fraud which will no doubt land him in jail."

Melody Paradise scoffs at this.

"You're overreacting Martin. Remember, it's only a little village committee. If one of them's married to the local MP so what? MPs don't count for anything these days."

"Maybe not but he might get the local Chief Constable to decide this is an illegal gathering, which under the terms of the Criminal Justice Act it is, and then where will we be?"

"In a police cell," says Melody, not sounding too concerned, "but that's not so bad. We'd get out after a few days. Quite probably if we all got attacked by the police everyone would forget their differences and I could go to France leaving peace and tranquillity behind me. Would you mind a few days in a police cell?"

"Of course I'd mind a few days in a police cell!"

"As a cult author it could only do your career good."

"That's true. I could exaggerate it loads for my next book. Place myself somewhere between Che Guevara and Nelson Mandela."

I muse on this for a while. I can't really warm to the idea of spending a few days in a police cell, even to help my career. Probably it would just be better to make it all up and pretend I'd been arrested. Melody Paradise, a practical woman, agrees with me. She promises to back up my story if the need arises.

"It was funny how Magwyn saved the day."

"Magwyn didn't save the day," she snorts. "He deliberately arrived looking as shabby and filthy as possible to outrage the villagers and make me look bad. It was just luck that Mrs Fitzroy happened to be there and recognised him as the person who did the stained glass. He was trying to cause trouble for me."

This isn't really how I remember the incident but Melody Paradise says that I don't know Magwyn The Grim like she does, which is true.

"I'm starting to think we'd better make a reasonable job of the circus."

"It's a bit late for that."

"I know." says Melody "I'll talk to Rupert about it. It's another thing I could do without. I thought he'd be able to deal with the whole thing but maybe he can't. Have you read to the tree today yet?"

I shake my head, but promise I will. Melody thanks me for this because it is at least keeping The Tree Planters happy. Thanks to their ministrations, more of the sick trees at the top of the valley are starting to revive.

"Megan's got a sewing machine in her bus." says Melody. "She says she'll run you up a toga if you like."

"What?"

"A toga. You could put it on when you're reading to the tree."

"What for?"

"It would be very appropriate for reading ancient Roman plays wouldn't it? Think how happy the tree would be."

My head swims briefly at the cruel image of publicly putting on a toga to read Terence to a tree. I decline the offer quite firmly.

"But you said you liked togas."

"Forget it. And kindly tell Megan to mind her own business."

Over in the marquee everyone still seems happy. Mary is playing music and there is some dancing.

"Everyone seems to be getting on better."

"They are. And most people are here now. We're only waiting for The Contemplators and The Riverboat Tribe. And The Mushrooms. Maybe things are starting to work out after all."

I notice that there are now two pyramids in the field. The Universal Leyline Protectors have carried out emergency repairs while The Elemental Sunshine Family have erected their own. Each tribe stands guard over their pyramid and watches their rivals closely.

"The temperature's rising. The sun'll come out soon." says Melody.

"I wouldn't go that far. The best we can expect is hot rain. Who was that handsome man I saw you talking to?"

"That was Majic Day," replies Melody. "Rupert invited him down to help."

Sweep arrives on his unicycle. Ploughing his way slowly through the mud he does not look very impressive. No chance of anyone mistaking him for young Lochinvar riding out of the west. He waves hello. His wheel becomes stuck. He falls on top of Melody Paradise. Melody is quite gracious about it.

"Do you think she was upset?" Sweep asks me afterwards.

I shake my head.

"Of course not. Why would she be? After all, Melody's a healer. A few cuts and bruises can't mean that much to her."

Sweep crawls into my tent and hands me a beer, part of the large consignment brought here duty free from France by The Galactic Navigators, as ordered and paid for by Melody Paradise.

153

"My heart aches for Melody," he says, getting straight to the point. "I love her and I can't get near her. Rupert keeps plying her with wine and dope, her family keeps getting in my way and Pixie seems to have nothing better to do than follow her around trying to grope her. And Eko keeps hanging around her making stupid predictions."

"I thought you buried his runes?"

"I did," says Sweep, momentarily triumphant. "He's been moaning all day about not being able to find them."

His face falls.

"It didn't stop him though, he just whipped out his I Ching and started predicting again. He says the I Ching definitely foretells that Melody is fated to go off with a man who's name began with the letter 'E'. What a fraud he is. And now there's this new menace, Majic Day."

"The handsome man?"

"I wouldn't say he was particularly handsome," objects Sweep.

"Wouldn't you? I thought he was. Still, I'm not the best judge. But Megan was very impressed. I think it's the way he has his dreadlocks so long but still keeps them that shining natural golden blond that does it. 'Nordic God' springs to mind. With a perfect, lightly tanned complexion. It's funny the way he's travelled all round the world and kept his complexion so perfect. Melody commented on it after he told her about the time he walked on his own through the Amazonian jungle and helped the local Indians win concessions from the Government."

"I don't believe a word of it," says Sweep.

"No, it's true apparently. I saw the tattoo the Indians did for him to say "thank you". It's a condor, it sort of fits in well over his stomach muscles, when they ripple it looks like it's flying."

Sweep clutches his own slightly saggy stomach and looks thoughtful.

"But I think it was his finely chiselled features that most impressed Melody. She and Megan were looking in my book of Greek myths to see which God he reminded them of most. They decided on Apollo, I think."

"Will you stop going on about how handsome Majic Day is?"

says Sweep crossly.

"I wasn't going on about it."

"You were comparing him to Apollo."

"No, Melody was comparing him to Apollo. I thought he looked more like the ancient portrayals of Alexander The Great. He was telling me about journeying round the borders of India and seeing a shrine marking the spot where Alexander died. He's certainly an interesting guy."

Sweep taps his foot rather angrily on my sleeping bag. He starts drinking his beer in a moody fashion. Realising I have been rather tactless, I try to change the subject.

"It's still raining."

Sweep grunts.

"But the temperature is rising."

Sweep grunts again.

"It's getting quite humid."

"For God's sake will you stop pretending to be a BBC weather forecaster?" growls Sweep. "And stop trying to change the subject. I want to talk about Melody Paradise. What can I do to get through to her? I've been rushing round the valley like a madman, clearing up rubbish like nobody's business. Melody's grateful but it's not enough. What else can I do? And kindly don't suggest I save Megan's baby from a runaway train."

"Now Sweep, the baby fiasco was at least as much your idea as mine."

"It was you that got me blamed for the whole thing. Some friend."

"The fortunes of war, Sweep. Had it been me floundering in the river and you on the bank I'm sure you'd have blamed me. Anyway, it's forgotten now."

"No it isn't. Megan hides Pookie when I'm around."

I point out to Sweep that he will soon have an excellent opportunity of impressing Melody Paradise.

"How?"

"The circus. You're actually performing there which is more than Rupert is. I hope you've got something dazzling prepared?"

155

Sweep nods his head. He's been practising some new routines with The Ancient Secret Knife Society and is looking forward to showing them off.

"You're right. I might make a big hit if I give a good performance. But that's two days away. I can't wait two days to be impressive. Not with Rupert, Majic Day and Eko all struggling for space around Melody Paradise. It's not right you know. They might allow the poor woman some peace."

I sip my beer and consider the situation.

"You know Sweep, we might have overlooked the one obvious way of scoring points with Melody Paradise. What's most important to her right now?"

"Ending the arguments in her family."

"Exactly. Don't you think that anyone furthering that aim would make a good impression on her?"

Sweep stares at me wonderingly as if seeing a person of real intelligence for the first time. He crumples his empty beer can triumphantly.

"Of course! If I could help end some tribal feud she'd be impressed. And pleased."

"Delighted."

"Ecstatic."

"Thrilled beyond measure."

There is a long pause.

"So how am I going to do it?"

This is a tricky question. The feuds seem so deeply ingrained that even the best efforts of Melody Paradise have so far failed to heal them. I confess that I can't think of any way to help.

Sweep sits for a while, musing. After a while he departs, heading for The Galactic Navigators encampment to pick up another free beer. Melody has entrusted the running of the bar to The Navigators, leaving it to them to decide how much free beer people can have, and when people will have to pay, to replenish stocks. Quite a weighty responsibility this, and not one I would necessarily have given to The Galactic Navigators, but Melody trusts them completely. She says that Nemo and Catherine make excellent barkeepers.

Outside the rain beats down. I do a little more musing. I can't help worrying about Eko and his hunt for The Magic Hat. Who knows what mischief he might do, poking around and asking questions? It really would be very unfortunate for Melody Paradise if the truth were to come out. Somehow it seems worse now Irene's got involved. Eko is a bit of a dreamer but I can imagine Irene showing dogged determination in pursuit of the truth.

It strikes me that Irene is far less likely to spend time looking for The Magic Hat if she is getting on well with Finan. After being dragged to countless road protests in the past few weeks, I know that Finan is keen on having a restful and enjoyable holiday. Presumably this enjoyable holiday will involve hanging round with his girlfriend, and sleeping with her. Finan is bound to be keen on sleeping with her. He hasn't had a girlfriend for ages and he and Irene can't have had that much sex yet. They've spent most of their time chained to trees or padlocked to bulldozers.

The obvious thing to do is ensure that Finan and Irene keep getting along well. If they're hanging out and having fun in bed together, Irene will surely be too busy to help Eko's investigations.

Finan crawls into my tent, a desperate expression on his face.

"Hide me," he pleads, "if Irene comes looking for me, don't tell her you've seen me."

I stare at him aghast. Rarely has a plan of mine crumbled so quickly. There is a rustling noise outside my tent. Moving far quicker than I've ever seen him before, Finan is under my sleeping bag in a flash. The flap of my tent is yanked open but the person who tumbles in is not Irene but a bedraggled looking Sweep.

"Hide me," he squawks. "They're after me."

Again there is a noise in front of my tent. Sweep panics. Before I can say anything he dives for cover under my sleeping bag. There is a brief struggle between him and Finan before both bodies disappear beneath the damp bedding.

Once more my tent flap is yanked open. It's odd the way these people all just feel they can use my tent as a home from home. Patrick thrusts his face in.

"Have you seen Sweep?" he demands, and glares around him suspiciously.

"Not for a while," I lie. "I think he went to get a beer."

"He'll need more than a beer after I get hold of him," rasps Patrick, irately.

Patrick is one of Melody's larger brothers, muscles well-developed from continually building pyramids no doubt. He looks threatening and insists that Sweep was last seen heading in this direction. I assure him that he hasn't been here.

"Well, if you see him tell him I'm going to ram his unicycle down his throat. And anyone who hides him."

Patrick casts one last suspicious glance around my tent before storming off. I feel myself sagging. I knew the festival was going to be bad but I never envisioned having two wanted men hiding under my sleeping bag.

Irene shoves her way into my tent.

"Is Finan here?" she demands.

I shake my head wearily.

"Haven't seen him all day, Irene."

"Well, if you do see him tell him I'm not very pleased with him. Not pleased at all."

Irene also storms off. I zip up my tent flap. No real protection of course as almost everyone in the valley apparently feels free to just barge their way in at will.

"You can come out now."

Two troubled and guilty figures emerge from under my sleeping bag. Each sits down heavily and stares at the ground.

"What have you been up to?" I demand.

Both of them have sorry tales to tell. Slowly and with some embarrassment, Finan tells me that his nerve has gone.

"It's Irene," he sighs. "I love her but she never gives me a moment's peace. Everything was great when we met. It was fine with me when she wore a cream blouse and blue skirt and worked in the restaurant. Since she changed it's all gone wrong."

I find this surprising, and say so. Usually men like it when women share their interests and manner of dress. Often, in fact, they

158

insist on it.

"Maybe," says Finan, "but she's gone too far. I liked it when she dreaded her hair and got her nose pierced and bought her first pair of stripey tights but then she started going to all these protests and reading all the leaflets there and taking in every single word. Remember she wouldn't let me wear leather shoes any more? Now I'm wearing these dumb canvas things and my feet are practically rotting away. And that was just the beginning. After that she insisted I threw out my comfy leather armchair from my caravan and after that I had to become a vegan and start drinking soya milk. I really detest soya milk on my corn flakes. Not that I'm allowed corn flakes any more. Irene buys special organic wheat flakes. They're horrible. Now she says she's toying with the idea of us becoming fruitarians. All I'll be able to eat is fruit. And even then I'll have to wait till it drops off the tree so we aren't harming the natural cycle of things. A man could starve to death waiting for enough apples to fall off a tree to make a decent meal."

There is more. Irene is now wondering about the propriety of them wearing their hair in dreadlocks having been told by someone that it is a bad thing for white people to do.

"Exploitation of black culture apparently," says Finan, running his fingers anxiously over his own treasured locks, "though don't ask me why. Also she doesn't approve of me mixing didgeridoo sounds into the tracks I'm doing with Mary."

"Exploitation of Aboriginal culture?"

"Exactly. There seems to be practically nothing I can do that isn't exploiting some person in some way or another. Or some animal. Or a plant. Even so, it wouldn't be so bad if I ever had a moment's peace but I don't. Every single minute of the day Irene wants to be protesting about some damn thing or other. She loved it with The Militant Children Of Lemuria. Attacked the bailiffs like a kamikaze pilot. I don't have the energy to protest every single day. I need a rest every now and then. And you know what Irene wants to do now?"

"What?"

"Hunt-sabbing. Right this minute. That's why she's looking for me. She wants to go and to meet the local hunt saboteurs and help disrupt the fox hunt. Hunt-sabbing scares me. The huntsmen hire guards and they're violent. I get frightened. Irene doesn't. And anyway, can't I have a day just to rest? Even The Militant Children Of Lemuria have given up protesting for a day or two so they can enjoy Melody's festival. Irene's obsessed. It's making me miserable."

"But you won't leave her because you love her?"

"Exactly."

Finan mutters a few more things about Irene's forthcoming activities which would seem to include the disruption of road building, fox hunting, falconry, hare coursing, badger baiting, angling, factory farming, live animal exports and a picket of the French embassy to protest against nuclear testing.

"And more next week," he wails, before falling into a gloomy silence.

I turn to Sweep.

"What tale of woe do you have? Why is Patrick from The Universal Leyline Protectors threatening to shove your unicycle down your throat?"

"Because he is a violent brute who won't listen to reason," replies Sweep.

"And?"

"And I destroyed his pyramid."

"You destroyed his pyramid? Why?"

"I didn't mean to. It was a complete accident. Could have happened to anyone. I'd have explained it all in a minute but you know what these people are like about their pyramids. Patrick chased me twice round the valley before I managed to give him the slip."

"So what happened?"

"I was just trying to do my bit towards ending the arguments," explains Sweep, in the voice of a man who has been hard done by.

"To help Melody Paradise. You know The Universal Leyline Protectors don't get on with The Militant Children Of Lemuria after The Militant Children accused them of cowardice and stupidity for sitting in the next field when they were meant to be protecting the last trees due to be destroyed to make way for the motorway?"

I nod. Melody's description of The Universal Leyline Protectors declaring that the next field contained one end of an important leyline to the Crab Nebula was not something I would forget in a hurry.

"Well, after a few beers with The Galactic Navigators it struck me I could probably make it up between them," continues Sweep. "I'm quite friendly with Breed. I hid her in my house for three weeks after the poll tax riots when the police were looking for her. So I took her a few beers from The Navigators giant freezer truck – have you seen that? Excellent piece of organisation by Melody Paradise – and suggested maybe she should patch things up with Patrick. Which Breed was quite willing to do, after the beer. Their argument was quite a long time ago and The Militant Children are all in a good mood after their last protest. So Breed picked up the beer crate and climbed on my shoulders."

"What?"

"Climbed on my shoulders. We were going to ride through the valley in a symbolic manner."

"Sweep, do you mean that you went to visit The Universal Leyline Protectors riding on your unicycle with Breed sitting on your shoulders carrying a crate of beer?"

"That's right. It was a peace offering. Very decent of Breed I thought."

He pauses.

"It's very muddy out there."

"Hard to ride a unicycle, I imagine. You already fell on top of Melody."

Sweep winces.

"I know. And it's started raining hard again. Breed wasn't a very good passenger. Kept shifting around and saying she was going to fall off. She seemed quite nervous really. Strange for someone who's always battling with the police."

This doesn't sound strange to me. Many people would rather risk battling with the police than ride on Sweep's shoulders on a unicycle over muddy ground. I hardly need to ask what had happened next.

"Close to The Leyline Protectors, we went out of control. Breed was just shouting to Patrick that she had something for him when the wheel stuck in a puddle. She catapulted right over my shoulders and into their pyramid."

"Badly damaged?"

"Completely destroyed," says Sweep grimly. "Flattened. The Universal Leyline Protectors were furious. So was Breed. Her and the beer crate went through that pyramid like a cruise missile. I think she's all right though. On my second lap of the valley I saw Melody Paradise giving her medical attention. So now The Universal Leyline Protectors are after me."

Poor Sweep. Another disaster. And, I imagine, another feud made worse rather than better. I have no doubt that The Universal Leyline Protectors will look on it as a deliberate attack by The Militant Children Of Lemuria. Melody Paradise won't be very pleased, though out of delicacy for Sweep's feelings I don't mention this.

"Melody Paradise won't be very pleased," says Finan.

Sweep rests his head on his knees. He and Finan share a silent depression over the miseries caused by their love affairs.

I glance out of my tent. It's raining heavily. The temperature has risen again. It feels like there may be a thunderstorm on the way.

A disgruntled group of Leyline Protectors are picking through the wreckage of their pyramid. Many hostile glances are directed towards the encampment of The Militant Children Of Lemuria. More hostility is directed towards The Elemental Sunshine Family, who, gathered around their own undamaged pyramid, would still seem to be laughing heartily about the whole affair.

The Motorbikes Of Merlin, The Ancient Secret Knife Society and The Flying Dementos have never performed together. It is Rupert's task to produce their show, and Magwyn's to build it. Various others, mainly from The Galactic Navigators, are helping with the construction. One further act has cancelled but Rupert is still anticipating the arrival of three more which he says should be enough to put on a reasonable show. Happily for Melody Paradise, Rupert does seem to have matters in hand. The organisation of the circus proceeds reasonably smoothly so it seems that even if the performance is going to be somewhat smaller and cheaper than Chelwyn Village anticipates, it will at least happen.

I suspect that Rupert has sunk some of his own money into this performance. It would not surprise me if he is paying some of the acts, out of his own pocket. The wealthy jet magnate is not short of money and he might well be willing to spend a little to impress Melody Paradise.

I don't want to introduce any unnecessary dramatic tension into my own story here. No one is fighting against the odds to mount a spectacular circus performance for the Chelwyn Village Summer Fair. There is no expectation from any one that the circus will be much good. It is merely a case of Rupert managing to put it on in a manner which will not outrage the Committee so much that they take out a lawsuit against us.

There is a need for some spare bodies to take the part of extras in the circus, to perform such tasks as lying on the ground while motor bikes jump over them, or standing still while people juggle axes around their heads. One of those asked is Florimel, who scornfully declines. She declares that there are few things in the world she would like to do less than have axes juggled around her head in a circus organised by Melody Paradise and Rupert. Florimel despises Rupert which is a point in her favour. Unfortunately, she is also implacably hostile to Melody and seems to have come to the festival only to cause bad feeling. She is consistently sarcastic and critical. Her friend Mirabel is worse. Mirabel wonders publicly where all the money from the Summer Fair Committee has gone.

"I haven't seen much sign of it," she says, implying that, apart from paying for a few crates of beer, Melody Paradise has pocketed the rest.

Melody is very upset by the accusation. A few tears form in her eyes which she quickly wipes away. No one else really suspects her of taking money for herself but in the light of Mirabel's accusation she feels obliged to give an account of what she did with it all. This financial statement, delivered under the mistrustful gaze of The Nomadic Daughters Of Lilith, makes for an incongruous moment in the middle of the festival.

"I used the money to help everyone," says Melody. "I sent money to Magwenwy to help repair her boat. I sent some to Breed to pay The Militant Children's bail and I paid for new tepees to replace the ones torn down by the police. I paid for The Mushrooms to get three trucks back after they were impounded in Cornwall. And there was money for The Golden World Eternal Party Tribe to fix their marquee and pay for repairs to their amplifier. I paid for a new gear box for Pixie's van and a new exhaust for Catherine's bus and the axle repairs for Bernadette's caravan. I sent money to Iris The Peaceful to help her back across the Channel and to The Tree Planters to repair their instruments that got damaged last year. I sent boots and blankets to The Night Time Elves when they were cold and wet in the mountains but couldn't give up on the Unicorn Survey. I paid for the repair of the Leylines Pyramid after it got damaged at Glastonbury and I'll pay for it again if there's any money left. I travelled halfway round the country just to take food and money to The Elemental Sunshine Family when they ran out of petrol and got stuck on the motorway. And everything that was left I used to make it a good festival. I hired fire-extinguishers and tools. I gave Jane The Jeweller a string of silver wire to make earrings for everyone and I bought Moonshine a new piercing gun. I bought records for Mary, sent The Galactic Navigators to Calais to bring us a truckload of beer and sent messages everywhere to buy the best drugs I could afford, all of which you're entitled to have free. Who else has ever done that for you? And what was left I didn't keep. I sent some to the Traveller's Schoolbus Charity and I sent more to the fund to pay fines for road protesters. And Mirabel, you and Florimel said you couldn't afford to come because I'd ruined your benefit claim so I sent you as much as I could afford to make up for it."

Melody comes to a halt. Mirabel shows no signs of reconciliation but Mary walks over and takes her arm. She tells Melody Paradise that she is very appreciative of everything she's done. She thanks her for the help she's given The Golden World Eternal Party Tribe. The dispute over the generator is quite forgotten. Afterwards Mary and Melody are seen dancing together so at least one argument is over.

Also dancing closer to Melody Paradise is Majic Day. Majic Day has proved to be a popular newcomer. Although he is a friend of Rupert's, he displays none of Rupert's bad points. He is neither arrogant nor officious. He laughs a lot without making other people feel that he's laughing at them. His tales of travel and adventure bear signs of being truth rather than fantasy. They are told in a manner modest enough not to outrage anyone who never made it past Dover before their bus broke down. He is even modest about the incident where he helped the Amazonian Indians win concessions from their government and the encroaching mining organisations. Just a coincidence that he happened to be there really, and knew how to translate the Indian dialect into six other languages thereby helping the United Nations team out of an awkward predicament.

He carries with him a beautiful embroidered bag, given to him by the Zumi Indians of North America. From this bag he takes a handful of intricately patterned clay beads and gives them to Melody Paradise. Melody is pleased by this, pleased enough to stop dancing in the marquee and start platting them in to her hair. Megan helps her while the rest of The Tribe Of The Last Free Moonbeam stand in readiness in case of unexpected complications. Sweep, usually happy to watch The Tribe Of The Last Free Moonbeam directing their total attention to the upkeep of Melody's hair, is displeased.

"Just a coincidence he happened to be there and spoke the Indian dialect," snorts Sweep. "The man's a fraud. I don't believe he's ever been to the Amazon. Probably never left the country. I expect if Eko investigated him we'd find out he's spent his entire life working as an insurance clerk in Barnsley."

"Please Sweep, don't talk about Eko investigating things. It'll only lead to trouble."

"I think there should be a lot more investigating," says Sweep crossly. "Expose some of the phoneys here."

Just then Eko arrives. He looks suspiciously at Sweep.

"Very strange the way those runes disappeared," says Eko, "but I'll get to the bottom of it."

He marches off, feet sinking in the mud. Sweep is looking rather pale.

"The man's a menace," he says. "He has to be stopped."

Patrick is walking towards us. Melody Paradise has already told her brother that he is not to inflict any revenge on Sweep for the pyramid catastrophe. Patrick has grudgingly agreed but Sweep does not want to put temptation in his way so we leave together.

Some of Melody's hopes have been realised and there is now a slightly happier atmosphere in the valley as people mingle, dance, or do nothing together. Many things remain to be put right however. The Nomadic Daughters Of Lilith's antipathy towards The Tribe Of The Last Free Moonbeam is undiminished. Apart from the obvious disharmony caused by this, further stresses are appearing in the ranks of The Moonbeams as both Rooster and Rag attempt to court Florimel. Melody Paradise says that this is entirely fine with her but Megan and some others seem to think that in paying such attentions to a woman who is so critical of Melody, Rooster and Rag are being disloyal. Naturally enough, Rooster and Rag resent this. Even more naturally, they have started to dislike each other intensely.

Further to this, the Nomads have proclaimed loudly and clearly that their idea of a good festival is one at which The Galactic Navigators do not appear. They've already threatened Hawk, Mulberry and Pixie that they'll run them over with a Land Rover if they come anywhere near their encampment. The two pyramid building tribes openly despise each other and after Sweep's destructive attempt at reconciliation which plunged Breed straight through one of these pyramids, The Militant Children Of Lemuria and The Universal Leyline Protectors loathe each other more than ever. Sundry members of The Tribe Of The Last Free Moonbeam, upset by what they see as the wilfully disruptive effects of The Leyline Protectors and The Sunshine Family both building pyramids in the valley, have been heard reviving the old grudge about Livia's treatment at the hands of Cabot. This is still a very sensitive subject with The Elemental Sunshine Family. They state unequivocally they were unaware that Cabot was regularly abusing Livia but it would seem that they at least feel guilty about being unaware of it.

"But we'll sort all that out tonight," says Melody. "All the pyramid people are going to show us how to astral travel and it'll be so much fun no one will want to argue."

The Clan Of The Night Time Elves have not managed to repair their differences with The Tree Planters and this has exacerbated the dispute between John and Ali. Ali and his friends are still camped some way away from their erstwhile Tree Planting companions. The Night Time Elves have themselves suffered a similar fate in being sundered by the after-effects of Mary's attempt at making up with them. Boot, Caddy, Starshine, Moonshine and Sunshine have moved down the valley and set up their benders far away from Willis and the main bulk of The Elves. They say that they're fed up with the dispute with The Golden World Eternal Party Tribe and want it ended. No one seems likely to end it. Willis Elf is too outraged about Mary's harsh criticism of the Unicorn Survey.

There are other arguments going on which mar the festival but I won't list them all just now. It's too distressing. Barring a sudden visitation from Solomon The Wise, I don't see how they are ever going to be resolved.

I will just mention one further source of friction. I imagine that Rupert did not count on the impression Majic Day might make on Melody Paradise when he invited him to the festival. I would say that he is now regretting the invitation.

Magwyn The Grim makes another of his rare appearances. After consulting with Rupert he approaches Melody Paradise. As before, he seems to find it hard to say what he wants to say and they again stand awkwardly looking at each other, the atmosphere frigid.

"What sort of wall do The Motorbikes Of Merlin need?" he says finally, which is something of an anti-climax.

"Ask them," says Melody, stiffly, "or Rupert. He's doing the circus." With that she takes Majic Day's arm and leads him off to her van. Magwyn The Grim glowers at them as they depart, and answers a tentative greeting from a friendly young Nightime Elf with an expression of silent loathing.

Finan is nowhere to be seen. Presumably he is again hiding from Irene, the great love of his life. Thinking of Finan reminds me of Irene's proposal that they become fruitarians. I knew a fruitarian once. All he ate was fruit that fell from trees and he expressed strong disapproval for people who went around wilfully ripping up vegetables from the earth. He was, however, a heroin addict which I could not help but feel spoiled the whole thing. After all heroin isn't a fruit. When I pointed this out to him he said it was a different matter altogether and refused to discuss it any further. In fact, he refused to discuss anything with me ever again. Possibly living only on fruit made him overly sensitive, and not fond of conversation.

Sweep accompanies me to the lair of The Tree Planters. On our way we are joined by Megan who maliciously asks me if I'm sure I wouldn't like her to run me up a toga on her sewing machine. I decline with dignity.

"Trees are responding well," reports Peggy as we arrive. "They're pleased we're clearing the rubbish out of the valley. Once The Navigators get their lifting equipment into operation and move these hulks by the river it's going to look a lot better. Your fig tree is making some progress. It's still sick but it's getting stronger."

While not particularly happy to hear Peggy refer to it as "my fig tree", I'm pleased to be useful.

"Hello, fig tree. Today I'm going to tell you the story of *The Eunuch*, one of Terence's best known plays, and another fine romantic comedy. It was written in 161 BC In the introduction to the play, Terence says he can't be blamed if he isn't original because everything has already been said. As a writer I take great comfort from that. If everything had already been said by 161 BC, no one can be blamed for a bit of plagiarism two thousand years later. So sit back, pretend you're in sunny Rome, and I'll tell you the story of the love affair between Chaerea and Pamphila, involving sex, slavery, money, lies, deception, cross-dressing, passion and lust. You'll laugh and you'll cry. It's one of his best."

"Another satisfied tree. Did you see the way it's branches were waving at the end? It was thrilled. I might get a whole new career out of this. Trees revived by the classics."

Sweep isn't listening to a word I'm saying. He excuses himself vaguely and hurries off. I let him go. As he hasn't seen Melody Paradise for an hour or so, I expect he feels the need to be in her company.

I might have cheered up the tree but I can't pretend I had much effect on The Tree Planters. Since splitting into two parts, depression has settled over them. The Peaceful Grove brings them little peace. The blackened stump of the old Wishing Tree is a dispiriting sight. There is a general longing for Iris The Peaceful to arrive and restore the Grove.

The rain still falls and the small river that runs through the valley has swollen alarmingly. The rising water has forced Magwyn The Grim to move his truck further up the bank where it hangs like a monstrous dark beast. If the river rises any more Magwyn will have to either withdraw from the valley or come closer to the main site. No one wants him any closer.

I'm near his truck. He doesn't seem to be around. I'd like to take another look at his stained glass portrait of Melody Paradise and am debating whether or not to risk it when Magwyn The Grim appears from behind a tree and stares at me in his usual disconcerting manner.

"Still raining," I say, by way of opening the conversation.

Magwyn, unkempt and unfriendly, does actually reply.

"If you've come to talk about the weather I'll kick you in the river," he says.

I suddenly feel very annoyed. I've coped with too many mad people in the past few days.

"Lighten up for God's sake. If you're so anti-everything and everyone here, what did you come to the festival for?"

He stares at me, very intensely. I back away.

"Melody Paradise," he growls, and walks back to his truck, and slams the door.

It is now dark. A few camp-fires, sheltered by trees, splutter cheerlessly in the damp air. The marquee is illuminated but little of that light reaches out to the edge of the valley. Here it is so dark that on the few occasions the clouds have parted I've been shocked by the number of stars visible in the sky. In London you can see very few stars at night. Out here in the country they cover the sky in their millions. This unsettled me at first. I had no idea there were so many. I pick my way very slowly and carefully back towards my tent. With the continual rain the valley is now a treacherous place. Traversing any sloping piece of ground requires great concentration. I make it safely back almost to the centre of the site where I come across Melody Paradise gazing into space. Should I relate to her what Magwyn said? I decide to test the water.

"I just saw Magwyn,".

Melody spits on the ground. I've never seen her do that before.

"Don't tell me about it. You know he was going round the valley causing trouble with The Galactic Navigators today? How dare he pick fights at my festival. He's trying to ruin it."

It seems best to drop the subject.

"How's your arm?"

"Much better," I lie, and look at her anxiously to see if she guesses I'm lying. She seems not to. I don't want to upset Melody Paradise by telling her that heat and healing no longer flow from her hands.

Melody gazes meditatively at the mud oozing over her bare feet.

"Things could hardly be worse," she says.

"At least you're friends with The Golden World Eternal Party Tribe."

"True."

170

She gazes over at the giant marquee. The Golden World Eternal Party rave tent is now fully operational, and very impressive it is. Inside Mary and her fellow DJs play trance and techno at a satisfyingly deafening volume. They have far more in the way of lights and decorations than I had anticipated. The inside of the marquee is completely covered with bright banners and cloth hangings showing mystical and psychedelic scenes. Some of these are colourful abstracts, some show pictures of Indian deities, others have Celtic designs. There is even one with fairies on it. When darkness falls they turn on their laser lights which spin and turn to shoot multi-coloured beams in every direction. Alongside these are fixed beams with rotating filters which illuminate the wall-hangings in continually changing hues.

Mary is a fine DJ. At times, when the lights are lancing through the air and the music is thundering on and the smoke machine is blowing out clouds of white smoke, a sort of mass delirium sets in, and no one there would rather be doing anything else than dancing to the sound of The Golden World Eternal Party Tribe.

I have never seen people enjoying themselves as much as they do while dancing in Mary's marquee. The friends of Melody Paradise are certainly enthusiastic dancers. Perhaps that's all they'll need to start getting on together again. Even Florimel looks happy as the laser light plays over her long white dreads, and she waves her hands in the air, and shouts out something which is lost beneath the music.

Melody, number one dancing enthusiast, is heading for the tent to dance her troubles way. She is interrupted by a horrible grating noise reverberating from the road above the valley, the noise of vehicles being driven extremely badly. Gears crunch, tyres squeal, engines splutter and roar; mixed in with it all there is a great deal of cursing as frustrated drivers attempt the difficult task of entering the valley in the darkness.

Wheels slipping, the first vehicle skids down the lane, apparently out of control. Inside voices whoop with laughter.

"The Mushrooms have arrived," says Melody, with an air of doom.

A battered old estate car, which I recognise as that belonging to Fluffy, Tuffy, Bug and Simple, the terrors of the nation's highways, leads an array of incredibly beaten up vehicles down into the valley. Even in the darkness, it is easy to see that these vehicles set new standards in poor maintenance and general disrepair. Melody flinches as the single-decker bus belonging to her sister Bernadette roars past, its front door tied shut with string and its windows held together with gaffer tape. Like its companions, its exterior is daubed with psychedelic paint work. Nine vehicles, each one seemingly worse than the last, plunge down the side of the valley. Three of these vehicles are towing caravans and Melody and I are forced to jump for our lives as the caravans sway crazily towards us.

"I don't like the look of this, Melody," I say, from behind a tree.

"They would have to arrive in the middle of the night," she replies.

We gaze after the procession.

"Where are they going?"

"They are going to stop aren't they?"

"The estate car doesn't seem to have any headlights."

Melody starts running after the cars and buses. Unwilling to risk my safety I remain securely behind the tree. It strikes me briefly that the very last car in the procession seems to be out of place. It is new, undamaged, and not painted with any psychedelic designs. I don't study it for long however. My attention is diverted by the car containing Fluffy, Tuffy, Bug and Simple. Finally settling on a straight course, it heads directly for the pyramid of The Universal Leyline Protectors. Panic breaks out on all sides. The Leylines spill out of the marquee and scream at The Mushrooms to stop. Their pleadings are in vain. Fluffy, driving without headlights and almost certainly in a hallucinogenic world of her own, ploughs straight through the pyramid. Rebuilt at record speed after being demolished by Breed, it is again reduced to matchwood. Further up the valley, The Elemental Sunshine Family can only watch in horror as The Mushrooms head towards their own pyramid. It too is reduced to rubble in the blink on an eye. Nine vehicles and three caravans trundle unstoppably over the wreckage and on towards the marquee.

Rarely can such chaos have broken out among a group of revellers. Travellers who only seconds before were dancing with abandon find themselves confronted by a lethal oncoming convoy, and panic accordingly. Mary runs for her life clutching her mixing desk, wires trailing behind her. Others stampede in all directions, some of them struggling furiously as they become entangled with the wall-hangings. Anorexia and Belladonna become hopelessly caught up in a banner depicting Laxmi, Hindu Goddess of Good Fortune, and have to be dragged to safety by Florimel and Mirabel. They are rescued just in time. The Mushrooms plough straight into the marquee, utterly destroying it. Laser lights point briefly to the sky before being extinguished under their wheels.

The valley is now a scene of absolute pandemonium. The Mushrooms seem to be completely oblivious to their surroundings. People are fleeing for their lives, gathering up their children and treasured belongings as the demented Mushrooms lurch uncontrollably from one scene of destruction to the next. Florimel sprints to her Land Rover and throws herself behind her steering wheel. The engine screams as she reverses desperately in an effort to avoid Bernadette's bus. She almost escapes but the bus makes a sudden unexpected change of direction and rams her. Florimel's Land Rover flies backwards into Anorexia's vehicle and overturns it. Belladonna and Anorexia curse The Mushrooms furiously but are obliged to turn and run as a pink and yellow transit van bears down on them like an avenging chariot.

Soon, as people try desperately to get themselves and their vehicles out of the way of The Mushroom juggernaut, the valley is full of buses, trucks, ambulances and caravans careering round wildly in all directions. I have never seen anything remotely like it. Half of the vehicles are trying desperately to escape, the other half are...well, I'm not quite sure what The Mushrooms are doing. Looking for a place to park, presumably.

In the chaos, benders and tepees are flattened, whole encampments levelled. The banners of The Clan Of The Night Time Elves are cut down and dragged through the mud. Pixie, showing more athleticism than I would have given him credit for, actually vaults over an upturned car to escape destruction at the hands of an oncoming truck. I notice Sweep frantically climbing a tree to escape from the pink and yellow transit van. From the relative safety of a branch he shakes his fist at The Mushrooms and hurls abuse quite out of keeping with his gentle nature. Eventually, The Mushrooms grind to a halt. By this time there is nothing left to destroy. Fluffy, Tuffy, Bug and Simple stumble out of their estate car.

"Are we here yet?" says Tuffy.

"Think so," replies Fluffy. "I thought I noticed a big tent somewhere."

Seeing that the carnage has now come to an end, I hurry back to my own tent. Miraculously, it is still standing, one of the very few things to escape destruction. The smart car I saw following The Mushrooms has hung back, also avoiding destruction. Two men emerge from it and look around. Megan rushes up to me with Pookie.

"What a disaster," I say, scanning the wreckage.

"Never mind that."

"Never mind? The Mushrooms have ruined the festival."

Megan impatiently waves me quiet then thrusts Pookie into my arms.

"Take these as well," she says, and hands me a bottle of milk and half a bag of nappies.

"What for?"

"The Social Services have come to take Pookie. Pretend he's yours."

She departs at a run. I take Pookie into my tent where he immediately starts to cry. I'm not surprised. It's been a stressful day. Outside there is so much confusion that it's difficult to tell what is going on but even in the cacophony I can hear Florimel, Mirabel, Belladonna and Anorexia bellowing for revenge on The Mushrooms. I can't hear the social workers but I can imagine that they are now questioning Megan about the whereabouts of her baby.

I gaze down at him.

I'm not actually sure how serious the baby-kidnapping with which I will no doubt soon be charged will turn out to be. Pretty serious I imagine. "You did, Mr Millar, wilfully conceal Pookie from his rightful father, and will now suffer the full penalties of the law."

I presume that tonight's entertainment is now cancelled, and we will not now astral travel with The Universal Leyline Protectors. It's all too much for me. Staring forlornly at the child, I am once more completely unable to fathom why I ever agreed to attend the accursed festival as organised by Melody Paradise and The Tribe of the Last Free Moonbeam.

6th August (Day 23)

After Livia rejoined The Tribe Of The Last Free Moonbeam she was often in the company of Melody Paradise. I sometimes met them together at Sweep's flat, and drank tea with them. Livia was Italian, one of a large group of young foreign travellers who passed through south London. As well as Italians there were Spaniards, Dutch, Germans, French and various other Europeans, beside the ever-present contingent of Australians and New Zealanders.

Livia was very attractive, and had a habit of wearing lycra sports clothes. This was not unknown among crusties, squatters and travellers but usually it would take the form of black cycling shorts worn under a baggy jumper or floppy t-shirt. Livia however would often dress in a small white lycra vest and shorts so that from the neck down she resembled an athlete, though her red and green dreadlocks and multiple ear and lip piercings would have looked unusual at the Olympic Games.

She had her navel pierced, not so unusual nowadays, but also her tongue, which was still a relative rarity. When she spoke you could see the stud in her tongue if you were rude enough to stare, which of course I was, being an author and keen to gather up information.

Dressing in white made her very distinctive and easily recognisable in a crowd. At a rave in Cooltan, the Alternative Arts Centre, you could pick her out from anywhere, her white clothes reflecting the ultraviolet light far more strongly than the generally dark attire of her fellow dancers.

I can think of two more instances where white clothes have been very distinctive in a darkly-clad crowd. The first goes back a while to the time I used to share a flat with Andi Sex Gang. Andi was a good friend of mine. He sang in a band called the Sex Gang Children. They were a mixture of punk and gothic and their fans always used to dress in black with black make-up and long black hair. At one gig, I remember a young woman turning up, with stunning incongruity, in full wedding costume. She wore a long veil, an embroidered bodice and sweeping skirts, all in dazzling white. At a gig full of gothic punks it was a spectacular success and everyone admired her for her daring.

The other instance was at a fetish nightclub where absolutely everyone was dressed in black leather or PVC. Although there were many subtle variations on this theme - carrying a whip, for instance, was not mandatory, and only a certain proportion of the men there wore high heels - no other form of dress other than black PVC or leather would have seemed at all acceptable. And yet, triumphantly, a woman appeared wearing a bright white tennis outfit. Not only was she wearing a white tennis shirt and short pleated skirt, both resonant of the fifties, she also had on a pair of old fashioned tennis shoes, again dazzling white. To complete this she carried a wooden tennis racket of dated design. The whole outfit was a fine re-creation of times gone by - a 1950's tennis player about to have a few friendly games with her neighbours. Again, this was a spectacular success. Everyone else, dressed in their black leather, could only marvel at the audacity of this woman, arriving at the fetish nightclub in such a costume.

7th August (Day 24)

The Contemplators rolled steadily through France.

"Tell me," said Fuzi, "about the time you met Janis Joplin riding through California on a unicorn."

Iris The Peaceful laughed.

"It wasn't a unicorn. Unicorns were extremely rare in the North Americas by the time Janis Joplin was around."

"What was she riding then?"

"A pink cadillac."

"That's not a mythical creature," objected Fuzi.

"Not now," agreed Iris, "but one day it might be. After all, unicorns were quite common once upon a time."

As the afternoon grew hotter they stopped to rest. Fuzi, anxious as ever about the possibility of missing the festival, found resting difficult. She had too much energy.

"Let's go into the woods and look for a Wishing Tree," she suggested.

"In a while," replied Iris. "I have to make a daisy chain first."

As the other Contemplators lay sprawled on the overgrown grassy bank, and Iris got on with her daisy chain, the young Pakistani woman diverted her energy into practising a juggling trick.

Iris The Peaceful was impressed.

"Who taught you that?"

"Sweep. Last time I was in London."

Iris nodded. She understood that it was hard for anyone to meet Sweep without at least some attempt being made to teach them a juggling trick. Fuzi dropped the balls but persevered with her practice. Iris mused on events back in Britain.

"I feel sorry for Sweep," she said, after a while.

"Why?"

"He has a passion for Melody Paradise."

"Does he?" said Fuzi.

Few people would have noticed the change in Fuzi's voice, but to the perceptive Iris she sounded just a little disappointed.

"Why are you sorry for him?"

"Because I can't see it coming to anything," Iris told her. "I've never known Melody fall for a person like Sweep."

"Why not?" asked Fuzi, sounding rather more pleased.

"Not romantic enough. You can't get to Melody with shyness

and diffidence. Of course, Sweep might just get lucky, like Tuffy."

At the mention of this grim disaster in Melody's life, Iris could not help smiling. In spite of all the trouble it had caused, there was definitely something humorous about Melody Paradise being found in bed with Tuffy The Mushroom and then claiming it was all a misunderstanding. Iris The Peaceful was not entirely convinced that it had been a misunderstanding. She suspected that Melody may simply have been having a final fling before committing herself to travelling with Magwyn. If that was the case, Iris didn't think it was really so bad, though she regretted that so many bad things had happened as a consequence.

"Yes," she mused out loud. "Things certainly went bad after that."

"After what?"

"Will you move that damned horse-drawn piece of junk and let me through!" came a harsh voice.

"After Magwyn started acting foolishly again," said Iris, still smiling.

The rest of The Contemplators looked with disgust at Magwyn's truck. They often met people they knew on the road abroad, but it seemed like an overly bad piece of luck to meet Magwyn The Grim twice. Hugh's caravan was occupying several inches of road. There was plenty of room for Magwyn to get past but evidently he was in the mood for an argument. He leaned out of his side window, muttering impatiently while Hugh went to move his caravan.

"Stay a while, Magwyn," suggested Iris The Peaceful brightly. "Have a rest and some food."

"Forget it," snorted Magwyn. "I'm not in the mood for any stupid stories about you riding centaurs round the Hanging Gardens of Babylon."

"That was a unicorn. I took the centaur to Sparta."

"You should have taken it to a lunatic asylum," said Magwyn.

Iris laughed.

"What's the hurry, Magwyn?"

Magwyn The Grim did not deign to reply. As soon as Hugh successfully cleared the road he put his truck into gear and roared off down the dusty lane, leaving The Contemplators choking in his wake.

Iris laughed again. Fernhadzi was surprised to see her so amused. "What's funny?"

"Magwyn," replied Iris, placing her daisy chain round her neck.

"I always enjoy the way he says I belong in a lunatic asylum. At least when he does speak he speaks his mind."

"He was heading south last time we saw him," said Green.

"I expect he changed his mind. He must be hurrying back to get to the festival," said Iris.

There was a groan from all her companions at the thought of Magwyn The Grim attending the festival.

"Surely he won't go to anything organised by Melody Paradise?"

"Of course he will. Magwyn wouldn't miss it for anything. I'm surprised it took him so long to make up his mind. Magwyn hasn't finished with Melody Paradise just yet."

"Is he going to do something bad?" gasped Fuzi.

"That depends on your point of view," replied Iris, and started on another daisy chain for her horse.

In her wagon Iris The Peaceful had presents for everyone. She had a parcel of beads from India and shells from Sri Lanka for Melody Paradise's hair. She had a Nepalese jacket for Megan, black with small patches of red, blue and green. She had a print of an ancient Chinese unicorn for Willis. She had sand from Egypt in two parcels, one for The Universal Leyline Protectors and one for The Elemental Sunshine Family, to go with their pyramids. For Florimel she had a picture of Lilith, bought in Israel, and a pair of Israeli army surplus boots, very functional. There was an unnamed stringed instrument from Afghanistan for Peggy. The Tree Planters would like it, they could play anything. Then there were three twelve inch singles, bought in Germany, for Mary. Iris, who knew little about dance music but knew that a DJ like Mary had to have exactly the right tracks, hoped they were suitable. As they were freshly pressed by a man who owned a studio in Germany she hoped they would be.

Fuzi peered at the labels. All that was written on them was 154 BPM.

"Funny name for a band," she said.

Iris agreed that it was.

"But these techno people are always obscure."

For The Galactic Navigators she had a parcel of sarongs, which they had requested, and some Spanish tunes for the Irish musicians who travelled with them. For The Mushrooms she brought a giant Balinese mushroom which grew in water, doubling its size every day. She brought blue hats for The Militant Children Of Lemuria, who always needed new hats. They were continually losing them while being arrested and thrown in jail. Iris wore one of the hats now, a very jolly blue woollen cap with a tassel that stretched down to her waist and made her look like a pixie.

Before they moved on, The Contemplators went wooding. In the middle of a small thicket Iris noticed a tiny sprig of hazel, just sprouting from the ground.

"That's a Wishing Tree," she said to Fuzi. Fuzi fell about with excitement. Iris remained calm. She studied the tiny sapling for a while, and received the strong impression that it would be quite happy to come with her to the Peaceful Grove. Iris dug it out carefully. She potted it in an urn Melody Paradise had given her specially. Melody had run her hands over the urn many times, infusing it with positive energy. Iris filled the urn with special earth given to her by The Tree Planters which they said was guaranteed to nurture any young tree. It was good to have Melody's healing urn and The Tree Planters best blessed earth but in reality Iris was not worried about the health of the sapling. She could have taken it home in an old bucket filled with sand. No plant was ever unhealthy while under the care of Iris The Peaceful.

"Full speed ahead," said Fuzi, excitedly, as The Contemplators went through the fairly lengthy process of harnessing their horses to their wagons. Everyone laughed. The Contemplators never went full speed ahead, but their customary gentle stroll would be enough to get them to the festival in time.

8th August (Day 25)

The Riverboat Tribe were finally ready to sail. Magwenwy, temper made brittle by the enforced delay, felt happy for the first time in almost four weeks. Being stuck on the riverbank had been a depressing experience. Magwenwy was a born traveller. Staying in one place made her unhappy, anxious, claustrophobic and miserable. The shortness of her temper had made the past weeks an unhappy experience for everyone. Her companions, each doing their best to refurbish her boat, had been obliged to suffer tirades from Magwenwy about their incompetence as the repair work progressed much more slowly than she would have wished.

Before the sun rose on the appointed day she cast off, beginning the long journey that would take her down to the valley near Canterbury. She and Amesh had calculated that they could still arrive in time for the start of the festival."

"Providing we don't have any problems."

"I never had any problems till The Mushrooms sank me."

"You're planning revenge on them, aren't you?" said Amesh.

"Yes."

"Why not just forget it?"

"Because I'm not Melody Paradise or Iris The Peaceful," replied Magwenwy. "Peace and love aren't my strongest points. I bear a grudge for a long time."

In her cabin Magwenwy had a large plastic bin liner filled to the brim with mushrooms, hand-picked in the woods. Later in the day she laid them out to dry, and she made sure that no one else saw them.

9th August (Day 26)

I was standing in Brixton's covered market talking to Melody Paradise and Finan about the possibility of everyone on earth being sent here from another dimension as part of an experiment in free will, when a middle-aged man, with every appearance of being completely insane, came up and started pawing at Melody's hair. He put his hands on her head, fingering her locks, all the time saying "nice hair, nice hair." Melody twisted and turned, frightened, as if she was being attacked by wasps. It took some time to disentangle her from her assailant. We hurried away. It was an upsetting experience though she coped with it well enough.

"At least he wasn't violent."

He seemed like someone who should be being looked after. Ever since the Government had closed and emptied a series of psychiatric hospitals, the streets of Brixton contained many people who seemed like they should be being looked after. The patients were now supposedly being cared for 'in the community' although who exactly was meant to be looking after them was something of a mystery.

Later, sitting in a cafe, Finan felt increasingly annoyed at the man's intrusion.

"I should've hit him."

Melody Paradise herself, after the shock had passed, was not annoyed.

"I'm glad you didn't. He wasn't well."

Finan was not sympathetic. Melody and I were. If you took people from psychiatric hospitals and threw them on the streets to fend for themselves, what else could you expect? Melody asked Finan to explain more about his space alien theories, to make him forget his anger. Finan got back to describing how the Earth was a popular place for aliens to come for an incarnation because here we had free will, and also fun, on occasions.

"So," said Melody Paradise, already cheerful again, "does that mean that in my next life I get to fly around in a spaceship? I can't wait. I'm going to fly it down a black hole and see what happens."

"That's the explanation for corn circles."

"What?"

"Aliens contacting us," explained Finan. "They don't show themselves openly because they only want to get in touch with people who are ready to meet them. So they do it discreetly with corn circles. Only people who are ready to meet them will follow it up."

Melody had a big bundle of letters to post, all connected with her festival, and we followed her down to the Post Office. Outside the Post Office there was a beggar I had often seen before, a very small girl who sat there with her very small dog. As always, it was raining. She had in front of her a cup in which were a few pennies, covered in rainwater. Round the corner from her was another young woman I'd never seen before with a cardboard sign saying 'Hungry and homeless, please help.' The sign was now disintegrating in the rain. She was sitting on the doorstep of an empty shop. Finan told us he used to squat in the flat above the shop before the owners evicted him. Since then it had been unoccupied.

"When I moved in I found a kettle. I've still got it."

He didn't know if it still worked. He kept it just in case.

A terrible argument broke out in the Post Office. A clerk, flanked by managers, was refusing to pay over money to some woman who had, I think, just handed in her child benefit book. They were accusing her of using a forged document. As the argument raged on with increasing vehemence, the atmosphere in the Post Office sank into one of general misery.

The same man who had molested Melody Paradise now came in. Melody shrank back behind Finan. Finan clenched his fists. Ignoring them, the man begged his way unsuccessfully up and down the queue. No one gave him anything. The community was offering him very little care.

Recently, the Government had been forced to modify its policy. They did this not because they cared about the mentally ill but because the most serious of these mentally ill were now killing people at the rate of one every two weeks. This looked bad for the Government.

The argument at the counter intensified. The woman accused of fraud started screaming and banging her fist on the glass that separated her from the clerk. One of the managers went to call the police.

It had not been a very good afternoon. Melody said she couldn't wait to get out of the city. Briefly, I was tempted to agree.

During that memorable period when Melody Paradise was organising her festival, Sweep's house was always busy. Most of The Tribe Of The Last Free Moonbeam were parked nearby. Friends of the Tribe's dropped by either to visit or to receive instructions from Melody, or perhaps just to ask if there was any news of Iris. Everyone was anxious that she should return with a new Wishing Tree. Melody had no news but maintained total confidence in Iris's success.

Whenever I went round there were a few people drinking tea in the kitchen and someone taking advantage of Sweep's bath. Sweep was happy enough about this as it meant he saw Melody Paradise often. I believe that the thought of Melody Paradise in his bath kept him well-entertained.

I sat with Melody at the table. She placed her hands on my arm and it went hot. Sweep and Megan were at the cooker, making food. Pookie dozed in a comfy looking carry-cot. Also there were Finan and Irene and Breed. Breed was in London to make a court appearance. A road contractor was trying to get her banned from the construction site.

This was the first time I had met Breed. Her locks were plain brown, but woven in among them were various coloured ribbons. Like Florimel, she wore them in two great bunches, one at each side of her head, the sort of hairstyle sometimes inflicted on five year old girls by their mothers. On both Breed and Florimel it looked good.

Breed had large dark eyes and an attractive face, which was to be expected from a natural sister of Melody's. She wore a tear-shaped jewel, or rather a piece of coloured plastic, in the middle of her forehead. Melody Paradise and Megan admired this so much that Breed promised to send them some from her supply, which she later did. By the time of the festival, Melody Paradise and Megan and Irene were wearing these jewels in the middle of their foreheads. They were called bindi. This seemed like fun. I'd have liked one. Unfortunately, or I suppose fortunately, I knew how stupid I'd look with a jewel in the middle of my forehead.

Finan related the tale of the deranged person grabbing hold of Melody Paradise's hair.

"It's a shame I wasn't there," said Megan, at the cooker.

"Why?"

"I would have calmed him down."

"How?"

"A quick prayer to Saint Dympna, patron saint of the insane. That would have calmed things immediately."

I was never sure if Megan was serious or not when she said this sort of thing. Finan scoffed at this idea but Megan defended herself.

"It worked before, didn't it Melody?"

Melody looked dubious.

"When?"

"Last year when that woman at the party went berserk and tried to hit you with the television. I invoked Saint Dympna and she ran out of the house."

"That's true," agreed Melody, "although she did run right in front of a truck."

"It still worked didn't it? Got her away from you anyway."

"Surely a saint wouldn't have let her be run over by a truck?"

"Well, I never asked Dympna to look after her for the rest of her life," said Megan. "Just to get her away from Melody. After that I guess she was on her own."

Melody Paradise asked Breed if The Militant Children Of Lemuria had made things up yet with The Universal Leyline Protectors. Breed replied quite emphatically that they had not.

"Certainly not. I'm still mad as hell with them. Protecting an empty field while we were all fighting the bailiffs and security guards right next to them? The most stupid thing I ever saw. If anyone comes to knock down their pyramid, they won't find us helping them."

Melody did her best to mollify her warrior sister, pointing out to her the necessity of accepting the various differences between them all. In this she was quite successful. She and Breed had always got on well. Breed agreed to forget the argument, although this was only after Melody and Finan promised that The Tribe Of The Last Free Moonbeam would attend another protest next week. As The Tribe Of The Last Free Moonbeam subsequently missed this event it all went wrong again, but for the moment Melody had produced some sort of peace and I was quite impressed.

21st August (Day 38) Fifth Day Of The Festival

Burdened with the heavy responsibility of looking after Megan's beloved child I immediately fall asleep. I'm woken some time in the night by Melody Paradise crawling into my tent.

"Is Pookie all right?" she whispers, shaking my arm.

It takes me a while to understand what she's talking about. I remember there is a baby present.

"Seems fine."

Megan is apparently hiding in Melody's van, having deemed it wisest to completely avoid the social workers.

"I told them Megan didn't come to the festival. I don't think they believed me. It'll be safest if you keep Pookie here for the night."

At this moment I don't care one way or the other. The stresses of the day, particularly The Mushroom rampage, have made me overwhelmingly tired. As soon as Melody departs, I again fall asleep. Unfortunately, this does not last for long. I am once more shaken awake, this time by Sweep.

"Why did Melody Paradise just crawl out of your tent?" he demands.

"What?"

"Have you been having secret liaisons with her behind my back?"

In the darkness I cannot make out his expression but I know he's glaring at me suspiciously, and quite possibly polishing his glasses.

"She came to check on the baby."

"Oh yes?," retorts Sweep, sarcastically. "You don't have a baby."

He bangs his fist on my pillow, or what he thinks is my pillow. It is, in fact, Pookie. Pookie starts to howl.

"Sorry, Pookie," he says, and starts trying to soothe him.

186

In no mood for Sweep's jealous stupidities, I eject him from my tent and try to placate the unfortunate infant with some milk and a few tales from Sophocles. This seems to work, which is fortunate. This baby care is hard work. It must be exhausting doing it all the time. Of course, parents don't normally have Sweep arriving in the middle of the night and pounding their children half to death. We both go back to sleep.

After what seems like a few minutes I am again wakened. This is turning into a nightmare.

"It's me," whispers Finan. "I came to see if the baby was all right."

"The damn child would be fine if you'd all just leave him alone," I say, quite crossly. Hearing my raised voice, Pookie wakes and starts to cry.

"He doesn't sound fine to me," says Finan.

"Well, he was all right before you got here."

I eject Finan and soothe Pookie. This takes rather longer than before. Pookie, quite reasonably, is starting to object to these continual interruptions to his slumbers. Finally he drops off. Satisfied that nothing else will happen, I follow suit. When I am shaken awake for the fourth time, I vow never to have children.

"What is it now? Can't you leave a man in peace for five minutes? Any more of this and I'm going to throw the kid out and let him fend for himself."

"How dare you say such a thing?" demands Megan, irately.

I apologise profusely, explaining that I really didn't mean it.

"I've been looking after Pookie to the very best of my ability. He's full up to the ankles with milk and I laid him on the comfiest bit of my sleeping bag. And I told him some stories. I just got upset because everyone keeps waking us up."

To my surprise, Megan believes me.

"Pookie looks happy. I think he's taking to you."

She thanks me for looking after him. Unwilling to be parted any longer from her child she spends the rest of the night in my tent. I am surprised to have suddenly acquired a family, but grateful to be able to sleep for longer than five minutes.

I rarely have fantastic dreams. They are usually quite down to earth. This night, for instance, I dream an anxious dream about being arrested and thrown in prison for my part in the hiding of a baby from social workers. Waking up brings little relief. Although it is early I can hear the sound of voices, and much banging and clattering. Presumably people are trying to get things back in order after last night's destruction.

I wonder briefly if The Nomadic Daughters Of Lilith have actually killed The Mushrooms in revenge but I'm distracted by Megan waking with her baby. She feeds him, cleans him with some pre-moistened wipes she has in her bag, changes his nappy, makes a fuss of him, then prepares to sneak across to Melody's van. She has not yet decided what to do, and asks me if I mind looking after Pookie for a while longer.

"I daren't risk giving him to any one in my tribe, the social workers might spot him."

"Do I have to stay hiding in my tent?"

"No, just carry him around like he's yours. No one'll suspect you."

While I was willing to help Megan in her crisis last night, I can't say I'm thrilled to be landed with this sudden unplanned parenthood. I am notoriously bad with babies. Just because I made it through one night doesn't mean I'm suddenly competent at child care. The social workers will certainly be suspicious if they arrive back suddenly and find me carrying him around upside down. Still, I appear to have no choice. Megan creeps off. I take Pookie out to see what is happening in the valley. I'm met with an incredible scene of destruction. It's hard to believe that so much devastation has been cause by one group of people, no matter how many mushrooms they'd eaten. Cars are overturned, small trees are flattened, tepees are strewn around like rags and pathetic bundles of unclaimed possessions lie soaking in the mud.

All around people are trying to put things right. The Galactic Navigators have some sort of towing bar at the back of one of their trucks. With this they are righting Florimel's Land Rover. Florimel,

188

for once not cursing everybody, concentrates on the job in hand. Behind them The Night Time Elves are pondering the wreckage of their encampment, trying to rebuild their benders and wondering if they can repair their banners.

As the corner of the valley occupied by The Tribe Of The Last Free Moonbeam was one of the few areas to avoid destruction, Melody, Finan, Rooster, Rag and the others are out helping their friends. The Tree Planters are fixing their benders and giving some attention to a damaged sapling nearby. Peggy studies it with meticulous care, hoping to save it.

"The fig tree's had a relapse," she tells me, mournfully. "Too much excitement."

I promise to call by later and do my reading. Which reminds me, when are the readings Melody planned for the festival? There was meant to be a storytelling night. That's one reason I'm here. It probably won't happen. Every other planned activity of Melody's has gone disastrously wrong.

The Golden World Eternal Party Tribe and some others from The Navigators are sorting out what is left of the marquee, prior to attempting its re-erection. Of Rupert there is no sign. I note with displeasure that his mobile home escaped the mayhem. Pixie is up and about, but not helping with repairs. It has all been too much for him and he's squatting under an undamaged tree smoking one large spliff after another.

Saddest of all is the sight of The Universal Leyline Protectors and The Elemental Sunshine Family sifting through the wreckage of their pyramids. As far as I can remember, this is the third act of pyramid destruction so far. The rain is again pouring down, turning what is left of their constructions into pulp. Each of them is determined to rebuild immediately.

Everyone is cursing The Mushrooms. The staff of the heavily damaged Druid Burger van swear they'll never serve them another veggie burger as long as they live.

Melody Paradise is helping Breed to knock the glass out of a broken window in her bus and cover up the hole with polythene. Breed mutters darkly that she's suffered attacks from entire police

189

forces that were less ruinous than that of The Mushrooms. Melody looks tired. She has been working most of the night. Apparently I'm the only one who slept. I get the impression that a large part of Melody's work was preventing the whole camp site from lynching The Mushrooms.

"How did you stop them?"

"Begged and pleaded," says Melody Paradise, wearily. "I told everyone if there was any violence the festival was over. But it was hard. Florimel only agreed to postpone her revenge till the festival's finished."

Melody sighs.

"Look at the valley. What a mess. After all the work we've done it's worse than ever."

The valley is in a sad state, once more strewn with debris. Worse than that, The Mushrooms' vehicles have cut deep gouges into the wet earth. Despite Melody's best efforts to prevent it happening, tyre marks criss-cross the valley in all directions. The incessant rain fills these gouges with muddy brown water. Melody Paradise is right. The place is a mess.

The Mushrooms themselves have withdrawn to the far end of the valley where their vehicles are drawn up in a wary defensive circle. Melody informs me that Fluffy and Tuffy had, on realising what they'd done, come down to apologise.

"Hawk and Mulberry drove them off with rocks. I was tempted to throw a few myself."

"At least everyone's working together now," says Sweep, looking on the bright side.

"That's true," says Melody Paradise.

"Mind what you're doing with that tow truck, you stupid bastard! Damage my Land Rover and you're dead!" yells Florimel.

"How about if we just drop your Land Rover in the river?" retorts Hawk.

Melody sighs.

"But I don't expect it'll last."

She strides off to help Willis look for his star-painted boots. The Night Time Elves have located one of them buried deep in the mud but the other is still missing. Majic Day is making himself useful to The Golden World Eternal Party Tribe and seems to be directing repairs to a whole batch of damaged sound equipment. Eko is meanwhile complaining to any one who will listen that he would have predicted last night's tragedy had someone not stolen his copy of the I Ching.

"First my runes and now my I Ching," he complains. "Someone is plotting against me. It's got to stop."

"Your I Ching is missing as well?" says Irene. "That's terrible."

"It certainly is," rages Eko, "and I'm starting to think it's all connected. Whoever took The Magic Hat is now trying to stop me getting to the bottom of things. Only someone despicable enough to steal the last part of the Wishing Tree would rob me of my runes and I Ching. What we're talking about here is a widespread attack on the New Age. Could there be a police spy in the valley?"

Sweep is pretending to be repairing a bender nearby but really he is listening in, enjoying Eko's discomfort.

"Make sure you keep a close eye on all your other possessions," advises Irene.

Eko replies that he certainly will. His Earth Mother tarot cards will not leave his sight.

"I rely on them completely. The Earth Mother Tarot never fails. It can tell you anything."

"Then why don't you ask them who stole you runes?" asks Irene, very logically.

Eko looks stunned.

"Of course! Why didn't I think of that?"

He hurries off to consult the cards. Sweep no longer looks quite so satisfied.

"Do you think Eko can really find out the culprit from his Earth Mother Tarot?" he asks me, obviously worried.

"Well, you said he was a fraud, Sweep."

"What if he's not?"

"Then you'll just have to deny everything."

Sweep pats Pookie on the head, apologising once more to him

for the unfortunate blow he dealt him last night. Melody Paradise arrives back at The Moonbeam's encampment and approaches her van where I believe Megan is still concealed. Melody is tired and, like everyone else, very wet and fed up. Carrying out large scale repairs in this downpour is an onerous task. Even the dogs look depressed. Depressed lurchers are a particularly gloomy sight. There is some shouting in the distance as an argument breaks out between The Elemental Sunshine Family and The Tree Planters over some branches The Family are cutting from a tree to help repair their pyramid.

"The festival from hell," mutters Melody as she squelches past in the mud. Attempting to climb into her van she slips and falls. Sweep hurries over and helps her to her feet.

I glance down at Pookie.

"Still, it's getting a lot warmer," I say, and check that his rain hat is still fitting snugly. "Wouldn't surprise me if there was a thunderstorm on the way."

Rupert avoids helping with any of the repair work by claiming that he is too busy with the circus. This may be true. Around lunch time another act arrives in the valley in a battered old Bedford lorry, some kind of rope-climbing thing I think. All the acts were meant to be rehearsing on the flat piece of ground across the river but have been unable to because of the rain.

A little order has been restored to the valley thanks to everyone's hard work. The giant marquee is re-erected, its splintered poles spliced together and the holes in the fabric covered with black bin liners. Inside Mary is testing her equipment, miraculously repaired by Majic Day.

"What a technician," she enthuses. "Fixed that amplifier with gaffer tape and silver paper. Learned how to do it in the jungle apparently, after his radio got damaged by a crocodile."

Magic Day, locks dripping wet but still shining and golden, is now helping Catherine fix the hydraulic equipment belonging to The Flying Dementos, also damaged in The Mushroom disaster.

The Flying Dementos are equally grateful as their machinery once more swings into action. Despite the bad weather they test it out so there is for a while the odd sight of six young female trapeze artists swinging high in the air performing tricks while dressed in thick coats and heavy boots.

When Melody Paradise makes her next appearance she still looks tired. Mud is etched into the slight wrinkles in her brow, exaggerating them. Majic Day approaches her to reassure her that most things are now back in order so she can rest and stop worrying. Thanks to the mechanical and engineering skill of the travellers, none of the damage has proved to be irreparable. Almost everyone here has at some time suffered either accidental damage to their homes or deliberate destruction at the hands of the authorities, so repairing things in a hurry is a way of life.

Melody is relieved. For a while her cheerful optimism seemed to be slipping but as she goes to sit under a tree with Majic Day and share some of his Amazonian herbal mixture, for relaxation and spiritual advancement, she is happier. Perhaps this is because of Majic Day.

"They make a nice couple," says Mary. Breed agrees, nodding her head so that her two fat bunches of locks sway back and forward.

There is furious activity in the middle of the valley where The Sunshine Family and The Leyline Protectors are busy rebuilding. Much of this work is carried out in the privacy of the large trucks owned by each tribe but every so often one of them will scurry out to the river looking for withy or some emergency equivalent while others scour the site for whatever else is needed. Fevered, gripped by the necessity to have their pyramids back in good repair, neither tribe assists any one else. In the pursuit of pyramid excellence they are completely single minded.

Although there is some relief that things are now back to normal the mood in the valley has not improved. Melody's comment that this is the festival from hell seems to be an opinion shared by most people. Some say quite openly that they can't wait to leave. There is little attraction in being here. The valley may now be a little tidier but it is by no means beautified. Enthusiasm for beautifying the valley has slipped considerably. No new friendships have been made and no old feuds have been forgotten. Everyone is so wet, so tired, so dirty and miserable that there is no chance whatsoever of any broken friendships being repaired. The only natural thing for anyone to do in these circumstances is to hate everyone else even more than usual.

Willis Elf, his starry boots now a sad shadow of their former glory, declares that he was less uncomfortable the time he got stuck up a mountain in Scotland. The breakaway camp of Night Time Elves are as unhappy as they can be. Boot, Caddy, Moonshine, Starshine and Sunshine sit huddled together in their benders wishing they were somewhere else. Breed, wringing water out of her long blue hat, reminisces fondly about some police cells she's been in which she swears were more comfortable than this valley. Various other Militant Children say that they were fools to miss some big illicit rave being held in the north of England to come here. The Galactic Navigators get drunk and sit around complaining about everything. Various of their members, like Hawk and Mulberry, are really quite objectionable when drunk. They are not above wolf-whistling at The Nomadic Daughters Of Lilith, which completely infuriates them, and even insult John and Ali for being gay.

"Drunken, macho, New Age travellers," snarls Mirabel. "Terrific."

When Hawk insults Magwyn there is very nearly a fight. Magwyn strides towards The Navigators, quite prepared to attack them all. Florimel and Mirabel, itching for a chance to get back at The Navigators, are ready to jump in on Magwyn's side and look frankly disappointed when Nemo and Catherine manage to separate the combatants before a blow is struck.

This is day five of the festival. The circus is meant to be staged on day seven. No rehearsals have taken place. Undoubtedly the whole thing will be a farce. Rupert asks people if they have been preparing for their parts as extras but no one can raise any enthusiasm. There are further complaints about why they have to do it in the first place.

"We just wanted to hang out. Why do we have to bother with

some stupid circus?"

So Melody has to explain all over again that it was her means of making the event legal, thereby circumventing the Criminal Justice Act and also bringing in some money. Everyone seems very unconvinced. Melody Paradise herself now seems doubtful about the whole thing.

"It seemed like a good idea at the time," she says, quietly.

If the circus is plunging full speed to disaster, so is my literary workshop. Two days left and I still don't know what to say. The Chelwyn Literary Festival has been going on all week. No doubt authors have been trooping in and out giving fabulous demonstrations of creative writing, making inspiring speeches or whatever it is we're meant to do.

I ask Finan for advice.

"What can I do to make my creative writing class a success?"

"Write creatively," he suggests.

"I can't be creative. I'm too wet. No one ever wrote a great book when they were wet. It just can't be done."

"Maybe you could base your talk on that," says Finan. "If anyone asks you how to write a book tell them to first make sure they're dry."

"Not a bad suggestion, Finan. Won't fill up the two hours though, I'll need something else."

First stage of creative writing, make sure you're not wet. What would be next? Wash your hands perhaps? It's hopeless. I can't think of anything in this miserable place. Melody Paradise's original idea was for everyone to arrive in the valley, make friends, frolic around happily for six days, clear up the valley, plant a new Wishing Tree, help do the circus on the seventh then head off happily together into the sunset. It all seems to have gone hopelessly wrong. There has been very little fun or frolicking these past five days and no one has made friends. I suspect that Melody may be giving up. Any time she has tried to end an argument it has gone wrong and I don't think she knows what to do any more except hope for the best. It's as if her powers of spreading love and peace have vanished along with her healing powers. Even Pookie no longer stops crying when she pats his head. Meanwhile the petty squabbles go on and on.

Magwyn The Grim is supervising the fixing of some sort of platform onto a flat bed lorry. As this lorry belongs to The Galactic Navigators, the whole awkward process is carried out in hostile silence. For some reason the platform will not fit onto the truck properly and the silence is broken by cursing from The Navigators. Both Magwyn and The Galactic Navigators work hard but it is a long slow process. They slide and fall in the mud and the rain. Their tools are cold and wet and awkward to handle, and despite their best efforts the wooden platform will not fit as it should. After stripping the threading off several bolts and cutting his hand in the process, Magwyn furiously kicks away his spanner and says that he'll have to take the platform back up the valley to adjust it. The platform is now half on and half off the truck, and jammed by the mis-threaded bolts, so the dismantling process is equally arduous and drives everyone involved close to despair.

Rupert is in a bad mood because Melody Paradise has gone off with Majic Day. He takes it on himself to start ordering people about, demanding they move their vehicles to give the workers some room. Needless to say this creates more bad feeling. Practically everything now creates more bad feeling.

Megan crawls furtively into my tent to look after Pookie. She has decided to stay at the festival. She'd like to take him and flee but feels that she can't leave Melody Paradise. Megan is making costumes for the circus and doesn't want to desert in our hour of need. Melody is herself unconscious in her van having followed up Majic Day's Amazonian herbal mixture with a liberal cocktail of drugs and alcohol, and passed out soon afterwards.

"Is she all right?"

Megan nods.

"Majic Day's with her. He wrapped her up in a blanket. She'll be fine."

It might seem unreasonable of Megan to be so unconcerned but to be honest, Melody Paradise collapsing in a stupor is not totally unknown. She's fond of liberal cocktails of drugs and alcohol, though usually when having a good time, not when trying to hide from a bad one. Dogs whimper. The rain pours down. John and Ali start shouting at each other. I tell Megan that I no longer expect to leave the valley alive but she's too busy with Pookie to even acknowledge my complaint. Either that or she's heard them too many times before.

The marquee is quiet. Before the start of the festival Melody arranged with The Golden World Eternal Party Tribe that they should play through the night but not the day, as not everyone likes to hear thundering techno music twenty four hours a day. Mary thinks this is strange, and would really rather be playing all the time but she accedes to Melody's wishes. Eko The Great takes advantage of the silence in the tent to hold court there. After making some enquiries he has come to the conclusion that The Magic Hat was not lost when Magwenwy's boat sank.

"It was seen in Magwenwy's cabin during the party. Fluffy and Tuffy quite definitely remember it being there. Of course, you can't trust their memories but Breed saw it too, and Melody Paradise. So did Pixie. He even tried it on. But Pixie swears it was gone before the boat sank."

There is general cynicism about this. As a witness Pixie is not that much more reliable than Fluffy or Tuffy. He's an amiable man, not given to lying, but he has been taking drugs regularly for thirty years.

"But that's what Magwenwy said as well, wasn't it?" Eko points out.

"She looked for it in her cabin before she went under, and it wasn't there. I firmly believe that someone removed it before the boat sank."

"Who?"

Eko doesn't know.

"But I intend to find out. Whoever has it is committing a shameful act. The Magic Hat should be shared by everyone. Anyone involved in predicting the future, for instance, should have full access to it."

"Who do you suspect?"

Eko refuses to speculate, rather implying that it would be harmful to the public if a man of his importance went around speculating. There is some suspicion that Magwyn The Grim might be the culprit but the only basis for this is that anyone detestable enough to pour weed killer on the Wishing Tree might quite easily steal its last remains.

I wish Eko would drop the whole thing. I don't want the truth to come out. Melody has enough problems without facing general ridicule. I'm troubled, but reassure myself with the thought that there is no way that the crime can be traced to Melody Paradise. No one even suspects her.

"I suspect Melody Paradise," says Florimel. "Why was she so keen to protect the hat if she didn't want it for herself? It's probably hidden in her van right now. Wouldn't surprise me if she killed the Wishing Tree in the first place. She's so dippy, anything's possible."

My heart sinks.

"How dare you say such a thing?" protests Sweep. "Melody Paradise would never do such a thing. She's the one that's trying to make everything better, unlike you."

"No doubt because she's wracked with guilt," retorts Florimel, but she laughs as she says it. I don't think she really believes or even suspects that it was Melody, but she enjoys casting aspersions.

Fortunately Eko seems unmoved by Florimel's suggestion.

"Of course it wasn't Melody Paradise. My thoughts turn more towards some of her more devious acquaintances."

With that he gazes at Sweep, who fidgets uncomfortably.

"It's at the bottom of the river," Sweep insists

"I think The Elves have it," says Roxanna The Tree Planter.

"Maybe The Riverboat Tribe just kept it for themselves," suggests Rowan, Mary's friend.

"Florimel's probably right," says Mirabel. "I've always suspected that Melody Paradise isn't the saint she makes herself out to be."

Sweep turns on his heels and departs angrily, although he spoils the effect by doing a little comedy routine with the guy rope at the door. Later in the day he complains to me at length about the behaviour of The Nomadic Daughters Of Lilith towards his heroine.

"They are so mean to her. Why? Just because she messed up Florimel's benefit claim? Melody Paradise was taking a big risk agreeing to do it in the first place. If she'd been caught signing on for Florimel she'd have been in big trouble. Why don't they like her?"

I shrug. There doesn't seem to be any real reason.

"Maybe they just don't like her because she's a nice person."

"That doesn't make sense," says Sweep.

"I don't know. It wouldn't surprise me. Sometimes in my books if I want a character to be disliked I make them too nice, and it seems to make sense if everyone hates them for it."

"Well, that's just in your books," says Sweep, implying that this bears little relation to real life. I don't argue the point. He's right. But I still say that being nice can get a person disliked. Aristides The Just got expelled from ancient Athens for much the same reason. People who'd never even met him got fed up with hearing him called 'The Just' and voted to ostracise him.

Finan and Irene have reached a truce. Finan, finding himself in deep trouble for again making Irene miss a day's hunt-sabbing, woke Melody Paradise from her stoned stupor and appealed to her for help. Melody revived herself with cold water, summoned up what energy she could muster, and rose to the occasion. She explained to Irene what the problem was, quite miraculously managing to do this in a way that did not cause Irene offence. As a result, Irene has agreed that for the duration of the festival Finan can have a holiday. She can't help feeling disappointed in him but she will accede to his plea for a few days off from militant action.

Reconciled, at least for the meantime, Irene and Finan head off to the small breakaway encampment of Night Time Elves. There, Moonshine is operating her body-piercing service, piercing gun and antiseptic swab always at the ready. As they leave, Irene is still undecided whether to have her navel done or maybe a second stud in her nose.

"Do you like Melody's lip piercings?"

Finan does, so they settle for that.

The kohl round Melody's eyes has smudged over her face and the jewel in the centre of her forehead has slid to one side. When someone points this out to her Melody retires to her van to repair herself. Even in these conditions Melody Paradise does not like to look a shambles.

Megan is in serious trouble. Having failed to turn up at the custody hearing she is now in contempt of court and liable to arrest. Furthermore, the Social Services will now be empowered to take Pookie into protective custody. Megan understands that she is in trouble but has no real plan apart from a vague intention of fleeing after the festival.

"I'll go to Spain," she says, "or Tibet."

I'm dubious about this. I feel that Megan should have pursued her custody battle through the usual channels. She and Melody Paradise are both full of stories about courts removing children from their mothers on the grounds that the mothers, as travellers, were not able to care for them properly. Even so Megan, as the mother of a healthy baby, must have a strong case, even if the father is wealthy and vindictive enough to hire good lawyers.

I tell Megan that she should hire her own lawyer.

"You'll win the case if you just do it right. If you run away they'll find you and take Pookie into care."

Megan says she doesn't trust lawyers or a solicitors. Anyway, she can't afford one and she didn't like the last one she had from legal aid. She even had problems claiming legal aid. Not having a fixed address made filling in the forms awkward and when she did fill them in it seemed to lead her into more difficulties as the benefit agency started harassing her about where she lived. This quickly became too much for her.

This, I think, is the problem. Megan finds it hard to deal with the outside world of forms and procedures and is therefore trying to avoid it. If your bus breaks down in the valley or your battery-operated fridge goes wrong or you fall sick or even if you get arrested there will be someone around to help, but in a complex child custody battle, no one really knows what to do for the best.

Megan simply decides to pretend that she isn't here. If any social workers appear she intends to give Pookie to someone to look after, and hide. A bad idea, it seems to me, although I don't have any good ones. I do have a long fantasy about suddenly qualifying as a lawyer, fighting and winning Megan's case and then vigorously prosecuting government agencies everywhere on behalf of The Tribe Of The Last Free Moonbeam, finally winning an epic battle at the European Court of Human Rights to restore the requirement for councils to provide sites for travellers. An entertaining thought, though not as good as the one about scoring a last minute winner for Scotland against Brazil in the World Cup final.

The patch of daffodils around The Tree Planters encampment was destroyed in The Mushroom rampage. Those flowers which were uprooted but not crushed, The Tree Planters have now put in their hair.

"Good to see you," says Peggy, with flowers in her hair.

"The fig tree is unhappy again," says John, also with flowers in his hair.

"Unhappy enough to have a relapse," says Roxanna, putting a few more flowers in her hair.

"I hope you've got a good story today," says Mark. A flower falls out of his hair. I help him put it back in. Might as well get into the spirit of things.

"I have. It had them rolling in the aisles in ancient Rome."

Terence was a slave at one period of his life but was freed because of his talent for writing. Unusually for an ancient writer, his complete works are still extant, probably because he only wrote six plays before leaving Rome and dying in mysterious circumstances. They were all based on earlier Greek works by Menander or Appollodorus, none of which have survived.

"Today, fig tree, is the story of Phormio, yet another fine

romantic comedy, featuring the talents of the aforementioned Phormio as a general fixer of problems."

"Like Melody Paradise?" asks John.

"Sort of, I suppose. Terence doesn't actually mention whether he was an out-and-out hippy or not. He was an adventurer though, so he probably travelled. And now I think about it, he does manage to fraudulently obtain money for his own purposes. He needs the money to enable his friend Phaedra to marry Pamphila, a beautiful lute player with whom he is hopelessly in love. As Pamphila the beautiful lute player is unfortunately a slave at the time, his father is against the marriage, figuring that it will drag down the family name.

"Phormio's other friend Antipho is in love with Phanium, the secret daughter of Demipho, his uncle. She's a secret because Demipho, the old rascal, had a wife in Athens and another one in Lemnos. Naturally enough, Demipho is keen not to let his first wife know about the other one so it is something of a problem for him when his son falls in love with the daughter. So Phormio has to sort out the problems and find a way for Phaedra to marry Pamphila and Antipho to marry Phanium. In the ancient world, love affairs never went smoothly. Much like today. Everyone wore togas then of course, but apart from that, nothing much has changed."

The telling of Terence's fourth comedy goes well. The Tree Planters are sufficiently pleased for them to offer me some of their spare flowers for my hair, but I decline.

"We'll give them to Melody Paradise," says Peggy.

She seems to have got over the upset caused by Melody's abortive attempt to end their dispute with The Clan Of The Night Time Elves, although this may only be because many more bad things have happened since then.

I walk back down through the valley, avoiding a goat on my way. The goat is one of several belonging to The Elemental Sunshine Family. They also have a few chickens. The livestock accompanies them on their travels.

The Galactic Navigators' vehicles are now protected by a circle of totem poles. Some of these are intricately carved, some little more than lumps of wood. They are very keen on totem poles. I would trade every totem pole in the world for a hot bath.

At the foot of the valley, Melody Paradise and Megan are watching The Motorbikes Of Merlin who are taking advantage of a break in the rain to rehearse. One of them is going to ride his motorbike through a blazing hoop. Rupert applies a flaming torch to the hoop. It doesn't ignite.

"It's too damp," he calls. "Just pretend it's on fire."

The biker revs his engine. It splutters, stalls, and won't start again.

"Just pretend he's riding his bike," mutters Megan. "The circus isn't looking too good, Melody."

"A disaster," I add.

Melody is about to say that it doesn't matter how bad the circus is but stops herself. It might not matter how bad it is, but there is no getting away from the fact that being associated with another failure is depressing to our spirits because everything else that's happened has already been depressing to our spirits. It all adds to the gloom. As we leave, Cinderella, nine year old mechanical wizard of The Galactic Navigators, is trying to get the bike started again.

"The Committee is coming," says Megan, who has been scanning the approach road for fear of social workers.

"Oh, no," groans Melody, and hurries across the makeshift bridge to see if she can induce the performers into some semblance of a performance. Melody Paradise and Megan are now both walking around barefoot. They like the feel of mud squelching up between their toes. I follow Megan, abandoning Melody Paradise to the Village Committee. I don't have the energy to pretend that my literary workshop is going to be any good, or the nerve to tell them I'm planning to bring them all out to the valley.

Will anyone turn up for my class? What will they be expecting? More than they'll get, I'll warrant. I can see it's going to be as successful as the time I toured the country as support act to Lydia Lunch, American performance artist. All of her audiences sat in bored silence while I read, wishing I would hurry up and finish. It was an interesting experience tramping off-stage to the sound of my own footsteps but not one I'm keen to repeat. I could always just feign illness and cancel it. But then I wouldn't be paid and I'd have suffered here for nothing. There seems no alternative but to grind on with it. Perhaps Iris The Peaceful will arrive today with the Wishing Tree. If she does I'm going to be fighting my way to the front of the queue to make a few wishes.

Pyramid mania continues unabated. The Universal Leyline Protectors have now finished their rebuilding and are standing around in a circle, proudly chanting some sort of mantra to usher in a new age of leyline protection. Patrick is particularly pleased because some recent astronomical calculations have proved that the distance from the foot to the apex of their pyramid is exactly one eight billionth of the distance between the Earth and Alpha Centauri. Apparently this is of the greatest significance.

In between chanting mantras, The Universal Leyline Protectors are not above some down-to-earth gloating over finishing their new pyramid before The Elemental Sunshine Family.

"Lightweights," scoffs Patrick's friend Alamo. "Can't take the pressure. We've had to rebuild three times since we got here and look at our pyramid. Perfect. Magnificent. Better than ever. You can practically see the energy flowing into it from the skies."

I nod and smile pleasantly. I pat the pyramid gently and tell Alamo and Patrick that it certainly is looking magnificent. I even pretend I can feel the energy surging through it. With luck, no one in London will ever find out I've been patting pyramids. Or reading to trees.

"Look at them," continues Alamo, waving his hand contemptuously at the nearby Elemental Sunshine Family.

"No sign of any pyramids in that direction. Not a trace. Completely pyramid-less. They're beaten. They might as well go home and start stringing love beads."

I leave The Universal Leyline Protectors happily chanting and follow the trail of Megan's footprints. I am desirous of a few words with her about Melody Paradise. Megan's bus is comfortably furnished with rugs and carpets and a bed, none of them new but none of them in bad condition. Some of the windows have been skilfully boarded up and the space used for book shelves. The old stove makes the whole place pleasantly warm. Clean dishes and pots rest on a polished wooden rack beside the sink. Pookie is asleep in his cot and looks content.

I accept a cup of tea and Megan rolls herself a joint.

"Megan, have you noticed anything about Melody Paradise and Magwyn The Grim?"

"They detest each other," she replies.

"On the surface, yes. But I suspect there are hidden depths."

"What hidden depths?"

"I think Magwyn is still in love with her."

Megan explodes with laughter which is always disconcerting if you've just advanced a theory.

"That's very silly," she says, when she manages to stop laughing. "All Magwyn wants to do with Melody Paradise is run her over with his truck."

"Wanting to run someone over with a truck doesn't necessarily mean you don't love them. I wouldn't be surprised if it was one of the most common desires of lovers everywhere. Okay, Magwyn gives every impression of hating and detesting Melody. I just think he's kidding himself. Maybe not even that. Maybe he knows he's in love with her. But I'm sure he is."

Megan is far from convinced.

"Why do you think so?"

"Well, it's hard to say really. But I can feel it. Perhaps it's the way he stares psychotically at her. Or maybe it's just the way he called her an ignorant bitch last time they met."

"That hardly sounds like love."

"Well, there was definitely something special about the way he said it."

I can't convince Megan. Nonetheless I'm certain that I'm right, which doesn't really please me. Imagine what would happen if Magwyn The Grim and Melody Paradise got back together? Sweep would make my life a total misery. Megan is dismissive of my suggestion.

"Even if Magwyn does still love Melody, which I strongly doubt,

Melody doesn't harbour any secret longings for him. Definitely not. Melody loved the Wishing Tree. Killing it killed any affection she had for him."

"Do you think she might be ready to transfer some affection onto a deserving cause? Like Sweep?"

Megan considers this.

"Sweep is nice," she says. "Not really Melody's type but then how do you know until you go out with that type? Melody's going to need someone to cheer her up after this damned festival. She always used to like having boyfriends, though the bad experience with Magwyn put her off for a while. Sweep would make a nice companion providing he stopped juggling for a while. Do you think he could stop juggling for a while?"

"I'm sure he'd make an effort."

"Well, perhaps," says Megan, "we should do something to encourage it."

"Do you think Melody Paradise might be getting interested in Majic Day?"

Megan thinks it is possible. I wonder out loud if we should do something to discourage this. Megan doesn't think so.

"We don't want to get carried away here. We can't start trying to run Melody's life for her. If she finds Majic Day's dazzling good looks, attractive physique, winning personality, really beautiful golden dreadlocks and all-round pleasant nature a bigger attraction than Sweep's baggy jersey and juggling skills, so be it."

"Sweep does have quite nice floppy blond hair," I point out, in defence of my friend, "and also an all-round pleasant nature. And he'll really make my life hell if Melody Paradise goes off with Majic Day."

Beside me on the rug is a cheerful pink furry elephant.

"One of Pookie's?"

"No, that one's mine," says Megan, "but we share our toys."

I play with it for a while, marching it up and down my leg. Tiny droplets of water form on the elephant's feet, rubbing off from my trousers.

"You know it has now rained every day for the past thirty

eight days?"

"Are you still blaming me for that?"

"Possibly, Megan. It might be industrial pollution changing the world's climate but I'm still suspicious of the way it all started after you insisted on invoking Saint Swithun. If it keeps up till the end of the festival it'll have rained continually for forty days and forty nights. After that I presume the world comes to an end."

"It hasn't rained continually."

"There have been very occasional breaks in the downpour but probably only because the Atlantic Ocean had completely emptied itself into this valley and needed a few minutes to fill up again."

"It hasn't turned out to be the best of times for Melody to hold the festival," agrees Megan. "She was sure we were going to have a hot dry summer. She used to be good at predicting the weather but she lost the talent after the Wishing Tree was destroyed. About the same time she started being clumsy. And everyone started arguing."

I play with the furry elephant for a while then notice that Megan is staring rather vacantly into space. The makings of a new joint lie in her lap but she seems to have forgotten about it. I finish my tea, put down the elephant, and depart. There is an odd noise coming from the floor of the valley. Ululating would describe it, I think. I hurry down to find out what's happening.

Once past the trees and into the open I come across an astonishing sight. Patrick, Alamo and the rest of The Universal Leyline Protectors are staring in amazement at the enormous new pyramid produced by The Elemental Sunshine Family. This has apparently been made in sections in the removal van before being brought out in triumph. As I arrive, they are lowering the top section into place, completing a vast construction some twenty feet tall, more than twice the height of their rivals'. The ululating is coming from the joyous Elemental Sunshine Family.

The Universal Leyline Protectors can only watch in dismay as, with the help of The Galactic Navigators' lifting equipment, the top section is successfully attached. The Elemental Sunshine Family roar with delight and begin a triumphal dance round their pyramid.

Perhaps as some sort of initiation ceremony, or else just for fun, The Elemental Sunshine Family have decorated their faces with red and blue face paint and are looking very tribal indeed. Hearing the commotion, travellers appear from everywhere to gaze wonderingly at the new construction. So impressive is it that spontaneous applause and cheering breaks out round the valley.

"You won't get much power from Alpha Centauri now," shouts Michael to Patrick, cruelly. Michael can't resist tormenting Patrick. The enmity between them is very strong.

"Call that little toy a pyramid? Looks more like a shoe box to me."

Michael and the rest of the Family continue their gyrations. Seeing people dancing is too much for Mary over in the marquee. She breaks her agreement with Melody and starts playing loud music even though it's daytime. It is quite an appropriate thing to do because everyone is eager for a little enjoyment after last night's Mushroom trauma. People start to dance. Once more there is fun in the valley.

This fun does not extend to The Universal Leyline Protectors. All defiance knocked out of them, their own previous triumph abruptly overturned, they can only stand forlornly in the shadow of their rivals' construction and stare miserably at the partying hordes.

Still, apart from their misery, the sudden appearance of the huge structure has certainly lent a joyous air to the proceedings. The friends of Melody Paradise are always eager to have a good time. Seizing on the face paint as an obviously good idea, members of other tribes begin to decorate themselves. Red, blue and yellow faces appear everywhere. Despite the poor weather, people discard their coats and jerseys to paint their arms, filling in the spaces between their celtic tattoos and colourful woven wristbands.

All this is very entertaining. Sweep arrives on his unicycle, juggling clubs in a cheerful manner, though he takes good care to avoid the new pyramid. The Flying Dementos start rolling and tumbling around, showing off some of their ground-level acrobatics while the genial Pixie breaks into a lumbering dance, his light blue cut-off kaftan fluttering around his body. The young Moonshine, Starshine and Sunshine, previously unhappy in their breakaway encampment, can be seen cavorting around merrily. Even The Nomadic Daughters Of Lilith join in. Florimel's twin bunches of white dreads whirl round her waist as she dances with Mirabel. Rooster and Rag are dancing nearby though Florimel ignores them.

Where is Melody Paradise, I wonder? She should be here enjoying this. I know she'd like to join in with all the dancing and face-painting and drinking and general enjoyment. Ah, there she is. Coming this way with the local Member of Parliament. Oh dear. I suspect that for the first time in her life Melody may not be thrilled to see a party going on. The MP and his attendant Committee members are looking rather bewildered.

Only Mrs Fitzroy seems at all happy to find everyone partying and even she blanches slightly when Pixie does a sort of friendly war dance right in front of her face. Mr Pitt's expression changes from bewilderment to annoyance. I can tell that Melody Paradise is trying to make some sort of explanation although she is again hampered by the noise.

I quickly review the situation, making one of these swift decisions for which I am well known. I decide it's time to pack my bags and go home. We cannot now convince the Chelwyn Village Summer Fair Committee that there is anything other than an illegal festival going on here. The MP will complain to the police. The police will come and arrest us. Leaving immediately is definitely the only thing to do.

Unfortunately Melody Paradise is fleeter of foot than I. She bounds over, grabs me by the arm and starts dragging me towards the Committee.

"Help me explain," she says.

"Get Rupert to do it."

"Rupert's disappeared."

"Wise move. I'm disappearing myself," I say, and start to struggle.

"Coward."

"I prefer 'trenchant realist'. Anyway I'm leaving."

It's too late. The Committee are now by our side. Rooster dances past. He seems to have put a larger bone in his nose specially for the occasion.

"I was just telling Mr Pitt about our rehearsal," says Melody, with what charm she can still muster.

Mrs Fitzroy actually laughs. She is a nice woman. I wouldn't be surprised if she started dancing herself. Unfortunately, no one else shows any sign of amusement.

"Is this really part of a rehearsal?" demands the MP "It looks more like a drunken orgy to me. Which bit of the circus is it meant to be?"

Melody opens her mouth but no words come out. For the moment she is all out of explanations, and is completely at a loss for a reply.

"It's the eh...eh...it was all detailed in our proposal. Martin will explain it to you," she says, and looks over at me rather apologetically.

Everybody else looks at me. At the mention of the proposal I feel slightly faint. Trapped, cornered, I cast around wildly for some sort of explanation.

"It's the literary, historical, classical, biblical, pageantry part of the production," I stammer. "A sort of 'Pyramids Through the Ages' act with motorbikes and elephants. No, no elephants, just motorbikes. But lots of them. They're not here yet. Cinderella is still fixing them."

"Cinderella?"

I curse the child for having such a stupid name.

"That's what everyone in the circus calls her. You know these circus types. Have to adopt stage names. Cinderella's a fine mechanic. Much older than she looks. Not nine years old and should be at school. Though if she was nine I'm sure her parents would be teaching her plenty. Wouldn't let her smoke dope, not a chance. The travellers have a school bus you know."

"Travellers?"

"I mean travelling circus. With the biblical motorbike pageant. We're rehearsing the part where Pharaoh Sixtas sacks Solomon's temple in Jerusalem. Hence the pyramids. Not that the Pharaoh actually took the pyramids with him to attack Jerusalem of course, they're just symbolic. Symbolic of him being Egyptian. Afterwards his soldiers ran about in wild debauchery which is what we're rehearsing here. We've had to hire a lot of extras, very expensive, cost far more than the grant, yes sir, we've certainly put that money to good use, not a penny wasted around here. Wouldn't even consider buying beer, too much work to do. Incidentally, modern scholarship has cast doubt on it actually being Pharaoh Sixtas. It might have been some other pharaoh. This, of course, does not obscure the essential truth and meaning of the story as told in The Bible. Are you familiar with the books of First and Second Samuel?"

I grind to a painful halt.

"I see," says Mr Pitt, slowly, "but why is everyone's face painted red and blue?"

"To keep out the cold," I reply.

Melody looks at me in horror.

"I mean, to...to..."

I haven't a clue what I mean.

"Standard Egyptian battle array," says Melody Paradise, swiftly. "You can still make it out on some of the hieroglyphics in the British Museum. The motorbikes are staging the scene in full Egyptian costume."

"It all seems very strange to me," complains Mr Pitt. "Hardly like a circus at all."

"I think it looks rather splendid," says Mrs Fitzroy, who is turning out to be an angel. "I like that man with the bone through his nose. What does he do?"

"He's our accountant," says Melody, and starts leading them away.

Before they depart, Mr Pitt informs me that his wife has booked into every single creative writing class at the literary festival.

"She hasn't actually come across your work before but she's looking forward to hearing you talk."

Melody leads them off up the valley to their cars. I watch their umbrellas disappearing into the distance and wonder if we've got away with it. After my rambling excuses, probably not.

Rupert appears.

"Was that the Committee?"

I nod.

"Unfortunate time for them to arrive."

"It certainly was. Where were you? You're meant to be looking after all that sort of thing, not leaving it to Melody."

Rupert doesn't reply to this, but looks at me suspiciously.

"You seem to spend a lot of time with Melody Paradise."

"She needs me," I reply, which is only a joke, though Rupert doesn't find it funny.

Melody Paradise returns.

"What on earth was that all about?" she enquires. "Elephants? Egyptians? A literary, biblical, historical, pageant on motorbikes?"

"I'm sorry. I panicked. It was the first thing that came into my head. I'm no good in a crisis."

Having made such a mess of things, I'm expecting Melody to be annoyed but instead of being annoyed she smiles. Then she laughs, for a long time. Eventually, she manages to tell Rupert that they should now prepare themselves for a biblical motorbike battle in full Egyptian costume, then laughs so much she has to sit down in the mud and rest.

Once Melody manages to stop laughing she tells me Mrs Fitzroy had hinted to her in a friendly manner that murmurs of disquiet have been heard in Chelwyn about the strange group of people now ensconced in the valley.

"But she said it would probably be all right. We're not fooling Mrs Fitzroy but I don't think she minds, really. Her son is still away travelling in India, and we still have a lot of credit with her thanks to Magwyn's stained glass. And she's on the council. We only have to hold them off another day or two."

I suppose this is true, although it is avoiding the main point. Even if we do manage not be arrested or chased out of the valley, Melody's stated intention of spreading love and peace will have failed. All we'll have achieved is the putting on of a circus, and that was always the least important thing. I don't say this to Melody.

212

I expect she is sick of my pessimism already. I certainly am.

"And looking on the bright side," she adds, "it's not so bad. Everyone dancing and partying didn't look too good to the Committee but at least they are dancing and partying. Look, even Florimel's enjoying herself. And Willis's talking to Starshine again."

"Belladonna just shared a bottle of cider with Pixie. That's progress. And The Tree Planters and The Night Time Elves seem to be mingling."

"It might turn out well even now," says Melody, and breaks into a huge smile. "I can feel the weather improving. It'll be sunny tomorrow. When Iris The Peaceful arrives we'll have a festival to remember. If we can just keep going till she gets here with a new Wishing Tree everything'll be fine. You know, I can feel my problems just evaporating away. Are you ready to read tonight?"

"Read? Tonight?"

"Yes. Poetry and storytelling under the stars. We'll all sit round a big fire and tell tales and read poems and sing and it'll be fun."

I nod my agreement. I could do with a bit of practice before I hit the Chelwyn Village Literary Festival.

"And now," says Melody, "I'm going to dance."

Melody's eyes flash with pleasure at the prospect of dancing, and a new Wishing Tree arriving and her problems ending. She looks happy. A little thinner than before perhaps, but happy. She takes her hair in two handfuls, covers her face with it for a second then throws it into the wind where it billows behind her like a vast multi-coloured sail. She holds her arms in the air, the palms of her hands turned towards the sky, and tilts her head upwards allowing the rain to pour over her face and down her neck.

"I love the rain," she says. "It feels good. Come and dance."

Before Melody can dance she is interrupted by Rupert.

"Going to dance with Majic Day?" he says, disapprovingly.

"Maybe," replies Melody.

"Some of us have to work."

He looks rather pointedly at Melody, before turning and leaving. Melody falls over. I help her up.

"To hell with it," she says. "I'm still going to dance."

John appears at our side.

"Melody," he wails, "Ali just set fire to my bus."

Ali runs up.

"I did not. I was trying to put the fire out."

"You started it."

"No I didn't. I told you it was bad luck parking under an elm in August."

They start to fight.

"Pixie just stole my cider," screams an irate Belladonna, and mounts an immediate raid to reclaim it.

"It's Fluffy and Tuffy!" screams Hawk.

The young Mushrooms, not wishing to miss out on the party, have ventured down from their refuge but are met with a strong barrage of rocks and mud.

"Stop doing that!" screams Melody and runs over to protect them. She trips and falls over Irene and Finan who are struggling on the ground. The sounds coming from them are confused and hard to follow, but I think they're having an argument about falconry.

"Stop throwing mud at our pyramid," demands Michael, marshalling The Elemental Sunshine Family into a defensive wall. Some of the mud is coming from The Universal Leyline Protectors who, under the pretext of driving off The Mushrooms, are taking the opportunity of pounding their rival's pyramid. Worse still, Mulberry, drunk, is attempting to climb it. The Sunshine Family drag him off and more pushing and shoving ensues.

"Well, I don't fucking care what excuse you make now," screams Breed, waving her fist angrily at Rooster. "You turned up six days late at the protest. The Tribe Of The Last Free Moonbeam is a waste of space."

Behind them The Clan Of The Night Time Elves and The Tree Planters would appear to be hitting each other with sticks.

"Stop this at once!" screams Melody Paradise at the top of her voice. No one heeds her. A fierce argument between Florimel and Mary breaks out and recriminations are again bandied around about the time The Nomadic Daughters Of Lilith had to pay to get into the Golden World charity event.

"Are you trying to tell me you didn't pocket half the money?" demands Florimel.

Even the ferocity of Florimel's accusations is lost among the general chaos. Pushing, shoving, fighting, screaming and bawling hordes plunge this way and that, breaking in waves over the beleaguered defensive wall of The Elemental Sunshine Family. Is all activity in the valley doomed after the destruction of the Wishing Tree, I wonder? Or is Melody Paradise really cursed for stealing The Magic Hat?

"Give me back my Earth Mother Tarot cards!" yells Eko, tackling Sweep on his unicycle and bringing him crashing to the ground.

Majic Day walks into the fray, arms raised, trying to calm the situation. A huge lump of mud hits him on the ear and he goes down struggling under the feet of John and Ali. At this moment the rain starts falling in a way that puts to shame all previous downpours. It falls so heavily that it's no longer possible to see who is arguing with who. The weather conditions succeed where Melody failed. There is a general disengagement. Unable to come to grips with their opponents, everyone slips and crawls their way back to their own encampments.

I struggle back to my tent. My tent has collapsed. I crawl under the remnants. Twilight is short and the night comes early. The Golden World Eternal Party Tribe do not restart the music. The evening of poetry and storytelling underneath the stars is cancelled. A very poor end to day five of the festival, I must say.

11th August (Day 28)

Magwyn The Grim drove his truck around the world with no greater aim than to get away from the last place he'd been. There was nowhere that he liked to be and nor was there any person he wished to be with. He would live for weeks on end without exchanging a single word with another person.

His solitariness did not make him happy. He suffered from

terrible loneliness. He had discovered that it was possible to shun society entirely, and to miss it dreadfully.

After splitting up with Melody Paradise he had found himself unable to tolerate company. He never had been a friendly man and since the break up it had got worse. To try and find some peace he drove his van to the quietest, least frequented parts of the country but it was no use. Wherever he went, whichever unused and hidden scrap of land he settled on, someone would object and he would be moved on. He had been moved on by the police thirty times in the past year, and arrested seven times. On three occasions he had been involved in violent struggles with local vigilantes. Inevitably, their greater numbers would win out over his ferocity and he would be chased away, bruised, and filled with hatred.

Magwyn did not ask anyone for help, which was just as well. Not even the most radical land rights protester would have campaigned for Magwyn The Grim to be allowed to live on someone else's land.

He was aware that everyone disliked him. He was also aware that he deserved this. His conduct when in any sort of society was abominable and always had been. He was drunken, violent, unpleasant, abusive and mean. His only period of happiness had been his time together with Melody Paradise. Before that everything had been bad. After that it had been worse.

Magwyn's loneliness was driving him slightly mad. He realised this but there seemed to be no way out. He hated everyone too much to ever rejoin society. Loneliness is terrible. Magwyn had nightmares about it and when he woke up the nightmares were true. So he sat, huddled in a blanket against the cold in his cheerless truck, hating everyone, and especially Melody Paradise.

He angrily rejected Rupert's original offer of work at the festival. The continual evictions and persecutions became too much for him and he drove across to France and Spain, looking for peace. He didn't find it.

Why he eventually accepted the offer and was now on his way to the festival he was not sure, except that it would pay him, and he needed money. He used to make a living from his stained glass but recently he had done nothing except paint horrible dark intense paintings of ugly shape and morbid colouring. Painting was at least something to do. Even Magwyn The Grim, mad, bad and lonely, could not spend every single minute of the day staring angrily at the bleak interior of his old army truck.

He stared at the postcard of the Cistine Chapel that Iris had given him. One of the angels reminded him strongly of Melody Paradise. He crumpled it up and threw it away. A minute or so later he retrieved it, and smoothed it out, the same as he had done last time, and the time before.

12th August (Day 29)
With five days left till the festival I decided not to go. I told Melody this when she came round to visit.

"I'm not coming. It's too dangerous."

Melody Paradise smiled.

"It won't be dangerous at all. It'll be wonderful. I promise you'll have a good time. And you wouldn't let me down, would you?"

"I can't leave my video city at such a crucial point in its development."

"Very bad for your sore hand," said Melody. "Destroy it in an earthquake."

I was shocked at Melody suggesting such a thing.

"Why do you keep playing? You keep saying you can't get enough people to come to your city."

I shrugged.

"Let me see it," said Melody. I plugged in my machine and loaded in the game. Melody studied my on-screen city for a while.

"It doesn't look like a very nice place to live," she said. "Needs more trees, and some fountains, and a nice big park in the middle."

"No room for that, I need to keep building commercial units."

"No," said Melody. "It needs a big park right there. I can feel it. If you build a big park there, I'm certain more people will come."

She asked me how to use the controls, and after some practice succeeded in knocking down a large area of buildings to create a park with lots of trees, flowers and fountains.

"Perfect," she says.

"Well, it might be if the game had been programmed by hippies. Unfortunately it wasn't. You've ruined it."

"No, I haven't," said Melody Paradise. "Just wait and see."

13th August (Day 30)

With four days left till the commencement of the festival Iris The Peaceful was in the north of France and making good time. As they journeyed north, the weather worsened. The past week had seen intermittent rain which now intensified. Iris said that this was to be expected, joking that it was almost inevitable that the festival would be held in the mud. Fuzi was disappointed but Iris was unconcerned.

"Don't worry. It won't make any difference. The valley we're going to is beautiful. The Peaceful Grove is still beautiful, even without the Wishing Tree. Count it as a good omen that the ground will be fertile when we plant the new tree."

Fuzi did her best to count it as a good omen.

"But it's a shame for Melody if it rains."

"It's fine. It won't be a problem. Once Melody and everyone else gets to that valley they'll have a great time. I guarantee it. Everyone always has a great time with Melody Paradise."

"Why?"

"Her unusual gift for spreading love and peace I suppose."

Hugh mentioned rumours he'd heard that Melody was growing clumsy and awkward. Iris scoffed at this.

"No one is more graceful than Melody Paradise."

Green mentioned rumours he'd heard that since the destruction of the Wishing Tree everything had started to go wrong, and everyone argued all the time, and even Melody couldn't make things better.

"How pessimistic you all are," proclaimed Iris. "Everything will be fine."

Iris The Peaceful was now entirely happy. They had a new Wishing Tree and were going to make it to Melody's festival on time. She hadn't met Simon on the road, and still wondered where he might be, but this was no more than a vague dissatisfaction. Surely they would meet again somewhere.

They travelled on. Some miles along the road a large truck, hurrying to reach the coast, rounded the corner behind them and ploughed straight into the back of Iris's wagon sending it crashing down the bank where it broke into pieces. Iris flew through the air, landed heavily and lay still. Her horse whinnied in terror as it too was dragged down with the wreckage. The rest of The Contemplators horses panicked and fled. It was sometime before anyone could regain control and make their way down to where Iris lay bleeding at the bottom of the bank. Beside her lay the urn that Melody Paradise had given her. It was smashed to small pieces, and the tiny sapling of the new Wishing Tree was crushed and broken.

14th August (Day 31)

With three days left till the start of the festival, The Riverboat Tribe were not even close to the site. Disaster had followed them everywhere. Reeds had fouled their propellers, locks had jammed, swollen waters had made travel difficult and Amesh managed to knock himself out jumping ashore. They were held back for two days by wreckage from a collapsed bridge and, on top of all this, Magwenwy's boat was almost impounded by local officials when she left it for half an hour to go shopping.

"Are we ready to set off yet?" demanded Magwenwy, after yet another delay.

"Not quite," replied Amesh. "Bit of a problem with my steering."

Their progress was dreadfully slow, and Magwenwy fumed. They would not now arrive in time for the start of the festival. The Riverboat Tribe all loved festivals. No one had any doubt that Melody's festival would be wonderful. They gave little credence to reports from The Tree Planters that the atmosphere may be less than genial.

"So a few people are arguing," said Magwenwy. "So what? Melody'll sort it out. When did anyone ever argue with Melody

Paradise around? She'll make everyone forget their grudges."

Amesh asked Magwenwy if Melody would make her forget her grudge against The Mushroom Clan, but Magwenwy answered that this was different.

"It won't be much fun if it keeps raining."

"It'll clear up. It won't rain on Melody's festival. I can't wait to be there. I need a holiday."

The outside world was a difficult place. Magwenwy needed to forget it every now and then.

22nd August (Day 39) Sixth Day Of The Festival

"Let's just forget it," says Livia. "Drive away somewhere else."

"No," says Melody. "I'm not leaving while everyone's arguing."

"Maybe we should give them some time to settle down?" suggests Livia. "Maybe try again in a year or two."

"We can't leave," says Megan, practically. "We still have to do the circus, and we're still waiting for Iris The Peaceful."

Melody hopes that Iris's arrival might yet improve matters but even her loyal supporters now find this hard to believe.

"Is the rain ever going to stop?" asks Rooster.

"Don't ask me," replies Melody Paradise. "My weather predicting skills seem to have declined sharply. They were never really that good, to tell you the truth."

She winces as some raised voices reach us from the trees where an argument is taking place over a piece of firewood. A loud voice, easily identifiable as Florimel's, threatens to break it over her adversary's head if he doesn't let go of it.

"Interesting that even gathering firewood now produces such ill feeling."

"There is nothing my family won't argue about," says Melody, dryly. "What a disaster this is turning out to be. Honestly, I had more success when I handed out plastic flowers to the police in Trafalgar Square than I've had here."

"You handed out plastic flowers to the police?"

Melody nods.

"Went down quite well actually. Policemen are all right in ones and twos, it's only when they get into gangs they behave so badly."

She walks into the trees where Florimel and Magwyn are angrily confronting each other over the piece of wood. As there is plenty of dead wood all around there seems to be no particular reason for them to argue. Magwyn seems to see the truth of this for as we approach he mutters to Florimel that she can have it, and walks off. Florimel departs in triumph.

"What a stupid argument," mutters Melody.

"At least it didn't end in a fight," says Megan.

"In fact Magwyn just conceded," I point out. "Maybe he's doing his bit to spread love and peace."

"I doubt it," replies Melody, and is of the opinion that Magwyn only relinquished the wood in embarrassment, on seeing her approach. If Melody Paradise is prepared to put up with endless displays of irrational behaviour on the part of her family, she certainly will never give Magwyn the benefit of the doubt. She really does seem to loathe him. Which is a lesson for all lovers. Never destroy your girlfriend's Wishing Tree. She'll hate you for it.

Sweep is upset because Melody is upset and hangs around moodily. Rupert marches up. He's wrapped in a thick Mexican blanket and frowning angrily. He demands to know what is happening.

"I'm meant to be putting on a circus tomorrow. Nothing's ready. Where's Magwyn with the new platform for the truck? Where are my helpers? Why have The Motorbikes Of Merlin fallen out with The Flying Dementos?"

Melody shrugs. She doesn't know why The Motorbikes Of Merlin have fallen out with The Flying Dementos. Nor does she know why the Druid Burger van has shut up shop and is refusing to serve Druid Burgers any more, or why Jane The Jeweller is threatening to stab Mulberry with a kilt pin, or why Patrice, resident yoga and meditation expert of The Galactic Navigators, chased Hawk all over the valley with a big spade in her hand. I get the strong impression that she is on the verge of saying she doesn't care. She controls herself, and trudges off with Megan, refusing all offers of comfort from Sweep or Rupert.

Sweep now seems too sad to speak. I ask him to help me fix my tent. He nods and walks back with me and we struggle with it in silence for a long time. Some escape from the outside world this turned out to be.

The Riverboat Tribe arrive, with little ceremony. They're five days late. Seldom can a group of travellers have been so disappointed upon reaching their destination. They expected to find a happy, sunny, friendly event; a joyous festival at which they could relax, get stoned, meet their friends, dance, and generally enjoy themselves. More than this, they had expected to find a festival so perfect in every way that it would pass into legend to be forever talked about as a highlight of their lives. Arriving instead at this rain-soaked, miserable, hostile valley, they are appalled, and sulk in their boats. Only Magwenwy remains on land for long, talking to Melody Paradise and trying to discover how exactly things reached their present dismal state. Melody is unable to explain it fully.

"It just all went wrong," she says, and no one else can provide much better explanation than that.

The sixth day of the festival is notable for some strange behaviour by The Mushrooms and some foolish behaviour by Sweep. The strange behaviour of The Mushrooms consists of them behaving like normal, if rather dazed, human beings. Fluffy, Tuffy, Bug and Simple wander down from their encampment and look around with a puzzled air. Unusually for them, they do not crash into anything, or commit any outrageous acts of accidental sabotage. It's the first time since their calamitous arrival that they've risked visiting the main site and Melody, despite her multitudinous problems, endeavours to make them welcome, assuring them that they won't be attacked.

"I feel funny," says Fluffy.

"Me too," say the others.

They wander off, still with a slightly puzzled air about them.

"They're behaving oddly," says Melody Paradise.

"They always behave oddly."

"But this was different. There's something the matter with them."

"Poisonous mushrooms?" I suggest, hopefully.

Rehearsals are progressing sporadically on the other side of the river but Rupert has new problems to contend with. Inevitably, The Motorbikes Of Merlin have fallen out with The Flying Dementos. The Ancient Secret Order of Knives soon get fed up with both of them and refuse to rehearse any more. Rupert threatens to abandon the whole thing and go home. Melody Paradise wearily goes off to try and sort it all out.

"Morons," she mutters under breath. "They're all morons."

I return to my tent and worry a little about my creative writing class. Sweep interrupts me. He wants to worry about Melody Paradise, which takes precedence.

"No wonder she's so sad. Who wouldn't be with all this arguing going on? Everything's falling to pieces. Well, I'm going to put a stop to it."

"How?"

"I'm going to get everybody to make peace."

"Good idea Sweep. Melody will certainly be impressed if you do. How are you going to manage it? A conciliatory goodwill mission on your unicycle perhaps?"

"D' you think that would help?"

"No. And nor would your stilts or your fire-clubs. I doubt if a mission from the United Nations Peacekeeping Force would help. Forget it, all these people are mad. No one can do anything with them. How did Melody Paradise ever manage to grow up spreading love and peace when all the rest of her family are sociopaths?"

"Because she's wonderful," says Sweep.

"Stop being nauseating."

"I'm not being nauseating. Melody Paradise is wonderful."

With that Sweep departs. Now used to the ways of this place, I know he is inevitably going to meet with disaster. By this time I have already determined to write about Melody and her family, and the doomed festival. I doubt if Melody will be pleased to read my account of the fiasco, but that's life.

I wonder if any progress has been made on 'Young Socrates'. Might there be a message on my ansaphone saying, "We love your idea and we'd like to talk about it over lunch?" Nemo has a mobile phone. I could use it to phone up my own number and listen to my messages, if I knew how to do it. Unfortunately, as with every single piece of electrical equipment I've ever bought, I was unable to understand the instructions. How to call up and listen to my own messages will forever be a mystery.

An agitated Sweep plunges back into my tent clutching Pookie, and gibbers in an unintelligible manner.

"Well, Sweep, what catastrophe have you initiated this time? Any deaths?"

"Social workers," he says, zipping up the flap. "I just ran to warn Megan and rescue Pookie."

It's strange being oppressed by social workers. I don't have anything against them normally, in fact I'm sure they do an excellent job. Usually I'd expect to be in sympathy with their aims. In the case of them pursuing Pookie however, I'm finding them infuriating, and I truly wish they would leave Megan and her child alone. I suppose it's the fault of the father rather than the social workers.

"What'll we do?"

"Stay hidden," says Sweep.

"What if they find us with Pookie?"

"Pretend he's ours."

"What do you mean 'ours'?"

"We'll say we're his co-parents," says Sweep.

"Sweep, you are a fool. Do I look like a co-parent?"

"Yes."

"No, I don't. And I don't look like your boyfriend either."

"Well, what would a boyfriend of mine look like?"

"Senile and demented. If the social workers storm this tent I'm telling the truth. I refuse to pretend to be joint parents of Pookie with you. It's preposterous."

"I don't see what the problem is," objects Sweep. "Gay couples look after babies nowadays. I saw a documentary on television about it. You're not prejudiced against gay couples looking after babies are you?"

"No, I'm not. But I'd have a hard time pretending I was in a family relationship with you. And you'll have a hard time convincing them he's your child if you don't take that juggling ball out his mouth."

Seeing Pookie about to cram the entire juggling ball down his throat, Sweep overreacts and starts trying to wrestle it free. Pookie howls in protest. Anxious not to draw attention to ourselves we frantically try to calm him. In this we're only partially successful, reaching a sort of stand-off where Pookie doesn't actually scream the place down but neither is he entirely silent.

Someone starts unzipping the flap of my tent. We're trapped. It's all over. I'll give evidence against Sweep in return for a short sentence.

Megan's head appears.

"They weren't social workers," she says. "Just sightseers from Chelwyn, come to look at the hippies."

"Oh," says Sweep. "Sorry Megan."

Megan gathers up her child.

"I can't stand all this arguing," she says. "It's not what I was expecting to happen. I don't understand why everything's gone so badly. Do you think Melody Paradise might be cursed or something?"

"Only by having friends like these. Do you realise that Rupert's meant to be staging his circus tomorrow?"

Sweep ventures a little optimism here.

"It might still be all right. All our performers are good."

"It would help if they were talking to each other."

"Well, I'll be good anyway," says Sweep, who is determined not to let Melody down, and is planning a stupendous display of juggling.

The whole of The Tribe Of The Last Free Moonbeam trudge down to the marquee. Gloom and depression have settled over them all.

"The sooner we head off to Spain the better," says Livia, and no one disagrees. Their present misery rakes up bad memories. There are painful stories of their past few years of continual evictions, of being harried by the police from one place to another, of park-ups raided by vigilantes, vehicles impounded and destroyed by councils, festivals cancelled, work drying up, sites being fenced off and dug with ditches to make them uninhabitable, and almost everything going wrong.

"It might still be all right," insists Melody Paradise, "and we've made the valley look a lot nicer."

Melody plunges head first into a massive wheel rut.

"We'll have to do something about these," she says, as Megan hauls her out.

Melody Paradise has an array of flowers in her hair, a present from The Tree Planters, so it is obvious that she is making maximum efforts to spread love and peace. According to Megan, the flowers only go into Melody's hair at moments of extreme crisis. Despite the flowers, Livia scoffs at Melody's optimism.

"Stay here much longer and something really bad is going to happen."

"It has already," says Melody. "My healing powers have disappeared."

Through immense force of personality Melody has managed to persuade everyone to gather in the marquee. The marquee itself is rather forlorn. The Golden World Eternal Party Tribe has been either unwilling or unable to restore it to its former magnificence and only a few bedraggled banners now decorate the walls. Inside the atmosphere is grim. The indomitable Melody Paradise apologises to everyone for giving them such a bad time.

"I thought it would be the best festival ever," she says, "and it hasn't been. I'm setting off for France tomorrow night and I wanted to say goodbye to everyone in a happy place but it just hasn't worked out like that. But we can still have a good time before we leave.

"We want to leave now," says Michael, and there are more than a few murmurs of agreement.

"Before having a good time?"

"Come on Melody, no one's going to have a good time. This

226

whole event has been cursed from start to finish."

"Cursed? Nonsense. I admit we've had a few minor problems. But look on the bright side."

"What bright side?"

Melody thinks for a few moments.

"Well, there's the fig tree. Making a good recovery I trust?"

"Close to death," report The Tree Planters grimly. "Hanging on by a thread. It's only holding out till it hears the complete works of Terence."

"Oh," says Melody, disappointed. "Well, I'm sure it'll get better. And look how nice we've made the valley."

"Soil's starting to give way from the tyre marks," says Nemo. "Fatal erosion, I reckon. Be a desert next year."

"Dustbowl probably," says Catherine, shaking her head grimly.

"It will not be a dustbowl. It'll be lovely. And there's a new Wishing Tree on the way."

"Iris isn't coming," says Patrick. "Probably couldn't find a new tree."

"Might have been knocked down and killed," says Mirabel.

"Dangerous things, these horse-drawn wagons," agrees Florimel.

"I expect we'll read about it in the papers," says Anorexia.

"Unless she's mangled beyond recognition," adds Belladonna.

"Oh, for goodness sake, will you all stop this?" says Melody, exasperation in her voice. "Let's all try to think positively."

Rupert, Eko and Sweep, all thinking positively about being closest to Melody Paradise, get in each others way and start scuffling. Majic Day separates them. Melody continues with her exhortations.

"And remember, we have to do the circus. We can't get out of it, we've been paid. So Mary, please stop refusing to do the lights for Rupert, and Catherine and Nemo, please help with the mechanical repairs and everyone else please just help so we can get it done as painlessly as possible."

This is met with a grudging acquiescence.

"What are these Mushrooms doing here?" demands Florimel. "I told them to keep out of my sight."

Fluffy, Tuffy, Bug and Simple and a few of their companions have wandered down unexpectedly to Melody's meeting. They stand there blinking and looking confused, not really seeming to register the hostility that is directed against them.

"Let's throw them in the river," says Mirabel.

"Good idea," agrees Hawk.

"Please," says Melody, "stop this. Can't you all try to get along with each other for once?"

"Get along with The Mushrooms?" says Florimel, "after the destruction they've caused?"

"It was all an accident."

"An accident? How many more accidents do we have to suffer at their hands? Two nights ago they wrecked everything in the valley. Before that they sank Magwenwy's boat."

"And don't forget the time they burned us out of our tree houses," says Breed, who is still angry at the memory.

Breed, Florimel, Hawk, Mulberry and various others advance menacingly, obviously having decided that throwing The Mushrooms in the river is a good idea.

"We didn't do it!" wails Fluffy.

"What didn't you do?"

"Burn down the tree houses," says Fluffy.

Breed glares at her scornfully.

"Oh no? It was your camp-fire that got out of hand, no doubt when you were all off gathering mushrooms. I nearly killed myself jumping out of that oak tree."

"But we weren't there," protests Fluffy "We left someone to look after the fire while we went to get water."

More suspicious looks are directed at Fluffy.

"How come you never said so before?"

Fluffy shrugs.

"I couldn't remember it before. I don't know why it's just come back to me. I've been feeling strange all day. I keep remembering things. We weren't there when it happened."

"Well, who was in charge of your fire?" demands Breed.

"Melody Paradise."

There is a stunned silence. All eyes turn on Melody.

"Is this true?"

"Ehhh..." Melody seems lost for words.

"Were you responsible for the notorious Oak Burning Incident?" demands Breed.

"Well, I don't think so," says Melody, rather uncomfortably. "I mean, I was there, and I do remember talking to Fluffy, but it's a bit of a blank after that. Did you really leave me in charge of your camp-fire?"

Breed explodes in annoyance.

"So it was you! The Mushrooms left you in charge to look after things and you got stoned and forgot about it and nearly killed us all!"

Melody Paradise, a fair-minded woman, has to admit that this is one possible reconstruction of events.

"You almost wiped out The Militant Children Of Lemuria!"

"Sorry," says Melody. "I really didn't mean it. And everyone escaped."

She smiles brightly.

"So that's that affair cleared up then. Mushrooms completely innocent. Isn't that good to know?"

Half the people in the marquee are outraged at the revelation and the other half seem grimly amused. The Tribe Of The Last Free Moonbeam shift around nervously, unused to seeing Melody Paradise condemned on all sides. Florimel and Mirabel leap at the opportunity of berating Melody, taking great pleasure in pointing out the incongruity of anyone going around pretending to spread love and peace and actually almost burning half her family to death.

"And don't forget she wrecked your pyramid," says Florimel to Michael. Michael replies that he hasn't forgotten.

"Wait a minute," yells Megan, striding up to Melody Paradise. "No need to start treating Melody like some sort of criminal. After all, no one was killed. Just a few bruises and one or two scorched trees."

"Eighteen dead oaks," interjects Catherine, angrily.

"Well, yes, eighteen dead oaks. But I'm sure the wood has

repaired itself by now."

"No, it hasn't," says Breed. "The fire ended our protest. They built a motorway over it the week after we left."

"Well, you can't blame Melody Paradise for that. It's not fair for you all to turn against her. Look what she's done for you all. She's helped everyone. Why, The Riverboat Tribe have just sailed in and they wouldn't be here at all if Melody hadn't paid for the repairs to Magwenwy's Boat."

"After The Mushrooms sank it," says Finan, cleverly trying to shift attention away from Melody.

"Absolutely true," agrees Sweep. "Melody Paradise has helped everyone and the oak-burning-incident was an accident. Could have happened to anyone. It pales into insignificance compared to the boat sinking. You should all thank her for helping The Riverboat Tribe."

At these exhortations from Megan, Finan and Sweep, hostility towards Melody Paradise does seem to ebb a little. Melody herself has recovered from the shock, putting it down as one of these little surprises life deals us every now and then.

"Absolutely right," says Eko, lending support. "Concentrate on important matters. The oak burning is no more than a minor misdemeanour compared to The Mushroom Clan sinking Magwenwy's boat."

"But we didn't sink it," wails Fluffy.

"Oh, yes you did," rasps Magwenwy. "You're not getting out of that one. It was your double-decker bus that sent me to the bottom of the canal."

"But we weren't near it at the time. We left it at the top of the bank. The hand brake was loose but it should have been okay because we jammed a big wooden wedge under the back wheel to keep it safe. I remember now, I was over at the trees watching the whole thing."

"Are you trying to say you didn't sink my boat?" demands Magwenwy.

"Yes. I remember now. The truck was fine till the wedge was moved."

"Well, who moved it?"

There is an awkward silence.

"Melody Paradise," says Fluffy, apologetically. "I think she used it to stand on when she was trying to pick an apple."

There are gasps from the crowd.

"Well?" demands Magwenwy.

Melody Paradise screws up her face, striving to remember.

"Err...well, now Fluffy mentions it, I do seem to recall gathering a few apples. And standing on a piece of wood I picked up. Was that really holding your bus in place?"

"Yes," say Fluffy, Tuffy, Bug and Simple.

"Oh," says Melody. "That's a pity."

There is now complete uproar. Melody Paradise is in utter disgrace, reviled on all sides. There seems to be no major calamity for which she has not been responsible. Magwenwy is absolutely livid and shouts abuse at her sister. Melody does her best to placate her.

"I'm sorry Magwenwy. I hardly even remember doing it. I must have had a few joints too many I suppose. But it was an accident after all. I'm really sorry."

Melody's apologies are of no use in soothing Magwenwy, or Breed, or anyone else. With The Mushrooms inexplicably regaining their memories, disaster upon disaster is now revealed to have been Melody's fault. Faced with this blanket hostility, Melody's bewilderment and embarrassment eventually changes to annoyance. Even the saintly spreader of love and peace can only take so much abuse.

"Well, all right," she says, raising her voice above the clamour. "It seems it was me that burned the tree houses and sank the boat. And wrecked the pyramid. I'm sorry. I have been a little clumsy recently."

"A little clumsy?" shouts Breed. "It's a miracle any of us are left alive."

"I'll make it up to everyone," says Melody

"Don't come near us when you're making up," says Florimel.

"The woman's a menace," says Mulberry.

"A walking disaster," agrees Hawk.

231

"Probably meant it all along," sneers Mirabel.

"She's a psychopath," says Florimel. "Puts flowers in her hair to disguise the truth."

"I do not," protests Melody, waving her arms in an agitated manner. "How dare you say such a thing. They were all accidents. I've never done anything malicious to any of you in my life."

It is unfortunate that at this moment Melody raises her arms in the air causing a small gap to appear between her brightly coloured waistcoat and her brightly coloured leggings. The Magic Hat falls to the ground.

"The Magic Hat!" screams Florimel. "Melody Paradise stole The Magic Hat! Thief! Cheat! She stole the hat!"

The cry is taken up and soon the whole marquee rings with the painful accusation that Melody Paradise has purloined The Magic Hat for her own selfish ends.

There is a limit to anyone's resilience. Melody Paradise has now reached hers. The Tribe Of The Last Free Moonbeam withdraw swiftly from the scene leaving pandemonium behind them. The shocking revelation of the whereabouts of The Magic Hat is the final nail in her reputation. Mocked and abused on all sides, there is nothing to do but flee. Streams of outrageous accusations fly in her wake. Anyone who has suffered any misfortune in the past decade now seems to believe that it was all Melody's fault. Suspicions are voiced that she may be a police informer gathering information about travelling subversives.

I follow her up the hill, catching her up as she slides in the mud and falls heavily. Sweep and Megan help her to her feet.

"At least I've rehabilitated The Mushrooms," says Melody, again displaying her uncanny knack of looking on the bright side.

The Tribe Of The Last Free Moonbeam stand loyally by Melody Paradise though even they are shaken by this turn of events.

"What a disaster," says Megan.

"I don't know," says Melody. "It's not all bad. Something good may well come out of it. I mean, on the one hand, the festival is a cold, wet, miserable, unhappy disaster. On the other hand, I am now revealed as the orchestrator of a series of dreadful calamities, which means...which means...eh...I seem to have lost the thread of my argument. Well, it might all turn out well anyway. Does anyone have any spare flowers for my hair?"

Sweep brings news that The Motorbikes Of Merlin have been fighting with The Flying Dementos. The Flying Dementos and The Ancient Secret Knife society hate each other. They all hate Rupert. The rope climbing act has left in disgust.

"So the circus is looking good," says Melody. "How's things with the creative writing class?"

"I haven't thought what to say yet," I admit. "Do you still want me to bring them all out to the valley?"

"Of course."

"But it's a mess. And everyone's quarrelling and fighting. That's hardly going to impress them."

"They'll press for eviction on the spot," says Megan, agreeing with me.

"Probably won't even wait for a court order," says Livia. "Just run us off the land."

Melody Paradise brushes this aside.

"I still think they'll stop objecting to us being here when they get to know us."

Poor Melody Paradise. The recent stress must have unhinged her completely. The whole tribe is crammed into her van, supporting Melody and protecting her from the outraged masses.

"I can't believe I caused all these disasters. No wonder everyone hates me."

"I'm sure they don't hate you," I say. "Although it was a bit of a blunder letting the hat fall at the precise moment."

Melody shrugs.

"It was bound to happen. I told you I was cursed."

She sighs, and wonders out loud why it is so difficult to spread love and peace. There is a knock on the door.

"A lynch mob, I expect," says Melody, and goes to open it.

It isn't a lynch mob, it's Majic Day, come to be friendly. Greatly to Sweep's distress, Majic Day now seems to have gained the position among Melody's suitors. He makes light of the shocking affair of The Magic Hat and supports Melody, which she appreciates. Megan now thinks that he is going to ask her to travel with him. More than that, she thinks that Melody might say yes.

I leave them to it and head off for the fig tree. I'm disappointed that it's had a relapse. Peggy says it's just too weak to cope with all the bad feelings flying round the valley. I determine to give a good performance. Perhaps I can pull it round in a heroic manner, thereby saving the day. For this reading there is a smaller audience. Only Peggy and Roxanna are here. The other Tree Planters are too depressed to leave their tree houses.

"John is missing Ali but won't admit it. Everyone else just wants to leave."

"What about the trees?"

"I expect they'll manage," says Peggy, dourly. Peggy is very annoyed at Melody. Burning down eighteen oak trees has put her well out of favour.

"It could have happened to anyone," I say, in Melody's defence.

"Really? Do you know anyone else who's burned down eighteen oak trees?"

"I suppose not."

I say hello to the fig tree.

"*Hecyra*, usually translated as *The Mother In Law*. Another pleasant romantic comedy."

"Do we have to have romantic comedy all the time?" demands Peggy.

"I thought it was appropriate. You don't want me to start depressing the tree with tragedies do you?"

"Wouldn't matter," says Roxanna. "It's going to die anyway."

It's strange how six days in this valley have transformed previously happy people into prophets of doom. If Jerehmiah was to wander along now he'd be right at home. It just goes to prove what I've said all along, that everyone would be better off living in comfy armchairs in the city. At least we'd be out of the rain. Water now runs in small rivers down the sides of the valley, washing away grass and soil and making some places virtually impassible. In the distance, there is the sound of glass being broken. I ignore it, and get to work, giving one of my finest performances. Peggy and Roxanna might not appreciate it but I swear the fig tree looks more cheerful afterwards.

The festival now learns the truth behind the strange behaviour of The Mushroom Clan, and the mysterious return of Fluffy's memory. It is the result of Magwenwy's terrible revenge. She sneaked up to their encampment and stole every single hallucinogenic mushroom they had, and poured away their tea. She then substituted a very similar variety of dried mushrooms she picked secretly. The permanently dazed Mushrooms did not notice the difference with the result that Fluffy, Tuffy and their friends found themselves drinking, instead of their normal hallucinogenic concoction, a healthy vegetable beverage. Since then they have found themselves unwilling participants in the real world, and quite miserable.

Magwenwy's triumph is tempered by the realisation that The Mushrooms were not responsible for sinking her boat in the first place.

"There again," she says. "I've probably done them a favour. It can't be good for them, being stoned every minute of every day."

The Mushrooms beg her to return their hoard but Magwenwy has thrown it in the river, and it is no more. A frenetic hunt by the Clan has failed to find any more Pscilocibin in the vicinity and they are now reduced to the dire straits of sitting around clutching cider bottles, glumly wandering what to do with themselves.

"I refuse to go back to being a bank clerk," says Tuffy.

After my reading I head for Megan's bus to get warm. Megan is wide eyed with excitement.

"Guess what happened! Magwyn The Grim came down and told Melody Paradise he loved her! He said he was sorry that everyone hates her and he was sorry he was mean to her and he brought her a present to make up for it. A portrait of her in stained glass. It was beautiful. I've never seen anything like it."

"What happened?"

Megan's face falls.

"Melody Paradise was furious. She said to Magwyn how dare he come down here telling her he loved her and bringing her presents when everything was his fault in the first place. She said things would never have gone so wrong if he hadn't killed the Wishing Tree and then she said she was going off travelling with Majic Day and she hoped she never saw Magwyn again unless it was after he'd had a serious accident. And then she smashed the stained glass!"

"Smashed it?"

"That's right. Picked up a hammer and smashed it to pieces. Luckily she'd bought a new tool kit before the festival."

I'm not surprised Megan is agog with excitement. This is surely the first ever recorded act of violence by Melody Paradise.

"So I was right. Magwyn does still love Melody."

"You were," agrees Megan, "but I was right as well. She certainly doesn't love him."

"So she's really going off with Majic Day?"

"That's what she says."

Elsewhere in the valley, it's business as usual. Everyone hates everyone else with the addition that they now also hate Melody Paradise. Circus rehearsals have ground to a halt. Rupert has no better plan than to drive everyone out there tomorrow and hope for the best. He and some of The Galactic Navigators have gone over to Chelwyn to start setting up the arena for the circus. It's being staged in a field outside the village so I'd say that the best hope is for it to be rained off.

Everyone who was meant to be helping is now causing difficulties. Only two people are now working with any real effectiveness. One of these is Magwyn The Grim who, after his rejection by Melody, sets new standards in hostile behaviour, but carries on working. The other is Majic Day, who carries on cheerfully. He seems to believe that the circus can still be successful. He even maintains some optimism about the festival.

"I expect Iris The Peaceful will arrive tonight. I can sort of feel it. Once she's here with the new Wishing Tree everyone will feel better. We'll get the circus done and still have a good time afterwards."

"Aren't you ignoring the fact that everyone now detests Melody Paradise?"

"They'll get over it. How could anyone be upset with Melody for long? We can still enjoy ourselves. All it needs is a little sunshine and a few better tempers. I remember being in the middle of a war in Afghanistan and once the sun started to shine everyone made peace and started dancing."

Majic Day seems to be a man of relentless good humour. Admirable I suppose, but a bit trying after such an unhappy week. Down below us, The Universal Leyline Protectors are enlarging their pyramid, building new sections to fit over the existing structure.

"It never struck me before what a pain these pyramid builders are," says Melody Paradise. "Don't they have anything better to do?"

The staging for the circus is not ready and the acts have not rehearsed but there is no time to do any more.

"How about appealing to some saints for a bit help?" I say to Megan.

Megan fishes a sheet of paper out of her pocket.

"I already have. Saints Bonaventure, David of Sweden, Donald, Swithun, Vladimir, Helier, Plechtelm, Stephen Hardin, Tenenan, Alexis, Kenelm, Martyrs of Scillium, Arnulf, Edburga of Becsterm, Edburga of Bishester, Macrina the Younger, Aril, Margater of Antioch..."

"All right Megan."

"...Wilgefortis, Wulmar, Laurence of Brindisi, Praxededes, Victor, Mary Magdalene, Wandrille, Apolinaris, Bridget of Sweden, Cassian, Apolnuos, Magi, Christine, Wulfhad and Ruffin, Boris and Gleb, Lewinna, Christopher, James the Great, Hoachim and Anne, Pantaleon, the Seven Sleepers, the Seven Apostles of Bulgaria..."

"Megan..."

"...Botvid, Samson, Lupus, Martha, Olaf, Simplicius, Sulian, Abdon and Sennen, Peter Chryologus, Tatwin, Germanus of

Auxerre, Ignatius Loyola, Joseph of Arimathea, Neot, Justin de Jacobis, Helen of Skovde, Alphonsus, Ethelwold, Kyned, Maccabees, Etheldritha, Eusebius, Plegmund, Sidwell, Stephen the first, Thomas of Hales, Manaccus, Waldef, Molua, Sithney, John Baptist Vianney..."

"Please Megan..."

It's no use. Megan is unstoppable and carries on like this for a long time. At the end of her recitation I feel dazed. There certainly seem to be a lot of saints. No danger of a sudden shortage.

"So we should be getting some help from somewhere," says Megan.

"Did you have to ask all of them?"

"Always safest not to leave anyone out. We don't seem to have received much saintly help yet but tomorrow's the twenty third of August and there's loads of saints for that day. I'm sure they'll come through for me in the end."

Outside Megan's bus, I am harassed by a goat, and rescued by Melody Paradise. Florimel strides past with a sneer on her face. Melody retreats into her van to listen to *The Archers*, a farming soap opera which she and Megan follow. One time in *The Archers* some travellers arrived in the village, bringing general consternation to the inhabitants, but it all worked out well in the end.

"Better than things have worked out for us anyway," says Melody.

Night falls. The Golden World Eternal Party Tribe refuse to start up the music on the grounds that there are too many miserable people around for them to play. The Tree Planters announce that they have now disbanded their tribe, unable to carry on in the face of continued internal divisions. Sweep, having heard the news about Melody and Majic Day, is inconsolable, and says he'll never juggle again. The temperature rises and there is some thunder and lightning in the night. As I huddle in my tent this seems to me like a very bad omen.

15th August (Day 32)

Iris The Peaceful lay in her hospital bed, covered in bandages and surrounded by her friends.

"Don't worry," she told them, "I'll be fine. How's my horse?"

"Shocked and disturbed, but no injuries."

"Good. How's the Wishing Tree?"

"Dead," wailed Fuzi, receiving an elbow in the ribs from Hugh, who had told her not to give Iris any bad news till she recovered.

"Oh." Iris looked disappointed.

"I don't suppose we'll make it to the festival now anyway," said Fuzi.

"Why ever not?" asked Iris.

"We can't leave you here."

Iris lay back, tired and sore. She thought about the festival. She was battered and bruised, but not seriously hurt.

"I'll be able to travel soon," she said. "We still might make it before it finishes. Was the truck driver injured?"

"No," answered Hugh. "In fact, he's waiting outside to see you."

Hugh fetched him in. He stood beside Iris's bed looking sheepish.

"Simon," said Iris The Peaceful. "How nice to see you again."

Simon blurted out apologies for crashing into Iris and knocking her off the road.

"I was trying to get to England in time for the festival. I thought you'd be there, I didn't expect you to be just round the next corner."

"You always were a terrible driver," said Iris. "What happened to your motorbike?"

"Wrecked it in Australia," admitted Simon, kneeling down beside Iris and taking her hand. "I've given up biking."

"Good," said Iris. "The world will be a safer place. Although not that much safer, the way you drive a truck."

Simon apologised again. The rest of The Contemplators tactfully left them to catch up on their recent histories.

"How romantic," said Fuzi, outside the ward.

"Extremely romantic," agreed Hugh. "Mowed down by a truck driven by your long-lost lover."

"In the French countryside," added Fuzi, implying that this made it even better.

"Do you think we can make it to the festival?"

"Maybe the last day, if Iris is really up to travelling. But we don't have a Wishing Tree any more."

16th August (Day 33)

I borrowed a tent, took it home, threw it on the floor in disgust and wondered what excuse I should use not to go to the festival tomorrow. Whatever the excuse was, the obvious thing to do was avoid Melody Paradise. If I saw her I knew she'd persuade me to come. I decided to write her a note claiming illness, barricade the doors and keep the lights turned out for the next three days.

I turned on my video game and let it run while I was making tea, and then settled down for a long session. Something was wrong. The city looked different. Population was growing rapidly. Happy messages from the citizens kept flashing onto the screen as they flocked to enjoy themselves in the parks and woodland created by Melody Paradise.

I was amazed. I realised it must be true. Melody Paradise really did have unusual powers of spreading love and peace. She could even spread them to a video game. My on-screen city, Megara, was the happiest city I'd ever seen.

I was finally convinced that I should go to the festival. It seemed at least possible that Melody could protect me from the miseries it would entail. I started packing medical supplies and warm clothing, and several months supplies of cigarettes, just in case I got stranded somewhere.

23rd August (Day 40) Seventh Day Of The Festival

I don't want to do a creative writing class. I'm not going to do it. There is no law saying I have to go to Chelwyn and do a creative writing class. No one can force me.

I determine to remain resolutely in my tent for the whole day. My tent starts to move. Slowly and gently, it starts sliding down the hill. As the tent poles fall around me and it gathers momentum I realise that the last remaining pegs have pulled loose from the sodden ground. My tent, pitched on a gentle incline, is now heading for the river. The flood waters are carrying me away. Faced with the unusual and unnatural fate of drowning in a tent I start panicking and trying to fight my way out. The entire structure collapses about me, wrapping me up in a wet and cloying ball of nylon which starts to roll, gathering speed as I struggle.

"Help!" I wail, plunging downwards towards a watery grave.

Something solid bangs me on the head, stopping my descent. There are a few moments of confusion as someone tries to unzip the flap. Seeing daylight above me, I burst free and grab hold of the nearest object, which turns out to be Melody Paradise.

"Good morning," says Melody, laughing.

"I've been washed away! I could have been drowned! Thanks for saving me."

"I told you tents were useless," says Melody, still laughing. "You wouldn't catch a bender sliding down the hill."

I see that Melody Paradise has recovered some of her good humour.

"All set for your creative writing class?"

"I'm not doing it. I can't face a gathering of stockbrokers right now. What do they want to write for anyway? It's lousy, no one pays you any money."

"They won't pay you if you don't show up," Melody Points out, which is unfortunately true, and a powerful argument.

"What am I going to say to them?"

"Whatever comes into your head," replies Melody.

"What if nothing comes into my head?"

"Make a virtue of it. Tell them silence is creative. Don't worry, it can't be any worse than the circus is going to be."

The circus is now assembling. I have never seen a more sullen group of people. Some of The Motorbikes Of Merlin seem close to tears.

"More arguments with The Flying Dementos?"

Melody nods.

"I don't suppose the summer fair has been much of a success," she says. "All this rain must have spoiled it. Little do they know the worst is yet to come."

"You don't think Rupert might still bring out the best in them? Inspire them to a marvellous performance?"

"No," replies Melody, "I don't. Rupert is in a terrible mood and refuses to speak to anyone. He asked me to go away travelling with him. I told him I was going away with Majic Day. He wasn't very pleased."

The motorbikes are loaded into trucks and form up in a small convoy behind the other acts. Nemo is taking me to my reading in his truck before going on to the circus.

"So, Nemo. How's life in The Galactic Navigators?" I enquire.

"Dreadful," replies Nemo. "One eviction after another and then this damned festival. And now Melody Paradise turns out to be a sneak thief."

He shakes his head, as if to show he doesn't know what the world's coming to.

Mrs Fitzroy meets me at the door of The Queen Elizabeth The First, the country tavern in which I am shortly to make a fool of myself in an upstairs room. Hospitably, she offers me a drink in the downstairs bar. The Queen Elizabeth is an elegantly fitted establishment in which I feel quite out of place, though I'm reassured when I notice someone in the bar who is much, much scruffier than anyone I imagined I'd meet in this rich little village. He's utterly filthy, unkempt, unshaven, and his clothes are hanging in rags. The poor man is a terrible sight. It looks like he's been sleeping in a ditch for the past six months.

I realise that I'm looking in a mirror. The bedraggled specimen is me. No wonder Mrs Fitzroy blanched when I rolled up in Nemo's truck. Being a polite and pleasant woman, however, she doesn't comment on my appalling appearance. I request a whisky with my beer and ask her how the Summer Fair is coming along

"Not too well, I'm afraid. We had to move the fete inside because of the rain and the church hall is still undergoing renovations so that was a bit of a let down. The horse gala was cancelled and the circus has been rather a disappointment, so we're all looking forward to Melody Paradise's, the modern version, especially the teenagers. We've never had anything like it here before."

I wouldn't call it fortunate.

"How about the literary festival?"

"Much better," says Mrs Fitzroy with enthusiasm. "We've had some really excellent readings and the creative writing classes have gone splendidly."

"Splendidly?"

"Absolutely. Yesterday's talk by Salmon Rushdie was nothing short of inspiring. I'm sure people are dusting off their computers all over the village. You have a large crowd waiting upstairs."

My last hope has gone. Had there been only two people in the audience, I could have pretended to be insulted and stormed out. That now seems to be out of the question. I could feign a heart attack. As Mrs Fitzroy leads me upstairs I have the distinct feeling that I'm climbing a scaffold. How did this happen? Where did I go wrong? How did I let Melody Paradise talk me into this? Why have I failed to come up with anything?

I'm carrying my complete works in a Tesco carrier bag. My complete works are now soggy and illegible and leak muddy water onto the carpet. The staircase is furnished with a mahogany banister over which I leave a thick trail of mucky fingerprints. The man chairing the event makes no effort to hide his shock. Nervous giggles sound in the room.

I gaze around me with displeasure. There do seem to a be a lot of people here. Well-dressed women, mainly, all of whom I know have never heard of me but want to attend every day of the festival. Everyone is waiting expectantly. I smile. A few people smile back. I have no idea what to say. The silence becomes awkward.

"Any questions?" I ask.

No one has any questions.

"We thought we'd have questions at the end," says the chairman, "after your talk."

"Right. After the talk. Yes, I suppose that makes sense. After the talk. Although if any one does have any questions I'm quite happy to answer them now. Or after the talk, I suppose."

There is another extended silence. Panic rises and I seriously consider fleeing the scene. Mrs Fitzroy is between me and the door. The window perhaps? Author plunges to grizzly death after creative writing tragedy. I place my carrier bag on the table. Muddy water dribbles out and runs over the table. The chairman looks very unhappy. That makes two of us. Playing for time, I try and offer some explanation for the state I'm in.

"Eh...you may be wondering why I'm so filthy. It's because I've been living in a field for the past week. Very muddy, with all this rain, and nowhere to take a bath. Of course, there is a river but you can't really trust rivers for getting washed in these days with all the pollution everywhere, so what with one thing and another I just got very dirty, I do usually get shaved occasionally but, well, that was difficult to do and...eh...of course most people there are much cleaner than me, don't go away with the idea that travellers are dirty, well, not that they actually are travellers having a festival or anything, just advance workers for the circus. Might travel occasionally I suppose, but wouldn't, I imagine, come under the auspices of the criminal law, not gathered illegally or anything like that, just clean circus workers, very clean, do a few motorbike tricks then get washed immediately, remarkably clean really, given the difficult circumstances, quite heroic efforts on the part of Melody Paradise and her friends to keep clean no matter what the consequences, cleanest bunch of people you could meet, no question about it, children inordinately well-looked after, hot bath everyday, remarkably clean children..."

I grind to a halt. I seem to have exhausted the topic. The audience is gaping at me. I wish I wasn't here. I wish I'd drunk more. I wish that woman in the front row wasn't craning forward with a pencil in her hand waiting to take notes. I cast around for something to say.

"'How can I improve my technique?', young writers often ask me. Read your book to a tree is my invariable advice..."

The circus is now set up in a field outside the village. Majic Day is mainly responsible for this. Rupert, outraged by Melody's rejection, refuses to co-operate. Majic Day has taken over the task of organising people, marshalling The Galactic Navigators who arrive with the props and staging equipment. Magwyn The Grim angrily shuns all offers of assistance in setting up his props but he works hard and, by dint of his and Majic Day's labour, the circus is ready to begin almost on time.

The performers, having argued over billing, timing, length of performances, past grudges and various other matters, now refuse to communicate with each other, and sit around with an air of indifference.

"So you'll come on right after Sweep does the motorbike leap?" says Majic Day.

"Don't care," reply The Flying Dementos. "Just get it over with so we can get out of here."

Megan has done a fine job on The Ancient Secret Knife Society's new costumes and they're parading round in colourful mediaeval cloaks and hats. Despite this, they lack spirit, and flourish their knives with little real gusto. Gusto is in very short supply. For a circus it is remarkably cheerless. The performers puff gloomily on joints and make no effort to warm up. The utter misery of the festival followed them here and nothing can shift it. Starshine, Moonshine and Sunshine, also in mediaeval costume, are meant to be wandering through the crowd doing bits of juggling and shouting out old-fashioned street cries, thus creating some atmosphere, but their half-hearted attempts are sad to see.

"Come and see the circus," says Moonshine, almost inaudibly.

"Greatest spectacle on earth," says Starshine, sounding like a judge pronouncing a death sentence.

"Death-defying motorbike thrills," mutters Sunshine, then sits on the ground and buries her face in her hands.

Mary is providing the music but the sound keeps going wrong and she curses behind her decks. Even Sweep is unhappy. Normally the prospect of performing transforms him from his normal shy self into a confident, even ebullient person, but the bad news about

Melody Paradise going away with Majic Day has crushed his spirit.

Around half of the people in the valley have come over to view the performance and sprawl behind the area from which the acts will enter the field. The spectators are gathered around the other three sides on red plastic chairs which sink deep into the damp earth. Melody Paradise, dented but not crushed, wanders round smiling at everyone, handing out flowers and charming the audience. The extreme difficulties in which she has found herself at the festival have not prevented her from arranging her hair to perfection. Some of her tresses now reach down to her knees and there are more colours, more shells and beads, more silver rings, a huge ocean of colour ebbing and flowing in the breeze. Even the most staid of villagers cannot prevent themselves from gazing admiringly at her incredible locks as she waltzes past with her basket of flowers, and bells jingling on her ankles. Travellers children mingle with children from the village, following her like a little band of happy disciples.

"Hello," she says, handing me a flower. "How did the creative writing class go?"

"Quite a lively affair."

"They liked it?"

"Not exactly. I've been warned never to come back to the village."

"It was that bad?"

"Afraid so. Halfway through the chairman denounced me as an impostor and claimed I'd never written a book in my life. Widespread dissatisfaction among the audience nearly led to rioting. It came to a shocking end when someone bounced a Maeve Binchy omnibus off my head. If Mrs Fitzroy hadn't calmed things down, I'd never have got out alive."

"What went wrong?"

I shrug.

"I don't know. I did my best. I told them all about reading to trees. They thought I was making fun of them. The woman who runs the Post Office led an assault on the stage. That's the trouble with these country villagers, no appreciation of nature."

"What about the young people?"

"They just looked bored. They wanted to hear about drugs and sex and music, not trees. Most of them left after the first five minutes. I'm afraid I've failed you Melody. I can't bring my creative writing class out to the valley to see what nice people you all are. I was planning to get them all enthusiastic about reading to the trees but it all went sadly wrong. Incidentally, Mrs Fitzroy knows you're holding a festival in the valley. I don't think she cares."

"I know," says Melody Paradise. "She's a nice woman. I think if she didn't like us, we'd have been chased off by now, circus or no circus."

Melody Paradise doesn't seem to mind that I failed in my task of bringing villagers to the valley. Perhaps she knew it was no longer a good idea with everyone being in such bad humour and the valley in such a poor state.

"Excuse me, Melody, I think these people are staring at me. I'd better go and hide with the performers."

Melody lets me go. She herself is unable to hide with the performers as the performers are surrounded by her family and her family is now shunning her. Poor Melody. The Tree Planters hate her. The Riverboat Tribe detest her. The Militant Children Of Lemuria are threatening to take out an injunction if she ever comes near one of their protests again. Even Rooster and Rag have been heard sniggering at Florimel's cruel jokes against her. Who could have imagined Melody would ever become such an outcast?

I secrete myself behind the motorbikes, well away from the villagers, and await the performance. If recent events are anything to go by, this will surely be one of the most disastrous events ever staged. Sweep will inevitably be run over by a motorbike. The Flying Dementos will plunge to their deaths, probably taking some of the audience with them. I am confidently expecting the worst, and I'm not the only one.

Everything that was expected to go well has utterly failed. The circus, which is expected to fail, goes very well. The costumes look cheap, the props are rickety, and the choreography between the acts non-existent, but when the acts do manage to make it into the field they perform excellently. I can only assume that they are all overtaken with professional pride when they find themselves in front of an audience. No one gives a bad performance. The crowd, though bored by the long gaps between acts, is impressed.

The Motorbikes Of Merlin, eight in all, their riders dressed in shabby leather and rusted metal, roar into view waving flags and chain-saws. They then race round the field, round each other, through flaming hoops, into flaming oil drums, and over and along the artificial walls, planks and runways as constructed by Magwyn. This involves a lot of near-collisions, a great deal of noise and copious amounts of fire and smoke. The Motorbikes Of Merlin find it unsatisfactory to ride over anything that isn't burning fiercely and soon a great pall of smoke hovers above the field, adding to the drama. They chase each other with chain-saws, cut one bike completely in half, reduce another to smoking wreckage, ride five people on one bike then one person on five bikes, leap, spin, roll over, and perform many other next-to-impossible feats of biking skill.

The Motorbikes Of Merlin depart to great applause. Majic Day announces the next act as The Ancient Secret Knife Society. After an interval of twenty minutes or so during which there is a great deal of struggling and cursing off-stage as last minute adjustments go wrong, they troop into the arena to give of their best.

The Ancient Secret Knife Society are a cross between jugglers and knife throwers and acrobats. They run along tightropes juggling chain-saws while their companions toss knives at them, or juggle scythes and axes over the heads of the audience. They stage a mock battle during which so many blades whiz through the air that it seems inevitable that someone will get killed before they storm into their grand finale, the chainsaw spectacular. Adults scream and children gaze in wonder as whirring chain-saws are sent spinning through the air, plucked effortlessly out of the sky and sent spinning off again. The Society have called quite heavily on the services of Starshine and her piercing gun, which all adds to the effect. Children applaud wildly as men and women in mediaeval garb with multiple piercings rush by, each juggling two chain-saws and a broadsword and passing them through the air to each other as if it was the easiest thing in the world.

The Ancient Secret Society of Knives also leave the field to great cheering. They bow to the audience, and themselves seem much more cheerful than when they arrived. I notice that they are congratulated by The Motorbikes Of Merlin.

Next on is Sweep. This is poor timing as Sweep is basically a juggler and we have just seen some spectacular juggling. However, as several acts failed to turn up at the festival it was inevitable that this would happen. Sweep is aware of the problem. He's intimated that he has the matter well in-hand and has worked out a few new routines that will delight any audience. Dressed as a mediaeval jester with a poor sense of colour he enters the field on his unicycle. This now stands an impressive fifteen feet off the ground. The club juggling with which he starts his act is rather tame compared to the other acts but is still impressive given that he is perched precariously on his one-wheeled bicycle, swaying to and fro like a ship in a gale. Majic Day is in close attendance, retrieving the occasional dropped club, and lighting fire-clubs when required. Sweep rides his unicycle round the field juggling three fire-clubs and when he adds a fourth he gets a great round of applause. He rides a smaller unicycle along a tightrope, stopping in the middle to juggle, and tumbles athletically off the end of the rope before announcing that he is now going to perform his greatest trick, a leap from one motorbike to another while juggling any three items tossed to him by the audience.

Two of The Motorbikes Of Merlin race onto the field. Sweep mounts one of them, clutching a shoe, an orange and a potted plant, as donated by the crowd. When Sweep stands up on the pillion of one of the bikes I wonder if this is the start of the anticipated disaster, but he pulls the stunt off magnificently. As the fast moving bikes draw level Sweep leaps from one to the other with tremendous skill, all the while juggling the shoe, orange and potted plant. The crowd bays its appreciation and Sweep exits in triumph.

After another very long gap, The Flying Dementos' lorry lumbers onto the field. The hydraulic apparatus raises a platform thirty feet into the air. Three trapezes and several ropes hang in a row from the platform. The Flying Dementos swarm up the ropes and position themselves on the trapezes. There are six of them, all women, all dressed in orange lycra jump suits and each with bright pink hair. They look spectacular, though they also look very young to be performing such dangerous stunts.

The Flying Dementos exhibit vast enthusiasm for their work. The trapeze artists I've seen have often struck me as rather cold, if skilful, but The Flying Dementos are anything but cold. They whoop and scream as they perform, pulling faces at the crowd, as if scared that at any moment they might plummet to the ground. After each terrifying stunt they waste no time in posing but hurry on to the next part of their act. The six acrobats clamber this way and that over the ropes and trapezes and over each other, swinging on a trapeze three and four at a time, hanging on to each others' wrists or ankles. At the highest point, the women let go of each other to somersault through the air before grasping the next trapeze, or being plucked out of the void by another passing Demento. Many times it seems that they have misjudged the distance and must fall to the ground but each time a hand or foot appears above them and drags them to safety.

The Flying Dementos appear to be in such continual danger that it's exhausting to watch. Their finale, a complicated manoeuvre which sees all six of them hanging in a line from one trapeze and each in turn climbing up the bodies of the other, all the while swinging high in the air, before carrying out a mass triple somersault on to the next trapeze, and then the next, leaves me, and the rest of the audience, gasping for breath.

The Flying Dementos stand on each others' shoulders, high above us, and acknowledge the applause. The lorry drives off the field with the acrobats smiling and waving goodbye. The circus is over. It was shorter than was intended but other than that Chelwyn Village can have no complaints because it was a fine performance in every way. As the performers run back onto the field to take a bow the villagers and tourists applaud them loudly and various members of the Fair Committee stride forward to shake their hands.

Melody Paradise looks very happy. It has all been a great success, the only success of the festival. It may have been the general opinion that no one cared what the circus was like but now it has gone so well everyone is pleased. There are congratulations all round; to the performers, to Rupert, to Majic Day, and even to Magwyn. And Melody Paradise, mingling with the throng, does not seem to be as unpopular as she was this morning.

The good feeling generated by the circus lessens the bad feeling around Melody Paradise. As the bikes and equipment are packed up, Melody wanders round congratulating everyone and most people are reasonably friendly towards her. Her main detractors are not here but Breed seems to be speaking to Melody again.

"I suppose you burning us out of our tree houses was good practice for dodging bailiffs," says Breed, and manages a rueful smile. Breed, who is not given to mysticism, is not really concerned about Melody's theft of The Magic Hat.

"So can I come to your protests again?" says Melody.

"Of course," replies Breed. "It always helps to have someone handing out flowers to the police."

Despite her slightly hard exterior, Breed is a good-natured woman. I like her. I'm pleased she likes Melody again. Faith in Melody is restored sufficiently for Ali to plead with her to do something to bring him back together with his boyfriend.

"John is a fool who doesn't know anything about trees or people," he says, "but I miss him terribly."

Melody Paradise promises to do what she can.

In one area misery is unbounded. After the excitement of his performance, Sweep suffers a terrible come-down and the sight of Melody Paradise holding hands with Majic Day is too much for him to bear. He takes the first available lift back to the valley where he plans to throw himself in the river. Poor Sweep. And poor

Rupert, I suppose, though it's hard to feel sympathy for someone I dislike so much. He only rouses himself from his brooding to accept congratulations on the staging of the circus, and claim all the credit for its success. Magwyn The Grim refuses to even acknowledge anyone's praise for his contribution to the event. He turns his back on the world, tosses his tools into his truck and departs without a word.

I ride back to the valley in Melody's van.

"Things are going better now," she says. "Okay, I admit I made a few blunders, wrecked a generator, burned down some trees, sank a boat, stole The Magic Hat, destroyed a pyramid, but these things happen. Life goes on."

"Everyone will forget them soon," says Majic Day.

"Thanks for all your help," says Melody, and squeezes his hand.

"Isn't the festival ending tonight?" I ask, rather anxious that it might not be. It is high time I was back in the city earning a living.

"Maybe not," Melody informs me. "I was speaking to Mrs Fitzroy. You were right, she does know all about it but she doesn't mind. She thinks the other members of the council probably won't mind either if we stay on a few days, after we entertained the villagers and didn't loot the shops or burn any cottages. So unless the police take it into their heads to turn nasty we should be all right for a while."

"But I have to get home."

"Why?" says Melody.

"I need my comfy armchair."

"Come and sit in mine."

"I need a bath."

"I'll heat up some water for you on my stove."

"Melody, stop trying to spread love and peace in my direction. I want to go home. I'm miserable."

"Stay and have fun."

"Like the fun I've already had?"

"Unfortunate circumstances," says Melody, waving her hands in the air, a bad idea as she is still driving at the time. "Things'll be better now."

I'm worried by the prospect of having to stay longer but comfort myself with the thought that it's unlikely to happen. Melody Paradise is again being carried away by her optimistic nature. Just because the circus went well does not mean that love and peace will now reign in the valley. All the travellers are already packing up to leave. Even in the unlikely event of Melody persuading them to stay, some new calamity will drive them away.

Pyramid rivalry is still rife in the valley. The Universal Leyline Protectors have now extended their pyramid so that it is larger than that of The Elemental Sunshine Family, which pleases them, though no one else much cares. They will in any case have to dismantle it soon. Everyone is packing up to leave. Tatting down, Megan calls it. The Clan Of The Night Time Elves are folding up their damp and mud-stained banners and The Golden World Eternal Party Tribe are starting to dismantle the marquee.

"This won't do at all," cries Melody, leaping from her van. Unfortunately, exposure as the purloiner of The Magic Hat has not cured her clumsiness. She sprawls in the mud, taking Majic Day with her. They roll down the slope, coming to rest in a large tyre rut. Already lying in the tyre rut are Bug and Simple, insensibly drunk. I help them all out. Melody wipes the mud off her face and rings some stagnant water from her shirt. Simple has been sick and the mess covers the front of his jacket.

"If you do write about us," says Melody Paradise, "be sure not to glamorise it too much."

I promise not to. Melody Paradise goes off to try and persuade everyone to stay a little longer. The Universal Leyline Protectors form up into a defensive line in front of their pyramid as she passes.

"Run for your lives," shouts Florimel. "It's Melody Paradise, the Hippy Terminator."

I decide that no matter what, I'm leaving tomorrow. If Melody insists on staying, I'll hitch a lift to London and if I can't do that I'll walk over to Chelwyn and catch a bus. My tent has collapsed again. I determine to say some very harsh things about festivals in my next book. I will expose them altogether and warn everybody never to attend, particularly if there is any danger of The Tribe Of The Last Free Moonbeam being there.

Sweep is slumped in his bender. He has decided that rather than throw himself in the river he is just going to lie there for the rest of his life.

"How could she go off with Majic Day? I can't believe it. They're not suited for each other at all."

He props himself up on one elbow.

"Do you think it'll last?"

I shrug.

"I don't know."

"I must find out," says Sweep. "If it's only a temporary infatuation I might be able to last it out. I know!"

He leaps to his feet.

"I'll ask Eko to read the future for me!"

Sweep rushes from his bender, eager for a prediction. Some time later he trudges back in, shoulders drooping.

"I can't ask Eko," he says. "I buried all his predicting things."

"All of them?"

"All of them. His runes, his I Ching, his Earth Mother Tarot cards, his Past Life cards and his book of shamanistic rituals. Archaeologists may one day think this was a major site for making predictions."

"Don't lie around moping. Come with me while I read to the fig tree."

Sweep looks up at me, his eyes gleaming in a contemptuous manner.

"I have just lost the love of my life and you want me to listen to you reading to a fig tree? I never realised it before but you're mad. No wonder I never stood a chance with Melody Paradise. I should never have listened to your advice. Throw Pookie in the river indeed."

Stung by this despicable and unfair criticism, I take my leave with dignity, and walk up the valley towards the tree.

"Hello Peggy. How's the fig tree?"

"Who cares?" answers Peggy.

I'm shocked. The demise of The Tree Planters has really affected her badly.

"Well, Peggy, I thought I'd finish off the works of Terence anyway, you know. It would be a shame to miss a day."

Peggy glances over at Roxanna. They both shake their heads.

"Mad person," says Roxanna.

"Goes around reading to trees," says Peggy, with weary sympathy.

"You better take care," advises Roxanna. "Once these manias take hold they're difficult to shift."

"I heard they ran you out of Chelwyn after you told them all to read to trees," adds Peggy, and they nod wisely to each other.

"I'm only reading to the damn tree because The Tree Planters asked me to."

"The Tree Planters are no more," says Peggy, and turns her back on me.

I leave them to their packing.

"Sorry, it's just me today, fig tree. The Tree Planters were, er...too busy to come. I'm sure they'll say goodbye to you before they leave. Well, this is the sixth time I've read to you, and the last, which works out conveniently enough because Terence only wrote six plays. This one is a slightly more complex affair so you'll have to pay close attention. It contains some elements of family rivalry and hostility between fathers and sons but don't worry, there's a good amount of romantic comedy in it as well. I know you like romantic comedy. I like romantic comedy. I don't like anything with adventures or suspense. I get enough adventure and suspense just trying to pay my electricity bill."

I realise that I'm starting to tell the tree my problems. This could, I suppose, be construed as aberrant behaviour.

"Well, enough of that. On with the entertainment. *The Brothers*, or, in Latin, *Adelphoe*. First performed in 160 BC, and later adapted by Moliere. Moliere was French. You probably knew that already. It starts off with Micio complaining about young people having no manners..."

"We're all doomed," cries a voice in the wilderness. "Melody Paradise's shameful relations with Majic Day will bring destruction on us all."

"Hello Eko."

Eko is too busy going on about doom and destruction to acknowledge me.

"Melody Paradise living in a van with Majic Day is a great abomination. Great misery will come in the wake of this unnatural action. The flood waters will wash us all away."

I have to object to this.

"Come on Eko, you're just annoyed because you wanted her for yourself."

Eko sniffs, and says he is not going to discuss matters of importance with a man who publicly reads to fig trees.

"But mark my words. Melody Paradise will bring about the destruction of the new Wishing Tree when it arrives."

Well, there's a thought. The new Wishing Tree. What happened to Iris The Peaceful? Members of The Elemental Sunshine Family and Universal Leyline Protectors jostle each other as they pass.

"You see?" cries Eko. "It's starting already. Terror in the valley. First The Leyline Protectors and The Sunshine Family massacre each other. Then War, Famine, Pestilence and Plague ride through. We're all doomed."

As evening falls, Eko can still be heard ranting away to himself, but I doubt if Melody Paradise teaming up with Majic Day can bring any more terror to the valley than already exists.

"Take care of Pookie will you?" says Sweep. "Megan's hiding from social workers again."

"Why me?"

"Because I can't be bothered. I'm going to lie in my bender and pine away. Melody's in the Peaceful Grove with..."

His voice tails off. Tears form in his eyes. He thrusts Pookie into my arms and hurries off. The baby starts to howl.

"Fancy a visit to the Peaceful Grove, young Pookie?"

The journey over the treacherous terrain is as difficult as ever, with the additional hazard of drunken and confused Mushrooms lying around in unexpected places. Still unable to cope with their enforced return to normality they have started to drop to the ground no matter where they are, cradling beer or cider bottles in their arms as protection. This alcohol has been kindly donated by others, as The Mushrooms have none of their own. The bar is now closed. Melody had reserved some money to restock it for the end of the festival but has deemed it to be not worth while. She now intends to use it to help with the countless repairs to vehicles and property necessitated by the chaos at the festival.

I had expected to find only Melody and Majic Day in the Peaceful Grove but find instead a large gathering.

"What's going on?" I whisper to Mary,

"Melody is having one last desperate throw at spreading peace and love."

"It's a lost cause."

"It's already gone badly. Magwyn The Grim arrived and Melody sent him packing. Told him he had no business being in the Peaceful Grove seeing as on his last visit he massacred the Wishing Tree."

I'm feeling a little sorry for Magwyn these days. It must be hard being the only person in the world that Melody Paradise hates.

"Get on with it Melody," shouts an impatient Golden World Eternal Partyer. "We're meant to be tatting down."

"Don't leave," says Melody "Now the circus has gone well no one will disturb us for a while. We really should finish clearing up the valley before we depart. And then we can all stay and enjoy ourselves."

Loud and raucous is the laughter which greets this suggestion.

"Stay and drown more like."

"It's stopped raining. It'll be sunny tomorrow."

More raucous laughter.

"It's time to start getting along with each other."

On cue, John and Ali start fighting and a furious squabble breaks out among the ranks of what were The Tree Planters. Melody Paradise drums her fingers against her thigh and looks as if she may be tempted into her second ever act of violence. She restrains herself.

"Please stop fighting," says Melody, placing her hands on John and Ali. All of a sudden they look ashamed of themselves, and stop fighting.

"Please stop fighting," says Melody again, and rests her hands on Peggy's arm. Peggy and the rest of The Tree Planters immediately stop fighting.

There is a moment of surprised silence. No one expects Melody's words to have any effect any more. Pookie starts to cry. Melody Paradise pats him on the head. Pookie stops crying, and gurgles happily.

"Melody, your powers must be returning!" cries Breed.

"Melody's Paradise's powers are returning!" cry a few others, although many remain unconvinced. We all stare at her, wondering if, despite everything, she might have recovered her superhuman talent for spreading love and peace. Melody reaches behind her and picks up a large clay urn.

"Iris The Peaceful has not arrived with the new Wishing Tree," she says. "So we'll just have to do the best we can with the old one. I'm sorry I took The Magic Hat."

There is some hostile muttering as Mary produces the hat from her bag.

"But I'm now going to make up for it," continues Melody Paradise. "I'm going to plant it."

The audience is stunned. Almost any weird behaviour is acceptable among Melody's family but planting a hat does seem to be going a little too far.

"You're going to plant The Magic Hat? Why?"

"Because it contains the last sprig of the old Wishing Tree. Since Magwyn poisoned it everything's gone wrong, so I'm going to replace it the best I can."

"But it's just a dead twig. It won't grow."

"It might. Even if it doesn't there will at least be a part of the Wishing Tree where it should be. And I'm giving it plenty of encouragement. Me and Peggy have prepared our finest magic growing water, full of good vibrations and loving, positive thoughts."

Melody brandishes the clay urn. She now has the complete attention of the assembled tribes. Even Florimel is intrigued by the idea of planting a hat and fertilising it with magic water. Melody places the hat in the hole. Majic Day takes the urn and prepares to pour the water over it.

"You're sure it's not weed killer this time?" says a voice from the shadows.

At this moment it starts to rain again, quite heavily. Rupert emerges from the darkness, a very unpleasant expression on his face.

"What do you mean?"

"I mean the last time you used that urn to pour water on the Wishing Tree you poured weed killer on instead. And killed the tree."

At this shocking accusation, the Peaceful Grove explodes in amazement. Moonshine and Starshine, perched on top of the standing stone, fall off in astonishment and even a slumbering Mushroom in the corner briefly raises his head. Rupert smiles in grim satisfaction at the uproar.

"You're lying," screams Melody Paradise. "It was Magwyn The Grim."

"I wasn't. It was you!" screams Rupert. "You ridiculous hippy. You don't know what you're doing from one minute to the next. I remember it if you don't. The Tree Planters put the weed killer in your van for safekeeping while they went to look after a tree."

"But it was in an oil can," protests Melody Paradise.

"No it wasn't. It was in that urn. You had to put it there because the oil can was leaking. And then, being the fool you are, next morning you forgot about it and thought it was your ridiculous blessed water. Which you then dumped on the bush and killed it."

Rupert smiles coldly.

"And blamed Magwyn afterwards," he adds, maliciously.

"Is this true?" screams John The Tree Planter.

"Eh..." says Melody Paradise.

John turns on Peggy.

"Was the oil can leaking?"

Peggy nods.

"And did you put the weed killer into Melody's urn?"

"Not exactly," replies Peggy, after a pause. "Melody put it in. Sorry Melody. I guess it must have been you that did it after all."

"Try spreading love and peace now you preposterous fraud," sneers Rupert. He turns sharply, trips over a Mushroom, staggers out of the Peaceful Grove and leaves the valley. He leaves the valley in malignant triumph. Melody Paradise is meanwhile at the lowest point in her career and is mocked and abused on all sides. Angry festival go-ers spill out of the Peaceful Grove to spread the news that not only has Melody Paradise subjected them to a week of misery and torment in the valley, she was responsible for all their problems in the first place.

"Melody Paradise killed the Wishing Tree," they cry. "No wonder she's cursed. The woman's evil. Run for your lives!"

The Nomadic Daughters Of Lilith howl with rage. Rag and Rooster join in, declaring that they are now leaving The Tribe Of The Last Free Moonbeam.

"It's the only safe thing to do. Imagine what might happen if we stay?"

There is now no question of the festival continuing. It is over. The valley will remain a mess, and the tribes will remain at war. Pursued by jeers and catcalls, Melody Paradise and Majic Day troop slowly out of the Grove and head for their vehicles. The rain pours down in torrents.

"Don't leave," says Megan, loyally.

Pookie starts to howl. Melody pats him on the head. He again stops crying, so I know that Melody's powers are indeed returning, too late.

"I killed the Wishing Tree," she sighs. "No wonder I'm cursed."

Melody climbs into her van.

"Don't leave," say David and Livia and Finan. So Melody Paradise, though reviled, is not completely deserted. Despite this she has no spirit for remaining in the valley. Nor it would seem, any enthusiasm for travelling off with Majic Day.

260

"I'll meet up with you later," she says, and climbs into her van alone. Left behind, Majic Day looks hurt and confused.

"Where?" he asks, but Melody Paradise doesn't reply.

"Poor Magwyn," she mutters, and starts her engine.

"Magwyn," mutters Megan.

Indeed. It strikes me that not only is Magwyn The Grim still in love with Melody Paradise, but that he must have known all along about the Tree, and taken the blame to protect Melody Paradise. The man is a romantic hero, after all.

Abuse is still coming from all directions. Melody starts her engine and releases the clutch. The van is parked on a slope and the grass beneath the wheels has turned to mud. Melody Paradise is a poor driver, and her van is in a state of perpetual disrepair. As she releases the brakes she startles everyone by roaring off backwards rather than forwards, and plummets in reverse down the valley towards the river. There are horrified screams as Melody Paradise thunders down the slope out of control, destroying everything in her path. Rarely can a group of people have exhibited such anguish as The Universal Leyline Protectors, as Melody's van hurtles through their pyramid, razing it to the ground for the fourth time in six days.

"Jump!" screams Megan, but it has all happened too fast, and Melody does not jump. Her van flies down the river bank, crunches onto Magwenwy's boat, and they both sink without trace.

Absolute pandemonium now breaks out in the valley.

"Magwenwy!" scream The Riverboat Tribe, pouring out of Amesh's narrow boat.

"Melody!" scream The Tribe Of The Last Free Moonbeam, sprinting down the valley as fast as they can go and sliding and falling in the mud. Everyone runs frantically towards the river. Even The Leyline Protectors forget their ruined pyramid and charge down the hill, howling in the rain and darkness that Melody Paradise is dead, or will be unless somebody saves her.

I'm knocked off my feet by Florimel who sprints ahead of the crowd, stripping off her jacket as she prepares to dive to the rescue. The nomadic and athletic Daughter Of Lilith easily out-distances everybody apart from one other, Magwyn The Grim. Florimel and Magwyn hit the water simultaneously and disappear beneath the surface.

At the river bank panic and confusion have set in. People are screaming, wailing and waving their arms about, and straining over the bank for a sight of Melody, Magwenwy, or their rescuers. Others splash about in the inky water. Amesh and The Riverboat Tribe dive in to help and The Galactic Navigators shout for their lifting equipment. Not that there will be time to use lifting equipment. The river is not very deep, but it's deep enough to drown in, particularly if you're trapped.

To my immense relief, Melody quickly rises to the surface. She's freed herself from her van and swum clear. She wades towards the shore.

"Sorry Magwenwy!" she cries. "I didn't mean to sink your boat again."

She pauses, looking round.

"Where's Magwenwy?"

"Still under the water!" screams everyone on the bank.

"Oh no!" wails Melody, and dives beneath the surface.

It is very dark. The lights from the nearby boats cast just enough light to illuminate the grim scene. Cheers break out as The Riverboat Tribe suddenly rise to the surface with Magwenwy in their arms.

"I'm all right!" cries Magwenwy. "Where's Melody Paradise?"

"She went back under looking for you!" yells the crowd.

"Oh no!" says Magwenwy, and to the dismay of The Riverboat Tribe dives back under the water.

Magwyn and Florimel now surface, spitting out water and looking panicky.

"We can't find them!" screams Magwyn.

"They went back under to look for each other!" shouts Pixie.

Magwyn immediately flings himself back beneath the surface. Florimel, with a look of some frustration, does likewise.

The next person to surface is Magwenwy.

"Melody's in trouble!" she calls. "Her hair's caught in my boat!"

At this grim intelligence, Sweep leaps into the water to join in the rescue, and he and Magwenwy sink into the depths.

There is more splashing. Florimel and Magwyn appear.

"They're still underwater!" screams Megan. "Melody's in trouble."

Magwyn and Florimel disappear. Mirabel, Michael and Patrick, fearing that more help is required, now throw themselves into the water.

Almost immediately, Melody Paradise rises into view.

"I think I lost a lock!" she says. "A green one. Where is everybody?"

"Underwater, looking for you," is the reply.

"Oh dear," says Melody, and submerges again.

Somewhere in the far distance there is a rumble of thunder. Florimel, water streaming off her long white locks, river weed trailing from her limbs, rises from the depths like a river goddess. Mirabel is with her and they're supporting Michael, who has got into difficulties and swallowed a lot of water. They drag him to the bank where he's hauled ashore. Magwyn again appears, this time with Patrick.

"Melody's trapped!" he shouts.

"No she isn't," shouts back Megan. "She freed herself. She went back to look for Magwenwy."

"We haven't seen Sweep for a while," yells Mary. "He can't swim very well.

"Melody!" screams Magwyn in a voice of anguish. "Where are you?"

With that he once more hurtles into the depths of the river.

"Oh for God's sake," says Florimel, shaking her head, and follows him under.

Once more there is an anxious silence, broken only by Fluffy.

"They're all dead!" she wails, which is not the most helpful thing she could have said. The rain teems down, making the riverbank treacherous. Pixie falls into the river and floats like a whale.

Florimel, Magwyn, Mirabel, Magwenwy, and Patrick now rise in a group, carrying with them the unfortunate Sweep, who is spitting out water and gasping for breath. Pixie floats into their midst, waving genially.

"Is everybody here now?" demands Florimel, standing up to her waist in the water with her hands on her hips.

"Melody's missing," yells Megan. The crowd groans. The rescuers groan. There is an attempt at another mass dive but Florimel rudely grabs her companions and tells them to stay where they are.

"Stop getting in the way," she demands. "You can't move down there for flailing bodies. I'll look for Melody. You stay here. And if she appears, don't let her go under again. What the hell's the matter with the woman?"

With that Florimel again launches herself into the depths. Despite her admonitions, Magwyn determinedly follows her. The other rescuers, blowing hard, remain where they are, standing in the water. Oddly, Majic Day has not joined in the rescue, but stands anxiously on the bank. There is this time a longer gap. A worrying amount of time passes and no one rises to the surface.

"They're dead!" screams Fluffy.

"Please stop saying that," says Megan, as Pookie starts to cry.

Magwyn and Florimel finally surface, bearing Melody. Not surprisingly after her numerous trips under water, she's now looking rather the worse for wear. Magwyn holds her upright as they struggle towards the shore.

"Have we got everyone now?" demands Florimel.

Everyone agrees that they have.

"Good. If anyone else goes under they're on their own. I'm fucked if I'm rescuing anyone else."

They all start wading towards the bank. It is at this moment that Iris The Peaceful and The Contemplators make their long delayed appearance.

"Hello," says Iris. "Having a swim?"

This cheerful line is answered by a confused barrage of greetings, complaints and explanations.

"Melody Paradise and Magwenwy nearly drowned!"

"Magwyn and Florimel rescued them!"

"Melody sank Magwenwy's boat again!"

"Again?" says Iris, questioningly, being unaware that she had sunk it even once.

"It's true," admits Melody Paradise, still up to her waist in water.

"I'm sorry about your boat, Magwenwy. Again."

Magwenwy turns on Melody.

"You're a menace to society," she rages, shock turning to anger. "Particularly my society. What's the matter with you? Can't you leave me alone for five minutes? Do you have to keep sinking my boat?"

"I'm sorry," repeats Melody, woefully. "And Magwyn, I'm so sorry I kept blaming you for the tree when it was me all along."

"What?" says Iris from the bank.

"Melody Paradise killed the Wishing Tree!" cry a chorus of onlookers.

Magwyn, while keen not to let Melody Paradise drown in front of his eyes, does not seem so keen to accept her apology. After harbouring his love all this time and loyally keeping Melody's terrible secret safe, he now obviously feels that the recent public humiliation of being ejected from the Peaceful Grove was one humiliation too many. He stands in the river in haughty silence.

"Melody burned the trees as well," says Mary to Iris.

"And she keeps wrecking my pyramid," complains Patrick, from the river.

"I'm completely sick of your pyramid," says Megan.

"Me too," agrees Florimel.

"Well, I'm sick of you going round like some warrior queen with an attitude problem," retorts Patrick.

At the uncommon sight of her friends standing up to their waists in the river in the middle of the night, arguing with each other, Iris The Peaceful looks perplexed.

"What's been happening here?" she asks.

"Countless disasters," snarls Florimel.

"Well, at least everyone's safe," says Iris. "Shouldn't you all get out of the water now?"

They all take heed of this sensible suggestion, and haul themselves wearily onto the bank.

"My boat," moans Magwenwy.

"Don't worry," Iris reassures her. "We can refloat it in the morning. I'm sure Melody's van won't have damaged it as much as The Mushroom's bus."

"Maybe not. But everything will be ruined."

Magwenwy, tired and displeased, trudges off with The Riverboat Tribe to the warmth of Amesh's boat. Majic Day helps pull Melody Paradise out of the water. He embraces her, and feels obliged to apologise for not joining in with the rescue, for the good reason that he can't swim.

"Ha!" cackles Sweep. "Can't even swim."

Melody Paradise doesn't seem to care one way or the other. She hurries over to the departing Magwyn and prevents him from leaving by grabbing his shoulder, hauling him round to face her, and putting her arms round him. She then kisses him.

"I love you," she says.

I believe that a small tear might form in Magwyn The Grim's eye. With the persistent rain, it's hard to be sure.

"I love you," says Magwyn.

The crowd looks on in bewilderment. Iris approaches the couple.

"Go and get dry," she says, and gives them a gentle push. Magwyn and Melody disappear into the darkness, arm in arm. While others are surprised to see Melody comfortably ensconced in Magwyn's arms, with Majic Day reduced to the role of onlooker, Iris The Peaceful seems to accept it as natural.

Melody Paradise turns round to call over her shoulder to Iris.

"It really was me that killed the Wishing Tree!".

"Never mind," Iris replies. "I've brought a new one."

So no one has suffered any serious injury during the second boat–sinking–incident, which is extremely fortunate. It was a potentially lethal accident, bad even by Melody's current standards. The poor woman is undoubtedly cursed. Nothing seems to be safe while she's around. I resolve not to return to London in her van.

"Nonsense," says Iris, spookily reading my thoughts. "A few minor accidents. Could have happened to anyone. Now tell me about the festival."

Iris The Peaceful wanders up the valley, listening to everyone's tales of woe; how bad it has all been, and how every disaster that has befallen them in the past year has turned out to be Melody's fault.

"We're lucky to be alive," claim The Militant Children Of Lemuria. "We're just hoping we can make it safely through the night."

"It's not safe to be in the country with Melody Paradise any more," says Catherine. "She has superhuman powers of destruction. It's like living alongside Genghis Khan."

"Nonsense," laughs Iris.

But no one else can quite bring themselves to share Iris's benevolent view of things. While there is immense relief that Melody was not injured in the accident, there is also a great amount of muttering against her. Everyone has some complaint or other and all the diplomacy of Iris The Peaceful is not sufficient to smooth them away.

"Melody Paradise is a menace," proclaims Willis Elf. "Brought us here to kill us all, I shouldn't wonder."

He glares angrily around him.

"And I wish this rain would stop, we haven't been able to hunt for unicorns all week."

I'd forgotten about the unicorns. How remiss of me.

"It'll be sunny tomorrow," says Iris The Peaceful, confidently.

More Days

I'm dissatisfied with myself. My standards have slipped. Only a week ago I was quite capable of discerning that anything suggested by any of Melody Paradise's family of demented hippies was sure to be either untrue, ridiculous, or dangerous to my health. Now, repeated exposure to them has weakened my defences. For instance, I actually believed Iris The Peaceful when she said it would be sunny today. As I awake, a thunderstorm is bludgeoning the valley. This, I suppose, was to be expected. We have now had forty days and forty nights of rain, so Armageddon cannot be far behind.

The Nomadic Daughters Of Lilith are doing Tai Chi Chuan in the thunderstorm. Lightning flashes overhead, which is impressive but worrying. The morning is hot and sticky and the thunderstorm brings people to their doors, staring like myself with dubious fascination at the skies above. These skies are almost black and the rain is falling in torrents.

The Galactic Navigators are meant to be recovering Melody's van and Magwenwy's boat with their lifting equipment but the storm will make this impossible. Even if Melody's van is recovered from the river she's obviously not going to be able to drive me home in it. I'll have to travel with Megan and Pookie. Do social workers set up road blocks, I wonder?

Iris The Peaceful claims to have brought a new Wishing Tree. I hope it's a good one. I could do with a little help from somewhere. You can't expect a TV executive to spot a quality script like 'Young Socrates' when it lands on his desk. New Wishing Tree not withstanding, everyone is still eager to depart.

"Just stick the tree in the ground, Iris, and let's get out of here," is the general advice. Iris declines to just stick it in the ground, insisting that there must at least be some ceremony to mark the occasion.

"We can't attend a ceremony with Melody Paradise," protest the frightened travellers. "It's bound to end in tragedy. It was bad enough before. Who knows what atrocities she might commit now she's back with Magwyn?"

There is at least general agreement that no one should leave while Magwenwy's boat is still at the bottom of the river. The only people not entirely in sympathy with Magwenwy are The Mushroom Clan who are rumoured to have drunk a toast to Melody Paradise for teaching her a well-deserved lesson. They're all coping with the real world now, but coping with the real world is not The Mushrooms' prime aim in life.

"Magic mushrooms must be in season somewhere," says Tuffy.

"Just enjoy having a clear head for a while," suggests Iris.

I struggle through the storm to beg food and shelter from Megan. As Megan opens the door a startled scream rises above the furious thunder.

"It's Melody Paradise riding on a unicorn!"

"Let me in Megan. I can't cope with any more mad people."

Megan doesn't move. She stands transfixed in the doorway, staring over my shoulder into the distance.

"It's Melody Paradise riding on a unicorn," she says, softly.

I turn round. There at the top of the valley, with the lightning flashing around her, and the rain battering down onto her psychedelic hair, Melody Paradise, completely naked, is riding down the hill on a unicorn.

The unicorn pads slowly down the slope, rain bouncing off its flanks. It is white, unblemished, with a long narrow horn on its forehead. Melody sits astride it, naked, expressionless, and very pale. Alerted by the uproar, the travellers pour out of their benders. Shock and wonderment and awe are visible on every face, including mine. For the besieged, bewildered, and half-drowned multitudes, it is all too much. The Clan Of The Night Time Elves start trembling and shaking. Several people faint, and have to be supported by their neighbours.

Melody Paradise draws nearer. Her hair covers most of her figure and splays over the flanks of her mount. A few timid souls, unable to cope with the strangeness of Melody Paradise approaching on a unicorn in the midst of a violent thunderstorm, start to back away. When Melody is around thirty feet from us she halts, holding up one hand as if delivering a blessing. At that moment a shaft of sunlight escapes from the clouds and pierces the valley. There is more moaning and sighing.

"It's a ghost!" wails Starshine. "Melody Paradise died in the night!"

Lightning splits the skies above. Moonshine and Sunshine now faint. I clutch at Megan for support. The pale spectral figure in front of us could well be the spirit of the departed Melody Paradise. Another shaft of sunlight breaks through the overcast sky just as an immense clap of thunder shakes the valley. Pixie sits down heavily in the mud.

"Melody, Melody!" wail the crowd.

"Peace," says Melody Paradise, arm upraised. At the sound of her voice some people are unnerved completely and hide behind trees.

"It is time to stop arguing with each other," continues the pale figure. "Love and peace must reign in the valley."

"They will!" scream a dozen people, agonised by the thought that their arguments have driven Melody Paradise into an early grave.

"Come back to us Melody!" cries Patrick. "We don't blame you for killing the tree. I don't mind that you wrecked our pyramid. And I'll never cause an argument again!"

"Neither will I," yells Michael, taking his rival's arm.

A peal of thunder shakes the valley. The unicorn paws at the ground. Another shaft of sunlight strikes its horn. In front of me, Sweep is rigid with shock, his mouth hanging open.

"So will you all start behaving better?" demands the unicorn-mounted phantom.

"Yes! yes!" is the universal reply.

"Good," says Melody Paradise, hopping nimbly off the unicorn. "It's about time."

With that she unfastens the unicorn's horn, revealing it to be an artificial construction attached to the horse's nose by a thin piece of white elastic. She brandishes it briefly at the crowd before falling on the ground and rolling around laughing.

"Ha, ha, ha!" chortles Melody, "You ridiculous hippies." And with that she dissolves in a great gale of laughter, and rolls about some more. Furthermore, she is not alone in this because Iris The Peaceful does exactly the same thing. At the sight of her own horse disguised as a unicorn, Iris entirely fails to be peaceful and laughs so much that she soon falls to the ground herself and rolls about beside Melody.

More shafts of sunlight break through the clouds. The rain diminishes to a drizzle. The audience is stunned, not quite knowing what to make of this deception, or the sight of Melody Paradise rolling around naked in the mud, laughing at them all. Then Florimel, of all people, throws back her head and roars with delight at the ridiculous concept of Melody Paradise riding down the valley on a unicorn and everyone believing it. Florimel's laughter proves to be infectious. The Nomadic Daughter Of Lilith, The Universal Leyline Protectors, The Elemental Sunshine Family, even the remnants of The Tree Planters all join in, holding onto their neighbours for support and eventually ending up in the same position as Melody, on the ground, in the mud, rolling about.

Megan laughs. Pookie, delighted at all this merriment, giggles tremendously. Even Sweep, victim of much recent disappointment, joins in. As the thunderstorm passes away and the summer sunlight streams through a rainbow into the valley, the whole gloomy place is transformed into a mass of laughing, guffawing, cackling, near hysterical souls. One of those laughing is Magwenwy, and another is Magwyn who, I notice, is looking a lot cleaner since his extended swim in the river. Willis is disappointed that it was not a real unicorn but he laughs along with everyone else. He claps Starshine heartily on the back and says it is high time The Clan Of The Night Time Elves got together again, and Starshine, in between laughing, agrees that it is.

A long line of items stretches along the river's edge, drying in the sun. Beds, cushions, carpets, batteries, fridges, lanterns, shoes and clothes lie in neat rows on the grass. These are the belongings of Melody Paradise and Magwenwy, rescued from their sunken craft. Magwenwy's boat has now been refloated and Melody's van hauled out of the river. All this has happened in one morning. As soon as the boat and the van have dried out, the combined engineering, mechanical, metal-working, carpentry, electrical, plumbing, painting and decorating skills of the travellers are poised to repair them.

Under the benevolent direction of Melody Paradise, work is going on to clean up the valley. The discarded trailers have been removed, the rubbish gathered into sacks and loaded onto trucks for disposal. By mid-afternoon, the valley is already much improved and with everyone working away eagerly it will not be long until it is beautiful once more. Melody's powers have returned and anything now seems possible. Magwyn The Grim may even become a friendly human being. He isn't quite there yet, not having had time to adjust to Melody Paradise being in love with him again, but he's improving. He's barely uttered a harsh word since Melody kissed him. He did direct some very hostile looks towards Tuffy while the young Mushroom conversed with Melody, but even a saint would find it hard to completely forgive the person last found in bed with the great love of his life. No doubt Melody will soon erase the memory.

Hawk and Mulberry forget to be anti-social and help with the clearing up. Only Pixie, some of The Mushrooms and Majic Day decline to help, all of whom Melody excuses.

"Pixie has been a dedicated traveller for thirty years," she says. "He's entitled to a rest. And The Mushrooms are still adjusting to not being, eh...mushroomed all the time."

Tactfully, she does not mention the cause of Majic Day's discontent. As the natural order of things takes hold, people start bringing their problems to her.

"We can't find any more material to fix our pyramid," says Patrick.

"Why don't you and The Elemental Sunshine Family share a pyramid while we're here?" suggests Melody Paradise.

Patrick looks surprised and goes away to confer with his tribe. Some time later they enter into a conference with the other tribe. Some time after that, The Universal Leyline Protectors and The Elemental Sunshine Family can be seen sitting peacefully around the same pyramid.

"Melody, John still won't let me in the van," says Ali, still clutching his pathetic piece of polythene.

Melody takes Alistair by the hand, leads him up to John's van, speaks a few gentle words to John, then shoves Ali inside and closes the door.

"Well, that's that sorted out," she says, and she's right.

After the rapprochement between John and Ali, The Tree Planters just naturally gravitate together again. Soon they're all going around talking to the trees together like nothing ever happened.

Melody Paradise uses much the same tactics to re-unite The Clan

Of The Night Time Elves, to end the feud between The Nomadic Daughters Of Lilith and The Golden World Eternal Party Tribe, and to heal the rift between The Militant Children Of Lemuria and The Universal Leyline Protectors. She just takes someone's hand, leads them to whoever they have been arguing with, suggests they stop arguing, and they do. It works like magic, every time.

"Why couldn't she do that before?" I wonder out loud. "It must have been the curse of The Magic Hat. Or the curse of the Wishing Tree."

Megan disagrees.

"I don't think it was either of these. I think it was the curse of not being in love with Magwyn."

"Weren't her powers returning before they got back together?"

"Only in small matters," says Megan.

Well, Megan may just be a romantic at heart. Or maybe she's right. Whatever the reason, Melody Paradise is certainly back at full power. Birds hop down from the trees when she passes. Pookie gurgles happily whenever she comes into view. Children play at her feet. She is no longer clumsy, and the heat has returned to her hands. When I try and excuse myself from carrying a heavy bag of rubbish up the valley on the grounds that my arm is sore, Melody rests her fingers lightly on my wrist and the warmth flows into my limb.

"Better?" she says.

"Much better," I say, "but I probably should rest it a while anyway."

The hot sun is already drying out the soaking earth, and passage up and down the valley is becoming easier. I decide to seek out Sweep and comfort him because while he suffered great misery at Melody's apparent teaming up with Majic Day, her re-uniting with Magwyn is an even greater blow.

Sweep is sitting cross-legged under a tree. He is not alone.

"This is Fuzi," he says, introducing his companion to me. "I'm teaching her a juggling trick."

I study the young woman closely. As far as I can see she is submitting quite willingly to being taught a juggling trick. Sweep looks happy. I get the impression that Sweep would rather be alone with Fuzi, so I leave them to it and walk further up to see how the fig tree is getting on.

The Tree Planters greet me enthusiastically.

"The fig is well on the way to a full recovery," says Peggy. "It's very grateful to you. So are we. Will you read it some more before you go?"

I promise I will. I have a great bond with this fig. It is a fine tree, and a much better audience than the villagers of Chelwyn. Thinking about the villagers sends a slight shiver down my spine. What a disaster that all was. But it seems to be fading into the distance, like all the other bad things that have happened here.

"It's going to be a great festival," says Roxanna from the upper branches of a tree, where she is hanging a large silver banner and smiling broadly.

The Druid Burger van is once more open for business, and shovelling out Druid burgers by the score to feed the hungry masses. Jane The Jeweller has set out her wares on a red tartan blanket. Melody Paradise is trying on some new anklets, and shaking her feet about to see if she likes the sound of the bells. She is incidentally still naked, apart from The Magic Hat, which she wears by general agreement. Iris The Peaceful and Simon are sitting on a log, watching the world. Pixie is slumbering in the sunshine. As this seems like an excellent idea, I find a shady spot, and go to sleep.

Finan has been to Alpha Centauri.

"Great place," he enthuses. "Much more colourful than I was expecting. There was a stream of particles shooting off for three hundred million light years and we all went sliding down it."

"Really Finan?"

Finan nods happily. He has been astral travelling with The Universal Leyline Protectors. Most people have, and are now lying on their backs studying the skies, trying to recognise the places they've just been to, or claim they have. Quite what this astral travelling involved I'm not certain, as I didn't participate, not feeling the urge to lie in a circle around the pyramid and let my astral self float through the cosmos. However, it was a big success and everyone enjoyed it.

Finan's happiness may be temporary. Irene has announced that she is going away with The Militant Children Of Lemuria at the end of the festival.

I've been spending time at the bar which consists of a tarpaulin pulled over the open end of a truck. Melody sent Nemo over to Chelwyn with the last of the money to restock it. She had again wondered about using the remaining money for vehicle repairs but her friends were of the opinion that they were bound to be able to repair their vehicles anyway, with so many mechanics here. Given this, they thought they might as well load up with beer and enjoy themselves in the process.

A vast bonfire is burning down by the river, which is convivial, although the sudden and miraculous change in the weather means that even the nights are now warm and dry. The Golden World Eternal Party Tribe have redecorated the marquee and are poised at their turntables, ready to play as soon as the new Wishing Tree is planted.

The midnight ceremony goes without a hitch. Iris plants the tree. Melody pours on her magic water, cheerfully accepting some gentle mockery concerning weed killer and other disasters. Eko does a dance which he claims incorporates important shamanistic rituals for protecting the new tree. Providing the sapling survives the shock of Eko leaping over it with his face painted blue and a plastic unicorn's horn in his hand, it might work.

The unicorn's horn with which Melody Paradise fooled everyone was made for her by Magwyn. She has now donated it to Eko on the understanding that he stops prophesying doom for everyone, which he does, in public at least. Privately, he's still shaking his head and muttering dire warnings about the awful consequence of Melody and Magwyn travelling together. His forebodings may be shared by a few others, but as everyone remembers how well they used to get on, and now appreciates that almost every problem they had was Melody's fault, there is a quite rapid acceptance of the situation. Melody is happy and radiant, Magwyn is happy and friendly, and that's good enough for now.

The tree being planted, blessed, and made to feel welcome, everyone goes off to dance. Because the night is so warm, The Golden World Eternal Party Tribe have rolled up the sides of the marquee and the revellers spill out onto the grass. All through the night everyone from the youthful Cinderella to the not-so-youthful Pixie can be seen dancing all over the valley. I drop off to sleep around dawn leaving Melody and various others still dancing enthusiastically, oblivious to anything else.

I awake to the tinkling of small bells. Melody Paradise is skipping past and the sun is shining overhead.

"What time is it?"

"I don't know."

"What day is it?"

Melody shrugs.

"I'd like to hear some stories tonight. Do you want to read one?"

I nod agreement, and go back to sleep in the sun. When I waken later for a Druid burger I find the valley clean and peaceful and full of small groups of people just sitting around contentedly, doing nothing in the sunshine. Apart from some swimming in the river, there is almost no activity. It is all very peaceful and everyone is happy.

The storytelling is held among the trees at the top of the valley. All of these are now making a recovery and Peggy says they'll enjoy the company.

"What are you going to read for the fig tree?"

"I'm not sure. I've finished Terence and I don't know any more Latin romantic comedies. What about Juvenal's fine fifth satire concerning the terrible scandal of authors never being paid enough money?"

Peggy and Roxanna are dubious.

"The fig tree might be a keen classicist but what about everyone else?"

I look round. Right next to me, Fluffy, Tuffy, Bug and Simple are making a huge bong out of cider bottles sunk into the earth. Peggy may be right.

"Tell us a story about fairies," suggests Melody Paradise, "I'd like that."

The fairy story goes down well, which is encouraging. I may bring forward my plan for unleashing another fairy book on the public, only this time with less harsh reality in it, and more wandering round in fields picking daisies. The most interesting tale of the night however, comes from Iris The Peaceful after Belladonna and Anorexia ask her if it's true that the Wishing Tree she found in France was destroyed when Simon ran her wagon off the road. They've heard this from Patrick, who heard it from Roxanna, who heard it from The Mushrooms, who heard it from Megan, who heard it from Magwenwy, who heard it from Fuzi.

"That was meant to be a secret," says Iris, cross-legged under a tree.

Fuzi apologises. It just slipped out when she was swapping travellers' tales with The Riverboat Tribe.

"Why was it a secret?" asks Anorexia.

"And how come you managed to find another Wishing Tree so quickly?"

"I didn't," admits Iris. "I just picked up the first sapling I saw and threw it in Simon's truck. Found it in a garden centre in Dover, actually."

"You found a new Wishing Tree in a garden centre?"

"Well, it isn't really a Wishing Tree. Not yet anyway. But I think it shows promise."

Iris spreads her hands, pacifying the astonishment around her.

"I had to bring something, didn't I? I didn't want to let everyone down. And it worked. Everyone likes the new tree. I'm sure it's as good as any other for granting wishes."

"Well, what about the first Wishing Tree?" asks Melody "Was it a real one?"

"Who knows?" replies Iris The Peaceful.

"You said it was."

"Only after a flagon of cider," says Iris. "I didn't expect everyone to believe me. Anyway, it's nice to have a Wishing Tree in the valley, don't you think?"

"Yes," agrees Melody Paradise. "It is."

Afterwards there is general satisfaction with the new Wishing Tree, despite its dubious origins. Even if Iris The Peaceful did just pick up the first sapling she saw in a garden centre, there is no lack of wishes directed towards it and everyone agrees that it suits the Peaceful Grove very well.

And More Days

One day Melody Paradise wakes up, disentangles herself from Magwyn, stretches in the sun, and looks thoughtfully at Megan, who is playing with Pookie a few yards away.

"What Megan needs is a good lawyer," she says.

"True."

"Mrs Fitzroy is probably a good lawyer. Well, she's got a lot of money. Does that mean she's good?"

"I don't know. It might. But she wouldn't help Megan."

"Why not?"

"She's probably not the right sort of lawyer. She might only deal with big business clients, or criminal cases or something."

"Maybe. That doesn't mean she couldn't help Megan."

I think Melody is off on the wrong track here, and tell her so.

"Just because she likes you Melody doesn't mean she's going to drop everything to take part in some family court case in Leeds. Anyway, don't you need a solicitor before you get a lawyer?"

Melody Paradise doesn't know, and nor do I. No one knows anything about the law, except it's best avoided.

"Well, I'm sure she'd help anyway," says Melody.

I sigh. The success of her festival has caused Melody to forget that things usually don't go so well in the outside world. She heads off for the blat motor.

"You better put on some clothes," says Magwyn, accompanying her.

The Tribe Of The Last Free Moonbeam are recovering from last night's dancing and lie sprawled in the shade of a huge oak tree. Nearby, The Galactic Navigators are playing football with The

Militant Children Of Lemuria. Over at the edge of the valley, Boot is crawling through the undergrowth with Caddy, checking out the local butterflies. Mary is playing on a swing constructed by Cinderella. The Sunshine Family and The Leyline Protectors are painting Magwenwy's boat. Sweep is sitting contentedly listening to Fuzi's tales of her travels abroad.

Later in the day, Melody Paradise arrives back with cigarette papers and good news.

"Mrs Fitzroy will be happy to help Megan. Delighted in fact."

She skips daintily over a log. To the relief of all, Melody's clumsiness has vanished.

"Why?"

"Because I asked her," replies Melody. "If you want something, just ask for it. You were right, Megan does need a solicitor first and Mrs Fitzroy is going to put her in touch with some solicitor she's associated with and make sure there's no problem with the legal aid forms."

"What about Megan missing the court case?"

Melody says that this should not be too much of a problem, providing Megan has someone proper to represent her. So Megan's problem also starts to melt away.

"Another triumph for the Catholic saints," says Megan.

"Unfortunately," continues Melody, "Mrs Fitzroy also said the council's about to evict us."

The good feeling generated by the circus is starting to fade. Villagers are complaining about our continued presence in the valley.

"But we're miles from them, we're not doing them any harm."

Melody shrugs, meaning that this is the way of the world.

"How long have we got?"

"A few days."

Melody Paradise does not seem upset by this news. We have, after all, been able to stay here for a good deal longer than she anticipated. She has beautified the valley, and caused everyone to stop feuding.

"Are The Tribe Of The Last Free Moonbeam still heading off to France?"

Melody isn't sure. She's happy with Magwyn and doesn't much mind where they go. She's going to leave the decision up to the rest of the tribe.

The Galactic Navigators are leaving soon, off to a large festival where they are being employed to set up and clear up. The Militant Children Of Lemuria are due at a road protest in the north of England next week. The Riverboat Tribe are planning to cross the Channel and spend some time sailing the canals of Holland. The Contemplators are going to set off on their horses, and just see where they end up. Just seeing where they end up is a popular option with many others here. Simon has given up his truck and is going to try sharing a quiet life with Iris The Peaceful.

"Will that work?"

"Yes," says Melody Paradise.

"What about Finan and Irene?"

"No," says Melody Paradise.

"Can't you make it work?"

Melody shakes her head, and says that she is unable to change people's personalities. Finan wants to lie around making music and Irene wants to travel around being militant and there doesn't seem to be anything to be done about it. Perhaps it will work out some time.

"What are you going to do?" Melody asks me.

"I'm going to write my ancient Greek book."

"The one only ten people will read?"

"That's right. I'm sure the ten people will be thoroughly entertained."

"Good," says Melody.

The evening is long and very warm. The Golden World Eternal Party Tribe ask Melody Paradise when she would like to start dancing.

"Right after the unicorn hunt. That's the last remaining thing to do."

This calls for a big conference with everybody exchanging ideas about the best way to go about hunting for unicorns.

"We should attract one by staking out Iris The Peaceful in a clearing," suggests Willis.

"Really, Willis," says Melody. "I'm sure that isn't necessary. Iris would stay in the clearing if you just asked her to."

Willis looks a little disappointed. He has the clear impression that hunters should stake out some bait but Melody tells him he's getting confused between unicorns and tigers.

I retreat to the bar. Okay, I admit I've been reading to trees, I patted a mystic pyramid, I attended a shamanistic ceremony to plant a new Wishing Tree, I've conceded the point that Melody Paradise does have unusual powers for spreading love and peace and I might even believe that Iris The Peaceful once rode a centaur to Sparta but, as the millennia draws to a close in a world riddled with war, starvation, poverty, misery and disease, I'm not going out hunting for unicorns.

"A beer please, Nemo."

Nemo bangs the beer down on the bar.

"Last orders," he calls, which is something he's never called before.

"You're closing?"

"Temporarily," he says.

"Unicorn hunt," explains Catherine.

"We figure The Galactic Navigators are just the people to find one."

"I don't know about that," object Livia and Finan, beside me at the bar. "The Tribe Of The Last Free Moonbeam are more likely to find one. After all, we've got Melody Paradise, she's bound to attract a unicorn."

"Preposterous," say Hugh and Fuzi. "The Contemplators will do it. All Iris The Peaceful has to do is walk into the woods and whistle and herds of unicorns will come flocking around her."

Creeping through the undergrowth some time later with Megan, my money's on Melody Paradise.

"Stands to reason," I say. "Melody Paradise is that sort of person."

"Shh," whispers Megan. "You'll scare them away."

Also by Martin Millar

The Good Fairies of New York
ISBN: 1-85702-217-3

Ruby & The Stone Age Diet
ISBN: 1-85702-216-5

Lux The Poet
ISBN: 1-85702-215-7

Dreams Of Sex And Stage Diving
ISBN: 1-85702-213-0

Milk, Sulphate & Alby Starvation
ISBN: 1-85702-214-9